CORRUPTION

Books by Jessica Shirvington

THE VIOLET EDEN CHAPTERS
Embrace
Entice
Emblaze
Endless
Empower

Between the Lives

Disruption
Corruption

CORRUPTION

JESSICA SHIRVINGTON

HarperCollins*Publishers*

HarperCollins*Publishers*

First published in Australia in 2014
This edition published in 2016
by HarperCollins*Publishers* Australia Pty Limited
ABN 36 009 913 517
harpercollins.com.au

HarperCollins*Publishers*
Level 13, 201 Elizabeth Street, Sydney NSW 2000, Australia
Unit D1, 63 Apollo Drive, Rosedale, Auckland 0632, New Zealand
A 53, Sector 57, Noida, UP, India
1 London Bridge Street, London SE1 9GF, United Kingdom
2 Bloor Street East, 20th floor, Toronto, Ontario M4W 1A8, Canada
195 Broadway, New York NY 10007, USA

National Library of Australia Cataloguing-in-Publication entry:

Shirvington, Jessica, author.
 Corruption / Jessica Shirvington.
 ISBN: 978 1 4607 5219 7 (paperback)
 Shirvington, Jessica. Disruption series ; 2.
 For young adults.
A823.4

Cover design by Stephanie Spartels, Studio Spartels
Cover images: Girl by BONNINSTUDIO / Stocksy.com / 779873;
City by carlosgb / Getty Images
Typeset in Palatino LT Regular by Kirby Jones
Printed and bound in the United States of America by LSC Communications

To a world where
compassion triumphs over technology,
children come first,
and chocolate is fat free!

*I'm going to tell you a story about a girl
who lost her dad and had her world fall apart.
And then I am going to tell you the story
about the woman she became.*

Gus Reynolds

One

They fed me. Just enough.

Submerged in darkness, I had long since lost track of time and day. Reality wasn't far behind. The four windowless walls and secure airlock door of my underground prison were all I now knew. A faceless, nameless guard rapped on the door at regular intervals, opening the bottom hatch to pass through my carefully controlled rations, and my sluggish mind speculated that this might be a daily occurrence. But with no light to gauge the passing of day to night, time had become elusive.

If the guard's schedule was daily and my mind wasn't playing tricks on me, somewhere between four and six weeks had passed. That was, until he stopped coming altogether. I knew that he'd been gone for longer than usual because the hunger pains were almost unbearable.

I kept to my routine as best I could, trying to force my muscles to work. Trying to stand when all I wanted to do was lie still. Even so, I knew I was sleeping much more than was normal.

That was what the darkness wanted.

Darkness is like that ... it seeps into you in an indescribable and unavoidable way. It becomes part of you until eventually you become part of it.

I worried that it would take over, that in the end there would be nothing of me but the silent dark, but until that time came, I continued to fight the despair, continued to push past the physical and mental barriers as much as I could.

And at my lowest moments, I thought of him.

I imagined him speaking to me, making me laugh, making me frown and, fleetingly, I would indulge in thoughts of him forgiving me. Most of all, I saw him hating me.

None of it was bad.

He kept me grounded, gave me a reason to endure the maddening silence.

Because it was his right. *His* to hate me. *His* to destroy me.

If anyone, it was he who held the right to sign my death warrant and if he chose to use it, then so be it. These bastards would not steal that right from him.

And still ... there was a part of me that held on. The part that knew I had things to set right. Things that went beyond me and my suffering, and even him.

'Quentin,' I whispered to the darkness, my voice cracking with misuse, my lips pulling apart from having set together. 'I was wrong. About everything. About you.'

Silence answered me, but in my mind he was there, watching over me. Still deciding.

And perhaps it was simply that – the smallest shred of hope that love could conquer all – which forced me to my unsteady feet yet again. I started stiff laps around my cell, using what energy I did have to ensure that if my chance came, I would be able to make the most of it. Of course, I wasn't stupid and saw the blatant irony in my reasoning. The irony that I would tear down a man, take away all of his hopes and dreams only to have my own stripped away, and then hope in vain that his love for me would go on. It made me a hypocrite and ultimately selfish, but since it was all I had to hold on to, I wasn't going to talk myself up onto higher ground.

Tiring of my walk after a dozen laps – which didn't equate to much – I dropped to my hands and knees, but persevered, forcing a round of push-ups despite my heavy breathing. After ten attempts, I stopped. Not because I needed to, though I probably did, but because if I did more, I was sure they would scale back my food and water. I was well aware they were monitoring my movements and vitals through my M-Band. If they felt they were giving me enough food to maintain any level of fitness, they would immediately make an adjustment.

I had learned how to walk the tightrope. Maintain enough strength so that I could try to get away if I found an opportunity, maybe even fight. But not so much that they reduced my rations.

With a sudden thought, I shuffled into a better position, ignoring the sharp pain as my ankle bone scraped roughly against the ground, and started to pat the floor around me. Inexplicably frantic, I navigated my way across the familiar grooves in the cement until I felt the leg of the cot, then stretched out my arm until my fingers came in contact with my supplies. As always, I exhaled with relief when I found them – as if someone could have snuck in and stolen them. Crazy, I know.

One energy bar and less than half a bottle of water was all I had left. I opened the bar, enjoying the sound of the wrapper crinkling, took a small bite followed by a sip of water and breathed as calmly as possible as I carefully put them back in their safe place beneath my bed.

I must have fallen asleep or passed out some time after that because the next thing I knew I opened my eyes to see a dim blue light surrounding me.

I was sure I'd been on the ground, but now I was on my bed. Waking up after an unknown period of time wasn't a strange occurrence. And while there was a good chance it was paranoia, I was certain that on some of those occasions I had been moved and I'd often felt different when I woke up. Sick. Running a fever. And sore all over. I didn't like to think about it.

But the blue light? That was new.

Nervous and struggling to get my mind to switch on, it took a few moments for my brain to connect the sounds I was hearing with the door. It wasn't just the hatch; the entire door was opening.

I shuffled back on my small cot, watching as two uniformed M-Corp guards entered my cell and approached without hesitation.

Eyes wide, I felt their hands – the first human contact I had experienced in a long time – grip my arms and lift me like I was nothing. On some level, deep in the part of my brain that still functioned, I considered my chance of putting up a fight.

And quickly discounted it.

'Oh man, she stinks,' one of them said. 'This is worse than clearing out a clean-up hub.' It made me flinch, knowing that he was comparing me to clearing away dead bodies.

'Breathe through your mouth. We just have to put her in the pod,' the other one replied.

I wanted to defend myself. But even I could smell the stench I'd been living in. Hell, I hoped it would make them pass out.

My thoughts kept moving back to the water and half-eaten energy bar under the bed. Food had become everything and I now regretted not storing it on my body somewhere. What if there was no more food where I was going?

The tunnel they moved me into was lit with a red light and it caused me to squint. It felt like a lifetime since I had really used my eyes. The guards paused briefly, one of them letting go of me long enough to pull out a pair of glasses from his jacket. He put them on my face. I blinked, adjusting to the new tinted vision. Instantly darker. More comfortable.

'Leave them on until you adjust, otherwise you'll blind yourself.'

Until I adjust to what? Jesus, I was starting to panic. Were they taking me to see my father? Were they taking me above ground? Outside? My breathing sped up even as I tried to pull myself together.

'Where are you taking me?' I managed to rasp out. They ignored me.

'Should we sedate her?' the one on my right asked. He was chewing gum and I could smell the mint on his breath.

The other one shook his head. 'You're a real bastard. You know that, right? Look at her, she's already half dead and you want to pump her full of drugs. Have you forgotten how awful this shithole can be?'

No surprise they were negs. Or what the public like to call 'rehabilitated' negs.

'Can you help me?' I asked the one who'd defended me, leaning in his direction.

He turned to me, meeting my eyes. I noticed that each of the many creases around his eyes were almost crying out with a story to tell. None good. But beyond that, his eyes were … empty. He wasn't going to hurt me, but he wasn't going to help me either. Down here it was survival of the fittest and I was most definitely lowest on the food chain right now.

I didn't even blame him, knowing that I myself had turned and walked away from others just as desperate, just as in need as I was. It was one of the things I would never forgive myself for. Or my father.

'I know ways to get out of here. I can help you get out,' I tried.

'Sorry, girl. After enough time down here, you understand there is no escape. You'll learn for yourself. Best advice I can give you is, do what you're told. That way we won't have to hurt you.'

His face softened slightly, but it wasn't comforting. Mostly because I knew he was telling the truth. He would kill me if I tried to get away from them. The alternative was simply not an option for him. And again, I understood.

We started moving down the long hallway again with me walking between them. After a dozen steps, I stumbled. My legs shook. Hell, who had I been kidding when I told myself I was keeping fit in that cell? The guards slowed their pace, giving me a chance to get my feet under me.

After a few turns, we went through a set of doors and back into the darkness. At first I wondered if this was a new cell, if they were relocating me. But then my eyes adjusted.

We were in the transit tunnels. And there was a transit pod idling with its door open.

'Get in,' the first guard said, pushing me towards the opening.

As I got closer to the pod, I started sweating. My steps were so small I was barely moving.

Sensing my hesitation, the guard to my right nudged me forwards. 'Get in, or we throw you in.'

I nodded, attempting to wet my lips with my sandpaper-dry tongue. My leg shook as I placed my foot tentatively on the first metal step.

Don't get me wrong, I wanted to get on this thing and hoped to God it would take me out of hell, but I'd just gotten out of one very small, very confined, extremely isolated place. Convincing my body to move into another …

I turned to the guard at my left, swallowing nervously. 'Are you coming with me?'

He shook his head. 'More guards will meet you at the other end. You need to go now; they don't like waiting.'

As if his curt words prompted the other guard, I was suddenly pushed from behind, my hands clutching the edge of the door to stop myself face-planting on the pod floor. 'I said, move it, bitch!'

But he didn't wait for me to move anything, instead choosing to place his booted foot on my upended ass and shove me again, hard, until I was inside the pod.

Before I managed to sit up, the doors were closing. My eyes fixed on those of the more humane guard. Even as his cold eyes stared back at me – a look I knew well, one I had delivered myself – I found myself nodding to him with acceptance before he flinched, turned, and walked away.

The high speed of the pod ride was disorienting and I managed little more than to stare at my hands for most of it. Firstly as a point of focus. Then out of fascination. My palms were raw and blistered. I wasn't sure exactly what had caused the damage – perhaps my attempts at exercise; perhaps my pathetic moments of lashing out when I had pounded on the door and walls, screaming for my father to show himself. There was a good chance it was something I'd done and simply not been aware of doing. And, no, that was not a comforting thought.

My fingernails – those that remained – were caked in dirt. The cell itself hadn't been overly dirty. The floor and walls were painted concrete so it wasn't as if I'd been digging, although that was what it looked like. Tentatively I lifted my fingers to my nose and smelled. I quickly returned my hands to my lap as the pod came to an abrupt halt.

Two guards stood outside the door as it opened. The lighting was harsh here and I pushed the glasses closer to my sensitive eyes.

It suddenly occurred to me that I hadn't used one second of the pod journey to devise any type of plan to escape. It was a sure sign that my grip on reality was shaky at best, and that my grip on myself was all but gone.

The guards silently led me from the pod and across the junction, down another tunnel, through a door and then into a corridor. I tried to activate my brain, blinking a few times and thinking back to what the old Maggie – the one who would do whatever it took, at any cost, to get what she wanted – would do right now. I glanced to my left and right. The guards were much bigger than me. They were armed. My sluggish eyes moved down to their M-Bands and I saw red lights flashing. Their camera zips were activated, streaming directly to whoever had decided to watch.

Was my father watching?

Even for the old Maggie, I was almost certain this was not the right moment to pick a fight. My M-Band gave a short beep and I wasn't surprised. The screen remained blank, just as it had since the day they imprisoned me, but I was fairly certain that the beep was a heart-rate monitor.

I was scared.

Mostly, it was fear I was being taken to Garrett Mercer. My father was a close second. I knew it was likely the next time I was brought before either one of them, it would be for the final act. Garrett Mercer wanted me dead. But he wanted me to pay too. Maybe I was about to find out which one he wanted more.

I glanced up at the curved ceiling and wondered where we were. For all I knew, I was metres away from thousands of people going about their daily business. That was the strangest thing about the tunnel network that travelled all the way from Washington DC, beneath the Potomac River, under the city of Arlington and out to Bluemont, Virginia. What had once been part of the FEMA organisation was now controlled by the private and all-powerful entity of M-Corp, and there were similar underground locations just like this one around the country. Around the world, I had no doubt.

But this was where it had all begun. *This* was the devil's kitchen. And while I had always known that Garrett Mercer was the devil, I now also knew that my father was his cook.

I tripped over my own feet, the guards not slowing their pace as they tightened their grips on my arms to stop me going over. I struggled to get my footing back, my legs like jelly.

Focus!

But it was so hard. My mind was erratic and childish, its only consistent line of thought revolving around the remaining energy bar I'd left under the bed.

We reached a large door and one guard moved ahead to enter the code, causing the door to slide open.

I gasped.

My M-Band beeped.

My legs gave out momentarily and the other guard hauled me back onto my feet. 'Breathe,' he instructed.

It was impossible to stop my body shaking as it argued with itself – one part wanted to move towards the light, the other shied away. The guard, clearly aware of my internal battle, suddenly produced a baseball cap, holding it out for me.

I fumbled with trembling hands to put it on and reduce the unsympathetic glare of sunlight – something I had convinced myself I would never again see. I lowered my head just in time to conceal the stream of tears.

'This way,' the guard said, wrapping a firm hand around my upper arm and pushing me forwards. I let him lead me to the doorway, and noticed the other guard had already made his way outside and was standing by the open door of a black Jeep with heavily tinted windows.

I turned to the guard beside me. 'Where are you taking me?' I asked.

Wordlessly, he walked me towards the waiting Jeep. The other guard held out a long dark coat and they fixed it loosely around my shoulders, covering up my filthy state. He then gestured for me to get into the car.

'Please. Where am I going?' I asked again, noticing there was a driver and yet another guard already sitting in the front passenger seat.

The guard beside me shrugged. 'This is as far as we go. Get in.'

I swallowed nervously, but did as I was told.

As soon as I was inside the car, a privacy divider slid up between the front seats and the back and the vehicle began its journey to God knows where. Once again, I was alone.

I looked out the window – which did not open, like the door – and after a short while I realised with a start that I was beginning to recognise the landscape.

They were driving into Arlington.

They drove through the city. Eventually the streets became more and more familiar and I felt a desperate cry fall from my cracked lips. I was so close it was cruel.

Once again, I tried the handle, but the doors remained locked. I looked around for something to smash the windows with, but there was nothing – without the right tools, car windows are a lot harder to smash than they look. Instead I closed my eyes, shoved my putrid fist into my mouth and bit down on my cries.

Suddenly the car pulled over and the door locks clicked open. A loud beep sounded and I flinched, then stared down at my M-Band. The screen was alight. It was back online.

Holding my breath, I reached out and opened the door, half expecting someone to hold a gun to my head.

Cautiously I stepped out of the car onto the kerb and closed the door behind me, surprised when the black Jeep simply drove off, leaving me there. Alone. Outside. In the light.

And that wasn't even the best part.

Convinced I must be dreaming, I refused to turn around, choosing instead to watch the Jeep as it travelled to the end of the road and slowly took the corner. Once it was out of sight, I finally braced myself and turned, falling to my knees instantly. My fingers sank into the damp grass and I wept uncontrollably as I looked up towards my garage.

They'd driven me home.

Two

They had held me prisoner for just over four weeks. The date was the first thing I checked on my newly reactivated M-Band.

The knowledge of how much time had passed was both a relief and disorienting. I could've sworn they had kept me locked in the dark for months.

Somehow I picked myself up off the damp grass and started moving. Only two things dominated my thoughts. One, get out of the open. Two, find food.

Everything else could wait.

I made it into my room above the garage and double-checked the time and day, not fully trusting my M-Band. It was 6 a.m. on Thursday. Mom should be home from the night shift at the hospital and passed out in bed by now.

I hurried to my desk and opened a drawer, crying out with relief when I found an old box of chocolate-chip cookies. I usually kept a stash of food in my room, but I had never been so grateful to find an unopened box. I tore the top off, causing half of the cookies to fall onto the ground. I stuffed one in my mouth before getting down on my hands and knees to collect them, shoving another in my mouth before I'd finished the first.

Once I had recovered every last broken piece of cookie and had the box tucked tightly to my chest, my breathing began to slow. I savoured the third cookie, each mouthful sinfully perfect, then I packed the box away for later.

I stumbled towards the bathroom and stuck my head under the faucet, taking several gulps of cold water into my mouth. It was heavenly. I stared at the running water – just hours ago I would've done anything for a tap with running water.

Now that I had food and water – not enough, but then, I wasn't sure I would ever have enough again – and was in my garage, I knew I needed to start thinking beyond the necessities. I kept the light off and closed the blind, leaving just a small crack of daylight filtering in. I turned to face myself in the mirror, carefully removing my glasses. I stared at my reflection, my eyes brimming with tears at the shadowed sight of me.

'Bastards,' I croaked, sucking in a broken breath.

I was covered in dirt and shockingly gaunt. The small amount of skin that was visible beneath the grime was sallow, my hair matted with what I knew was a cocktail of dried blood, sweat, vomit and worse. My dull eyes took all of this in, while I smelled the overall feral stench that seemed to be coming off me in waves. Ignoring the random tear that slipped down my face, I turned on the shower and began to strip off my tattered pieces of clothing, throwing them straight into the bin bag in the corner. I'd think while getting clean.

I shook with desperate relief when I stepped into the warm water. Strange how such simple things now felt entirely surreal. I hung my head, letting the water pound my weary body, and watched the stubborn stains gradually relinquish their hold and swirl down the drain.

I wanted to cry. To scream and let it all out. I wanted to throw things and crumple into a heap on the floor. But I knew if I started …

And I had to think.

Why had they just let me go? It made no sense.

What did they expect me to do? *Want* me to do?

It was a trap. I wasn't a complete fool. I just had no idea what game I was playing. Only that the teams were not evenly matched.

I reached for the soap and loofah and scrubbed hard, ignoring my quivering body. They'd just left me there. In the dark. For weeks and weeks. Now I was out, but that did not make me free. I was still there in my mind. Still locked away. At least I was sane enough to know what the real question was at this point – just how broken was I?

When no response came to mind, I slumped down to the shower floor and turned my attention to washing my hair.

Sitting helped.

'Think, Maggie,' I ordered, clutching my hair. 'Cry later. Think now.'

The smart move was to run. Fast. Far.

I could ditch my M-Band and use my black-market one until I had enough money to get the microchip that was implanted near the top of my spine removed. It would mean living off the grid for the rest of my life – there were no replacement chips, and no counterfeit ones had ever been successful. Not to mention the removal operation was incredibly risky. The chips were embedded near the spine for a reason – an inexperienced surgeon digging around so close to the spinal cord could easily leave you a quadriplegic. But with the right money and contacts …

Then I remembered: I didn't *have* any contacts.

Gus?

I whimpered.

Could I try to contact him?

There were a few people I could think of who might agree to try to get a message to him. But even doing that was a risk. My father's words, if nothing else, had stuck. Even now, I could feel his laugh crawl over my skin as he gloated that all of my contacts were loyal to him first. I gritted my teeth and went back to rinsing the grunge out of my hair.

I shampooed my hair three times and even after dousing it in conditioner, I still couldn't get a brush through it.

After I towelled off, I cut off half the length of my hair until the worst of the matted clumps were gone and I could drag a brush through the rest. It was a nasty hack job, but I threw it into a ponytail and moved on.

I sat on the edge of my bed, intermittently glancing at my calendar on the wall, pretending I hadn't already made up my mind.

I couldn't go to Gus. The fact was, I already knew Gus was long gone.

I *should* run. Leave a note for my family and disappear.

Instead, I dressed in a pair of jeans that were once skin tight and now hung loosely from my hips and a black tank top. I'd thrown my boots out with the rest of my other clothes so I shoved on an old pair of navy Converse, before collapsing back on my bed.

Four weeks locked up on the brink of starvation really takes a toll.

I wanted to sleep, and yet knew I couldn't. After a few minutes, I forced myself upright. I looked in my cupboard for my black-market M-Band, but after turning the cupboard inside out, I sat back on my heels. It was gone.

After a moment, I fisted my hands. Feeling powerless wasn't going to help me do what I had to do, so I got up, grabbed my backpack – pausing to stuff in the box of chocolate-chip cookies – and headed to the house.

I was in danger and my family would be safer without me. But I had to be sure that Mom and Sam were okay first.

I wasn't sure what I was expecting. If Mom had picked up an extra shift, she might not even be there. And if Samuel worked at Burn last night, there was a good chance he'd never even made it home. Either way, I certainly wasn't expecting to walk down the hall to the sound of voices and peer around the corner to see both of them up, dressed and sitting at the kitchen table. Between mouthfuls of bacon and eggs they appeared to be discussing a pile of papers in front of them.

The smell of the food attacked my senses.

'Uncle Liam said he had an old college friend he might've kept in touch with. We should try that,' Sam said.

Mom shook her head. 'I've told you a hundred times. He didn't keep any of his friends. He was too smart for that. We won't find him, Sam.'

He slammed his hand down on the stack of papers. 'Damn it, Mom! Then what are we going to do? I've run out of people to ask and every day that goes by … I don't know what to do! We can't just give up on her!'

They were talking about me. A pain shot through my chest. They were looking for me, just like I had for Dad.

'We're not giving up!' Mom snapped back vehemently. 'We just need a new plan.' Her shoulders slumped and she put a hand over her face. 'It's all my fault, Sam.'

Sam leaned forwards and put a hand on her back. 'Not all yours. Mine too. We made this choice together. We couldn't have known she'd do this. Jesus, Mom, we still don't even know where she went.'

Mom whimpered and I felt a tear trickle down my cheek. 'She's like him, Sam. Smart. And too determined for her own good. If anyone was going to do this, she was. I should've known.'

I took a step into the kitchen, grabbing the countertop to help me keep my balance. Sam and Mom both looked up and gasped in unison.

I smiled pathetically, knowing I pretty much looked like Death's cousin. 'I promise you, Mom, I'm nothing like him.' I gripped the straps of my backpack tightly and couldn't stop my eyes from darting to their food. I had to force myself not to launch towards it.

Mom's face scrunched up tight, but she couldn't hold in the wail as she leaped from her chair and crushed me to her. She kept trying to talk, but her racking sobs choked her words every time.

I looked over to Sam and caught him wiping away his own tears.

He cleared his throat. ''Bout time you got home, Mags. Mom's been a total mess.' He coughed again and turned towards the sink, busying himself with the dishes.

Mom finally loosened her grip and got her breathing under control. She stepped back and took a better look at me. She gasped again.

'Oh God, Maggie. What did he do to you?' she cried, leading me to a chair. 'Why are you wearing sunglasses?' she asked hesitantly.

I swallowed, embarrassed. 'It's bright for me at the moment. They help.'

Her brows pulled together and I knew she was fighting for control. 'Here, let me take your bag,' she said, reaching for the straps on my shoulders.

No! My food was in there!

Mom saw my reluctance and, after glancing towards Sam, dropped her hands, leaving me with my bag.

'Did you know he was never really a neg?' I asked quietly.

Mom's quiet sob was answer enough.

Samuel placed a glass of water and a plate in front of me. Two slices of plain toast with butter – as if he knew I would struggle to stomach anything more.

'Thanks,' I said, watching as he sat opposite me.

He met my eyes and spoke softly. 'No one will take your things, Maggie. You can keep your bag if you want, or put it down by the chair. Either way is fine. You're safe here with us.'

I swallowed nervously, slowly releasing my hands from my bag so that I could eat my toast. It seemed to be enough and Sam said no more even though I didn't – couldn't – remove it from my back.

I looked at the papers spread out on the table: old business documents. And some photographs I didn't realise Mom had managed to keep. When Dad was first arrested, M-Corp security had done a sweep of the house and his offices. Unapologetically they took everything that related to him, explaining it was standard procedure. I had managed to save one photo, but everything digital had been wiped and the rest they confiscated.

I tilted my head to look at one of the photos of Dad on the kitchen table. He was smiling and shaking hands with a man wearing a lab coat. The man looked about the same age as Dad and I vaguely remembered seeing him once or twice when I was a kid.

'Who's that?' I asked, shifting the picture towards Mom.

'Mike Peterson. He worked with your father for a few years before he got offered some big job in Chicago. Your father was furious. He thought the job should've been his.' She frowned. 'In some ways he was never the same after that.'

We were all silent and I concentrated on eating. My throat was raw from swallowing the cookies, but I didn't care. The sensation of eating my first warm food in over a month was indescribable.

'Did you know, Sam?' I asked him, after finishing the first piece of toast.

'We both knew, Mags. We'd seen his experiments, figured out what he was doing. Mom tried to talk to him, tried to get him to stop, but he was … obsessed, and eventually he just stopped talking to us.'

'How could I not have known?'

Sam shrugged. 'You were busy with school and Dad used to take you out to those dinners at the diner once a week and that seemed to be all you needed. You thought the sun shone from him and we didn't want to take that away from you.'

'Once the world believed he was a neg, we didn't want to make it harder by telling you that it was even worse than that. As far as you were concerned, he never left us, but was taken, and we thought that was best for you,' Mom finished.

My eyes pricked with fresh tears. 'And you did that, knowing that it made me think the worst of you two.' I'd thought Mom had given up on him too soon and that Sam had turned his back on the family. That he should have fought alongside me.

'We all handled things after Dad in the only way we knew how. We hoped you'd think he'd been sent to a rehabilitation farm and that eventually he'd be reintegrated into society somewhere,' Sam explained.

'Oh, wow,' I said, 'we've really been running circles around each other.' They had no idea I'd put any hopes of that theory to rest a long time ago. How could they? I knew things about M-Corp that no one else knew. That was why they'd asked what *he* had done to me, and not what the Mercer Corporation had done.

And if I told them everything, I'd be putting them in danger too. Hadn't I dragged enough people down with me? Lost in thought, I realised I was staring at my empty plate. Mom stood up and put a banana in front of me.

'You'll need to take things slowly, Mags. I don't know the whole story, but I'd say it's safe to guess you haven't eaten much for the past month, would that be right?'

I nodded, pressing my quivering lips together.

'Oh, my sweetheart,' Mom said. I could hear her voice thicken with emotion. 'You'll want to eat a lot of everything right away,' she said, fighting to keep her voice level. 'Your body will even accept quite a bit, but be careful. It will also reject the sudden return to a normal diet. Try to take it easy and stick to plain food for a few days.'

I nodded again, unable to admit I'd already been taught this lesson while imprisoned in the dark.

'Maggie, what happened?' Sam asked. I respected the fact that he just came out with it.

I took a small sip of water and measured my words carefully. 'I found Dad. He put a gun to my head and told me the truth. That he'd been watching me all along while I'd been trying to find him and that he wished I'd never bothered looking.'

Mom covered her mouth with one hand and grabbed mine in her other. I squeezed it back before moving my hand away.

'He locked me up and kept me prisoner. I think …' I swallowed, seeing my cell around me again. 'It was to scare me out of ever looking for him again.'

'Half killing someone will do that,' Sam said, taking a good look at me.

I nodded. 'He's a very bad person. He … The things he does. He sells his technology and a lot of people suffer because of him.' I took another sip of water and let out a deep breath. 'The best thing he ever did was leave us. I'm sorry I ever looked for him.'

'How did you get away?' Sam asked.

I shook my head, still wondering the same thing. 'He just let me go,' I said, avoiding any talk of M-Corp. 'But not out of compassion. He'd kill me in a heartbeat.'

I looked up, meeting first Mom's and then Sam's eyes. 'He'd kill any of us.'

I watched until I saw understanding settle on their faces.

My M-Band beeped with my programmed morning reminder. *The bus.* I looked back at Mom and Sam. 'I had someone with me and I need to make sure he's okay. But first, I need you both to do something for me and it's big.'

'What?' Sam asked cautiously.

'I need you to pack up and leave.' I ignored their wide eyes. 'Get out of the city and use whatever money you have to buy GPS hazers so you can't easily be tracked.'

'And what about you?' Sam asked.

I shook my head. 'He'll have someone tracking me. My M-Band's already been hacked and I'm sure they won't let me out of their sight. You're safer without me and I have to make sure my friend is okay. Please. I'm begging you, Sam. Get Mom away from here. It isn't safe. I'll find you when I can.' I held his eyes, letting all of the horror I'd been through flow from me to him.

When he shrunk back in his chair, his hand running quickly through his hair, I knew I'd made my point.

'No, Maggie,' Mom said, shaking her head. 'We just got you back. We're not leaving you now. And I have my job, we can't just –'

Samuel cut her off. 'We're leaving, Mom. Go pack.'

'What?' Mom said. 'Why?'

Sam was still staring at me and an understanding passed between us. He would do this for us. For our family. I just managed to withhold the strangled cry that threatened to escape from my lips. After all this, it would be Sam who held the family together. Not me. It was never me.

'Look at her, Mom. Do you think he'd hesitate to do the same to you or me? Jesus, she was his favourite! We leave in an hour.'

'But we can't leave Maggie behind!' she yelled.

Sam clenched his teeth. 'Do you think I want to do that? But we have no choice. This is on us, Mom. We kept the truth from her. We didn't trust her and she paid the price.'

'Maybe I could talk to him.'

'No, Mom,' I said softly, but she already knew.

'I've still got most of the money you gave me,' Sam said.

I nodded. 'Good. Those zips are untraceable, but try to save most of it. You'll need a lot for the hazers. Do you know anyone who could help you get them on the black market?'

'There's someone. Maybe,' Sam said.

With no other alternative, I'd have to trust Sam could work this out. I turned my attention to Mom. 'I know it's hard to leave. But trust me when I say that I'm stronger than you think. I've been doing things … things that I'm ashamed to admit, especially now I know I was doing them for such an evil man. But the point is, he's not done with me yet and I can't fight him the way I need to unless I know you're safe.'

Mom stared as me, tears streaming down her face. She still wanted to argue. 'You're my baby girl,' she whispered. 'I'm the one who's supposed to protect you.'

I nodded. 'There's no better protection for my heart and mind than if I know you're safe. It will give me the strength I need.'

'I'm going to get us a set of wheels,' Sam said. He stood behind Mom and placed his hands gently on her shoulders. 'This time we're going to trust Maggie. She'll get to us when she can.'

Eventually Mom nodded.

I stood up and Sam pulled me into a hug. 'I wouldn't be letting you do this if I didn't ... Let's just say I've learned a lot about my little sister by being out on the streets the last month looking for you.'

I nodded into his chest, moving back for a little space. I could only imagine the things he'd heard.

'I'm so sorry, Mags. For everything. I've been the world's shittiest brother.' He dropped his voice so only I could hear. 'I'll get Mom to safety, but then I'm coming back for you. Do you understand me?'

I threw myself back into his arms and shook my head. I didn't want him to come back. I was a lost cause.

He pulled me tighter. 'Get word to me when you can.'

I didn't respond, too afraid the ache in my chest might turn into sobs if I opened my mouth. Too afraid I might plead with them to take me with them. So instead I stepped aside and let them go.

Three

Obsessing over your failures is a slippery slope into self-pity-ville.

As much as I wanted to free-fall, I couldn't. I needed to find Quentin. I needed to know he was alive. Was free. I needed to see his steel-blue eyes as they met mine. And the only place I could think to start was school. If I was lucky, maybe I'd find a lead.

I was weak, both physically and mentally, but having a task helped keep me together, and there was no time to rest. M-Corp guards could show up at any moment to take me away again, and right now I wouldn't be able to stop them. I needed to start rebuilding my strength. I already knew there was a chance I was going to have to go back into the tunnels to break Quentin out, and that meant being strong, fast. And smart.

If I found nothing to work with at school, I would try to find Sebastian, Quentin's brother. It was a risk, but the one time I'd met him it had been obvious he cared about his brother – and Quentin always spoke well of him. I had to hope Sebastian wasn't as cold-blooded as his father and that he wouldn't want Quentin locked up and wasting away.

The bus ride was worryingly short, and as I stepped off, I wondered if I'd slept or even been passed out for the majority of the journey. But the most surreal thing was walking through the front doors of the school and drifting down the corridor with swarms of my fellow students. I'd been locked away for over a month, had been on the brink of death, had discovered life-shattering truths, but here ... nothing had changed.

A few people gave me a curious second glance. Perhaps because I'd been missing for weeks or, more likely, because I was emaciated and probably still looked half feral. When I reached my locker, I took a few deep breaths and closed my eyes. The sounds, the smells, the movement ... It was overwhelming my senses. I was dripping sweat and breathing way too fast. My M-Band was continually vibrating, alerting me that something was wrong – as if I wasn't already keenly aware. I'd learned enough about myself over the past couple of years to know I was verging on a full-blown panic attack. And I also knew that couldn't happen. I needed to keep focused.

'Maggie, good to see you.'

I jolted at the sound of the too-close voice, my eyes springing open to see Morris Delaware standing beside me. His locker was two doors from mine.

'Hi, Morris,' I said, trying hard to control my breathing.

He looked me up and down, his eyes flittering beyond me a couple of times. 'I've missed seeing you around the halls. Not to mention in the gambling ring.'

I licked my dry lips and shrugged. 'Been kind of tied up lately,' I said.

He studied me with obvious concern. 'Well, you take things easy today,' he said with a gentle smile.

I nodded and stepped back to encourage his departure.

He glanced at me one more time. 'I like the glasses. They look good on you.'

'Thanks,' I muttered, adjusting the light-activated lenses. They weren't as effective as the sunglasses, but Mom had given them to me before they'd left so that I could keep them on during class.

Once Morris had walked away, I concentrated again on my locker. I took a deep breath, shoved a handful of chocolate-chip cookies into my jacket pocket, and collected my books.

Bags weren't allowed in the classroom.

I gave myself a pep talk as I made my way to my first class. The time for feeling sorry for myself was over. My father was lost to me. All that mattered was getting Quentin out. I would make sure he was safe. Then he could either finish me off or cut me loose.

If he let me go, I'd leave. I'd do what I could to set things right here and then find somewhere I could melt into the background – somewhere that hopefully wasn't too far away from Mom and Sam. It would never be safe to actually live with them again, but I'd stay as close as I could. I would become a better person, just like I'd always planned.

It would be my penance.

I would become someone actually worthy of him, even though I'd never see him again. Never have him. And never love another in a way that could ever compare.

But in order to enter my self-imposed exile, I had to first ensure he was alive and safe.

The bell rang and I sighed. I'd wanted to get to class early to start asking people about Quentin, but I'd had to sit and rest a few times on the way, which slowed me down.

I took my usual seat in English Studies, turning to Gabriella beside me. She was finger combing her cropped, platinum-blonde hair.

'Hey, you haven't heard anything about Quentin Mercer lately, have you?' Okay, so I wasn't good at small talk. And I wasn't subtle.

Her eyes widened and she leaned a little closer to me, assuming a pitying expression. 'Not today. But then again, it is just the start of the day and with him, you never know.'

The way she said it …

'Hey,' she said, adjusting her white tank top, which barely covered her not-at-all-subtle fluorescent orange bra. 'Haven't you been away recently?'

I relied on old tricks to keep my breathing as even as possible. 'Has he … Has Quentin been at school lately?' I asked, ignoring her question.

Gabriella nodded. She opened her mouth to say something, then bit her lip.

'What?' I prompted, still trying to process the earlier information.

'Sorry to hear about your break-up.' She looked me over. 'They can be rough.'

My eyebrows shot up in surprise. I wasn't sure what part of that to grab onto first: that she had seen Quentin, that she knew we'd broken up, or even been together in the first place, or that she thought my current physical state was the result of a pining heart?

Gabriella leaned forwards, speaking quickly. 'With the way he's been acting ...' She cringed. 'You're probably better off without him.'

'Acting?' I asked.

'Ah, you know ...' she said, nervously glancing at my M-Band.

I nodded, wetting my lips briefly. I got it now. 'He's turned his Phera-tech on.'

She shuffled closer. 'Don't worry, though. I don't believe the rumours.'

Great to know. 'Rumours?'

'That you knew there was something up with his tech and so you told him you'd sleep with him as long as he kept his tech turned off.' She made a show of rolling her eyes, while studying my reaction closely.

'Wow. That's harsh,' I said, drumming my fingers on the table, trying to get my head around everything, including this latest titbit that apparently I was a slut. Brilliant.

'Not as bad as the others,' she mumbled.

'Others?' I asked, knowing I'd regret it. But there was a reason I'd chosen to sit next to Gabriella. She had no filter between her brain and her mouth.

'That you were trying to lure him into marriage because you were after the Mercer fortune.'

'Oh. That.' Correction. I wasn't a slut. I was a money-digging whore.

After that informative little chat, I was quite sure I was in the wrong place. Quentin didn't need me at all. He was just fine. He'd been at school, with his tech on, spreading ugly rumours about me while I'd been locked away. I knew he hated me, I just hadn't really allowed myself to accept it. I'd been too obsessed with the thought that he was locked up like I had been.

I shook my head at my own naivety. 'He's a *Mercer*, Mags,' I whispered to myself. Of course he hadn't been locked up.

I started to collect my books, determined to get the hell out of there, only to find my legs suddenly cement-heavy and my eyes glued to the classroom door.

Quentin had just strolled into the room with Ivy Knight on his arm.

He was dressed impeccably. More so than I'd ever seen him before. One of the things that had always drawn me to him was that even in his best clothes he managed to keep things just a little off-kilter. But not today. In his suit pants, crisp blue shirt and perfectly knotted tie, he looked very much the young Mr Mercer. He was surrounded by friends greeting him, girls kissing him on the cheek and guys slapping their hands in his. All the while, Ivy stayed glued to his side.

Quentin was smiling and, at first, I was so relieved he was safe that I was smiling too. He seemed genuinely happy and relaxed and … My smile quickly fell away. I swallowed nervously, waiting for him to see me, for the inevitable moment when our eyes would meet. I knew I would see so much in that moment.

But it never happened.

He never once even glanced in my direction. He had to know I was there, but he didn't look. It was as though I'd never existed.

He didn't care at all.

My eyes started to well up and I knew, despite my uncooperative legs, I had to get out of there.

What had I been thinking? That he actually needed me? Would want me to come anywhere near him after all that had happened? My chest tightened and my throat closed. But just as I started to force my body to cooperate, two guards walked into the room and my blood ran cold.

I held my breath, expecting them to charge in and rip me from my chair. But, like Quentin, they didn't even look my way. In fact, they moved so discreetly that none of the other students appeared even slightly surprised by their presence.

When Quentin took his seat at the back of the room and one of the guards took up position behind him, the scene suddenly made sense. They were here as his security.

Keeping my eyes trained forwards was almost impossible, but I did it. Why did Quentin have bodyguards? Was it for me? Did they think I might try to hurt him? I would never …

I heard the sound of his laughter and couldn't help but sneak a glance over my shoulder, then wished I hadn't. He knew I was there. He had to. But with Ivy sitting close and looking into his eyes adoringly, he hadn't once turned in my direction.

'Are you okay?' Gabriella whispered, leaning towards me.

I kept my head down and gritted out, 'Fine.'

'Must be really hard, huh?' she added. Man, she had no tact at all.

I took a deep breath when the teacher walked in and started the class. There was no way to escape now without drawing every pair of eyes in the room and I wasn't about to do that. I slumped down in my chair and told my heart that it could take it. Of course, if my heart could talk back it would've told me to eat shit and die. At least then I could've responded that it was no more than my stupid heart deserved. And no more than Quentin was entitled to dish up.

I heard Ivy giggle from the back and closed my eyes tightly for a few beats.

When Mr Ferris turned to the whiteboard, Gabriella leaned in again and rolled her eyes. 'They've been like that for the past two weeks. It's sickening.'

I swallowed over the lump in my throat. 'I take it they … rated?'

She nodded. 'They sure did. Apparently their original rating was incorrect. Some computer glitch or something.' She leaned back in her chair just as Mr Ferris turned around.

So that's how they had explained it all away. A glitch. You'd think people would ask more questions, but most are too preoccupied with themselves to worry about anyone else. Even so … they had to have some way of making sure the tech didn't get the blame. M-Corp would never let that happen.

How could he not even look at me?

I shook that thought away just as the door swung inwards and Headmaster Edwards walked in with two uniformed police officers.

I suppressed a groan. Coming to school had been a bad idea. Of epic proportions.

Mr Edwards addressed the class. 'Students Bennett, Mercer, Knight and Stevens, your immediate presence is required in the school hall.' He gestured to the policemen. 'These men will be escorting you.'

'For what, sir?' Nathan Bennett asked from the other side of the room.

Mr Edwards shot Nathan a disapproving glance. 'You have all been requested for an interview and retesting of your Phera-tech.' Mr Edwards all but rolled his eyes. 'Don't look so petrified, Bennett. There was a problem reported with your original uplink equipment. This is simply procedure.'

I collected my books and watched as Quentin stood confidently, taking Ivy's hand. They appeared to be pleased with this turn of events. Probably expected it. Nathan looked worried he might be about to lose the status he'd only so recently begun to enjoy.

Me?

I was sure my expression exposed nothing. But this was bad. And I was fairly certain this was also the precise reason I'd been let out of that prison cell. They knew I'd try to find him. And worse, Quentin would have known it too.

As we walked down the hall, I was surprised to see Quentin whisper something in Ivy's ear and then let her walk on as he turned to me. His eyes were all steel as he glanced first at his bodyguards and then at me. But only for a split second. Then his eyes settled on anything but me.

When he spoke, his tone was as cold as his glare. 'You'll end up exactly where you're destined to. *I* can promise you that.' I flinched, but he continued. 'I just want you to remember, no matter what you think you know, and after all you did ...' He leaned closer and pointed first at himself and then to me, his voice lowering. 'I *know* that you know. And *that* is all that matters.' Without another word, he looked ahead and sped up, retaking Ivy's hand and ignoring the tears in my eyes.

Could he be so cruel as to throw that back in my face? My heart ached so much I had to fight not to clutch at it. That was how he'd told me he loved me. How he'd explained that he had to say it, so that, no matter what, he would know that I knew how he felt.

Was it possible that that was still the case? I thought about it for a few steps, but I couldn't for long. Couldn't allow my mind to be weak again and tell me things that were not true. The look in his eyes had been answer enough. No. This was not about love.

Just the opposite.

'Miss Stevens, do you have any relationship to Mr Angus Reynolds?'

She'd been asking me questions for the last forty minutes. Each of us had been allocated one of the interviewers that had been set up and waiting with a small tech team in the assembly hall. I'd been lucky enough to get the one whose black hair couldn't be pulled back in a slicker bun and whose condescending tone made it clear she'd already reached whatever evaluation she was supposed to be in the process of making.

None of the questions really bothered me, but I wasn't a fool. I knew they'd get here eventually. Gus had been the technician on that day and they had obviously made the connection.

I maintained a blank expression. 'Yes. Gus and I worked together. We have for the past year at the M-Store in Clarendon.'

'Do you have any contact with him outside of work?' she asked.

Other than having blackmailed him on a daily basis? I would have preferred to lie, but right now that wasn't an option. I was connected to a truth zip. An accessory used by law enforcement agencies and others to monitor truth. They were extremely accurate – creating a readout that was produced via the pulse-rate monitor on my M-Band *and* the earphone my female interviewer wore, which was connected to the mic they had clipped to me. If I lied, my voice would distort through the earphone and sound much higher. Truths were delivered at a lower pitch.

'On occasion. Why?'

The woman didn't answer. Funny that.

'Have you seen Mr Reynolds lately?'

I held back the hollow laugh. Gus was so far out of this city I wouldn't be surprised if he'd crossed an ocean to get away from me. 'No. I've been a little cut off from the world the last month.'

She glanced at me, her eyes narrowing. 'In what way?'

I shrugged. 'I've been suffering and sick at times. I feel like I've been locked away in the dark for weeks.'

The woman made a note and went back to her list of questions.

'Your father is a neg, is that correct?'

'He produced that rating, yes,' I replied, taking my time to think through each question before answering. One thing I knew for certain was that this was a game, and I was not in good game form.

'Were you ever concerned that you might … follow in his footsteps?'

I couldn't hold back the frown. 'I hate my father. I'll never follow in his footsteps.' And yet, even as I said the words, memories of my deceptions plagued me. Had I not been just as terrible? Lying and cheating people in order to serve my goals? Had I not screwed up Quentin's life in order to get what I wanted? I hated my father, but I hated myself just as much.

The woman nodded and typed something into her computer. Finally she glanced back up at me, adjusting her glasses and pursing her lips. 'On your testing day, you claimed that you had an eighty-two per cent rating with Quentin Mercer. Is that correct?'

'It is,' I replied, glad she had worded the question in such a way. I *had* made the claim. Didn't mean it was true.

'Did you hope that this might mean Mr Mercer would pursue a relationship with you?'

'Not any kind of romantic relationship,' I answered, pleased again that I could answer the question without implicating myself.

'Miss Stevens, would you be surprised if we told you we have reason to believe that the rating you recorded with Mr Mercer was in fact incorrect?'

Here we go. I looked over to the other side of the room where Quentin was being interviewed. I wondered what his answers would be, and if he was getting the same questions. By the easy smile on his face and his relaxed posture, I was willing to bet they were not quite the same.

'It would seem believable since you're all here interviewing us,' I said, looking back at the woman who maintained an impressively blank expression.

'Okay.' She glanced at her computer then back to me. 'One final question, Miss Stevens.'

I nodded. 'Shoot.'

'Do *you* believe Quentin Mercer is a high probability match for you?'

My eyes flashed over to Quentin again. For the first time since we'd entered the gym, he glanced in my direction as if he knew exactly what question I'd just been asked. Our eyes locked and I glimpsed a flicker of emotion, his Adam's apple jutting out as he swallowed. Just as quickly, he looked away.

I blinked back the hurt. I had done this to him. And the guilt was just too much.

'I did,' I answered, my voice breaking.

'And now?' she pushed.

I had to let him go. He deserved to live his life the way he'd planned. Even if he had to tear out my heart in order to do it.

'Now I know I'm not worthy of anyone, least of all him,' I said, staring into space.

When I looked back at her, she was still making notes on her computer, and in some recess of my mind I understood that the interview had not gone well. I wasn't a fool. They were setting me up somehow. But there was nothing I could do about it. And anyway … I knew this was also their way of confirming Quentin's status. If I fought it, it would only cause him problems.

I really hoped Gus had gotten far away.

The interviewer put down her laptop and stood. 'If you'll follow me, Miss Stevens, we will be retesting your tech now.'

I followed her to the temporary terminal that had been set up. Nathan, Ivy and Quentin were already there. At the sound of approaching footsteps I turned to see Garrett Mercer entering the hall. My hands fisted as I watched two guards walk in behind him and another two take up position by the doors. This was in addition to the two police officers and Quentin's bodyguards. The show of force sent a clear message: there was no escape.

I kept my eyes on my feet, trying to fight the surge of fear at being so close to Garrett Mercer. I knew what this man was capable of. He was the one who'd kept me imprisoned with no food and no light. He was the one who controlled M-Corp. The one who took – So. Many. Lives. Him, and my father.

'Son,' he said, when he reached our group.

'Hi, Dad,' Quentin replied, sounding pleased to see him. I'd be lying if I said it didn't cut like a knife to hear him to talk to his father so warmly. After all he knew.

'Hello, Ivy. My, my, I barely see my son without you these days,' Garrett said lightly. I knew his words were intended for me.

'Hi, Mr Mercer,' Ivy said, giggling. I bit down on the inside of my cheek and told myself sternly that it wouldn't help to hit her. As gratifying as it would've felt, it wasn't her fault, and anyway, I really wasn't strong enough to make it count right now.

I didn't get a greeting from Garrett, but even with my head down, I felt his eyes on me.

The technicians reappeared holding plug-in zips. 'Once you have inhaled your cleansers and activated your tech, we'll plug these zips into each of your M-Bands, giving us the ability to see the readings from your Phera-tech. Normally we don't hack into the bands for this information, but given there's a concern about program tampering, we need to be able to verify the readings directly. Does everyone understand?'

There were various nods and murmurs of agreement. I noted no one looked in my direction for an answer.

The head technician nodded, then sent a file to each of our M-Bands. 'In that case, could you all please thumbprint the waiver under section 164 of the Privacy Act and return the file immediately.'

As we followed his instructions, the police officers and security guards began to move away from us so they would be out of range. When the technicians were ready, Garrett Mercer cleared his throat.

'Son, why don't you help by handing out the cleansing vials.'

Quentin gave a half-smile and nodded before grabbing the tray of vials. He delivered a vial to Ivy first, then Nathan. When he finally stood in front of me, he lifted a vial with my name on it and held it out.

'I believe you know the drill,' he said, his eyes not meeting mine.

I reached out and took the vial, our fingers brushing in the transfer. The jolt of emotion caused me to lift my eyes to his. And what I saw there was so strong. So determined.

Slowly, my eyes still on his, I tipped the contents of the vial into an inhaler and, in one sharp breath, took in the dosage.

Apart from a slight flexing of his jaw, Quentin showed no reaction as he moved back into position with his own inhaler. I glanced beyond him to see his father watching us closely.

Once everyone was in place, the head technician instructed us to turn on our tech.

I looked at Quentin as he turned on his Phera-tech. He didn't look my way, but I saw his jaw clench again, the only sign that he might not be as relaxed as he appeared. Somehow that gave me strength. The thought that, even though he would make me pay for my sins, there was still a part of him – however small – that possibly cared was comforting. At the same time, it triggered a new concern. Was Quentin as worried as I was, but for different reasons?

There was a good chance their plan was to prove the ratings taken on the original testing day were incorrect, and then to take me down as the conspirator behind the entire thing. Simple enough. But there was one major flaw. When we turned on our M-Bands, the ratings would expose Quentin and me as a true match. And if Quentin hadn't told his father the truth, then I couldn't imagine how that would go down.

My mind whirred with all the possible scenarios.

Ivy was bouncing on the spot, she was so excited. My antagonism towards her was only amplified when she reached over and ran her hand down Quentin's arm. Again. Nathan, on the other hand, looked so pale I almost wanted to reassure him that his ratings would be fine.

Did Garrett Mercer have any idea how badly this was going to go for him? The more I considered it, the more obvious it seemed that Quentin hadn't told anyone about our true rating – otherwise Ivy wouldn't look like it was Christmas morning. Whereas Quentin was clearly *not* looking forward to the results.

That hurt too.

My father's warning played in my mind. About how the Mercer family would never accept me as their son's true match. But none of that mattered now. Because Quentin was done with me.

'Miss Stevens, we're waiting on you,' the head technician advised impatiently.

'Please hurry up, Miss Stevens. We'd all like to get back to more important issues,' Garrett Mercer added.

With no alternative, I glanced around the room one more time before I activated my tech and waited for the inevitable.

But, even as I registered Ivy's jump for joy out of the corner of my eye, all I could do was stare at my M-Band.

Oh.

I'd been wrong.

So, so wrong.

Poetic.

Quentin's head was down, but he must have sensed my stare because he eventually looked my way. His eyes said it all. He knew *exactly* what my results were.

This hadn't just been about vindication and bringing me down publicly. This had been about revenge.

'To verify your readings, we'll now plug in the zip-readers,' the technician instructed, approaching Quentin first.

As he adjusted the plug-in readers, I considered the possible outcomes. Somewhere in the background I heard Ivy chant, 'Seventy-three per cent, Quinny. Seventy-three!' I wondered fleetingly if the bookies at school would try to recoup their losses from the original test results.

Well, they sure as shit weren't getting my winnings back.

When I heard Quentin chuckle and remind Ivy that he'd promised her it would all work out, it broke me.

As the technician approached, my eyes darted briefly to Garrett Mercer, who was watching with a satisfied smirk. Yes, I'd underestimated him.

I knew what this meant. I was going back underground. And though there was a very large part of me that wanted to turn tail and make a run for it, I stood firm.

I looked at Quentin. When I caught his eye, I gave him a small nod, which caused him to flinch. But if this was what he needed, then okay. The technician reached me and I held out my arm for him to connect the plug-in reader that would confirm my results. Confirm that I'd rated negative with Quentin.

Just as I had with everyone else.

But instead of plugging in the reader, the technician suddenly dropped the portable zip and grabbed the sides of his head.

The ear-piercing alarm, followed by a number of shrieking alerts from our M-Bands, warned us that this was a full-scale fire alarm.

The lights shut off.

The gym was windowless, so we were suddenly thrown into pitch darkness. I couldn't stop trembling. All I could think of was my tiny prison cell. I was quite sure in that moment that I would rather die than go back to that dark cell. The room, in all its blackness, started to spin as I stumbled back, looking for some kind of anchor.

I heard sirens approaching as the technicians yelled out that all of their computers had gone down. Even their remote laptops had lost power.

Continuing to stagger backwards, I heard footsteps running into the hall and two small torches lighting the way for a number of silhouetted guards.

My heart raced. I was on the verge of a full-blown panic attack as I braced for them to come and take me. But they went straight to Garrett Mercer, forming a protective circle around him as he yelled out orders. The guards, however, only seemed concerned with securing him and began to move him out of the gym.

The guards who were already in the room called out orders to the rest of us, directing everyone towards the main doors. And then, more thumping footsteps as another group of men entered the room. The spotlights on their helmets identified them as firemen.

I smelled smoke. Fear forced me back, even as they called out instructions. 'The building is on fire. This is not a drill and we are evacuating now. Please stay close to us until we are clear of the building!'

I heard everyone scampering towards the firemen and caught glimpses of their panicked faces in the beams of light from the firemen's helmets.

But nothing could stop me backing away. Maggie Stevens. Afraid of the dark.

Out of nowhere a hand grasped mine and spun me around so quickly I fell into my rescuer's chest. But I knew that hand, and that chest, instantly. I gasped, instinct taking control, my body clinging to his.

His hand slid around the back of my neck and he pulled my ear to his mouth. I looked down to where his other hand gripped my forearm and noticed that, oddly, he was wearing a glow-in-the-dark ring. 'Breathe, Maggie,' Quentin ordered.

I gripped him so tightly that later, looking back, I couldn't be sure if he was holding me or I was just clinging to him. But in that moment, it felt like he was the only thing holding me together.

All too quickly he pulled back, gripping my shoulders

tightly. 'You need to run.' He gave me a sharp shake. 'Now!'

I shook my head and clung to his arms. 'Run where?' I tried to sound like the old me, but I didn't. I sounded scared and weak and beaten.

Quentin didn't hesitate, he just squeezed my shoulders one more time before he spun me away from him into another set of waiting arms. I jerked back, thinking I'd been captured, but then heard another voice I knew so well.

'Didn't think I'd miss out on a chance to have you owe me one, did you, Mags?'

Tears were streaming down my face. From the time I'd been taken prisoner, to being released, arriving at school and everything going from bad to worse – I'd held it in. Until now.

'Gus?' I said, worried I might've completely lost my grip on reality.

'Who else would be able to orchestrate something so awesome?' He leaned closer. 'And manage to blow up a building in the process.'

I choked on a laugh.

He tugged my arm. 'Mags, we gotta book it.'

'Quin?' I asked with a cough. Smoke was rapidly filling the gym.

'He's safe, trust me.'

Before I could nod, Gus was dragging me away from the main entrance and towards the back door which lead to the changing rooms – and, I later discovered, to the small device he'd rigged to blow a hole in the wall. It didn't escape my notice that Gus was also sporting a happy face glow-in-the-dark ring.

They'd planned everything.

I was so weak, I could barely keep my feet moving. And yet, I could feel the lingering sensation of Quentin's touch and it urged me on. And Gus's hand was holding mine. I was weak, but they'd given me their strength.

Even when I didn't deserve it.

Four

'Why are we here?' I wheezed, hands on my knees as I tried to catch my breath.

We had run from the school to a car Gus had parked nearby. He'd had to support me with his arm at various points to help me along. After a short drive into the city, we'd paused only long enough for Gus to upload a GPS hazer onto my M-Band and dump the car before we started running again. It had only been a few blocks, but I was wasted. Gus had to practically carry me the last stretch.

'Jesus, Mags. You look like death. I mean, if death could actually heave like that.'

I collapsed into a booth. 'Why Burn?' I asked, looking around at the deserted nightclub.

Gus shrugged. He was standing behind the bar, helping himself. He walked over and handed me a glass of water while he sipped on something similarly clear yet an awful lot stronger.

'The bar manager lives upstairs. She owes me a debt.' He shrugged again. 'If we stay hidden, we're safe here. She's given us access to her apartment upstairs.' He studied me for a moment. 'Let's hope there's some food up there so you don't die overnight.'

I rolled my eyes. 'I'm not that bad.' But I entirely agreed about the food issue. In the midst of the explosions and escaping, I'd left my bag – and food supply – behind.

'Maggie, your collarbone sticks out about an inch from your neck. Trust me when I say it's going to take a whole lot of hot dogs to fix this.' I ignored the way my mouth watered at the mention of hot dogs. Gus shook his head and looked away.

'You're angry with me,' I said softly. It wasn't like I didn't expect it.

His fierce eyes came back at me. 'Not you, Mags. Your dad. I can't ...' He swung his arm out, sending his empty glass flying into the wall. 'I can't believe he just stood by! I know you wanted things to work out differently, but your dad's a total prick, you get that, right?'

'I get it.'

'Good,' he said with a firm nod, which made my heart a bit mushy for him. Sure Gus was all tough and uncaring on the outside, but we weren't so different.

I took a greedy gulp of water and snatched the bag of chips he'd thrown in the middle of the table. Gus raised his eyebrows.

'Sorry,' I said. 'I ... Food was hard to come by ...' I swallowed and stared at the packet of chips, ashamed. I opened the bag and put them in the middle of the table to share.

Gus poured himself a fresh drink and sat opposite me. He didn't reach for the chips.

'Tell me everything,' I said.

Leaning back, he took a large gulp, cringing as it went down. 'Quin was taken into a holding cell at the same time you were. They knocked him out with a sedative and when he woke up, his father was there. Garrett Mercer told him in no uncertain terms the way everything was going to go down. Quin figured out pretty quick that you'd be kept imprisoned and that if he fought for you, his father would make sure you never saw the light of day. I gotta give it to him, he definitely picked up a few tricks from you along the way. The man has been relentless.'

'So it seems,' I mumbled, not sure how I felt about him playing these types of games. He'd been through enough.

'Anyway,' Gus went on. 'He made sure his father believed that he hated you. That he'd only just figured out what you'd done to him and that he wanted you to pay big time.'

'I'm sure that didn't take much imagination on his part,' I offered.

'Probably not,' Gus agreed.

I appreciated the sting of his honesty.

'Did he tell his dad that …' I looked down, embarrassed.

Gus snorted. 'That you two crazy kids are a true match? And thanks, by the way, for letting me in on that one too.'

'Sorry, Gus. I just … I couldn't. I barely admitted it to myself.'

He shrugged. 'I can't know for sure, but Quentin says he hasn't said a word. And it seems that, for some reason, your father has kept quiet about it too, as far as we can tell.'

That was one thing, I suppose.

'So Quentin came back as if nothing had happened?'

'He might not have been locked in prison, Maggie, but I don't think life has been a party for him lately, if that's what you're thinking. He's being watched constantly. The security who were with him at the school are nothing more than a glorified prison. They report everything back to his father.'

'So … how?'

Gus grinned. 'Well, to start with, leaving the phone on was brilliant, Mags. I heard everything that went down while you guys were in that lab, including the conversations *after* you and Quentin were taken away. I knew where you were and that they were putting Quentin under guard. I have to admit, after Quentin found out everything, I didn't know if he'd …'

'Hate me?' I finished for him.

'Well, yeah. But he found a way to contact me through his friend, Morris. Through Morris, I managed to let Quentin know you were still alive and being held prisoner and that I was working on trying to get a message to you.'

That explained Morris's weird mood that morning. He'd known what was going to happen, but couldn't say anything. I nodded. 'I got the message. It was the only thing that kept me going in there, even though I wasn't sure if it was real or not.'

Gus slumped further into his chair. 'I can't imagine what you've been through. I know I've said a lot of hateful things in the past and most likely will in the future, but ...'

'I know,' I said, saving him from having to say anything more. 'And every hateful thing you've said to me I've deserved. And then some.'

He cleared his throat. 'Well, we looked at it from every angle, but there was no way to break in and get you out and we both knew it. So Quin came up with his plan to get his father to decide to let you out.'

'How?' I couldn't fathom how it could have been Garrett Mercer's idea to set me free.

Gus laughed, shaking his head. 'He told his father he wanted revenge. That he was entitled to it, and now that he knew more about the "family business" he also knew he was in a position to get the payback he desired. Garrett Mercer was tickled pink that his son finally wanted to embrace the family way. Quentin made it clear he wanted public vindication for his own Phera-tech and that he wanted you there so he could rub it in your face. He figured that once you all turned on your tech, it would expose the fact you guys were a true match and there'd be so much public attention it would ensure your safety.'

'So they just let me go? But I don't understand. Why keep me in the dark? Why didn't you just come to my house if you knew there was a chance I'd be there.'

He raised his glass as if I'd had a not-so-bright idea. 'Never an option. Quentin overheard discussions between Eliza Mercer and M-Corp security the moment your release was set in motion. There were guards watching you every second until the lights went out in that gym.'

I nodded, realising that Eliza's knowledge of M-Corp's underhanded dealings was no longer in doubt. 'Go on,' I said to Gus.

Gus pulled out his phone and tapped a few buttons before responding. 'Quentin assured his father that the combination of your hero complex and your puppy love for him guaranteed that you'd try to find him, starting with school.'

My heart sank at that, mostly because it was true. 'Oh.'

Gus rolled his eyes. 'Get over it. Anyway, they let you go, but at the last minute Garrett put his own conditions on their deal. He said that if Quentin was after true revenge, it had to be done properly. An eye for an eye.'

'So it was Garrett's idea to disrupt me and make me a neg?'

Gus nodded. 'Which basically ripped our plan to pieces. Hence plan B.'

'Which was?'

'Blow everything up.' He smiled widely. 'Frankly, I preferred that one from the beginning.'

I returned his smile. Because let's face it, so did I.

*

The fire at the school had been much more calculated and much less dramatic than Gus would've liked me to believe. He'd pulled in some favours with a few of the black-market crew and they'd rigged a number of small explosives. They were set off strategically in order to move people out of the buildings, and while there was actual fire, it was mostly smoke bombs.

Quentin and Gus had worn the glowing rings so they'd be able to identify each other in the dark. Quentin's job was to get me away from the masses – one I'd made easy for him by panicking – and Gus's was to get me out. Everything, it seemed, had gone off without a hitch. Although, apparently Gus had hit a small hiccup activating the smoke bombs. The plan had been to set off the bombs before we were given our inhalers. I guessed that explained Quentin's look of unease.

After we'd shifted to the bar manager's apartment and Gus had checked our food supplies and made me eat a sandwich, I asked him when I would get to see Quin.

He rolled his eyes. 'I'll try not to be offended that I'm not your first choice of company.'

'When, Gus?'

For the first time, Gus looked nervous. 'I don't know, Maggie.'

I pressed my lips together, biting hard from the inside. 'He doesn't want to see me.' It wasn't a question and, in fact, I realised I'd been ridiculous to even think he'd come.

'I don't know that either. Our conversations were limited at best and we used all of the time to align our plans. Whenever the subject came up of what would happen after we got you out, all he said was to lie low and he'd get supplies to us.'

'What supplies?'

Gus shrugged. 'I'm not sure. But, Mags, he got you out. He cares. For all I know, he'll turn up here tonight. But just ... don't get your hopes up. As I said, he's being watched like a hawk and he might not be able to slip them. Morris is helping him, but after everything that went down today ...'

I nodded, eyeing my last few bites of my sandwich. 'I get it,' I said, pushing my plate away. I was full and I needed to start acting normal again. Stuffing the remains of a sandwich into my back pocket would not be normal.

Before long, I was exhausted. There was still so much to discuss and work out. We would not be safe for long, but I was so tired. When I couldn't fight it any longer, I stretched out on the sofa, quickly drifting off to sleep. When I woke, Gus was sitting on the opposite sofa, working on his laptop.

'How long was I out?' I asked, sitting up and ignoring the head spin.

Gus glanced my way. 'It's morning.'

'I slept through the whole night?' I looked around the small apartment. We were alone and I was acutely aware that this meant Quentin hadn't come.

'That's usually the way it happens. And frankly, I'm guessing it wasn't long enough. You still look like shit.'

'Bite me,' I said, reaching over for the glass of water he'd left for me. My throat felt hoarse and, despite having slept for so long, my sleep had been full of nightmares.

Gus raised an eyebrow, but then just smiled.

'What?' I grumbled, stretching my body. Everything ached.

'It's the first time you've sounded like … you.'

Silence settled for a few awkward beats. I wanted to say something else, something to convince him that I was me, bitchiness and all, but …

'Why'd you come back for me?' I asked instead.

Gus kept tapping on his laptop as he replied. 'I barely left, Mags. Before I even hung up from our last phone call, I was driving back to town.'

'Why?' I didn't understand. 'I'd been blackmailing you for months, forcing you to help me.' I'd used him for his black-market contacts and threatened him with a long stint in prison if he didn't do everything I asked. Gus hated me.

'Because you'd do the same thing for me,' he said, as if it was the simplest thing in the world.

I opened my mouth, but no words came out. I had nothing. Mostly because he was right. I would've gone back for him.

I swallowed over the lump in my throat. 'Thank you.'

Gus put a hand behind his ear. 'Sorry? I think I missed that.'

My eyes narrowed. 'I said, thank you,' I repeated, this time at a more audible level.

Gus laughed. 'Oh, Maggie. You should see your face. Did those words actually hurt coming out?'

'A little,' I conceded with a small smile.

Still laughing, Gus went back to his work.

He was deactivating my M-Band. It was delicate work, considering we were acutely aware that, while the GPS hazer might be concealing my location for now, M-Corp was most certainly tracking any M-Band activity. Gus had a new, black-market M-Band that he'd reprogrammed to work with my microchip – now all he had to do was shut down any tracking devices in my current M-Band long enough to transfer my data to the clean band. It would still be risky being out in public. If I inadvertently walked past a chip scanner, I'd set off an alarm for wearing an unauthorised band. But that was an acceptable risk.

Truth be told, I wasn't exactly sure what it all involved, but Gus seemed tense so I stayed quiet on the sofa and watched the light filter in through the sheer curtains. I don't know how long I stared at the dust mites floating in the sunlight, but I quickly snapped out of it when the music started blaring around me.

I looked up to see a very satisfied Gus standing by the stereo, turning the volume even louder. He was playing an old song that I had always liked called 'Uprising'.

A few bands had remixed it over the years, but he was playing the original.

'I've decided we need an anthem!' Gus yelled over the music.

I figured this meant my new M-Band was up and running. I smirked at Gus as he headbanged his way across the apartment, arms out wide in worship to his own awesomeness.

When he grabbed my arm and yanked me off the couch, spinning me around, I laughed for the first time in what felt like forever. And the lyrics were right. M-Corp couldn't control us and I would do anything I could do to stop them from degrading every single one of us.

The words slowly seeped into me, filling me with a sense of strength that I greedily stole.

It felt good. Like hope.

After Gus's anthem breakout, I resumed my position on the couch and took stock. I was starting to feel better. Physically, my body was remembering to function and food was gradually becoming easier to stomach. What I needed right now was to do something normal.

Before I knew it, I was back on my feet.

It turned out I'd been staring at the window for a few hours so I padded my way to the kitchen and rummaged through the cupboards, collecting ingredients to make lunch.

Gus joined me after making a few calls. For the past month he had been trying to track down Kelsey – he told me she'd been MIA since the night before I was captured.

'Need some help?' he asked. 'You look like you might fall into the pot of boiling water.'

I glared at him. 'No help necessary.'

'I guess some things never change,' he murmured.

I didn't look up from my cooking. I'd decided on pasta and a very light sauce.

'Wanna talk about it?' he asked eventually.

I concentrated on chopping a small onion. 'It was dark.'

'Anything else?'

I shook my head. 'I'm planning on repressing it.'

'Solid plan.'

'Totally.'

And that was the end of our chat about my father who'd left me for dead and the darkness we both knew I'd never forget.

Focusing on cooking spaghetti and making the sauce while Gus worked away on his computer – setting up nearby surveillance by hacking into government street cameras – was comforting.

As I dished out the pasta into bowls, I glanced up and caught him watching me, sadness in his eyes.

I sighed. 'Did you always suspect?'

He wasn't surprised by the question. He gave a slight nod. 'Your dad had access to technology that was valuable. I knew that dose of neg disruption you had meant that he could make more. When you have that kind of a discovery sitting in the palm of your hand … power and money is extremely tempting. The only thing I could never work out was …'

'Why I thought he was such a great guy?' I heaped a few large spoonfuls of sauce onto Gus's pasta and just a drizzle on mine. I jabbed my fork into the bowl of spaghetti, hoping it would alleviate the bitter taste in my mouth.

'Pretty much. I figured he must've been taken, like you said, if he cared about you anywhere near as much as you did him.'

I swallowed back the bile. The whole thing was still so raw. But I couldn't pretend anymore and it was long past the point where I could avoid admitting to my failings. 'He didn't. I just never opened my eyes.' I took a deep breath and let it out slowly. 'Gus, I'm sorry.'

Surprising me, he reached out and covered my hand that was now repeatedly stabbing away at the pasta.

'Maggie, I hacked into your closed files six months ago and found the evidence and pictures you had on me.'

I blinked. 'What?'

He shrugged and released my hand.

'Wait, what?' I blurted again. Those files were hidden beneath a cyber shit-fight. I'd paid the kind of money that ensured that if you didn't know exactly where you were going, there was no way to find them. But if Gus *had* hacked my files, he could've deleted everything I had against him. There would've been no reason for him to keep being my … well, in his words, my bitch.

He shovelled a fork-load of spaghetti into his mouth. 'Someone needed to have your back.'

Christ, I was *not* going to cry. I copied Gus and concentrated on eating to give myself a moment to pull it together. When I finished, I looked back at him and simply said, 'You're my best friend, Gus.'

He snorted. 'I'm your only damn friend.'

There was that too.

So my new bestie and I spent the afternoon running through inventory and discussing my new plan – the one I'd been pondering for a very long time. Weeks ago, Gus had raided my room above the garage and collected everything he thought could work as a weapon. All up, we had a good stockpile, but I would've felt better if we had more.

'Maggie, stop whinging. You wouldn't be able to carry anything else anyway.'

I reloaded the tranq gun, then got to work on the smoke grenades. 'Yes, but I'd trade a lot of these for the two tech-bombs I'd been saving up.' Gus hadn't known I had them hidden in the ceiling of the garage, and we couldn't risk going back.

'They would come in handy,' Gus admitted.

That was putting it mildly. Tech-bombs worked like grenades, but when they went off they released a silent frequency that sent all tech within a two-mile radius haywire for a few minutes. Including M-Bands. People panicked when they went offline.

But they were damn hard to get hold of. And more expensive than gold.

The flashing images on the television in front of us caught my attention. I grabbed the remote and turned the volume up.

'What's all this about?' I asked.

'Riots in Mogadishu, Somalia. A group of rebel troops stormed the city and have been bombing and burning nearby villages.'

'Who are they?'

He shrugged. 'No one knows. They've come out of nowhere.'

I felt sick looking at the images: children injured, starving and homeless people now walking the long roads out of the city. 'Why isn't anyone helping them?'

'Somalia have been sending in their own troops, but it only seems to be escalating things. They've refused international aid.'

I shook my head. 'The world is going crazy.'

'Says the girl who's about to declare war on its most powerful single entity.'

'Someone has to,' I mumbled.

Gus looked back at our supplies, pushing aside the decoder and my toolkit. 'Everything here you're going to need, and we don't have nearly enough money to buy tech-bombs.' He glanced up at me. 'Of course, we wouldn't need the tech-bombs if you didn't insist on going back down there. The plan is bad enough without you risking your life. Plus ...' he threw a hand towards me, 'you're far from your best.'

I clenched my jaw. The idea of going back ... Just talking about it had me breaking out in a sweat. But if I didn't do this, I was no better than everyone else who made noise while achieving absolutely nothing.

'You and I both know that without physical evidence they'll put some PR spin on it and cover it all up. It's the only way to make sure people see the truth. But you're right, I need to get back in shape.' Thankfully, with our location now off the grid, we could use this as our base. For now at least.

'Well, it sure will stir the shit pot, but Mags, you gotta know they'll be looking for you and they won't be shooting with tranqs.'

'I know,' I said softly. I grabbed my utility belt and carefully placed the smoke grenades inside before looking up at Gus, hoping he would understand.

'And good luck floating this plan with *him*,' he added.

'I know,' I said, knowing he meant Quentin.

But this was something I had to do. And in a world where gambling was king, why not stake everything? Besides, as the hours continued to tick by with no word, I was beginning to wonder if Quentin even cared to know.

Five

Quentin did not come to me that night.

Or the next.

Or the next.

After some prodding – of the annoying variety – Gus sent a message to Morris using an old-fashioned handheld cell. I wasn't surprised to discover Morris also had a less traceable method of communication. He ran a number of established gambling rings at Kingly Academy and beyond. An hour later, we got our response.

Q being watched too closely.
Not worth the risk.

In some ways, I was relieved, even if I couldn't help wondering if he'd meant to say that *I* wasn't worth the risk. Still, the break was giving me a chance to get my strength back and … facing him right now, knowing he wouldn't be happy when he heard the new plan, wasn't something I was looking forward to. On the flip side, seeing the constant barrage of pictures – him on the news and in the social pages at M-Corp events standing at his father's side – was unbearable. And though I told myself the real Quentin was not the person captured in these images, I worried that the longer he spent with those people the more chance I had of losing him forever. Hell, I still didn't even know how he felt about the whole 'us' thing. For all I knew, he was just being Mr Nice Guy who would never leave someone locked up in the dark.

'Did Morris's message say anything else?' I asked between sit-ups. The exercise was frustrating. And painful. It felt like starting from the ground up, but I knew there was no other way. I did as much as I could during the day, and last night, thanks to my new black-market M-Band, I hid myself beneath a hoodie and went out for my first jog. I only made it a couple of blocks, but I would go out again tonight. I had to believe that the conditioning was still there and with regular food and training it would come back quickly.

Gus was going through blueprints. I should've been too, but once again, I'd slipped into daydream mode.

'Yes, he said that Quentin really misses you and that you're the only thing in the world that he thinks about.'

'Really?' I whispered.

Gus rolled his eyes. 'Of course not *really*. Christ, who are you and what have you done with Maggie-I'll-kick-your-ass-if-you-even-think-that-kind-of-crap-about-me? I would really like it if she would return and if ...' his nose crinkled, 'whoever you are would kindly exit the damn building.'

'Sorry. You're right,' I said, suitably chastised.

He grunted and we went back to the blueprints for a few minutes until I just couldn't help myself. 'So, Morris didn't say anything else, then?'

Slowly, Gus put down his coffee mug, gave me a glare to end all glares and then walked out of the apartment, stomping down the stairs, muttering about how we were all going to die.

I checked on him about an hour later. He was sitting in one of the booths in Burn with a bottle of tequila in front of him. When he realised I was there, he gave me another loaded look until I turned tail and went back upstairs to reflect on the fact that, yes, at some point I'd turned into a pathetic lovesick girl. I shared in Gus's repulsion. God, stalker tendencies were probably in my foreseeable future if I didn't seriously get a grip.

I went out for a run later that night, keeping my head down whenever I passed people on the street. I didn't realise I was heading anywhere in particular until I stopped in front of the Muay Thai centre.

The main lights were out, but I could see a glow coming from the back office, and suddenly I was in the back alley punching in the code that Master Rua had given me a year ago.

The door clicked. I glanced over my shoulder to check I was alone and then slipped inside.

Instinct kicked in and somehow I dodged the first strike. But the second hit me hard, a foot slamming into the side of my gut, knocking the wind out of me and throwing me against the wall, where I proceeded to crumble.

Even in the dark, I knew my attacker, and that he would not stop. I sucked in a fast breath and only had time to pant out, 'It's Maggie.'

The round kick paused millimetres from my cheekbone.

'It's Maggie,' I repeated.

Suddenly Master Rua was crouched beside me, pushing back my hood.

'I thought you were dead,' he said, and if I didn't know better I might have thought his voice was thick with emotion.

'I think I might be,' I groaned.

He grabbed my chin, turning my face harshly from side to side. Then he grabbed my upper arm, squeezing. 'You're weak,' he stated, standing up.

Yep. Definitely imagined the heartfelt moment.

He held out his hand and I let him pull me to my feet. 'Come. You need ice.'

I followed the Muay Thai instructor to the kitchen. When he reached for the light switch, I grabbed his hand.

'No more light. They could be watching.'

Slowly he lowered his hand and nodded.

'But …' I said, now with a distinct swelling of shame, 'could … would you mind if we went into your office?'

Master Rua stared at me, seeing through my words and straight to my fear of the dark. With nothing more than a grunt, he fished an icepack out of the freezer and led me to his softly lit office, closing the door behind us. I was sure he noticed my flinch at the sound of the door, but again, he said nothing until he sat on the chair opposite me. Even then, he simply repeated, 'You are weak.'

I held the icepack to my throbbing hipbone. 'Yes.'

'You need to be strong or you will die.'

I swallowed. 'Yes.'

He pondered this. 'Can you come here?'

I shook my head.

'Can I come to you?'

I considered the risk. 'Maybe. At night.'

He nodded. 'You let me know. We start tomorrow night. You run tonight and tomorrow morning.'

I bit my lip. 'Okay.'

'Will they come for me?' he asked, no accusation in his tone. He simply needed to know.

'I don't think so.'

'You found him?'

'I did.' I looked down.

'He is a bad man?'

Ignoring the sting in my eyes, I nodded.

'Are you ready now?' he asked. Master Rua had always been disappointed by my goals. He always wanted me to look at the bigger picture, but I was determined to put my father first.

I adjusted the icepack and winced. 'Yes. I'm ready.'

He leaned back in his chair. 'What do you need from me?'

I met his eyes. 'I need a meeting with Preference Evolution.'

He watched me for a few beats before responding. 'I'll arrange it for a week from today. We work at making you strong until then.'

I shook my head. 'A week is too long.'

He stared at me, unmoving.

I rolled my eyes. 'Okay. One week. But you can't tell anyone else you've seen me.'

'You come here to insult me?'

I grinned. 'No.'

'Get running. Eat carbohydrates. I take care of the rest.'

The next night, my training with Master Rua began. We waited until Burn was in full swing and then he slipped in via the back stairs. On first inspection, he complained that the apartment wasn't big enough, but after we moved back all of the furniture and explained the dangers of being seen together, he let it go and got to work.

We carried on this way for the next three days – Gus compiling information courtesy of my cyber files, and Master Rua turning up at midnight. For my part, I cooked. I trained.

And I waited for Quentin.

But it was becoming increasingly clear that he wasn't coming.

*

After my third consecutive night of training with Master Rua, I could barely make it to the bathroom. Every muscle screamed out in agony and it took everything I had not to drop to the ground and curl up in a ball. Thankfully my humiliation was limited since Gus had gone out to meet an old contact of his. He was hoping to use the last of our cash zips and tech secrets to trade for some extra intel, but the truth was, we were too low on money to make much happen and if we didn't work something out soon, we were going to have a very real problem.

Stubbornly I dragged my uncooperative body into the bathroom and tried not to cry out as I slid into the bath, which I'd half filled with ice. I shivered through the pain, trying to breathe deep and relax my muscles until the numbness set in. Ice-baths were torture, but they always helped.

After my bath and a sandwich, Gus still wasn't back, so I grabbed a tub of rocky road ice-cream and made myself comfortable in bed. Lately I'd gone from wanting to sleep all the time to avoiding it. Mostly because I was becoming increasingly aware of the nightmares that seemed stuck on repeat, and let's just say waking up dripping with sweat never leaves me in the best mood to start the day. The worst part was they sucked me in so deeply that I could never seem to get out of them until I woke in the morning. And something about that gave me the chilling thought that it might not matter how free I was – a part of me would always be locked away in that concrete cell.

But despite my reluctance, after a few mouthfuls of ice-cream my eyes became heavy and my need for sleep took over.

They always start the same now.

My eyes are open wide.

But I cannot see.

I am shaking and starving.

I hear my breathing.

My heartbeat.

I hear the ventilation fan.

I am alone, and yet ...

A hand suddenly grasps my arm, fingers digging to the bone.

Then he is there, close to my ear, his whisper echoing off the walls until it becomes a chant that swirls around me like a tornado.

'You chose this path, Margaret. You forced it when you should've left well enough alone.'

My father's voice mocks me. Then suddenly he is injecting something into my arm.

'I assured Garrett I would deal with the problem. And here we are.'

My breathing speeds up as I try and fail to struggle.

'Yes, here we are,' says a new voice. One that makes me cry out. But he is not here to help me. He stands beside my father, looking more like his own father than ever.

'Quin,' I whisper.

'For the greater good, sacrifices are often made. For Maggie's greater good, you were one of those sacrifices yourself,' my father says.

Quentin nods. First sad, then resolute, he turns his back to me. 'The testing?' he says.

I try to speak, to explain, but the tornado of words bouncing around the suddenly deafening room overwhelms me. And within the tornado come the faces. So many.

The faces of all the negs I have watched as they were gunned down, locked up. The faces I have turned my back on and walked away from. All because I was trying to save the man who had helped put them there.

My father holds my head up so I can see the chaos that is my own doing. He laughs and points at Quentin, who walks away from me.

'How could you have expected me to care about you, Margaret? Even your true match cannot bear the sight of you.'

Then they are gone and I am back in the cell. Alone. In the dark. Starving. Quivering. On some level I know it is a dream and yet I can feel the effects of the drugs my father has injected into me as they push me further into my sedated prison. I try so hard to fight it, to scream. But nothing comes out.

I start to convulse.

I think I see death, lurking in the corners of my vision. Like it wants me, but is patient and willing to wait.

Suddenly I feel the strain of my struggles and my body breaks out in a sweat. I feel cold and it only spurs on my battle against the demons that have trapped me.

I convulse again.

Then something hits me across the face.

Quentin's voice returns. 'Maggie!'

I look for him in my prison, but he is not there. His voice is far away.

I tremble. He has come back for more. It will go on forever.

'Maggie! Feel my hands, Maggie. Feel my hands in yours.'

I look down, but cannot see in the dark. I clench my hands. They are empty, and yet ...

I feel something. Distant.

'Again!' his voice orders.

I clench. This time I feel more. There is warmth and pressure. He is with me.

Somehow, he is with me.

I opened my eyes with a start.

'Shh, it's okay. You were having a nightmare.'

I looked around wildly, clutching at myself. I was in the apartment above Burn. I touched my cheek; it was wet. So was my hair.

'Shh,' Quentin coaxed again. 'Please calm down, Maggie. You need to breathe slowly.'

I looked down to see my body was still shaking uncontrollably, but I couldn't stop it. I swallowed and my throat was painfully raw.

'I didn't know what to do,' Quentin said, glancing guiltily at the empty bottle of water in his hand. 'I couldn't wake you up, but you were screaming and you sounded so terrified.'

I stared at him, trying to get control of myself. And failing. The nightmare played over and over in my mind and I couldn't stop the anger welling up inside. Some towards my father, some even aimed at Quentin. But the lion's share went to myself and I had to turn my face into the pillow to stifle the cries.

Suddenly I was wrapped in his arms as he cocooned me from behind. I was coming apart, but he held me together. He cradled me through the shaking and the tears. He soothed me as I struggled to breathe again and focus on my surroundings instead of the images still tormenting my mind.

Eventually his M-Band stopped vibrating, and after a while mine did as well.

A quiet settled over me and a semblance of self returned. But with that, also an acute awareness that Quentin was really there. The person I had lied to, deceived, betrayed, played. The person who was my true match.

My stomach sank. There was so much I needed to say to him, and yet my mouth was cotton-dry, and with each passing second I became increasingly unsure.

'I don't know what to …' I started. But he squeezed me gently from behind and shushed me softly.

'Not yet.' He disentangled himself from me and sat on the edge of the bed. I thought he was going to leave and felt instantly barren. But then he just took off his shoes and lay back down beside me.

My eyes fixed on the steel-blue eyes that haunted my dreams. But as they stared back at me, there was something in them that had never been in my dreams. Something uniquely Quentin. My M-Band vibrated again with a heart-rate alert.

He looked the same as ever, healthy and strong. But different too. Changed in some way I could tell was permanent.

'Roll over, Maggie,' he said.

I stared at him for a beat and then rolled onto my side, away from him. After an awkward few moments, his arm slid around my middle and I heard him exhale.

'Let's just hold on for tonight.'

I swallowed roughly, ignoring the tears in my eyes.

'Sleep,' he instructed, pulling me closer to him. 'I'll wake you in a few hours and we'll talk then.'

'But –'

'You need this, Maggie. I need this too. First. Before the talk.'

My heart skipped a beat and I was sure he could feel my M-Band vibrating again. All I could manage was a small, 'Okay.'

I breathed deeply, inhaling his scent and relishing the warmth of his embrace. When we woke up, we would talk for what I feared would be the last time.

I wanted to stay awake and cherish every moment, but after my training, ice-bath and nightmare, I was wrecked and eventually I slipped back into the darkness. Safe in his arms.

And holding on for dear life.

Six

I woke in a panic. My eyes darted to my side, even though I already knew.

I was alone.

No!

I sat up, curling over, my hands in my matted hair.

Had I imagined him?

No, he'd been there. He'd brought me out of my nightmares.

Oh my God, would I ever see him again?

Christ! I couldn't breathe.

'Did you honestly think I'd do everything I had to do to get here and not hang around to talk?'

His voice was low. The air that had been impossible to breathe a moment ago was suddenly filling my lungs. My fingers flexed.

But still, I couldn't look up.

I heard him sigh. 'I've made breakfast. I only have a few minutes and there's a lot to discuss.'

I heard his retreating footsteps and slowly looked up. He was here.

I took in a deep breath and dropped my face into my shaking hands.

It was time to face the music.

After throwing on a pair of jeans and a wrinkled T-shirt, I headed out to the kitchen, keeping my movements to a minimum. Every single muscle in my body ached and the day ahead held a whole lot more training.

'What time is it?' I asked Quentin. He was scooping scrambled eggs onto toast.

'Early. Just after five. I need to move soon.'

I nodded. It explained why it felt as if I'd barely slept. I only finished with Master Rua at 2 a.m.

I grabbed two glasses of orange juice and sat down at the small table, watching in a daze as Quentin placed a plate in front of me and sat on the opposite side. He started eating straight away while I could only prod at the food with my fork.

'You look better, Maggie,' he said eventually.

I looked up, confused.

'From last week, at school,' he clarified. 'You're looking much more like your old self.'

I gestured to my plate with my fork. 'Food does that.' And time. I'd been at the apartment for a week now.

Quentin swallowed, looking down.

Finally I couldn't stand it. 'Why are you here? I mean, I know you don't … I know you hate me,' I blurted.

Quentin sat back, his gaze on the table.

'I'm sorry,' I said. I was sorry for so much. 'But I ... I need to know.'

There. That went well.

Of course if I'd just shut up and said nothing that probably would've been significantly better. Now the silence was even more awkward.

Slowly Quentin put down his fork. 'I do hate you,' he said. 'I wish I didn't, but I do.'

My heart felt like it was being squeezed. I gripped the edges of my chair to stop myself from bolting out of the room and hiding away. No. I had to let him say this.

Time stalled, each second carrying more weight than the one before. Finally his voice broke the tension. 'But it also appears that isn't the only emotion involved when it comes to you.' He cleared his throat. 'Gus has filled in a lot of the blanks. But what I really want to know is, when did you decide on me?'

I stared at my food. 'Two years ago.'

I heard the intake of breath. 'You weren't even at Kingly then.'

I kept looking down.

'I'm the reason you were there.'

I nodded.

'Wow. No one could ever accuse you of lack of dedication. The entrance exams?'

It was a valid question. The entrance exams for Kingly were brutal. Definitely not the kind of exams someone just knocks over on their way to their next goal. I licked my dry lips and forced out the words. 'I studied for months. And I bought cheat sheets. Bribed the librarian to keep feeding them to me along the way.'

'And here I thought only my brothers had figured out that she was the weak link.'

I guess that explained how they maintained their excellent grade point averages. 'But not you?' I asked, even though I already knew the answer.

He shook his head. 'Just how stupid did you think I was?' he asked dryly.

I glanced up, hoping he could see the honest regret in my eyes. 'I thought you were a Mercer. I thought you knew exactly what was going on and that you didn't care.'

His tone hardened. 'So I wasn't stupid, I was a monster.'

'I was wrong,' I whispered.

'Did you ever care?'

I opened my mouth to answer, but he held up his hand. 'Don't answer that.' He took a deep breath and let it out, looking straight ahead, as if lost in his thoughts. 'I understand why … all the things you've done.' He cleared his throat again, as if the next words were hard to say. 'I don't agree with a lot of them and it hurt. Plain and simple, knife-in-the-back *hurt*.'

I listened. He had a right to say these words and I deserved every one of them.

'I fell in love with you, and you looked me in the eye and told me I was nothing. You let me believe there was something innately wrong with me and that one day, when the gene showed itself, I could do something terrible to another person. Do you know what that feels like? Thinking you carry something in you that others would call evil?'

I thought of my father, of our genetic link. Of overhearing my mother tell Sam how I was just like him. Yes, I knew what that felt like. 'I wanted to tell you the truth. So many times,' I said quietly.

'But you didn't. And I think, in some ways, that's the hardest part. You had your reasons for what you did, but … it's hard for me to believe that you ever felt anything for me.'

My eyes shot up defensively.

He raised his eyebrows, but his look remained impassive. Disconnected. 'How could I, when you kept up the façade to the very end?'

I wanted to argue that I'd tried to tell him in the lab. That at first I'd needed to stay the course, and then I was in so deep that I couldn't.

'I was scared,' was all I managed.

'Scared of what, Maggie?'

I was starting to sweat. I either had to put myself on the line or pretend I didn't care. The old Maggie would do just that, turn away and deal with the pain in private. But now …

'I thought about you while I was down there. All the time.' I shuddered at the recollection of my concrete cell. 'I wondered what you would say if I ever saw you again and I promised myself that if you wanted to be rid of me, or if you wanted to punish me, then that was okay. But for all those weeks, the hours that took lifetimes, I thought of you and it kept me going. Not because I thought you would forgive me and that we would live happily ever after, but because I thought you might be ...' I took a deep breath. I was starting to shake with the memories.

'You thought I might be down there,' Quentin finished for me.

I nodded. 'And that was on me. I couldn't take back all the wrong I'd done, but I could keep fighting in case I ever had the chance to try to get you out. So when I did –'

Quentin's hand covered mine briefly, stopping me. 'Do you think I didn't know that, Maggie? Did you think I didn't know that as soon as you were freed you would come for me?'

My eyes welled up with tears. 'Then on some level you knew I cared.'

He tilted his head. 'On some level. And I knew how fixated you could be as well. I knew if you thought you had put me in danger, you would try to save me.'

I could tell the comment wasn't meant as a compliment.

'Turned out you didn't need me though, right? I wasn't saving you at all. But the question is, why did *you* save *me*?' I looked into his eyes, searching for the answer.

'They would've kept you down there until you died,' Quentin rasped.

'So it was out of pity? Or is it that you wanted to deliver the killing blow?' I wrapped my arms around myself.

Quentin stood up and started to pace back and forth. 'You say you thought of me when you were down there? Well, you're all I thought of from the moment we were separated. I have questions and anger, and believe me when I say there is more of that to come. But, damn it, Maggie ...' his fist hit the table, jolting me, 'our fathers had you locked up and were doing God knows what to you and I couldn't do a damn thing!' He paused. 'You said you were scared. I need to know why.'

My leg bounced up and down beneath the table, but when my eyes met his, a calm spread over me. 'I was scared that ... What I'd done ...' I shook my head, and a tear slipped down my cheek. 'I couldn't even forgive myself, how could I ever expect you to understand? Yes, I loved you, but I didn't want to. I told myself it wasn't real, time and time again, until it became impossible to deny. And then things were so good, I just kept holding on. Even though I knew that eventually you'd see me for the monster I'd become.'

Quentin stood stock-still. 'Well, I guess we failed each other. You left me in my own personal hell, while I stood back and watched them drag you into yours.' He exhaled deeply. 'As much as you hurt me, I can only imagine how much hatred you have for me after my father locked you away and left you to ...' His breath hitched. 'I failed time and time again to come up with a plan to get you out of there. I don't know where we go from here. If there is anywhere *to* go.' His words were controlled. His expression gave nothing away. I didn't know what he wanted from me – if he wanted to hurt me or leave me or just twist the knife. And I knew that was how he wanted it.

I stood now too, needing to level the playing field. I lifted my eyes from my feet and felt my shoulders move back. 'I'm taking them down, Quin. I'm going after all of them and doing what I should've done in the first place.'

Quentin took a step towards me and shook his head. 'You're changing the subject.'

I held my ground. 'Yes, but you should know this. And you should also know I'm going back down there. I'm going to show the world the truth. And there's an extremely high likelihood that I'll be dead very soon.'

Quentin took another step, agitation now showing in his eyes. 'You're not going up against them alone.' His voice was hard.

'If you want your revenge, you can have it, I promise you. I live with my stupid decisions every day, and if I make it through the next few weeks alive, you can do whatever you want to me, but I'm begging you to let me do what's right first.' I was rambling, and he was getting too close.

Quentin took a final step and grabbed my upper arms. 'Is this all that matters to you?' he growled. 'Is this all you want to say to me?'

The façade had slipped and his eyes gleamed with such overwhelming emotion I felt my legs weaken. But his grip held tight, holding me in place.

Barely breathing, I closed my eyes and whispered, 'I don't deserve to say the things I want to say.'

We were so close I could feel his chest rise and fall with each breath. His scent enveloped me and I gave in. To him. Our match. Our love.

But Quentin didn't move. He stared at me like I was a puzzle he needed to solve. And I suddenly became acutely aware that he hadn't said anything to me to indicate that any of his feelings remained. All of his words had been about what he'd felt in the *past*. Apart from that, it had all been me.

I blushed, immediately uncomfortable under his scrutiny. But he was gripping my shoulders and I'd been backed into the wall with nowhere to go.

When I couldn't take it anymore, I whispered, 'What are you looking for?'

The intensity in Quentin's eyes didn't let up, but my words at least seemed to break him from whatever thoughts were controlling him. He blinked, but remained focused on my eyes as he tilted his head slightly.

'The lies, Maggie,' he whispered. 'I'm looking for the lies.'

I flinched. A bucket of cold water would have done less. But somehow I held my ground and blinked back the sudden sting in my eyes so that I could hold his gaze. 'And have you found them?'

Suddenly his hand was tangled in my hair, pulling me to him, and his lips slammed against mine. My body fell into his, even as my mind staggered to catch up.

His other arm, wrapped around my waist, pulled me even closer until there was no space between us. He tightened his hold on my hair, deepening the kiss that was jolting my entire nervous system back to life.

I wasn't sure whose grip was more desperate, but we clung to each other as if we both knew just how fragile our hope was.

Eventually the fear resurfaced. He meant everything to me, but after all I had done, I couldn't deny him his right to hate me; I couldn't hide from it. Somehow I managed to rip myself out of heaven and away from him. 'If this is a game … please,' I stuttered, 'I can't!'

I was trembling all over, my earlier bravado fading away. But Quentin was instantly there, his arms holding me together, keeping me up.

He brushed the hair back from my face and tilted my chin until my eyes met his.

He flashed a sad grin. 'I hate you.'

'I know that part,' I said quickly.

His eyes penetrated my soul and I hoped and prayed he'd find something there. 'The tech says we belong together, but how can we be when I don't know if I can trust you?'

I stared, waiting for what might come next.

'Maggie?' he asked, his eyes full of conflicting emotions. 'Don't lie to me again.'

I swallowed and nodded.

'Ever,' he added.

'Never,' I promised.

His hand wrapped around the back of my neck and he moved closer, his breath brushing my face. 'I forgot how damn beautiful you are.'

I bit my lip to hold back my tears. Mostly because the things he was saying about me weren't necessarily compliments and we both knew it. Lies and beauty were a troublesome combination and he'd once been my prey. I was sure that my eyes revealed my shame even as Quentin's showed his hesitation.

'Oh God, it's too early for this shit. I'll have you know these walls are paper-thin, *Mr Is-This-All-That-Matters-To-You!*' Gus – who had just walked out of his bedroom – scoffed. Quentin gently pulled away from me in time for Gus to stare at me pointedly. 'And you're no better, *Miss If-This-Is-A-Game-Please-I-Can't!*' His interpretation of my voice was entirely inaccurate.

Gus looked ridiculous standing there in his Spiderman pyjama bottoms and too-tight Incredible Hulk T-shirt as he flapped his hands in the air between us. 'I've given you two long enough to sort out your crap, so either take it to the bedroom and do something interesting, or change it up from dry humping and groaning to making me coffee and planning how we are all not going to die very, very soon.'

With that, he started towards the kitchen before turning to me with a look of genuine agitation. 'I much preferred you when you hated the world and everyone in it.'

'You're just cranky because you can't find Kelsey!' I snapped.

'Yep!' he called back.

Quentin kept his eyes on Gus until he disappeared into the kitchen and then glanced at his watch. 'I've only got a few more minutes, so we should probably catch up on whatever it is you two have been planning.' He furrowed his brow and I found myself staring even as I nodded. I was still struggling to process that he was here, and there was still so much more to say. Sure, we had kissed, but I had no idea what he wanted and if any of those wants included me. And something about that kiss had felt as much like a punishment as anything else.

Then again, I thought as I followed Quentin into the kitchen, maybe not knowing was for the best. Heartache is easier to ignore when it hasn't delivered its final blow.

Gus started to fix the coffees only to notice the plates on the table. 'Oh, well, this is nice. I suppose you forgot to make me some, did you?'

I rolled my eyes. He really was in a sour mood, even for him. Quentin nodded to a plate covered in foil by the stove.

'Oh,' said Gus. 'Thanks for that.'

Then we were all at the table drinking coffee while Gus inhaled his breakfast and we filled in Quentin on the plan.

'So let me get this straight,' Quentin said, his hands fisted on the table. 'You're going to meet with the Pre-Evo's and offer to give them all of your intel if they help you go into the tunnels again and break out an entire hub of negs?'

'Yes.'

'And you plan on going in alone?'

'Yes.'

'And why is that?' Quentin asked, his tone short.

I felt myself slipping into a more familiar version of myself. The Maggie who was able to separate need from reason and stay focused on the job at hand. I knew full well that this was the Maggie I needed to be to get these things done.

'I know my way around down there. I'll have people waiting on the outside, and Gus is devising a way to get the negs to safety.' I ignored the sarcastic noise that erupted from Gus's end of the table. 'The Pre-Evo's will then have everything they need, along with all of my files, to go public and show the world the truth about M-Corp.'

'And what about you? I haven't heard the part where you get out of the tunnels.'

I was silent as I considered my words. Finally I met Quentin's eyes. 'I've sent Mom and Sam away. Hopefully they have GPS hazers by now and are safe. If they don't hear from me within a month, they're going off the grid for good.' Quentin's eyes went wide at the thought that I'd gone as far as to contemplate M-Chip removal. 'I'm doing this. Of course I'll do everything I can to get out of there alive, but we both know I can't promise that.'

Quentin shook his head and looked at Gus. 'You agree that this is crazy, right?'

Gus nodded. 'Certifiably.'

'Maggie, you can't take on an entire hub. How will you even know how many guards are in there? What are you going to do – taser them all? Kill them and activate their death alerts? And what about the negs? Have you even stopped to consider how unpredictable they'll be?'

I looked at my hands, not sure how to explain to Quentin that, yes, I had considered all of these things, but it did not change anything.

'From the way you're refusing to look at me, I assume you plan to ignore my warnings,' Quentin pushed. When met with silence again, he said, 'You need help, at least.'

My head shot up. 'You're not coming. No way.'

He smiled sadly. 'You don't get to make that decision for me. But that's not what I meant anyway. I'm stuck on the inside trying to find out what the hell is going on in there. Even aside from the fact that I might find out something that could help you, I can't leave yet.'

'I never expected you to leave your family, Quin,' I replied softly.

He shook his head. 'They aren't my family anymore. But ... I need to be sure. I know Dad and Zachery are definitely knee-deep and I've heard Mom talking with security and making plans so I'm pretty certain about her, but ...'

'You need to be sure.'

He nodded. 'Sebastian and I were always ... Granted, I haven't seen as much of him over the past couple of years;

he runs PR for the company and he's been travelling more than ever as the face of M-Corp internationally, but I haven't figured out if he's part of it all yet, and I need to be sure.'

'I understand that,' I said, not mentioning that I dreaded the disappointment that lay ahead for him if he was forced to make the same conclusion about Sebastian as the rest of his family. 'It must be hard being there.'

He nodded sharply and I could tell he was fighting back his emotions. 'I won't know if I can get away and come with you until the last minute. It was difficult enough doing what I had to do to be here now.'

The way he said it triggered my curiosity. 'How *did* you get here?'

Quentin glanced at Gus. 'You didn't tell her?'

Gus shrugged. 'Didn't know if you would make it work and saw no point getting her hopes up.'

Quentin nodded uneasily and I shot Gus a look that he ignored.

'Tell me,' I demanded. Obviously I wasn't going to like it.

Gus was suddenly fascinated by his empty plate while Quentin rubbed the back of his neck, looking anywhere but at me.

'I was in the club last night. Gus set me up with Joy, the bar manager who usually lives up here. She helped me sneak away.' Joy, the bar manager, who owed Gus a number of favours it seemed.

'*How* exactly?' But really, I didn't need to ask.

'We danced for a while, made sure we were seen together. My brothers were there and when they were ready to leave I told them I was staying with Joy.'

'And apparently you and *Joy* had been convincing enough that they accepted this?'

His look held a challenge. 'Apparently.'

'How convincing?' I asked, my voice flat as I crossed my arms.

Quentin continued to hold my gaze. 'My brothers wouldn't have believed me if I hadn't made it good.'

'And I'm sure it was very good,' I said softly.

'Are you angry with me?' he asked, raising his eyebrows.

I shook my head. 'No. You did what you had to do. I know what that's like.' Besides, I had no claim on him. He was free to do what he wanted.

He half laughed and the bitterness hung in the air around me. It had possibly been a bad choice of words.

'None of this changes the fact that you need help, Maggie.' Quentin stood up. His eyes stayed on me for an extra beat and I wanted to believe what I thought I was seeing. But before I could be sure, he blinked and looked away.

'I have to go before I lead them here, but you two need to sort this out. Your entire plan is going to fail if you don't find some backup, and you know it.' With that, he headed for the door, giving me the distinct impression that I had just been dismissed. 'I've got some money put away that no one knows about. If I try to get to the money and then to you ...' He grimaced. 'It's too risky. When Morris contacts you, follow his instructions.'

'Are you sure you can trust him?' I asked, standing now too.

He gripped the door handle. 'I'm only sure of one thing these days, Maggie.' He flung the door open. 'If you need me, find Morris.'

I nodded, letting him go, despite the fact that I was dying to ask what the hell that one thing was.

Once the door closed behind him, Gus wrapped his knuckles on the table. 'The man makes sense, Mags.'

I slumped back into my chair.

'But I gotta ask you something,' Gus went on.

I stared at the door, unsure where things had been left between us.

'Mags!' Gus said, breaking me from my trance.

'What?'

'You asked him if he trusted Morris, but have you stopped to consider if we can trust *him*? He's been with his family this past month and they know he knows the truth about what they're up to. You really played him, Maggie – we both did – and that's gotta change a guy.' Gus watched as I absorbed what he was saying.

'You're asking if I think there's any chance he's switched sides?'

'Yes,' he said softly.

I thought of the way Quentin had looked at me. Of the hurt and anger I brought out in him. Of the way he challenged me with his stares and almost enjoyed my discomfort at times. I considered the way he'd asked for every detail of the plan, and even how I'd withheld some of that information instinctively.

I drummed my fingers on the table. Yes, he had changed. 'I suppose anything's possible, Gus. But I'm telling you right now, Quentin Mercer is not a murderer. And to play this game, to double-cross us ... that would make him something I could never ...' I shook my head. 'For once, I'm going to put my faith in the system.'

'Because he's your true match?' Gus's eye twitched slightly.

I nodded.

'But have you taken a rating with him lately?'

'True matches don't go away.'

Gus shrugged. 'Not that we know of. But you have to admit, your circumstances are pretty freaking unusual. You've both changed, Maggie. We all have.'

'He's not a killer,' I gritted out.

Gus raised his hands in defeat. 'You can't blame me for asking the question.'

'No.' I stood. 'But don't ask it again.' I started to clear away the dishes, pausing as I lifted Gus's plate. 'And it might be best to keep me away from Joy in the future.'

'Noted,' Gus said. He kept his head down, but I saw the corners of his mouth pull up.

I pressed my lips together and dumped the dishes in the kitchen sink. 'He was right about going in alone,' I called out to Gus.

'And?' he said from right behind me, causing me to jump.

I turned. '*And*, first Pre-Evo and then we're going to have to recruit.'

'Why do I have a feeling this is going to be more like a conscription?'

I smiled. 'Because you know how I like to get things done.' I snatched the last piece of toast out of his hand before I stalked towards the living room, pausing briefly to call over my shoulder, 'And because payback's a bitch.'

Seven

I was on my way to the meeting with Master Rua's Pre-Evo contact.

Over the years Gus and I had done our research on Pre-Evo, but we'd never found all that much information. They had offices in Clarendon and Washington DC. They were vocal protestors of the M-Chip and of Phera-tech.

They had made a number of small discoveries – at one point sheltering a neg within their ranks who claimed she'd been treated like an animal at a rehabilitation farm. Unsurprisingly the woman, who had once been a highly sought-after criminal barrister, was killed in a tragic head-on collision before she could tell her full story.

All in all, it was disappointing that with all of their resources – which had to be better than ours – the Pre-Evo's seemed to have done little more than draw posters and sing chants.

Master Rua and I walked through the parklands of Arlington Cemetery. The sun had set, but I could still smell the afterburn and feel the warmth of it on my skin. I let my fingers widen to feel the gentle breeze as I gazed up at a few stars persistently shining despite the pollution and city lights.

While I was locked in my cell I had dreamed of the sun, bartered with any god who would listen, offering up all I was and could ever be just for one more chance to see the sky and feel the sun. Now, looking at the moon above, I realised the sun alone would never have been enough. The city's darkness was stunning. Illuminated by the deceptively friendly city lights, it was different to the darkness that had overwhelmed me all those weeks underground. The world, for all our failures, still held wonder and beauty. Even in the dark.

I just hoped that it wouldn't swallow me whole once again.

'You said your friend had a connection to the Pre-Evo's as well?' Master Rua asked as we made our way towards the Memorial Amphitheatre. It was a weird place to have a meeting, but we weren't calling the shots.

'Gus was dating Kelsey. Her brother is the leader of the Pre-Evo's – and your contact.'

Master Rua absorbed this information with little surprise. 'Why not go through her, then?' he asked.

I shrugged. 'Last time Gus saw her was the night before I was captured. He was leaving town and they'd said their goodbyes. He hasn't been able to get in contact with her since.' A problem that had him increasingly worried. Every time he thought I wasn't paying attention, I knew he was looking for ways to track her down. Given how skilled Gus was at finding things, I was beginning to think he had good reason for his concern.

'Here we are,' Master Rua said, gesturing towards the amphitheatre entrance.

'This is all very Colosseum-like,' I joked to hide my nerves. But the truth was, I had no idea what lay ahead. I wasn't controlling any of this and something about the entire set-up had me sweating bullets.

Master Rua grabbed my arm at the top of the stairs, and pointed to his left. 'This is as far as I can go. You walk left. He said he will find you.' When I didn't immediately move, he nodded me on. 'You want me to wait?'

I did, but I had no idea how long things would take and I couldn't leave him out there in plain sight. I shook my head. 'I'll make my own way back and see you tomorrow night.'

'It will be okay, Maggie,' he said, his tone softer than usual.

Swallowing my fear, I stepped into the undercover walkway that encircled the amphitheatre. Each step felt heavy and, despite my rubber boots, made more sound than I was comfortable with.

Shit. I was out of practice. I shook out my jittery hands.

'Fake it 'til you make it, Maggie,' I whispered to myself.

I pushed my shoulders back and set my eyes straight ahead. I wasn't as strong as I once was, but I was a hell of a lot stronger than I had been just over a week ago. If I had to fight, I could. And besides – I patted the pocket of my hoodie, comforted by the feel of my taser and the knowledge that my tranq gun was in my backpack – it would be a shoot-first, ask-questions-later kind of night if needed.

Pep talk concluded, I shifted my attention to my surroundings. There was no denying the deserted amphitheatre had a certain sense of gravity about it. Perhaps because it was surrounded by graves that honoured deaths made in sacrifice. Perhaps because the structure was almost exclusively marble, giving it old-world grandeur while remaining dauntingly Colosseum-like. Or maybe it was something else entirely. A gust of cold air interrupted my thoughts and I bit back a shiver.

Ahead, a figure stepped out from behind one of the pylons. My stride didn't falter, even if I had stopped breathing.

I fixed my gaze on the figure – clearly a man – and kept my hand inside my pocket.

As I closed in on him, I was able to make out his face. In his mid-twenties, he was tall with dark hair that needed a trim, stubble that needed a shave and friendly eyes that I could instantly imagine lit up with contagious laughter. But this man, in his dark pants and long overcoat, was not laughing. In fact, he didn't look pleased to see me at all.

'Keep walking,' he instructed. 'We have one full revolution to speak. Say whatever it is you came to say quickly, because that's all the time you're getting.'

I bristled, but kept moving, albeit a little slower. One rotation would take five minutes, tops.

'Alex?' I confirmed.

He nodded once.

'I'm Maggie,' I said.

'I know.' He looked ahead, barely acknowledging me. 'You can take your hand out of your pocket. You won't need your weapon.'

I shrugged, leaving my hand exactly where it was. 'You're Kelsey's brother?'

'You're wasting precious time.'

'Look,' I huffed. 'You guys have been trying to contact me for the past six months. You came sniffing first, so why the cold shoulder?'

Alex continued walking and glanced at me briefly. 'You should have come to us when we first invited you. But instead, you went out on your own. You got caught. With Quentin Mercer at your side. Now, you're a liability.'

My eyes narrowed. 'You know I was captured?'

'Of course.'

This was news to me. 'That would mean you know about the tunnels.'

Still walking, he turned his head and stared at me with a flat expression. Clearly he wasn't going to bother with an answer.

'If you know, why haven't you gone public?'

'Because we need to handle the situation properly. And we need to control the flow of information. There are a lot of lives at stake, not just one.' I didn't miss the dig.

We had nearly finished a full circle of the walkway – my time was almost up.

'Look, I have files. Data that could help you go public. And I have a plan that will make sure the whole world knows the truth. I just … I need your manpower and resources. And we'll need help to disappear after.'

Alex sighed, as if he pitied my ignorance. 'Look, Maggie, the best advice I can give you is to run. You've sent your family away. You should do the same.'

I clenched my jaw. 'How do you know about my family?'

He shook his head. 'You're not listening.'

'I came here to see if we could help each other. We both want the same thing.' My irritation was starting to show.

Alex stopped. We were back to where we'd started. 'You have no idea what we want, Maggie. And –'

The sound of helicopter blades caused us both to look up.

I listened hard and also picked up the faint noise of sirens in the distance.

Alex pulled a small device out of his pocket and began pressing buttons. It looked like a cross between an old-style smartphone and the M-Band. When he finished, he glanced over his shoulder before looking back at me, moving close and speaking fast.

'You blew any chance of teaming up with us when they captured you.' He pulled out a piece of gum and popped it in his mouth. 'The smartest thing Pre-Evo has ever done is to never become a real threat. Our strength is in our ability to remain inconsequential. You threaten that. That helicopter?' He jabbed a finger towards the sky. 'Those sirens? They aren't coming for me, Maggie.'

'That's why I need to stay hidden,' I pushed, starting to shiver in the cold. 'Please, Alex. I've made mistakes, but I know how to bring them down. I need your help.'

Alex shook his head sharply. 'We're not bringing you in. We can't be sure you haven't been corrupted. We can't be sure your files haven't been altered. And we simply don't trust you – or the company you keep. Yes, there was an offer on the table before and that's why I met with you tonight, but that offer has now expired. Don't contact us again, Maggie. And I beg you to heed my advice and disappear. No good will come of your little "plan".'

I swallowed hard as I watched him stride away and open the passenger door to an unmarked car. He looked up at me, his eyes flashing, before getting in. 'And please ask your friend Gus to take a hint and stop calling my sister. It's pathetic.'

I watched the red tail-lights as the car sped off, even as the sound of the sirens intensified.

They would be there in less than a minute.

'Shit,' I whispered.

And then I was moving, sprinting for the tree line that bordered the cemetery.

The first thing to hit me was the helicopter searchlight. I pulled up sharply, slamming my back against a tree to avoid the beams of light. The sound of approaching sirens came in my direction and then I saw them. Two cars –

coming from opposite ends of the cemetery. If I could get to one first, maybe I had a chance.

Adjusting my hood to keep my face hidden, I made a run for it.

Arms and legs pumping hard, my ragged breaths confirmed my still-lacking fitness. But I kept going, running straight for one of the approaching vehicles.

I knew the moment they spotted me. The gunfire erupting from the passenger window was a total tip-off.

Dodging the wayward bullets – it's hard to hit a target from a moving car – I threw myself into another group of trees, panting for breath. The sound of screeching brakes quickly followed. I listened hard. One car door. Two.

I waited.

Then I closed my eyes briefly. Two car doors were better than four.

My eyes darted left then right as I tried to calculate my best mode of attack. The trees were good cover, the trunks thick and easy to hide behind. I looked up, contemplating climbing onto one of the branches. The extra height would be an advantage, but I couldn't rely on my fitness or risk the noise it could make.

The helicopter disappeared long enough for me to hear the first set of footsteps. He was good, treading carefully, but after my time locked up underground, with nothing but the hum of the ventilation fan to keep me company, my hearing was the one thing that had improved. I tilted my head, concentrating on calming my breathing and listening for the second set. But it didn't come.

When the first guard – dressed in an M-Corp uniform – passed the tree I was hiding behind, I had little choice. I could either let him walk by and risk the other car arriving, or do something.

Old habits died hard.

The helicopter was back, shining its searchlight in our direction, but we were well covered by the trees. I stepped out behind the guard, quiet as a mouse, and had the taser on his neck before he knew it. He jolted with the current and I kept it on him until he was on the ground. As I crouched over him, I saw the faintest shadow. But it was enough. I dropped and rolled. Just in time to miss the bullet that went straight into the shoulder of the man I'd just tasered.

As he screamed out in pain, I rolled onto my back, noting the second guard's shocked expression as he stared at his buddy.

Before he had a chance to look away, I rocked into a crouch and kicked out, my foot colliding with his knee, sending him off balance. It gave me the time to jump up and hit him hard across the face. My entire body jolted from the impact of my closed fist against his temple.

Gotta give it to him; the guy was tough and somehow stayed on his feet, even managing to hit out with a quick return jab that made my jaw feel like it was going to fall off. But it didn't matter. Because for the first time since I'd been imprisoned, I'd hit my groove. Fighting for your life does that, I thought with a grin as I rammed a series of fluid hits into the guard, not stopping when he dropped his gun, not for a second, until he crumpled to the ground.

He was still conscious so I bent over him.

He spat blood at me.

I ignored him and grabbed his gun, pointing it at him while I yanked his radio from his belt. 'Tell the chopper to back off,' I instructed, holding it out to him.

When he didn't do it, I moved the gun to his forehead. 'I'm not a counter. Do it, or I'll shoot.' I held his eyes, daring him.

He snatched the radio and pressed the talk button. 'Ground Team B to Sky Hawk 7, request you fall back to a half-mile radius while we conduct ground search. Over.'

After a moment, the response sounded. 'This is Sky Hawk 7, reading Ground Team B's request to move out to a half-mile radius. We are moving now. Over.'

I let out a breath.

Keeping my knee on the guard's throat, I wiped my prints from the radio and gun before tossing them both as far as I could. I dug around in my backpack, exchanging my taser for my tranq gun.

'They're coming for you,' he laughed, the sound gurgling as he coughed up more blood.

I smiled cruelly, sinking into the state of mind that had kept me alive since all of this began two years ago. I moved close to his face and spoke low. 'I bet I find them first.'

He didn't even see me position the tranq gun at his side. His eyes simply widened after the shot and I waited the few seconds until consciousness faded out.

I pulled up the base of his vest, revealing his hipbone and neg marking. All negs were branded when they were first removed from society. I shook my head, wondering if he'd been a neg to start with, yet knowing after looking into his calculating eyes that he was very much a neg now. Aware that I was losing time, I stumbled to my feet, looking around wildly as I attempted to assess the situation. I'd already heard the second car pull up. Three doors this time, which meant I was probably facing three negs, but there was a chance it could be more.

Both of the guards in front of me were unconscious. The new team would most likely be distracted with them for a few moments, giving me a small window of time.

It only took a few seconds to make up my mind. What I really wanted to do was stay and fight. Now that I'd started, it felt good, and as far as I was concerned, taking out some of my pent-up aggression on M-Corp guards seemed fair. But I couldn't take that chance. I was on my own now – Alex had made that clear – and if I wanted to keep my family and friends safe and expose M-Corp for what they really were, then I needed to stay alive. And free.

I heard the thump of approaching footsteps. Without another thought I broke into a flat run, dodging trees and staying away from open areas as I circled back to the northern end of the cemetery. I could hear them on my tail. Shouting out orders and then … the pop that coincided with the thump and plume of dirt less than a metre to my right. They had silencers.

I jutted to the left, using the cover of what trees I could, and weaved my way forwards, giving every ounce of strength I had to keep up my pace. Once I made it out of the cemetery, I kept going, walking fast and staying in the shadows until I made it to the Court House station just in time for the last train.

When I came out of the metro, I called Gus with one of my burn phones.

'Well?' he answered, knowing I was the only one who would be calling him.

'They're not going to help us.'

'Shit. Why?'

'Apparently I'm no use to them anymore.'

Gus snorted. 'Do they have any idea how much stuff we have on M-Corp?'

I shook my head even though he couldn't see me. 'No. They're done with us. And I'm done with them.'

'When you say *they* and *us* …?' Gus hedged.

I hesitated, which said it all.

'She's with them. She doesn't want to speak to me,' he said.

'I'm sorry. Alex told me to tell you to stop calling Kelsey.' I felt the unfairness of it all on Gus's behalf. Kelsey wouldn't even talk to Gus and he had no idea why. Aside from that, he was my friend.

'Yeah, well. It was never going to go anywhere anyway.'

I swallowed, at a loss for words.

'What now?' he asked. 'Do you need me to come get you?'

'No. I'm back in the area, just had to go the long way. M-Corp guards turned up.'

'Oh, super. Did you leave any standing?'

I smiled. 'None I came face to face with.'

'Nice to hear you're back in form. What now, then?'

I rotated my jaw a few times. That guard had got in a good hit. 'I don't trust the Pre-Evo's, Gus. Someone led those guards to me tonight.'

'And you think it was them? Pretty low for a peaceful group, don't you think?' he said dubiously.

'I didn't get a lot of peaceful vibes tonight – plus, they know I've been in touch with Master Rua. They could've been following him.'

'All the way to us,' he concluded. I could always rely on Gus to never miss a beat.

'We're getting a new base camp. Start packing. I'll call as soon as I have things sorted.'

'On it. Where are you going?'

I smiled, walking through the bustling nightlife of Ballston. It was time to get back to what I knew best.

'To kill two birds with one stone.'

Eight

The night's chill had well and truly wormed its way into my bones. My knuckles were badly grazed, my jaw ached, and I craved the warmth of a bed. But worst of all, I was consumed by the very unwelcome sensation of hunger – not something I let happen often these days. At least the streetlights and the comings and goings from the small club a little further down the street kept me sane as I waited in the small alcove.

I was rewarded for my efforts just after 3 a.m. when a familiar four-wheel drive turned into the narrow lane, pausing near my hiding place to wait as an electronic garage door opened. The driver was the only person in the car. Sloppy.

Beneath my hood, I watched intently as I held my position. When the four-wheel drive entered the garage, I waited until the very last moment before dashing across the road and dropping to a ground roll, making it inside just as the door closed.

It was almost too easy. I was on him the moment he tried to step out of his car, slamming the car door on him once, twice, three times, his grunts and groans a little more pathetic with each impact. Can't say it wasn't fun.

He fell to the ground and it took all my strength not to kick him. Instead, I settled for bending over him, just enough so that when he opened his eyes he saw my face beneath my hood. When I saw the spark of recognition, I aimed my gun at his crotch. His expression quickly morphed to all-out fear. Very satisfying.

'Hello, Travis. *Very* clearly, tell me the code to your apartment. If you give me the wrong one, I will happily shoot you before any alarm is triggered.'

He swallowed, attempting to inch back and move his … parts out of my line of fire.

I shook my head. 'Uh-uh.'

He froze.

I glanced towards the internal elevator on the other side of the garage. 'Is this your place?'

'Y-yes.'

'All of it?'

'Yes,' he hissed, his eyes darting between me and the gun.

'Is anyone else up there?'

He hesitated, but shook his head before I had a chance to ask again.

'The code, Travis.'

Sweat ran down the side of his face. I raised my eyebrows, enjoying the power. His eyes narrowed, but he knew there was no other way. 'Seven, thirteen, sixty-six, eighty-two, seven, alfa, echo, alfa, romeo.'

I recited the code back to him.

As soon as he nodded, I shot him. In the balls.

He was damn lucky I'd only brought my tranq gun.

One good thing about dealing with lowlifes was that they didn't bother with security surveillance. Sure, it had its uses, but with tech so easy to hack these days, most chose to go without. That is, unless they had someone like Gus to secure all the software. And Travis most certainly did not. Nonetheless, I did a quick sweep to make sure there were no cameras.

Kneeling by Travis's body, I patted him down, relieving him of his gun – a very nice Bexley & Moore glock that I would be donating to our collection – his pocket knife, and two handheld phones. Then I pulled one of the plastic ties from my backpack and zip-tied his wrists together, ensuring he couldn't fight if he came around and that he couldn't access his M-Band to set off any silent alarms.

After I had finished gagging him, I sat back on my heels and inspected my handiwork, double-checking that I hadn't forgotten anything. Mistakes meant failure, and that wasn't an option. I wiped the sweat off my brow and got on with the next stage.

Dead weight is a goddamn nightmare.

Travis was no friend of mine – he'd made that clear by double-crossing me and feeding my father the information that ultimately let to my imprisonment. So I figured I was being more than charitable when I paused twice, as I dragged him by his feet along the concrete floor, to adjust his arms from bending in unnatural ways.

As for the drag marks that were leaving a slight trail of blood ... well, he could live with that.

By the time I levered him up against the doors to the elevator, I was drenched in sweat and wheezing like a ninety-year-old stuck on a treadmill. But there was no time to rest. The tranq wouldn't hold out for much longer.

I pressed the elevator call button and leaned against the wall. When the bell dinged and the doors slid open, I used one foot to wedge them open, then grappled with Travis's limp body. Somehow I wriggled my hands under his smelly, hot armpits and heaved him into the elevator.

Making use of his pocket knife, I cut the zip-tie around his wrists so I could hold his index finger to the print recognition scanner while I entered the code. As soon as the code registered, I grabbed a fresh tie and yanked it tight around his wrists, then set about changing the security settings on the elevator. I couldn't do anything about the code, but I was able to lift the fingerprint requirement at least.

When the elevator doors opened, I stepped out slowly, my tranq gun poised and ready. But the dilapidated open space that looked like it had once been a factory was silent. It seemed Travis hadn't been lying. I scanned the thick exposed beams in the ceiling and the large pylons, both of which could serve as hiding places, before I re-entered the elevator, and dragged Travis out.

Then I got on with clearing the space properly.

Judging by the large stained areas on the old wooden floorboards and the two fixed tables that ran down one end of the thirty-by-ten-metre space, this had once been a textiles factory.

I spied four doors at the end of the open area and kept my guard up as I moved closer. The partitions were flimsy and recent. Breathing steadily, I opened the first door, discovering it was a bathroom. The next three were bedrooms. I took my time inspecting them. They were all similar, except only one of the beds had sheets on it and the only clothes I found were in that room too.

I looked through the galley-style kitchen in the main area. It was little more than a small bar fridge, a counter with a sink, a single burner working off a gas bottle and a microwave. And I discovered another small bathroom with no supplies tucked behind the kitchen area.

After a full inspection, I was sure that this was not Travis's only place of residence. In fact, I was beginning to think I'd been especially lucky that he'd stopped by tonight. From the contents of the rubbish bin alone, no one had been here for at least of few days.

Satisfied we were alone, I heaved Travis onto the sofa, checking his ties, and then called Gus.

'About damn time!' he answered.

'Aw, were you worried about me, Gus?' I teased.

'Bite me,' he snapped.

'No thanks.'

'Jesus, one night out and you've reverted to the She-bitch. And no, by the way, I wasn't worried about *you*, more like the trail of destruction you were leaving in your path and how it will all come back to bite me on the ass.'

'You've been thinking way too much about biting, Gus,' I said, enjoying the fact that he was fuming. I'd missed our chats.

'I wouldn't test me right now, Maggie. I have all of your supplies and weapons packed in my car. I could easily drive in the wrong direction and never come back.'

'Where are you?' I asked, dropping the chit-chat. Now that he'd mentioned it, I could hear the background noise of his car.

'Driving the streets. Once I packed and got everything loaded, I basically started to piss my pants. I wasn't about to hang around in that place waiting for M-Corp's finest to come pay me a visit, was I?'

I held back a smile. 'Well, it's your lucky day because we have a new place. You can drive straight in and park the car, just try to be discreet. I'll leave the garage door open.'

'And where, pray tell, is our new abode?'

'Remember when Travis brought us back from Roosevelt Island?'

Pause.

'Yes,' Gus said softly.

I grinned. 'Well, Travis has kindly offered up his place for the foreseeable future.'

'Maggie, please, please, please tell me you are joking,' Gus said in a low voice.

'Nope. And I suggest you get your butt over here instead of driving the streets where you can be seen in your very obvious car. The code for the internal elevator is seven, thirteen, sixty-six, eighty-two, seven, alfa, echo, alfa, romeo. Got it?'

'Tell me this is part of the plan, Maggie. At least tell me that,' Gus pleaded.

I walked over to where Travis was still knocked out, glancing back at the veritable treasure trove of weapons and tech I'd just found buried under the floorboards. 'It's part of the plan, Gus. Just make sure no one follows you here.'

'Says the girl who got caught,' he said with a snort before hanging up.

Gus arrived just as Travis started to wake up. By that time, I'd moved him onto a wooden chair and secured him with a possibly too-tight rope. Oops, my bad.

'Did you close the garage door?' I checked with Gus.

He threw me a dry look before taking in the scene in front of him. 'No, I actually left it open with a welcome sign out the front,' he deadpanned.

I rolled my eyes.

'Oh, and by the way, there's something you should know,' Gus said, scratching the back of his neck.

I glanced up from Travis who was groaning with his head still hanging down. 'What?'

'Quentin came to the apartment just before I left.'

My heart did that squeeze thing it does whenever I heard his name. I took a step towards Gus. 'Is he okay? You told him not to go there again, didn't you? It's not safe!' I was rambling and starting to panic. Gus simply smiled and crossed his arms which only infuriated me more. 'Jesus, Gus! If they find him out, they'll … He can't take those kinds of risks anymore!'

Just then the elevator pinged and the doors slid open. I launched myself at the weapons lying on the coffee table, snatching up Travis's Bexley & Moore glock just in time to spin around and aim … right at Quentin.

He stepped out of the elevator, carrying full garbage bags similar to the ones Gus had arrived with.

He stared at me calmly as I remained rigid, my brain refusing to accept that he was there. My eyes darted between him and Travis, who had chosen that moment to finally open his eyes and was staring straight at Quentin Mercer.

'Maggie,' Quentin said softly.

I jerked my head back to him.

'Think you'd mind putting the gun down, Mags? Or at least, you know, not pointing it at me?' he said with a quirky smile.

I blinked. I'd completely forgotten the gun. Which only made me mad.

'I could have shot you!' I yelled, lowering the weapon.

Jesus Christ, that would be just my luck. First ruin him, and then damn well shoot him!

Quentin put down the bags and slowly came to me. 'No, you couldn't have,' he said, sounding so sure of himself. Of me. He eased the gun from my hand and rested it on the table, swaying slightly as he straightened.

'You shouldn't be here,' I said, even as I let him pull me to his chest. 'Travis has seen you.' My mind was spiralling. If I didn't manage to keep Travis my prisoner now, he could turn Quentin in to M-Corp.

'They know, Maggie,' he whispered in my ear. I leaned back from him and looked into his steel-blue eyes.

I jabbed a finger at Gus, who I was entirely pissed off with. He should've told me the second he walked in about Quentin. 'Watch Travis.'

Travis, who was gagged, watched on, blinking furiously as if that would somehow convey whatever it was he wanted to say. He was just going to have to wait.

'Maggie, wait,' Gus protested.

But I held my hand up. 'Watch,' I ordered.

'But –'

'Watch!'

I dragged Quentin into one of the small bedrooms, closing the door behind us.

'Who?' I asked, feeling dread course through my veins like ice.

He shrugged, trying to blow it off, and collapsed onto the bed. 'I heard Mom on the phone. She was telling whoever was on the other end that they needed to stay close to me and get ready to take me out of the game.' His voice sounded distant, but he lay back on the bed, stretching out his arms.

'What does that mean?' I asked, fearing that I already knew.

'I like this bed,' he said in a very un-Quentin-like way.

I narrowed my eyes, studying him.

He sighed. 'I think it means that my mother just ordered my execution. Whoever she was talking to was clearly following her orders.' He sat up and rested his elbows on his knees. 'She instructed the person to leave Sebastian and Zach alone. That she had no doubt they were loyal. I just …' He shook his head. 'I guess I'd been holding out hope that one of them might be in the clear, but her voice … I've never heard her sound like that. So cold and …' He trailed off.

'I'm so sorry, Quin,' I said, feeling responsible.

He suddenly grabbed my hand and pulled me down onto the bed beside him. 'No more sorrys. We're in this together from now on, okay? I need someone on my side, Maggie. Please be on my side.'

I nodded. 'I'm on your side. Always,' I said, but froze when I felt him bury his face in my neck and inhale deeply. Once. Twice. On the third time I wriggled.

'Quin,' I said, pulling back to get a good look at his eyes. 'Are you okay?'

He brushed his fingers across my jaw, then brought my hands up between us, running his thumb over my sore knuckles. 'Part of me wants to stay mad at you.'

'I know,' I admitted.

One of his hands went to my hip, pulling me a little closer to him. 'Part of me wants to go back and never know the truth.' He half laughed. 'Can you believe that? Part of me would actually prefer to believe I was a neg than know you could betray me like that.' His hand travelled up the side of my body, his lips moving closer to mine. 'But in the end none of it matters. You know why?'

He was definitely slurring and his pupils were too big. I'd seen my brother with eyes like that before. His hands continued to move as he closed the gap between our bodies and, for the life of me, I couldn't seem to pull away. I craved him that much, and the feel of his hands on me made any attempts at talking impossible.

'Because I can't fucking breathe when you're not around. And all I want to do is be with you,' he murmured into my neck.

'Quin, have you taken something?'

He laughed. 'I want to kiss you, but I don't think I'll be able to stop.'

I swallowed. 'I want to kiss you too.' And I would never *want* to stop. But as much as I longed to hear those words, I didn't want them like this. 'Why wouldn't you be able to stop, Quin?'

When he didn't answer and just kept trailing his fingers over my body, I dug deep and tried to focus. 'How did you get away?' I asked, trying a different tactic.

His hands continued exploring. 'Morris helped with one of his overly elaborate plans. He staged a party at his family's city apartment in Old Alexandria. I turned up and played the part of the drunk, falling all over the band and spilling my drinks on poor girls with intolerably high-pitched squeals.'

I mustered a chuckle. 'Exactly how much of a method actor were you?'

He rolled his eyes.

I forced him to look at me. 'Quentin, have you taken a lust-enhancer?' I knew that if he had, then being around his true match would make it almost impossible to control his desires. Which would also mean I couldn't trust the words coming out of his mouth when it came to the subject of us.

'It was enough to have my "protectors" rolling their eyes and ignoring my antics,' he said, by way of admission. 'We planned to try to have me pass out in one of the bedrooms where I would then sneak away, but in the end, we didn't need to.' He glanced at me suspiciously. 'Something happened, and suddenly all but one went running off, saying they had to get to the cemetery.'

I winced.

Quentin raised his eyebrows. 'Maggie, Maggie, Maggie. What have you been up to?'

'I'll fill you in later,' I said, not bothering to add: *when you're sober*. 'Tell me the rest.'

'Not much more to tell. Have I told you how much I love this part of you?' he said, running his finger along my collarbone. 'I lie awake at night and think about doing this. Think about everything we could be together.' His voice ran like velvet across my body and I fought the need to lean into him. He saw, and smiled.

'Quentin, tell me what else happened tonight.'

He sighed. 'It's very hard to be good right now.'

I nodded. 'I realise that. And you're doing extremely well.'

He let out another heavy sigh. 'With only one guard left, I hit him from behind with a wooden chopping board and Morris gave me his bike. I ditched it a few blocks from Burn and backtracked another couple of blocks to make sure no one was following me. When I finally got to your place, Gus was on his way out.'

At least he'd gotten away cleanly. I hoped.

I lay with Quentin for a few more minutes before extracting myself with the promise to return shortly. I quietly closed the bedroom door and prayed he would drop off to sleep. I'd be lying if I didn't admit a part of me wanted to go back in there and jump into his waiting arms. For all I knew, it would be my one and only chance.

Gus was in the same place I'd left him, standing over Travis, prodding him in the forehead with one hand, the tranq gun in the other.

'How long did it take you to figure it out?' Gus asked me, keeping the gun poised while nodding towards the bedroom.

'Probably a little longer than it should've,' I admitted. I'd been too busy basking in Quentin's words to notice he was on something.

Gus rolled his eyes. 'If it's any consolation, it says a lot that, even on that stuff, all he wanted was to get to you.'

I shrugged, not wanting to get into it with Gus right then. As I got closer, I noticed Travis wasn't moving.

'Gus?' I queried.

'What?' he snapped. 'I did like you said, but you were gone a long time and my arm got tired.' He waved the tranq gun around and I ducked a few times. 'My finger just slipped! Could've happened to anyone.'

I pulled the tranq dart out of Travis's shoulder and sighed.

Nine

Courtesy of Gus, Travis was knocked out for at least the next few hours so I sent Gus to bed, planning to have a rest on the couch where I could keep one eye on the door and the other on Travis.

Gus, already yawning, disappeared in a flash.

A couple of hours later, Quentin came out of the bedroom. Looking sheepish, he sat beside me.

Eventually he took hold of my hand, his fingers outlining the grazes on my knuckles, sending bolts of electricity up my arms and straight to my heart.

He raised his free hand, gesturing to my face, which was now sporting a bad bruise. 'What happened?' he asked, a hint of gravel in his voice.

I shook my head and pulled my hand away. 'How are you feeling?' I countered.

He licked his lips. 'Pretty rough, but better. More myself,' he said.

I nodded. 'That's good.'

'At least I get to stop living the lie now,' he said, causing me to blink in confusion. He noticed. 'You didn't really think I wanted to be there? Please tell me you know me better than that by now.' His eyes locked with mine and I found myself nodding.

'I know,' I whispered. 'I just … I know what it's like to have everything you believe in torn down, and I feel sick knowing that I did that to you.'

'You *didn't* do that,' he said, gently running a finger along my forehead and brushing back a few strands of hair. 'My family – the people I believed were my family – did that.'

Unsure where to go from here and feeling self-conscious about what had happened earlier, I jumped to my feet. 'Hungry?'

Quentin, looking at me as if he knew exactly what I was avoiding, nodded slowly.

I found a couple of packets of ramen noodles and boiled them up, and we sat on the couch and ate in silence. At that moment, what was there to say? The world as we knew it would never be the same. The bad guys were hunting us down, and the people who were supposed to be the good guys had turned their backs on us. A trigger-happy tech genius was asleep in the next room. And a black-market criminal – whose place we had just commandeered – was tied up and gagged in front of us.

Silence seemed appropriate.

After we had eaten, Quentin searched the bathroom and reappeared with a small first-aid kit. He proceeded to tend to my grazed hands. He also found a tub of ice-cream and held it gently to my bruised jaw.

All the while, I stared at him, wondering if there was anything I wouldn't do for him. My need to protect him from those who would do him harm was extreme. Perhaps it was due to our status as a true match. I thought back to the pregnant woman at the Mercer Ball who had stood by and allowed her true match to gun down her husband, who was also the father of her unborn child. Would I allow that?

I hoped not.

But I couldn't say for certain.

'I'm sorry about your mom,' I whispered. We'd each settled back onto opposite sides of the sofa, and I was trying hard not to focus on where our thighs were touching.

'I'm sorry about your dad,' he echoed.

'Yeah, he's a real piece of work,' I said, suddenly exhausted.

He threw me a roguish smile right before he jumped up, pulling me up with him. Suddenly I was standing before him, and he was close, and I was fairly certain he was about to kiss me, and Christ I wanted that kiss. I wanted it more than I'd ever wanted anything before. His eyes fixed on mine as his lips moved dangerously close and my heart thumped in my chest. With every ragged breath, I felt the frenzy of emotions and our desperate need to be together. Our lips hadn't even touched yet and I was already overwhelmed by my desire to be owned and to own him.

Except, of course, when I heard a sound and realised we had an audience.

'Uh, Quin,' I murmured.

'Uh-huh,' he replied, his lips brushing mine, causing me to almost throw caution to the wind.

'Travis is awake,' I said before I could stop myself.

Quentin blinked and stepped away from me as though I'd just tossed a bucket of ice-cold water on him.

I wanted to laugh, but my attention was quickly on my prisoner. Seeing his eyes and the way he watched me reminded me of my imprisonment. My jaw clenched as I slowly stepped towards him.

Travis watched me and I could feel the nerves radiating from him.

He was scared.

He should be.

But he was also a career criminal. He knew how to play the game. And he had people who would start looking for him before long. I needed to close whatever deal I was going to make with him, and fast.

I walked up nice and close and put my fingers on the edge of his gag. 'I don't imagine your neighbours are unaccustomed to hearing screams coming from this place, but still ...' I smiled, as if this whole thing was completely normal, and glanced briefly at his gun in my hand. 'If you don't do as I say, the next thing to hit you won't be a tranq. Do you understand me, Travis?'

He nodded.

I pulled down his gag.

He heaved a deep breath before narrowing his eyes at me. 'You shot me in the balls!'

Quentin winced.

I continued to smile. 'What can I say? I was feeling sentimental.'

'What does that mean?' Quentin asked.

Travis huffed. 'It means the bitch already kneed me in the balls once before.'

Quentin glared at Travis. 'Then I suggest you stop pissing her off.'

Travis looked between us, his eyes settling on Quentin. 'You shouldn't be here, Mercer. However much ass you're getting for this, trust me when I tell you, she's going to get you killed. You should go back to your almighty family.'

'Not going to happen, Travis,' I said. 'At least not while there are people in this world who can expose him.' My threat was clear. And he saw the truth in my eyes. If it came down to it, Travis was a price I would happily pay to protect Quentin.

Travis's shoulders slumped. 'I tried to warn you, Maggie.'

I crossed my arms. 'Oh? When exactly was that? Before or after you sold me out and double-crossed me?'

'I told you to walk away the day after Roosevelt. I didn't know you when I made the deal with your father. I didn't even know he *was* your father until the very end when I worked a few things out. I'd already taken his money. There was no backing out for me. I had to hand over the intel. You know how it goes in our world. But I only gave him what I had to. You gotta believe me.'

'Yeah. You only gave him enough to capture me and leave me locked away in a cell with no light, no hope and barely any food or water for over a month!'

Travis looked horrified. 'Your own father did that to you?'

'His and mine,' I said, waving towards Quentin.

'Shit, you two really lucked out with the family trees.'

'And *you* are plain shit out of luck, Travis,' I threw back.

'Look,' Travis started, but then winced.

Quentin disappeared into the kitchen, returning a moment later with a bag of frozen vegetables. He dropped it in Travis's lap.

'Thanks, man,' Travis said.

Quentin shrugged and sat on the couch.

'Look, Maggie,' Travis tried again, turning to me. 'I'm sorry. I'm not usually in the business of double-crossing, but it was an easy score – it was win-win for me. I was getting intel from you and money from your father. I was cleaning up.' When he saw my face, he quickly added, 'Not that that's an excuse for what I did.'

I glared at him. 'It goes like this, Travis. You now work for me. You and your entire team.'

Travis choked on a laugh. 'Sorry, but you can tie me up and tranq me all you want, sweetheart. You won't get my team on board. They'll happily watch you kill me before they ever work for you.'

I waited.

When his smile faded, I continued. 'Your hands are tied behind your back so I forgive you for not noticing straight away, but if you wriggle around a bit I'm sure it won't take long.'

I waited.

Travis slowly started to move. It only took a second.

'You've got my M-Band.'

I smiled broadly. 'No, Travis. *I* don't. *Gus* does. I'm not sure if you ever did your homework on Gus. He's a man of many talents. He was the head programmer at the Clarendon M-Store, but he liked to moonlight as a hacker, restoring retired M-Bands and selling them on the black market along with some other bits and bobs. Basically there's nothing he can't hack or ... download onto an M-Band. Did I mention I filmed a portion of our meeting back on Roosevelt, including the part where you activated the mines that ended up destroying half the island and taking ... how many lives?'

Travis's face paled.

'You see, I've always been good at keeping evidence. We all have skills, and that is what I do very well, Travis. I also happen to have a number of other ... informative little moments documented from the following day. Let's just say, it will be crystal clear to M-Corp exactly *who* was responsible for hijacking all of their lust-enhancer labs over the past three weeks. The files have all been stored in your M-Band in a place where, I promise you, no matter who you go to or what you pay, you will never find. But the second you cross me again, the *second* I think I can't trust you, all the files linked to your M-Band will be sent to the police, and to M-Corp security.'

'They'll kill me, Maggie.'

I nodded slowly. 'At least I'm giving you the chance to dig your own grave. It's more than you ever gave me.'

I turned away from Travis to give him a few minutes and took the opportunity to glance at Quentin, who was watching on. I wondered what he thought of me at this moment. Was he disgusted that I could go this far and be so heartless? Did he think this was easy? Did it remind him of how I'd treated him?

I looked away, turning my attention back to Travis.

'Tell me what you need and I'll make it happen.' Travis shook his head. 'And for the record, if you'd knocked on my door instead of knocking me out and tying me up, I would've let you in and tried to help anyway, Maggie. Believe what you want, but I wouldn't have sold you out if I'd known you.'

I nodded. 'And for the record, I wish I had been able to trust you enough to do that.'

Travis lifted his chin at Quentin, but kept his eyes on me. 'But you trust him? A *Mercer*?'

It was the easiest answer I'd even given. 'With all our lives.'

Ten

Travis paced back and forth. We'd released him a few hours ago, and Gus had joined us to let Travis in on our plan.

'We're all going to die, you know that,' Travis stated.

Gus nodded at me pointedly.

I stared.

'You want to go down into the tunnels and free an *entire* neg hub?'

Gus nodded again.

I stared.

'And who exactly is in the ground team you're proposing?' Travis asked.

'Me. You. And four of your best men,' I answered.

'Her, you, three of your best men, *and me*,' Quentin corrected.

'No, that is not how it's going to happen,' I said through gritted teeth.

Quentin crossed his arms and leaned against the kitchen bench. 'Yes, it is. You're not going down there alone with him and his men. No way. I'm coming with you.'

Travis grinned and gingerly sat down. 'Well, I have to say, I didn't see that coming from a Mercer. Maybe you aren't full of shit.' He looked at me. 'I agree. He comes. Better for all of us. If my men think he's down there, they won't think he's up here double-crossing them. And clearly he's the only one around here who has any hope of controlling you.'

I glared at them all.

Gus started chuckling. 'What?' he said, when I turned a hard look on him. 'He's right. And anyway, Quentin's the only one besides you who's been down there before.'

Quentin cleared his throat. 'You should know that if they see me, they'll probably shoot on sight,' he said, hands in his pockets, looking at his shoes.

'Well,' Travis said, sensing the mood, 'that all but makes you one of us then.' He leaned his head back, blinking as if fighting to keep his eyes open. 'And what happens to all of us after we majorly piss off the richest bastards in the world? Have you got somewhere to go?'

I wiped a tired hand over my face, wishing I had a better answer. 'We'll go off the grid, maybe get our chips removed.' I exhaled. 'I don't know, Travis. We'll leave the city that night and hope that when everything comes out about the negs and the underground ...'

'What?' He laughed. 'That you'll be welcomed back with open arms?'

'No,' Quentin said. 'We're not naive. But if what we do is enough to create division in public opinion, it will inevitably cause a division within the power structures too. And a division makes us valuable to one side.'

'Yep,' Gus agreed with a sarcastic nod. 'And a goddamn target to the other.'

Travis pointed at Gus while looking at Quentin and me. 'You should listen to your friend. We do this, we will be the most hunted people in the world.'

'So you'll do it?' I asked.

Travis rolled his eyes. 'Well, apart from having no fucking choice, I wouldn't mind blowing a few holes into the M-Corp armour. I've got a few friends that turned neg all too suddenly for my liking. I reckon I owe them a little justice.' He paused and looked at me, his eyes softening slightly. 'I reckon I might owe you too.'

I studied Travis, his shirt stained with blood and dirt from being beaten with the car door and dragged across the floor, his wrists badly bruised from the zip-ties. He had every reason to hate me and betray us, and yet … I found myself nodding, knowing that if he did double-cross me, it would most likely end in all of our deaths.

'But once we're done, we go our separate ways. Something tells me I'll be safest as far away from you lot as I can get.'

He was a smart man.

'What about the guys you'll bring in? Do you trust them?' Gus asked.

Travis didn't hesitate. 'No. But these guys will do anything for the right money, and I think that's the best way to go on this one. We tell them what they're risking and pay them well, but otherwise we don't give them the dirty details. Best if that stays just with us.'

I was surprised to see Travis strategising so quickly, but then, why wouldn't he? He was going to have to go down there with us, and giving the wrong people the wrong information would end very badly for him as well as for us.

'Okay,' I said. 'Brief your men on a big money, high-risk job, but nothing else until the night so they can't go running off their mouths. And make sure they know this is a no-kill job. Not unless there's absolutely no other option.' I hadn't killed anybody yet. At least not directly, and I didn't want to start now.

Travis nodded. 'When are we doing this?'

I turned to Gus and Quentin. With each day that went by, we were in more danger of being discovered. I would've liked a few more weeks to get stronger, but I was fit enough to hold my own. 'Gus?' I asked, knowing that he would need a certain amount of time to get his end organised.

'Two days at least,' he said. 'And you're going to have to get into the tunnels via an entry you've never used before. Your dad was aware of everything you'd done, which means at some point he corrupted our contacts or people we paid off along the way. We need a clean slate.'

I bit my lip. It was Wednesday morning and there was a lot of organising left to do. 'We hit the tunnels tomorrow night,' I said.

Everyone nodded slowly.

'I need to get some sleep,' Travis said, standing with a grimace before limping towards his room.

'Travis?' I called out.

He paused and looked over his shoulder.

'You don't leave the apartment. Got it?'

He nodded, unsurprised.

'And Travis?'

He tilted his head to the side.

'About that big money?' I asked.

He looked to the ceiling and shook his head. 'I've got you covered, Maggie. But the tally is getting heavy on my side. When we get this done, you're going to owe *me* one. Or two.'

Gus shot me a warning glance. Favours in our line of work were never nice.

'If we get through this alive and you hold up your end, you're right, I'll owe you one,' I said. 'Or two.'

I knew Travis would hold me to my word.

I didn't care.

As soon as Travis was in his room – with his windows nailed shut and his M-Band along with all other means of communication confiscated, much to his wry amusement – Quentin grabbed one of the handheld phones.

'Who do you think you're calling? I asked.

'Morris,' he replied, barely looking up.

'Wait!' I screeched, panicked.

He glanced up at me. 'He has some of my stuff.' When I put my hands on my hips, he sighed. 'Maggie, do you think I hadn't prepared for this? I've been slowly downloading codes from my father's computer when no one was around. I don't have a lot because I was scared I'd trigger some kind of hidden alarm, but what I did get might be of use.'

I bit my lip. Codes, especially if they got us access to underground security doors, would definitely be useful. Gus still hadn't found a direct route into the tunnels that would cater to our needs. Still ... I shook my head. 'We don't know for sure if the codes will be useful, and the risk is too high. Your family might already be looking for you.'

'They won't have hit the panic button yet. It's worth the risk.' Quentin clenched his jaw. 'Besides, intel isn't all that Morris has. And he's expecting my call.'

I stared at him.

He gave as good as he got.

'Money, Maggie.' Quentin checked his M-Band. 'Morris is running a big event for Georgetown University tonight. I need to get this call in before he leaves his house so he'll be ready to meet me later on.'

My jaw dropped. 'You must be kidding. You can't go back there!'

'We're going to need money and I have it. Gus has already disabled my M-Band, and as soon as it's ready he'll transfer me over to a black-market one. Once that's done, I'm no longer a Mercer. I'll no longer have access to all the things I've taken for granted my whole life. *Things* that could keep us safe. But I was at least smart enough to have one thing that none of them knew about.'

'Money zips,' Gus said, joining us. Frankly I was still stuck on the part where he'd talked about keeping *us* safe.

Quentin nodded. 'I'm Morris's silent partner in the gambling ring.'

That got my attention. How the hell had I never figured that out?

'It's not enough that we won't have to make some money eventually. But enough to get us out of here and keep us hidden if we're smart,' he explained.

Damn. Damn. Damn!

He was right. It was one thing to get Travis to pay off his guys, but after that we'd still need money and currently had none. If there was a stash, we absolutely needed it – especially if I had any hope of keeping my mom and Sam safe too. I'd already given them everything I'd stockpiled and it was bound to run out soon.

I quickly considered the dangers. Apart from not wanting to be out on the streets, knowing we were already being hunted by M-Corp, the main risk was Quentin being recognised.

'Fine. Set it up and I'll go and meet Morris. You stay here.'

Quentin smiled as he shook his head. 'Never gonna happen. Even if I was pathetic enough to let you go and do my legwork, Morris won't hand over the money zip to anyone until he lays eyes on me.'

I gritted my teeth – he was clearly enjoying this. Didn't he know what was at stake?

I went back to running through the possibilities. Unless Quentin's mother knew he'd overheard her conversation on the phone, all they knew was that he hadn't come home last night, not that he'd left for good, or that he was planning their downfall. With me.

I blew out a breath, then looked myself over. Christ. There was dried blood mingled with dirt caked on my hands and all over my clothes. My clothes were ripped and my boots were covered in mud from running around the cemetery – and I didn't need a mirror to know I was sporting an impressive bruise along my jaw.

'We'll go together,' I said.

Quentin wanted to argue. I could almost see his mind in overdrive trying to decide on the best argument. I rested my hand on his arm. 'Together, Quin.'

His arguments fell away as he nodded.

After Quentin sent some kind of coded message to Morris and made a mysterious, brief call from one of the handheld burn phones, we continued with our preparations – Gus looking for our way in and out of the tunnels, Quentin taking me through a workout session and then studying some of my covert footage of the neg hubs.

When the handheld beeped, Quentin stared at it as if contemplating an important decision.

'What is it?' I asked, suddenly wary.

He shook his head at me. 'We're on for tonight. We need to dress discreetly – black if you have it.'

I gave him a sardonic look. Black was all I had.

He half smiled. 'I'm going to grab a quick shower. Can you be ready to go in twenty?'

He looked worried, and that made me worried. But this was something we both knew we had to do. I wished I could go without him and keep him safe. I knew he was thinking the same thing about me. But we were strongest together.

'I'll be ready.'

I took a quick shower in the second bathroom near the kitchen. The shower cubicle was tiny and the taps were rusted, but I didn't care. It was heavenly. Never again would I take for granted such basic necessities as soap and hot water. Not to mention a razor. Or a mirror.

Back in my small room, I pulled on one of my few pairs of underwear, groaning when I noticed that my dismally small garbage bag of belongings was almost out of wearable clothes. Gus had brought what I had from the apartment, but that only amounted to a few changes of clothes and I'd already ruined most of them the previous night. If I planned on making it back into the tunnels fully clothed, I was going to have to fit in a trip to the shops.

I sighed, pulling on what I had and yanking my hair back into a ponytail before heading out to the living room.

Quentin was already there, loitering by the elevator doors as he waited for me. He was in the same outfit from last night – a simple pair of dark grey jeans and a long-sleeved black tee beneath his denim jacket – and yet he looked his usual wayward self, which was also somehow perfect. How the hell did people do that? Was it that their clothes cost so much to start with that it didn't matter how they were thrown on, they'd still come out looking perfectly styled? Is that what it meant to have money? Why everyone wanted it so much? Because it made a person perfect? The thought had me clenching my jaw and thinking of my father.

Gus and Travis were in the kitchen discussing pizza toppings. Travis, like me, seemed happy to stick with all things unhealthy, whereas Gus liked to protect his health, arguing that until we didn't need to worry about ratings, his pheromones would give off nothing but good vibes to the ladies.

Their discussion was just morphing into an argument when Gus spotted me. He threw his hands in the air dramatically. 'Great. So you and him ...' he pointed at Quentin who had moved towards me, 'get to party the night away, while I'm on babysitting duty with the scary badass criminal you recently nailed in the balls and I *accidentally* but nonetheless shot with a tranq, and, oh yeah, who we just forced into a certain-death mission which also guarantees that, if we don't happen to die *during* it, he will take pleasure in hunting us down for the rest of our days. Is that about right?'

I bit back a smile.

Quentin slapped Gus on the back. 'You forgot the part where Maggie slammed his body with the car door repeatedly just for fun.'

Gus glared at Quentin. 'I actually thought I'd hit the highlight with the shot to the balls,' he mused.

Quentin laughed. 'You're probably right.'

Eleven

'So where exactly are we meeting Morris?' I asked as we got into a taxi. I reached forwards before Quentin could say anything and held out a money zip to the driver. 'No M-Bands,' I said, holding his gaze.

The driver didn't hesitate, taking the money zip, which would earn him much more than any ordinary cab fare. Fortunately, sideline revenue was common practice for anyone who wanted to earn some untraceable cash on the side.

'Where you going?' the driver asked.

Quentin sat back. 'The Mellon, in DC.'

The driver nodded and turned his attention to the road while I spun towards Quentin.

'DC?' I asked, my voice suddenly high-pitched.

He nodded.

'The Mellon is basically Capitol Hill. Are you insane?' God, I was going to be sick. Suddenly Gus's warnings about Quentin's intentions came flooding back. Was I being a complete fool? Was he leading me back to them? I shut my eyes briefly, confused by all the possibilities.

'Breathe, Maggie. It will be fine. It's the annual Diplomatic Ball for Georgetown. They run it every year, and in the past few years they've made it a masquerade ball. It's supposed to be a symbol of the way forwards – they invite some of the most powerful men and women in society and also some of the least privileged. Everyone's dressed to the same standard – if they can't afford an outfit, they're given one. And on arrival each guest is fitted with a jewelled mask. Some are fake, but others are the real deal – diamonds and precious gems. People leave their Phera-tech active, so they can see what kind of ratings they get. It's a last attempt at stripping back social structures and age barriers – the ratings do all the talking. It's the perfect advertisement for Phera-tech,' he explained, sounding increasingly ashamed. He looked at me sadly. 'It was always one of my favourite events.'

'Why?' I asked, again cautious of his behaviour. Was he leading me into a trap?

'Five charities are chosen to be represented on the night. At the end of the night, each guest has the chance to place their mask on the table of the charity of their choice.'

I caught on. 'Not knowing if their mask is worth nothing or a small fortune.'

Quentin nodded.

'I like that part,' I said, somewhat soothed by his explanation. 'But why are we meeting Morris there?'

He shrugged. 'It was always on our radar as a backup. With everyone watching out for you – and possibly me by now – it will be my last chance.'

'But they'll have scanners everywhere. It won't matter if they can't pick up our identities from our forged M-Bands – their scanners go directly to the M-Chip, Quin. We'll be in handcuffs before we get anywhere near Morris. I can't believe you were even contemplating this. We can figure out another way to get to Morris.' I leaned forwards to tell the taxi driver to turn around, but Quentin grabbed my arm, halting me.

'You mean *you'll* be in handcuffs.'

I flinched. His words were cold, his eyes guarded. Was this it? The moment I'd been waiting for? The moment Gus had warned me about? Had Quentin changed sides after my betrayal?

I swallowed in an attempt to kickstart my breathing.

'That's what you really mean, isn't it?' he went on, remaining calm and yet *not* at the same time. It was like watching a storm brew.

I managed to draw in a little oxygen and opened my mouth to speak, but when nothing came out, he let out a man-huff.

'I knew you'd consider it. The way your mind works, I knew you'd have to go there at some point, so I'm not surprised. But strangely it doesn't stop me from feeling incredibly angry now that I can actually see it.'

'W-what …?' I stumbled over my words, trying to catch up.

'You think I turned.'

Silence.

'You think I'm one of them. That at any moment, I'll hand you over.'

I wanted to scream, *No!* That was what my heart was telling me. But my mind … all the wariness and suspicion I'd had to develop over the past two years caused me to believe his betrayal was definitely a possibility. 'I wouldn't blame you,' I said softly.

He reared back, as if burned by my words.

'You wouldn't … blame me?'

I shook my head, avoiding his livid gaze. 'They're your family. And I've done nothing but let you down.'

Suddenly he had my chin in his grasp, forcing my eyes to his. 'Just because they're my family, doesn't make it okay, Maggie.' The words were hissed with so much venom, if he hadn't been holding my face so close to his, I would have shied away. 'What you're talking about, what *you* are contemplating that I'm capable of –' His voice caught. 'It's genocide.'

He leaned so close, his lips were on my ear. 'If you think I'm capable of that, you should take the knife I know you have strapped to your thigh and run it through my heart right now. Because I guarantee you, if I have turned, you and Gus and everyone else is as good as dead.'

His words were lethal. Whispered low and strong. My body tingled with the threat.

He leaned back to catch my eyes and I was sure he could see the myriad emotions and thoughts flickering through my expression.

But for every alarm bell and warning sign I knew I should acknowledge, another thought would stamp it out.

This was Quentin.

I'd followed him for two years. I'd thought I had known who he was, only to be surprised that he was so much more.

He had never betrayed my trust. He had been the one to find the way to get me out of that prison cell. He had held me through the night, chased away the nightmares. He might not have let me back into his heart, but he had done nothing to hurt me.

'You're my match,' I said softly, as though offering a confession.

'What does that have to do with this?'

I swallowed again, my mouth cotton-dry. 'I've done things ... things I can never make amends for. Things that have cost lives. I have become a person I can't bear to look at in the mirror. And you are my match.'

Quentin let out a breath, finally grasping what I was saying.

'That's why you can't trust me? Because you think I must be like you to be your match? And that you are so terrible that me turning on you is entirely possible?' With each question he sounded less angry and increasingly sad.

I nodded.

He tilted my face again to force my eyes to his. 'You're better than you think you are, Maggie. Maybe when you realise that, you'll be able to stop doubting me.'

My eyes stung with tears, but I held them back.

Slowly he released my chin and sat back. He took a deep breath, and when he started talking it was with a new resolve. 'This is the one night the scanners are shut down. The event is under tight security. Invite only and the invites are unmarked. The entire point is anonymity.'

I hesitated. But I needed to either move on, or do exactly what Quentin had said and draw my weapon – which, let's face it, was never going to happen. 'You can't believe people won't recognise a Mercer. And what if they're looking for you? They'll find you with me, and then you'll be exposed.'

Quentin was ready for this. 'Yes, being ... me makes me more recognisable, but being a Mercer also ensures no one would dare make a scene. That's the last thing my parents would want.' His eyes bore into mine. 'You have to decide – you either trust me, or you don't. Morris's family are one of the main organisers behind the event. He'll be ready for us.' Quentin looked ahead, remaining quiet as if he could sense my internal battle. I suppose there wasn't much more to say. He had laid out his challenge, and I knew he wouldn't back down.

In the end, so much of this came down to one annoying word. *Trust*. Quentin still hadn't said how he felt about me – apart from when he'd been high on lust-enhancers. But I knew I didn't have his trust. Even though he seemed so comfortable demanding mine.

But *could* I truly trust him? Trust anyone? My own father had just torn my whole world apart – could I risk giving Quentin the same power?

I'd chosen this life. This loner way.

Could I truly be the better person I'd always told myself I would be?

Was there anything more to me than being a liar and manipulator?

I felt Quentin's fingers link through mine. When he squeezed my hand, I stopped the spiral of thoughts and glanced up at him, knowing he could see all of my fears in my wild eyes.

'Stop overthinking. The world you see out there is about to change forever,' he said, his voice low so only I could hear. 'We're going to make sure of it. Right now, *our* world is the only real world there is. I don't know about you, but I'd take truth over a lie any day.' He looked as though he wanted to say more, but didn't – or couldn't.

And it didn't matter, because those were the words that I had needed to hear. I nodded slowly and breathed deeply. 'I'm sorry for doubting you, but I can't let him get away with this, Quin. Those people down there deserve their freedom and the world needs to know the truth. Maybe then I'll have a chance to finally wash away the stains.' Yet even as I said it, I doubted its truth. Stains never washed away. Not fully.

Quentin pulled me close and kissed the top of my head. I sank into the sanctuary of his strong arms, wishing I could stay there forever. 'You *are* going to save people, Mags. And your father, along with my family, is going to pay. I promise you that.'

I had to believe he was right. And for once in my life, instead of trying to think three steps ahead of the game, I was going to do something that went against my nature. And would no doubt piss off Gus.

I was going to trust him.

The taxi pulled to a stop outside The Mellon. A black-and-white chequered carpet led the way up the granite stairs of the imposing, temple-like structure. My eyes took in the six colossal columns, the central focus of the purple and green lightshow.

'Take us to the laneway entrance at the back of the building,' Quentin instructed the driver.

When the taxi pulled to a stop, Quentin moved swiftly, taking my hand and pulling me from the car. As soon as the taxi took off, the door at the back of the building opened and Ivy Knight stood before us.

I flinched, backing up a step. Quentin tightened his hold on my hand.

'What's going on?' I asked.

Quentin grinned. 'You said you wanted to come with me to meet Morris?'

I nodded cautiously.

'Then you had better get dressed.'

It was only then that I noticed the outfit Ivy was wearing – she was in a full ball gown.

Suddenly I felt self-conscious. Here I was in my torn-up Target jeans, my military boots still covered in dried mud, and a crappy out-of-shape faded black T-shirt. My face was covered in bruises. My hoodie was the only thing I had going for me, and not because of the state of it, but because it hid the hair I'd hacked away and hadn't bothered to fix up. And now, it was also hiding my blush.

I could only imagine how refreshing Ivy looked to him.

I glared at Quentin. 'I can't believe this,' I mumbled.

Quentin's smirk returned. 'Is this your jealous side?'

My glare turned glacial. He was enjoying this way too much.

'What the hell is going on?' I snapped.

Quentin shrugged and Ivy crossed her arms patiently.

'In order for you to be here we needed help, Maggie. You can't have it all your way,' Quentin explained.

I looked in each direction down the back laneway. I couldn't see anyone, but that didn't mean no one was watching. We couldn't stay out in the open like this and we both knew it.

But I just couldn't bring myself to go in there with his girlfriend. I took a step back and turned around when Quentin suddenly spoke. 'She knew!'

I paused, but didn't turn. 'She knew it was all a lie. From the moment I went back to school and struck things up with her again, she knew it was just a cover. She doesn't feel that way about me anymore, Maggie. She just helped me.'

I swallowed, still not turning.

'He's telling you the truth,' Ivy said, speaking for the first time. 'And if you want to make this ruse happen tonight, you're going to have to get over your issues and hurry the hell up.'

Damn it. She was right. I was being petty.

I could have pushed – I wanted to know more – but something in me stopped me asking any questions. Instead, I gave a small nod and turned, walking straight past Quentin and through the back door Ivy held open.

Twelve

Ivy walked us through a series of hallways, which appeared to be used only by service staff. She showed Quentin into a bathroom first. 'Everything you need is in there. Morris said he will try to get to you in the ballroom.'

Quentin nodded. 'Thanks, Ivy. I know what you risked, helping us.' His face was genuine and I could see they shared a bond. I didn't want to be jealous, but I couldn't help it. So when Ivy nodded and walked on, motioning for me to follow, I did so keeping my head down.

But Quentin clearly wasn't willing to accept that and he grabbed my arm as I passed, pulling my ear to his mouth.

His words were whispered. 'I already told you. There is only one thing I know for certain, Maggie. And a lot I'm still trying to figure out. But Ivy Knight is not even part of the equation.'

I felt my cheeks redden. Quentin released my arm and moved into the bathroom, leaving me to follow Ivy. I still wasn't sure what his one thing was, but the more I heard about it, the more I damn well wanted to know!

Ivy led me down another hallway and then into what looked like an office. As soon as she closed and locked the door, she turned to me, looking me up and down with a sigh. 'Strip,' she instructed as she reached around and started to unbutton her ball gown.

'Ah … sorry … I … what?'

She rolled her eyes. 'You are at a ball.' She spoke as if talking to a simpleton. 'You need to get into the ballroom unnoticed. There are a lot of people looking for you. And Quin.' She batted her eyes at me. 'Strip.'

Okaaaay. She was nuts. But I did as I was told.

When she was down to her underwear, she passed me her gown and grabbed my jeans and T-shirt. I cringed on her behalf.

'Sorry,' I muttered, seeing her pull on my rags.

She shrugged. 'I'm getting the better deal. That corset hurts like a bitch.'

I almost smiled as I fingered the delicate material. The dress was beautiful. Not me at all. But I could appreciate it wasn't your ordinary dress.

'I arrived early to help Morris set up so I've already done a few circuits of the room and talked to the people who would recognise me regardless of the mask. Once you get your mask and you go out there in this dress …' She crouched to where a bag was hidden behind the desk. 'And this wig,' she said, pulling a long platinum-blonde wig from the bag. 'They'll think you're me. Just avoid talking to people where you can.'

'You don't already have the mask?'

Ivy shook her head. 'They're alarmed. Once they are on, they can't be taken off unless it's to hand it in for the night. You're going to have to do that part yourself.'

'Okay,' I said, trying not to let my nerves go wild.

I took the wig from her outstretched hand and, still standing there in nothing but my underwear, jammed it on my head and stared at myself in the mirror.

'Well, that looks ridiculous,' I mumbled.

Ivy snickered. 'It won't when we have the rest of you put together. Don't worry, I brought supplies,' she said, now pulling out a cosmetics bag.

I stared at myself in the mirror, wondering how this was all going to work. I'd filled out a lot since leaving my cell, but still, my cheekbones were much more defined than before and the large almond-shaped eyes I'd inherited from Mom now seemed alien-large. I huffed, increasingly frustrated with my deficiency in all things beauty related. Gus would have looked better in this dress.

Ivy ignored me. She set up a table of makeup and pulled out a chair. 'Sit, we only have a few minutes.'

I looked at Ivy who was dangling a pair of high heels in her hands.

'I hope we're a similar size,' she said. 'Otherwise it could be a painful night.'

I narrowed my eyes. 'So Quentin just asked you to help, and you did?'

'He said there might be consequences,' she said with a no-biggie shrug. She kneeled and buckled me into the shoes. They were a perfect fit. 'But he's always been a touch dramatic.'

'Not this time,' I murmured, my mind already contemplating the 'consequences' for Ivy – and for us.

'I know what I'm doing,' she said. And though she couldn't possibly have known what she was doing – not really – I got the distinct impression that even if she had, it wouldn't have changed her decision. I tilted my head, confused, as I watched her hold up different shades of foundation to my face.

'You really knew all this time?' I said. 'You've really been helping him? Knowing that he and I … that we are … were …'

'Together?' she suggested with a raised brow. When I just stared at her, doing everything I could to look tough and not give away the fact I was tongue-tied over a guy, she lifted a shoulder and stood awkwardly in the middle of the room. 'We've been friends forever. We kind of got thrown together, you know. "The high-school couple." But when the ratings went wrong the first time … I realised I wasn't all that disappointed. I love Quin, but I was never *in* love with him. I've missed having him as my friend.'

'And now you're here, helping me? You do realise M-Corp are hunting me? That if you're caught helping me, you could be in serious danger?'

She nodded. 'But from what I understand, you guys need all the help you can get.' She gestured for me to look up and started efficiently applying makeup to my face and eyes. 'All I know is that you and Quentin – and by that, I mean *mostly* you – have made a lot of very important people very upset. But I've seen enough in the last month to know a few things: the first is that Quentin was followed everywhere by guards who frightened him, guards who were sent by his own family. In my book, that's wrong.' Instantly, my opinion of Ivy flew up a few notches.

'Secondly, whatever's going on between the two of you, I've never seen Quentin like this before. The way he talked about you …' She half laughed. 'I've never seen him so angry or desperate or passionate about anything or anyone before.'

'You realised you just used the words angry and desperate? It's not exactly a glowing report.'

She shrugged. 'You hear angry. But to me, it's the type of emotion that's only born from the kind of intense and crazy love most people never get to experience, so …'

I crossed my arms. 'So you just risked your own future and safety to help Quentin and me?' I asked, not bothering to hide my disbelief.

'He's my friend, Maggie. And maybe you need one too.'

We stared at each other as the seconds ticked by. Part of me knew this could be a trap and yet, watching Ivy, I felt nothing but confusion. Because as much as I should have run screaming, I found myself staring at the dress, the shoes, and then Ivy, who looked back at me with honesty in her pretty eyes.

I picked up a hairbrush and held it out. 'Any chance you know how to fix my hair under this wig?' I asked, embarrassed that I cared.

She nodded and took the brush. But as soon as she removed my wig, her expression became uncertain.

'What?' I asked.

She bit down on her thumbnail. 'We might need a pair of scissors too.'

For the first time since Ivy had opened the back door, I cracked a smile.

Twenty minutes later I stood in front of the floor-to-ceiling mirror on the back of the office door, trying to find something familiar about the girl standing before me. I scrunched up my face. 'I don't know if I can do this,' I mumbled.

'Of course you can,' Ivy said, not missing a beat as she continued to adjust the wig that made me a platinum blonde. Just like her. 'You're wearing the dress that many people have already seen me in. Your hair is ...' she glanced up, her nose twitching, 'as good a match as possible with a wig. And we're roughly the same height and weight,' she surmised.

'I only had to get locked up and starved to death,' I joked.

Ivy's hands dropped from my hair and her mouth fell open. 'I ... I didn't know ...'

I flashed her a grin. 'Don't sweat it.'

When her face remained frozen in pity, my grin turned to a glare. 'Ivy,' I said sternly. 'I said, don't sweat it.'

Finally she snapped out of it and nodded. 'Okay. I just, I don't know … How are you so … okay?'

I adjusted the high heels, noting I wouldn't be able to run for shit in them. 'I'm okay because I have to be.'

'And what about when that technique doesn't work anymore?'

'Excuse me?'

'People can shut things off all they want, but sooner or later it catches up. Eventually you can't stop it.'

I gritted my teeth. 'Thanks for the tip, Ivy. But I'm just fine,' I said, refusing to acknowledge that I feared the exact same thing. Sometimes it felt like I was holding on by the tiniest of threads. But what would it help to admit it?

'No, you're not,' Ivy threw back, surprising me with her boldness. Her expression softened. 'But lucky for you, Quin is one of the good ones. If you let him in, he'll be there for you.'

I bit my lip.

'It's not as simple as that. Quentin and I are …'

'Complicated?'

I nodded.

'So uncomplicate it.'

My eyes flashed up to hers. But I found myself lost for words when I saw her genuine smile. And suddenly my selfish concerns turned to guilt. Ivy was honest and kind. She was a true friend to Quentin whereas I had not been. She was from a powerful family, she was intelligent and beautiful and had the world at her feet – and still, she was here lending me her clothes, her *identity*, to help her friend.

'Thank you, Ivy,' I said.

When she looked confused, I gestured to myself. 'For helping me get ready. I couldn't have pulled this off without you.' I threw a hand towards her cosmetics bag. 'I didn't even realise what half of those makeup things were for.'

Her expression morphed into a smile. 'You're welcome.' She moved to the door and peeked into the hall. 'Okay. I'm going to tell you how to get to the mask room. I would take you there, but ...' She looked down at herself and I almost burst out laughing. She looked ridiculous in my torn-up jeans and hoodie.

'What are you going to do?' I asked.

Ivy shrugged. 'A night at home with a movie is well overdue for me.'

I bit my lip, overwhelmed that she could be this kind to me when there was seemingly no personal gain. 'Just point me in the right direction. I'll take it from here.'

Following Ivy's instructions, I kept my head down and approached one of the waitstaff dressed in a white tuxedo. When he didn't raise any alarm bells, I requested he escort me to the mask room. The man gave a curt nod and led me towards a large set of open double doors. He didn't say anything so I just nodded and entered the room, knowing that the sooner my face was covered, the safer I would be.

Inside the large sitting room I paused to watch a group of women collecting their purses and waited for them to make their way out. There was an excited bounce in their steps and they giggled and whispered as they hurried out to the ballroom. I pressed my lips together, wondering fleetingly what that would be like. What my life would've been like if my father had been a different man – a kinder person. And then I wondered what my life would've been like if I had been a kinder person too.

'Well, you have perfect timing. That group of ladies have left you the room to yourself,' came a gentle voice. I looked up to see a raven-haired woman in a long apricot dress that flowed like a water fountain from her waist. The effect of the shimmering material was remarkable. 'I'm Eva and I will be selecting your mask this evening.'

I nodded, avoiding any further introductions. This didn't seem to bother Eva, who simply smiled and took a small step back. 'Now, why don't you take a seat and we'll try a couple of these masks on you.' She gestured to one of the large swivel chairs. 'I think I have one that will go beautifully with that dress,' she murmured as she studied a tall stand adorned with a dazzling array of masks. 'Here it is!'

She turned to me, gracefully fitting the mask to my face and moving behind me to fix the ties and pin it to my hair. As she went about her work, I heard another person being escorted into the room and instructed to sit several spaces down from me. When Eva's hand slipped at one point, I felt the wig shift slightly. She felt it too.

I froze.

Time slowed down.

After what felt like a small eternity, she leaned close to me, placing a warm hand on my shoulder. 'Tonight is all about discretion, darling. Your secret is safe with me,' she whispered. 'Let me just ...' She readjusted the wig and inserted a few extra pins. 'There. That will hold better now.'

I swallowed nervously. 'Thank you.'

She spun the chair around. 'And we are all done! What do you think of the mask? Everyone has a right to refuse twice before their selection is locked in,' she explained.

I gazed at myself in the floor-to-ceiling mirror. But, of course, it wasn't my reflection I was looking at. My heart sped up and I felt my M-Band vibrate with a pulse alert. Everyone was staring at me – including the other guest in the room. I had to pull it together and get out of there.

Get a grip, Maggie!

My palms were tingling with fear and the wig suddenly felt impossibly hot.

'Well?' Eva asked.

I licked my lips.

'I think it's breathtaking,' came the familiar voice from the other end of the room.

Slowly, I turned to face Eliza Mercer, who looked like royalty in a scarlet-red gown.

Our eyes locked and I was sure she was looking right at me, beyond the mask and hair. She knew it was me.

'But that's no surprise. You have a memorable flare for fashion.'

I glanced down at my ball gown. Eliza's comment made no sense – I felt ridiculous in Ivy's lime-green dress with its enormous full skirt. But then I flashed back to the one other time I'd met Eliza Mercer – at the annual Mercer Ball when I'd unwittingly worn a vintage black wedding dress.

My M-Band vibrated against my wrist in a steady thrum of alarm. Every sound was amplified – the sound of laughter beyond the doors, of glasses clinking and high heels hitting the marble floors.

'It is a beautiful mask,' Eva said from behind me. 'But if you prefer another, I have some other options I think would work.'

Eliza stood and took a few steps towards me, her face breaking into a quizzical smile. 'Ivy? That is you, isn't it?'

Swallowing the lump in my throat, I pulled myself together just in time to nod. 'Yes,' I said as quickly as possible. I turned back towards the mirror, studying the mask properly for the first time. The base was charcoal grey, the eye area encrusted with what looked like diamonds. On the right side, a curtain of clear gems hung down so that it looked like I was crying diamonds. It really was extraordinary.

And probably glass.

I touched the mask with my fingertips. 'It's perfect, Eva. Thank you.'

Eva beamed. 'I agree. The alarm automatically activates when you leave the room so just remember you can't remove the mask until you hand it in at the exit doors.'

'Okay,' I said, running my fingers over the mask briefly. I nodded in Eliza Mercer's direction briefly. 'Enjoy your evening,' I said softly.

'You too, Ivy,' Eliza said slowly. 'And do be sure to let my son know that I would like at least one dance tonight. His father couldn't make it this evening, so it appears I'm partnerless and it feels like I haven't seen him in days.' She smiled knowingly. 'I imagine that might have something to do with you.'

Eva must have sensed my need for escape because she took my arm. 'You had better get on with showing the room your gorgeous mask and I had better get on with finding the perfect match for Mrs Mercer.' Eva turned from me and started towards Eliza. 'Now, we need something incredible to go with that dress ...' she began as I gratefully bee-lined out of the room before Eliza could say anything else.

Thirteen

I spotted Quentin on the far side of the ballroom easily. My eyes were drawn to him instantly and there was no mistaking the impressive way he filled out his midnight-blue tuxedo. Apparently I wasn't the only female aware of his presence, given the three-deep circle of fans hovering around him.

Looking around the room, filled with diplomatic representatives, I questioned again if this had been the right decision. We were out in the open and in the thick of political territory. We may as well have been in the lobby of M-Corp, considering Garrett Mercer controlled the government. At least – thanks to Eliza Mercer's comment – I knew Garrett wasn't there.

I wondered idly how many politicians or their family members M-Corp had turned neg in order to control, or silence. My hands fisted as I considered this, let alone the fact that M-Corp's facilities below ground were all once government property.

I started to make my way towards Quentin when someone tapped me on the shoulder. I spun around, half expecting to see a team of M-Corp security guards holding their guns in my face, but it was a guy. Slightly shorter than average, with a receding hairline and medium build. He was wearing a red tuxedo – yes, tuxedo colours were all the rage – and a green mask. He looked like a Christmas decoration.

'I'm sorry, miss,' he said with a charmer's voice. 'But I couldn't help noticing you and I had to say hello.'

God help me.

'Hello,' I said, knowing I had to play the part. 'Are you having a nice evening?' Isn't that what boring people with too much money say?

'I am. And when I saw you I instantly moved closer to see if we might have the kind of rating I suspect we would, however …' I didn't need to see behind the mask to know he was raising his eyebrows. 'I do believe having our Phera-tech in active mode is very much the point of the evening. Unless, of course, you are married?'

He was challenging me, knowing that even if I was married, if I moved in the right social circles, that wouldn't stop me from supporting this event and activating my tech.

I forced a smile and adjusted my M-Band setting, turning on my Phera-tech for the first time since Quentin had taken our rating. The tech activated instantly and a rating flashed up for the guy in front of me. My smile became genuine and I shrugged. 'Maybe next time,' I said, enjoying seeing his face drop at the measly seventeen per cent compatibility reading. That pretty much excluded us from everything, even friendship.

'I see you're still forcing yourself on unsuspecting victims, Justin,' said a man who approached us from the side and clapped the red tuxedo man on the back.

'I thought tonight was supposed to be anonymous,' the man grumbled as he shoved past the taller man who chuckled.

The man, wearing a more traditional black tuxedo, turned to me. He was wearing a white mask with silver markings and it covered most of his face, making it hard to see anything more than his mouth. 'I have incredible powers of observation,' he said with a slight accent I couldn't place. Maybe British.

'Oh?' I questioned with a small smile, playing along while I tried to figure out how to get over to Quentin. 'And what would your observations of me be?'

'You're distracted.'

My eyes flashed to the stranger. He held out his hand. 'And a dance would cure you of that.'

Before I knew what I was doing, I took the man's hand, hoping that a dance across the centre of the ballroom floor might get me over to where Quentin was being swamped by women who had clearly identified the Mercer heir. I had to let him know his mother was nearby, and we still had to find Morris.

'You're still distracted,' he said, turning me around the room with so much skill that he managed to make it look like I was actually something more than a ragdoll in his arms.

'Why do you think that?' I said, working hard to keep my focus on my dance partner.

'Because you agreed to dance with me, and yet you haven't once looked at your M-Band to check our rating.' He pulled me close. 'Which happens to be very impressive, by the way.'

My step faltered, but he held me up. Casually I turned the wrist that was resting on his shoulder towards me to read the rating.

I glanced back at him. 'It is ... quite good.'

'Seventy-nine per cent is a little more that *quite good*,' he said.

He spun me around and a flash of red caught my eye. I gazed up to one of the balconies that rimmed the ballroom. Eliza Mercer was standing next to a man in a black tuxedo and turquoise mask that matched the unusually coloured flower in his lapel. They were both facing the dance floor, as if ignoring one another, but I could see their lips move in fast conversation and then the man's shoulders dropped, as if he'd received terrible news.

I shook my head, wondering what Eliza Mercer was up to now. If she did know it was me in the mask room, I needed to be ready for anything. The only thing that kept me from making a run for it was Quentin's words from earlier. And he was right. She wouldn't make a public scene.

'Sadly for me,' my dance partner said as he turned us again and broke my line of sight, 'it's the highest rating I've yet to record.'

I blinked back to the conversation. 'Sadly?'

He nodded and, for the first time, smiled. The warm expression triggered something in me and I took a closer look at the stranger, my eyes narrowing. When he spoke next, he leaned close to my ear. The accent was gone. 'These things rarely work out well when the lady is already spoken for.'

I gasped, but he held me close and shook his head in warning when I opened my mouth to say his name.

'Took you long enough,' he murmured.

I pulled back enough to look at Morris's eyes through the mask. 'We have to get –'

He cut me off with a sharp squeeze of my hand before I could say Quentin's name, his eyes darting to his M-Band.

It was then that I saw the small amber light, indicating a recording device was in operation. Someone was listening in. All M-Bands were fitted with recording devices that could be activated remotely – for 'reasons of security' – by someone with a warrant. Or enough power.

And if they were listening … My eyes shifted from side to side. I suddenly felt like I was in a fishbowl.

'I was beginning to worry I wouldn't be meeting anyone tonight,' he said in a voice that let me know he was talking about his planned meet-up with Quentin. 'It seems everyone is on the prowl this evening. But when

I saw you walk in, I knew it would be my one chance. Nice … *mask*, by the way.'

'How'd you know it was me?'

'To be honest, at first I thought you were someone else, but when I got up close, I realised my error.' He grinned mischievously.

My curiosity was piqued. 'How?'

'Her boobs are bigger than yours.'

'Oh,' I said, glancing down then back at Morris. 'Good observation.'

He shrugged. 'I try to be thorough.'

'I don't like this,' I whispered.

'Neither do I,' Morris replied. For the first time, I registered his clammy palms and the way he kept licking his dry lips. He wasn't as calm as I'd assumed. Which meant I needed to get a grip and get us through this.

'Just keep dancing,' I murmured, pulling him closer. 'And let's both try to look as though it isn't some form of cruel and unusual torture.'

He smiled, his shoulders relaxing. We danced until we'd moved behind a large group who were all dancing together.

Morris's fingers were jittery on my back. When the group laughed loudly, he took the opportunity to lean close to my ear and whisper, 'You guys are in some deep shit.'

'And then some. Thanks for helping us,' I replied quickly.

He nodded, his eyes darting about. 'You know I'm good for it.'

'Are you?' I threw back, not caring if I offended him. The tension coming off Morris was causing my skin to crawl.

'Follow your instincts. I don't think they will mislead you.' Morris stared at me before glancing over my shoulder. He turned me slowly until I was facing the same direction as him. I spotted a man talking into his M-Band. He was in a black tuxedo with a sunflower-yellow pocket square. Morris discreetly turned me again and I spotted a similarly dressed man, then again, and again until I had counted twelve guards. And that was just what I could see in the room.

I looked back into his waiting eyes. Slowly I nodded, letting him know that I understood.

'My instincts say you're a trustworthy kind of person. For a stranger, of course,' I said in what I hoped came across as a flirty voice to whoever was listening. 'But I'm afraid I wasn't planning on having a late night, so I'm not sure I'm the best person for your lovely attention.'

The corner of Morris's mouth lifted. 'Unfortunately that might be true,' he said. I noticed that Quentin had moved closer to the dance floor and was looking in our direction. I prayed he didn't try to intervene. 'Are you driving?' Morris asked conversationally as he pulled a folded envelope from inside his jacket.

I shook my head. 'Train and bus,' I said, hoping to give some misdirection. Subtly I looked around. There were guards disguised as guests everywhere. God knows how many more were hidden where I could not see.

Morris carefully passed the envelope to me and I managed to quickly slip it down the front of my dress. But there was no way the transfer had gone completely unseen.

When I looked up, I saw that Quentin was moving towards us. No!

'In that case, I wish you a very good evening and safe travels.' He leaned close, kissing me just below the edge of my mask on one cheek and then dropping the hand with his M-Band as he kissed the other, and whispered quickly, 'Everything is there, plus a little extra that was out of my control. There's a black Range Rover across the street. The code on the outside of the envelope will activate driver privileges. Make sure you look in the glove compartment straight away.'

I nodded. 'I won't forget this.'

Morris tipped a finger to his head in mock salute, playing the part. 'I'm sure you won't.'

With that I quickly stepped past Morris, took two steps towards Quentin and grabbed his arm, squeezing hard in warning before I released him and walked towards the exit. When I chanced a look over my shoulder, I exhaled with relief to see that he was following me instead of Morris.

I made my way out of the main ballroom and into a hallway, following a waitress with large bag through a doorway. We were in a linen room. When the waitress turned and noticed me, she started to explain that this was a staff-only area.

I put up a hand to stop her. 'I know. I'm really sorry, but I ...' But what was I really going to say? I locked eyes with the woman, who looked like she was in her sixties. 'Please,' I begged. '*Please*. Just two minutes.'

At that moment, the door opened and Quentin slipped in, closing it behind him.

I looked between him and the woman, who put the incorrect-but-convenient pieces together for herself and rolled her eyes. 'Two minutes,' she said sharply, moving towards the back of the room, where she emptied the large bag of linen and started organising it.

'What's going –'

But I was on him in a flash, my hand on his mouth until he *finally* registered that something was very wrong. I'd talk to him later about his powers of perception.

'One, your mother is here,' I whispered. 'And she knows you're here as well.'

His eyes widened.

I looked down and deactivated the Phera-tech on my M-Band. Quentin followed suit, but not before we both registered our rating. Still a true match. After everything. I failed to stop the small cry that came from somewhere deep inside.

'Two, your father isn't, thank God,' I said, regrouping. 'And three, that guy I was dancing with was Morris. He's given me your zips, but he was being monitored and we need to get out of here fast. There's a black Range Rover across the street. Meet me there.' I pulled the envelope from the front of my dress and shoved it at Quentin. 'The code for driver privileges is on the front.'

Quentin watched as I attempted to straighten the dress, his eyes darkening. When I noticed and stepped back, he suddenly grabbed me around the waist and pulled me to his chest, slamming his lips against mine.

It was frantic. The kind of kiss that meant everything. Fear. Love. Life. Death. Hope. Devastation. Lust. It was all there, and coasting over the top of it all was the certainty that came with every touch – we were each other's match.

He pulled back, breathing heavily. 'I'm sorry, I just …' He ran a hand through his hair. 'I had to kiss you. Seeing you dancing with someone else, I almost lost it.'

I ran my thumb over his furrowed brow. 'Don't apologise.'

'You look beautiful.'

I wasn't sure how I felt about that, since I was dressed to look like Ivy.

'Though I prefer you in jeans,' he said with a half-smile, as if reading my mind. Then he made a frustrated kind of growl. 'I wish you didn't drive me crazy.'

'I wish I hadn't made so many mistakes,' I countered.

This seemed to sober him up enough to take a step back.

We heard people laughing just outside the door. 'We should wait until it's clear,' I whispered.

Quentin nodded and leaned back against the wall. 'I'm sorry about last night.'

When I didn't say anything, he went on. 'The lust-enhancer was Morris's idea and I was so desperate to get to you I went along with it.' He blew out a breath. 'Mostly I was scared. I didn't know if you'd still want me,' he said in a low voice.

'What do you mean?'

He ran his hand over the back of his neck. 'I left you down there, Maggie. For weeks and weeks, I failed you. I … I didn't know if you'd ever forgive me for that.' His eyes came back to mine. I was barely breathing, so afraid of what he was going to say that he had to tilt my chin up so I would look at him. 'I know this isn't really the time, but you look at me like you don't know how much I love you, and I can't take that anymore.'

The air whooshed out of my lungs. I looked away, blinking back the unwelcome tears in my eyes.

'It almost killed me seeing you that first day, Mags,' he said. 'Forcing myself not to look at you the moment I entered the classroom. I wanted to charge at you, scoop you up and run away. And instead I had to pretend I didn't care. I had to hurt you, knowing you had already been through too much for one person. I've never hated myself so much, and mostly because …' He trailed off.

'Because there was a part of you that wanted to hurt me,' I finished for him, no judgement in my tone.

He blinked in surprise. 'You knew?'

I put my ear against the door; I could still hear people talking just outside. We were stuck here until they moved on.

I looked back at Quentin. 'Sometimes giving a person a dose of his or her own medicine is tempting. Especially when they've hurt you so terribly.'

He scowled in frustration. 'It's still not an excuse.'

I swallowed hard and took his hand. 'Of course it is. I have a lot to make up for.'

'You did it all for your father, Maggie. I get that and I'm trying hard to let myself trust you again.'

'You shouldn't have to, Quin. If I'd just been honest with you from the beginning, maybe –'

He cut me off with a finger to his lips when we heard the sound of footsteps moving away out in the hall.

'We'll talk about this later?' he whispered.

I nodded. For the first time, I found myself daring to believe that Quentin might be willing to give me another chance.

I pressed my ear to the door again to check the hall was clear, then opened it. 'You go first. I'll follow close behind.'

Quentin looked as though he was about to argue, but the woman cleared her throat behind us, making it clear our time was up. He furrowed his brow at me before slipping out the door and heading straight for the main exit doors.

I waited ten seconds then followed suit, sending a small 'thank you' nod to the waitress who gave me a hassled wave.

I could see Quentin ahead, pausing briefly to shake hands with someone then making his way through the exit doors. I knew security would have spotted him. Being followed was not something we'd be able to avoid. I just had to hope Morris had a plan.

As I made my way past the ballroom doors, a loud cheer went up, followed by a round of applause. I paused at the doors to see what all the drama was about. My view to the main stage cleared just in time to see a man wearing a black tuxedo remove his mask, revealing his identity to the surprised and elated guests.

Even I was shocked to see the President of the United States smiling before the room, his turquoise mask in hand, the perfect complement to the matching flower in his lapel.

Fourteen

I hurried to the doors, but a large arm shot out and barred my exit. I closed my eyes briefly, my heart pounding. This was it. They had me.

Images of my underground prison swamped me and my stomach tightened at the memories of the horrific hunger pains.

'Ma'am?' he asked in a deep baritone voice.

I steeled myself and looked up. It was one of the door guards. Barely contained in his white tuxedo, I knew he'd have me on the ground in seconds if he made a move.

When I just looked at him, his arm still extended in front of me, blocking my escape, he cleared his throat and his eyes flickered to something behind me before coming back to me. 'Ma'am? Is everything okay?' he said, his voice holding enough accusation that I knew I wasn't going anywhere.

My hand twitched, thinking of the dagger I had strapped to my thigh, but with all the material of the dress I'd never get to it in time. So instead, I nodded. 'Everything is fine,' I said, keeping my head down.

'Ma'am, we're going to need you to hand in your mask before you can leave the premises,' he said.

'My … Oh, my mask?' I said with a jolt, my hand flying to my face as I spun around to see a woman standing behind five large glass bowls, each with a label in front of them noting a different charity group.

She smiled awkwardly and I realised they thought I was trying to take off with the potentially valuable jewels.

Reaching up, I hurriedly untied the mask, fumbling to remove it while also trying to keep my face down and to the side. 'Here,' I said, holding it out to the woman.

'You need to place it in one of the bowls,' she instructed.

I glanced quickly at the noted charities. They had a range covering domestic charity, child services, homeless shelters, armed forces, but my hand went straight to the international aid bowl, where I placed my mask.

'Thank you,' the woman said, noting down something on the screen in front of her.

I nodded awkwardly and turned back towards the exit, relieved to see the giant-sized guard had now dropped his arm.

'Have a nice evening, ma'am,' he said as I sped past him and outside, spotting the Range Rover already idling across the street.

I jumped in the passenger side, blowing out a breath as I glanced briefly at Quentin and then proceeded to search the back of the car.

'Paranoid much?' he said with a chuckle. He clearly thought the danger was over.

Ignoring him, I kept looking around, keeping most of my attention on the steady flow of tuxedo-clad guards filing out of the Mellon building.

Quentin followed my line of sight, catching on. But when he opened his mouth again, I was quick to put my hand over his lips.

Silently I opened the glove compartment and found an old-fashioned paper road map. I unfolded and scanned the map, my senses on high alert.

I flipped the paper over. Nothing. I clenched my jaw. There had to be something. I ran my hand over the flat surface and noticed a slight inconsistency. When I did the same on the other side, it was more obvious.

'Mags?' Quentin asked.

'Um …' I cleared my throat. 'Is there a pen or pencil in here anywhere?'

Quentin searched around and found a tiny pencil wedged into the coin compartment.

'We should get moving,' I said absently. I started to carefully shade in the indented area of the map, revealing the first arrow with the words 'park here' beside it, and then the second arrow with the words 'real car here', followed by a series of numbers I assumed were a numberplate.

Quentin backed out of the parking space. 'Which direction, Mags?'

I held up the map, pointing to the first arrow as I said, 'Just take us somewhere we can lay low for a while.'

'Got it.'

Quentin drove silently, observing the traffic laws and taking his time. I could see he was keeping his eyes on the rear-view mirror and trusted he was on the lookout, so I turned my attention back to the map that was directing us towards a museum called Hillwood Estate. There was no doubt Morris was being watched. If not by the guards I'd spotted, then by others, hidden in the shadows and ready to pounce. On top of that, thanks to Morris's clues, I was certain the car was bugged in more ways than one.

I glanced at Quentin. This was going to hurt him. Because if Morris was being followed and was as frightened as he appeared, it meant only one thing: Quentin's family truly had turned on him. I just prayed that Morris *hadn't*. And that he was as smart as he always professed.

We hit traffic on Irving Street, but made it to the entrance gates of Hillwood Estate within twenty minutes. Quentin glanced at me questioningly.

I nodded, telling him to drive in.

The museum was closed, but we parked in the signposted visitors area anyway and got out.

I paused to pull up the many layers of my skirt until I found my thigh and the tranq gun strapped to it. 'Let's go,' I said, not wasting time. Whoever was tracking us would be there soon.

We walked towards the front doors of the mansion-style museum. It was a traditional Georgian building of red brick with stunning white pillars. I made a bee-line for the two night-guards, who stood up when they saw us approaching.

'Sorry, folks, but the museum won't be open until morning,' one of the guards said.

'I know,' I responded, shooting him in the shoulder, then shooting the other guard. They clearly weren't pros – they were out before they even realised there might have been cause for alarm.

We dragged the guards into the shadows and made sure they were in comfortable positions before taking off.

I let out the breath I'd been holding. 'The gardens should be over that wall.'

I wrangled with my dress until I had the skirt under as much control as possible and we climbed the garden wall, breaking into a run the second we reached the other side. Quentin followed me as I sprinted in the direction Morris had marked on the map. Eventually we hit a small cemetery, which had me confused until I realised it was for pets. We kept running, both silent. Both panting. My only hope was that the zips would be worth it. And that Gus would be able to fix whatever the hell Morris had been forced to lump us with.

We made it across a bridge over the lake and to another garden wall. As soon as I'd climbed over it, I pulled out the map and tried to work out our position. Quentin looked over my shoulder, lighting up his M-Band to help us see. He seemed to get a handle on where we were faster than I did, because he pointed.

I nodded and followed his lead. About ten minutes later we arrived at a narrow road. We spotted the row of three cars about one hundred metres away.

'That one,' I said, pointing to the old-style Ford. I smiled and started patting down Quentin's pockets. 'There's a key in the envelope, isn't there?' I'd felt the lump when Morris had given it to me.

Quentin grinned, watching as I patted him down. 'Back pocket,' he said, barely containing himself. I rolled my eyes and pulled out the key.

The moment I opened the front door, we both saw the note stuck to the driver's seat.

Check the back.

We found a duffle bag in the boot. Inside was a stack of Quentin's clothes and a letter.

If you are Quin (or even Maggie), great! Read on. If not, I'd appreciate it if you would kindly fuck off and die.

We both chuckled.

Maggie, if it's you, I'm glad you aren't dead. We were seriously worried there for a while. Wish I could throw you a party or something, but it turns out you two are totally screwed and parties that end in bloodshed are bad for business – you understand.

I've done what I can, but don't come knocking again. It's too risky for all of us. I've called in every favour I could to get this stuff to you.

The Range Rover was bugged to the hilt so really hoping you got the hell away from it ASAP. This car is clean. I won it in a gamble. No one knows I have it and it can't be traced by the tech. That said, it's so bloody old it stands out like a sore thumb, so I wouldn't go cruising if you get my drift.

Quin, your money will be in the envelope I gave you, but watch out. Booby traps!! There will be at least two extra zips in there. Your father knew we were in touch and put the hard word on me. Agreeing to set you up (for your own good, of course!) seemed to be the only way – I just hope this works. Don't know exactly what they can do, but I do know they can track you. Pretty sure they can listen in. Maybe more. They're disguised to look like your zips, but I went old-school and marked them up like we used to.

Last thing. The money zips have been tampered with. They (idiots) tried to put them back before I noticed, but I had a few of my own booby traps and I'm positive they did something. If I'd cleaned them myself, it would have outed me before I could get them to you, so you're going to have to clean house yourself. DON'T trust the money until you scan the zips.

Good luck, guys. Don't know what you are doing. Don't want to. Just ... look after each other and stay alive.

The letter was typed and he didn't sign his name. He wasn't stupid.

Wasting no time, Quentin emptied the envelope of the small disk-like zips. In a world of no cash, money zips were the only form of untraceable money.

Quentin picked up a zip and, cupping both hands around it, held it up to his eyes. I watched on, wondering if he'd lost his mind, until eventually there were two piles. One with eight zips, the other with just two. And a game zip to the side.

I lifted the game zip, my question obvious.

'Morris designed it. To anyone else it is just a game, but for us, once you access level two and know where to go, it unlocks an embedded file.'

'The information you collected.'

He nodded.

Curious now, I picked up one of his eight zips and did as he had, cupping my hands around it like Quentin had so that I blocked out the light. Sure enough, there was a small mark in the centre. Invisible to the naked eye – except for when it glowed in the dark.

I shook my head, smiling. Morris wasn't stupid at all. He was a genius.

Fifteen

By the time I made it back to the car, I was wheezing uncontrollably.

'You should've let me go,' Quentin said.

I probably should have. I still wasn't at my best physically, but when Quentin had pulled up at the closest metro station I couldn't stop myself from snatching up the two booby-trapped zips and taking off at breakneck speed with nothing more than a 'Back in five' mouthed to Quentin.

'Done.' *Wheeze huff puff.* 'Now. They. Are ...' Keeping my words to a minimum wasn't a choice – I was seriously having trouble breathing. 'Going. Opposite. Directions,' I reported.

Quentin scowled.

I smiled. At least, I tried to, but I'm fairly certain all that resulted was more of a strangled whimper. Truth was, I relished the pain that came from bolting down the deep stairway to the platform so I could hide the zips under the seats of different trains. It was all worth it to send M-Corp and whoever else was tracking us on a wild-goose chase.

'Next time, I go,' he grumbled, driving us back towards Arlington.

I leaned back in my chair, forgoing a response in favour of air.

Once we were a safe distance from the station and I was satisfied we weren't being followed, I called Gus.

'If I happen to accidentally tranq Travis again, multiple times, would you be upset with me?' he asked as he picked up. 'And before you answer, do try to remember that he almost got us all killed recently.'

'Tranq him and I tranq you,' I answered.

'That's a little harsh,' Gus mumbled. 'The guy is doing my damn head in. He has the world's worst taste in music, and when I say that, I really can't stress enough what I mean by the *worst*. But let me just give you one word. Opera. Five fucking hours of opera.'

I smiled. Travis had been in the game for a long time. I would bet everything I owned – admittedly not much – that he was doing it on purpose.

'Deal with it.'

Gus snorted. 'Don't say I didn't warn you if you come back to find I've thrown myself out a window. Where are you anyway?'

'On the move. We have what we wanted, but there are complications. How are you going with everything on your end?'

'At a big bloody dead-end – and by bloody, I mean potentially *our* blood if I don't find a way through.'

'What do you need?' I asked.

Gus sighed. 'Mags, I need more than what we have. I've been thinking –'

'Don't,' I cut him off. 'Don't think, Gus. You and thinking always leads to the same thing.'

Gus scoffed. 'And what's that, oh great oracle?'

'To you looking out for numero uno, which ultimately leads to a plan that starts with: let's make a run for it.'

Gus was silent for a few beats. 'You're actually pretty good.'

I rolled my eyes. 'What do you need, Gus?'

'Access to computers and files I no longer have,' he said, now sounding tired and frustrated. We all needed more sleep. Nonetheless Gus's words sparked an idea.

'Would your old computer have what you need?' I asked, purposely not mentioning the fact that Gus's old computer was in the M-Store where we both used to work. Of course, Quentin swerving slightly off the road and looking at me with wide eyes tipped me off that he'd instantly put two and two together.

'Yes,' Gus said hesitantly.

I chewed on my idea for a minute, before giving myself a nod. Chance favours the bold and all that shit.

I turned to Quentin. 'How fast can we get there?'

Quentin was shaking his head in shock. 'Mags –' he started, but I cut him off.

'How long?'

He clenched his jaw. 'Fifteen minutes. But it's ten o'clock.'

'Be at the back door in twenty,' I instructed Gus.

I heard him groan, but he simply said, 'What do I do with opera boy?'

I bit my lip, but we were already too far down the road to stop. 'Bring Travis with you,' I said. 'Wear caps and keep your faces away from the security cameras.'

'I'll try not to be insulted by the ridiculous obviousness of that statement,' Gus said with a huff. 'You do realise we're all going to hell for this stuff?'

'Yes,' I admitted sadly. 'But we are going to take some terrible people with us.'

'Shitty consolation prize, Mags,' he said and hung up.

The car was torturously silent.

Five minutes.

Ten.

Finally Quentin broke. 'We're almost there.'

I nodded, keeping my focus on the task ahead. I had used the silence to get in the zone and work out my angle. You always had to be ready with an angle and then commit to it.

'Maggie, if you want to –'

'You're not coming in,' I said, cutting him off and deciding to keep it simple and direct. 'I need someone out front keeping watch; someone who'll be ready to get us the hell out of there.'

'But –' he started.

'No, Quin!'

Quentin didn't respond until we pulled into the street where the M-Store was. 'Front or back?' he asked, staring straight ahead.

I glanced at him, noting his white-knuckled grip on the steering wheel. Yeah, he wasn't happy, but I would deal with him later. The last thing he needed was to land himself on the morning news for breaking and entering into one of his family's stores.

'Just here is good,' I said when we were about one hundred metres away from the store. Quentin pulled over and I got out, turning back briefly. 'Stay here. If you see anything, beep the horn. We'll come to you.'

Quentin didn't look at me. I hesitated, wanting to explain why he shouldn't come in. Wanting to go through my plan with him, but instead I pressed my lips together and took his non-reply for agreement.

The M-Store was closed for the night. But like all M-Stores, it had night security. And for the eighteen months that I'd worked at the Clarendon store, I had never left a shift without first getting a coffee for the night-guard, Darren.

So when I walked straight up to him, smile on my face, and gave him a wave, Darren was quick to open the sliding door and come out to see me.

'Well, well. I haven't seen you in a while. I've been having caffeine withdrawals.' He laughed. 'Aren't you a sight to behold.'

I laughed back. 'I took a bit of time off to concentrate on school. You know how it is. But I'm hoping to come back to work once I finish school. I love my job here,' I said, taking a chance that he wouldn't have been informed otherwise. So far the Mercers appeared to see less benefit than gain in slandering my name to the world.

Darren's eyes crinkled. 'Good girl. You gotta put school first. But I know what you mean; the M-Corp family is a good one to be part of. They've always looked after me.'

I nodded. 'Actually, Darren, that's why I'm here. I was kind of hoping you might be able to let me in the back office. I left a few things behind.'

'Oh. Well, what did you leave in there? I can go in and get it.' He gestured to the door.

'Well, that's just the thing. They're kind of private. And ...' I looked away, wringing my hands together, 'it's all sort of embarrassing.'

Darren looked at me, confused.

I licked my lips. 'I just don't want this stuff getting in the wrong hands.'

His smile faltered.

I worked on building some tears in my eyes. 'I had a relationship with Gus,' I said softly. 'And now he's in big trouble for something and he got fired.'

Darren nodded gravely. 'I'd heard that they were looking for that boy. Always liked him, though.'

I nodded, blinking away a tear. 'Me too. And the stuff he's in trouble for, he didn't really do. I swear, Darren.'

His expression softened. 'If you say so, kiddo. There is a lot of crazy stuff that happens in the world these days, but I figure with the systems the way they are, if someone is a real problem, it's gonna come out in their ratings, right? That's what they say.'

I nodded. 'That's what they say,' I said, having another idea. 'Anyway, Gus and I, we rated really high.'

He beamed. 'You did? Well, that's no surprise. You two were always huddled away in the corner.'

I looked up at him with wide eyes. 'Please, Darren. There are photos on the computer of Gus and me and … and there's other stuff … messages he sent me. Love notes. I need to get it off the computer before someone else finds it. I really care about Gus, but I really want to be able to keep my job with the M-Corp family too.'

Darren watched me for a few moments, his fingers tapping his M-Band, which I knew was programmed to control all the locks. Finally he pressed a few buttons.

My heart sped up, not knowing if he was helping me or activating some kind of alarm. Subtly I glanced down the street to where Quentin waited in the Ford. At least if I was caught, he would get away. That was the most important thing. And even as I had the thought and acknowledged my obsession, I knew it was true. I had crossed the line. Quentin came first.

When Darren looked up, it was with a sly wink. 'Go on, then. I can't leave my post, but the back door is unlocked. I'll leave it that way for ten minutes and then I lock it back down. You clear?'

I nodded excitedly, playing my part. 'Thanks, Darren. You're a lifesaver.'

'You tell that boy to straighten himself out if he wants to keep rating with the likes of you,' he said as I started towards the side street.

'I'll make sure he knows,' I called back, before breaking into a jog to reach the back alley of the M-Store.

Gus and Travis were already there.

'Nice work,' Gus said as I approached.

'Thanks,' I said, making a grab for the door.

'I particularly like the part where you made yourself out to be innocent and me to be the guilty bastard.'

I flashed him a smile. 'I liked that part too.'

'You two have some kind of backwards relationship going on here, you know that, right?' Travis said, following us into the M-Store.

I put a hand on Travis's chest, halting him. 'You stay in the alley. Keep watch.'

He rolled his eyes. 'I'm not a goddamn guard dog, Maggie.'

'Until I give you back all of your files, you're whatever I say you are,' I threw back.

'Maybe she just needs to get laid,' Travis said to Gus.

Gus looked horrified. 'Please!' He put up a hand. 'I already have enough mental images for a lifetime of nightmares – there's no need to add to it.'

Travis sauntered back out to the alley to keep watch, but not before making a parting comment. 'When you say nightmares, are you sure you don't mean fantasies?'

My face screwed up.

'That dude has got to go, Mags,' Gus grumbled.

I nodded even as I got to work, pulling out the zips.

'Oh … money, money, money,' Gus said, rubbing his hands together.

'Yep,' I said. 'But there were two extra zips which had trackers and bugs in them. I've already gotten rid of those, but I need you to run a scan on these eight and the game zip to make sure there are no other surprises. Quin's intel is locked in a file hidden in level two. Can you get that done, along with whatever else you need to, in …' I checked the time. 'Eight minutes?'

Gus sat down without another word and got to work.

Three minutes in, he had cleared the game zip and all but three of the money zips. 'These two have action alerts attached to them. If you use them or download the money, it will activate a tracker.'

I bit my lip. Those two zips contained a lot of money. 'Can you clean them?' I asked.

'Sure, but not now. It will take at least an hour to clean each one to ensure I don't trigger any of the alarms.'

I pocketed the two suspect zips. 'Okay, but they're safe to keep with us?'

He nodded.

I pointed to the other zip he'd put aside. 'That one?'

'That one is bad news. I can't figure out exactly what it has, but basically it's like a sleeper. They can activate it any time they want. I wouldn't have found it if I'd been doing a general sweep; I only discovered it because I'm basically the superhero of hacking.'

I rolled my eyes as I slipped the suspect zip into my other pocket; I'd dispose of it somewhere soon. I didn't want to leave evidence behind where Darren could get in trouble. We were already leaving an electronic footprint.

Gus got on with his other hacking, finding whatever system information he needed in order to get us into the tunnels the next night.

'Okay,' he said at the seven-minute mark. 'I've got a possible entrance into the neg hub from a tunnel that connects the Court House Metro to an apartment building called Archstone across the road. It looks like a good possibility. Two ways in and out. The metro is public so if you send the negs out that way, it could work.'

'Sounds good, but we're out of time. Gotta go, Gus,' I said, tapping his shoulder.

Gus, never one to argue when it came to saving his own ass, was up in a flash. But before we made it to the back door, we heard the internal office door open and saw the beam of a flashlight.

Without a second thought, I grabbed Gus and pulled him into a hard kiss.

I hadn't told Darren I was going to let Gus into the office. This was all I could think of to make us look believable. And with that thought, I deepened the kiss that had left Gus in a state of stunned shock, and pulled him closer.

Catching on, Gus suddenly played his part. His hands slid around my back and gripped me tightly as he took control. He dominated the kiss, backing me into the wall. It was overkill, but I wasn't about to argue right then.

The sound of someone clearing his throat caused us to stop.

Keeping up the act, I sheepishly looked around in feigned shock.

But the shock quickly turned genuine.

Quentin stood there, arms crossed, glaring at Gus and me. 'If you two are done, there is an M-Corp patrol that just pulled up out front.'

'Quin, oh my God. It's not ...' I swallowed my words as he stormed past me.

'Darren won't be able to keep them occupied forever so I would suggest we leave now.'

I quickly stepped away from Gus. 'We thought you were ...'

'Save it,' he said, his expression shutting down as he held the back door open for us. 'The car is in the alley.'

I looked to Gus for support, for something ... anything. But he just stared at the ground as he followed Quentin's orders. My stomach sank. Looking into Quentin's stony eyes, I think he saw my confusion. But right then, it wasn't enough.

Sixteen

The trip back to Travis's loft was a cocktail of strained and awkward. Even Travis felt the tension and shut up.

After twenty minutes of backtracking and ensuring we weren't being followed, we pulled into the garage.

Gus was out of the car in a flash.

'I'm going out to get a drink,' he said, running a hand through his hair before pulling on his tweed fedora hat.

'Not a good idea,' I replied as I grabbed my bag. We needed to stay hidden.

Gus kept walking towards the door. 'No offence, Maggie, but it's midnight and I need a drink. And you two ...' He looked between Quentin and me as if he could see the iceberg forming. 'You two could do with me going out for a drink too.'

Travis fell in step behind Gus. 'The bar down the road is still open and they have a don't-ask, don't-tell policy.'

Gus nodded, sending me a brief smile. 'See? We'll catch you later.'

He and Travis disappeared before I could argue and suddenly Quentin and I were alone with nothing but the awkwardness between us. It was a terrible idea, letting Travis out of my sight, but right then I just didn't have the energy to drag him upstairs and tie him to a chair.

Silently I followed Quentin up to the loft.

He made a bee-line for the bathroom the moment we got inside, slamming then locking the door. A second later I heard the shower running.

I closed my eyes briefly, letting the guilt wash through me for a moment. I made my way to the locked bathroom door as my mind played over the events of the night. I'd been on autopilot. Determined to get us through to the next stage. To keep us safe, get the job done, all while ensuring Quentin's protection. I slid down the door, slumping into a heap on the floor. All in all, the night had been a success. We'd secured the money zips, found and destroyed the trackers and bugs, and managed to get into – and out of – the M-Store unscathed. And yet, why did I feel like I had caused irreparable damage?

'The kiss with Gus meant nothing,' I said softly against the door. I didn't know if he could hear me. If he was even listening.

No answer.

Somehow that made it easier to go on.

'I thought you were Darren, the security guard, coming to check on me. I'd spun him a story about Gus and me – that he and I were together, and that I was trying to hide any evidence of our relationship. That's how I got in. But when I heard him coming out the back, I panicked. I wouldn't have kissed Gus otherwise. I didn't know it was –' My words were cut short by the sound of a loud crash.

'Quin? Are you okay?' I asked, getting to my knees and pressing my ear against the door.

Another loud crack as something broke.

'Quin!'

No answer.

'Open the door!'

I tried the doorknob, but it wouldn't budge.

Trying to ignore the sounds coming from the bathroom, I took a deep breath, closed my eyes and focused. When I opened them, I was looking right at the lock. It was old – I could easily pick it with the right tool. I ran to the kitchen and grabbed a slim knife.

The bathroom had gone disturbingly silent, which only made me more desperate to get the door open. Forcing my hands not to shake, I lined up the length of the blade into the narrow socket and levered it until I felt the mechanism turn and the lock click.

I threw the door open only to stumble back a step, gasping at the sight before me.

Quentin had his back to me. He was still wearing his jeans, but his shirt was gone and his chest was heaving, his hands bloody and badly cut from the mirror he'd smashed.

I was shaking, but I managed to stumble towards him.

Not knowing what else to do, I threw my arms around him from behind and just held on.

'I'm sorry, Quin,' I whispered over and over. 'I'm so sorry.'

He was still for a moment, although his breathing was still ragged. Tears streamed down my face as I held on, praying that he would talk to me; that I could somehow fix this.

But, of course, the opposite happened. He straightened rigidly. As if he'd suddenly realised I was there.

Slowly and instinctively, my arms slid away from him and I took a step back.

'Quin, I ... Please talk to me.' I wished he would just yell at me and get it over with, but somehow I knew it wasn't going to be that easy. This was about so much more than just a kiss.

He hung his head.

'I can't be around you right now,' he murmured, his words barely audible.

I took a shaky breath. 'At least let me clean up your hands?'

After what felt like a short lifetime, he lifted his head slightly and nodded.

'I'll get the first-aid kit. Come out to the living room,' I urged him. When he didn't turn around, I left him to it, hoping that he would decide to follow.

As I gathered the first-aid supplies, I heard him turn off the shower. A minute later he walked out of the bathroom, his hands wrapped in a towel.

He dropped down on the sofa and I took up position opposite him on the coffee table, setting out the antiseptic and bandages.

'Can I?' I gestured to his hands.

He held them out and I gently unwrapped the towel, trying to hide my reaction to the deepest cut on his left hand.

I got to work cleaning the wounds and applying the antiseptic. The worst cut could have done with stitches, but I knew he would say no, so I got busy with the butterfly tape.

'He's in love with you.' Quentin's voice was raspy, like he'd had to force every word.

I glanced up to deny it. The look on his face quickly stopped me.

'He is. Even if you don't see it, that doesn't make it less true.'

My brow furrowed. Both at his assumption about Gus's feelings, and that his choice of words implied there was a chance I *did* see it.

When I didn't say anything, he went on. 'I saw it from the beginning, but I believed in you; that you were telling me the truth when you explained your relationship.'

I felt my shoulders drop. Well, shit. *The truth.* Something he'd discovered I could be very selective at telling.

'You don't trust me,' I said, knowing I'd given him more than a few reasons to reach that conclusion. And he was now applying it to seeing Gus and me kissing.

He swallowed, his Adam's apple working hard.

'I don't blame you for that,' I said.

He flinched as I added another bandage to his hand. They were already turning black and blue.

Eventually his eyes met mine. 'Have you rated with him?'

'No,' I said quickly. 'Ivy, Nathan and you are the only people I've ever rated with until earlier tonight when I had to turn on my Phera-tech at the ball. You saw me turn it off as soon as I could.'

'So you don't know if you're a strong compatibility?'

I shook my head. 'I don't know and I don't care.' I only cared about him.

When he didn't respond, I asked, 'How did you get into the M-Store anyway?'

He shrugged. 'I'm a Mercer. I can go anywhere I want if I'm willing to threaten someone with their livelihood. I told Darren I knew you were in there and that I'd just spotted a random M-Corp patrol. I gave him a chance to save his ass by letting me in, and he took it. If you'd taken a moment to discuss your plan with me before simply casting me aside, I might've been able to make the entire process a lot easier.'

I looked down, properly chastised. 'I wanted to keep you out of it, in case we got caught.'

His brow furrowed. 'And as frustrating as that was, I guess I understood. That is, until ...'

'You saw me kissing Gus.'

The silence spoke volumes.

'Did you feel it?' he asked eventually.

'What?'

'The way he feels for you.' His eyes flashed up, giving me a glimpse of his anger. It was rooted deep. 'He's good at covering it, but tell me honestly, did you feel it when he was kissing you?'

My knee shook nervously and Quentin watched it.

'Maybe,' I said. 'I don't know. He's been pining over Kelsey. She's the one he cares about.' But somewhere deep down, a part of me knew exactly what Quentin was referring to. I had felt something different for a few seconds during that kiss.

'You should rate with him, just to find out. So we all know.'

'No.'

His jaw clenched and he fisted one of his bruised hands. 'Why?'

'Because it won't change anything!' I bit back. 'I'll always choose you! I'll always want to be with you. I know I ruined everything you believed in, but you ruined me too!' I banged at my chest like a mad woman. 'If you can't trust me, I understand. If that means you can't be with me, I understand that too,' I said, calming down and taking a deep breath. 'But it won't change *me*. Or the way I feel about you. There will be no turning to someone else. No exploring other ratings or opportunities. For me, it's simple. It's either us together. Or me alone.'

'You're all I have,' he said, looking away. 'That's the way you planned it, right?'

My heart broke. 'Yes,' I whispered. 'And if I could give you back everything I took, I would.'

He shook his head. 'I don't want it. I told you that. But … I also don't want to be fooled again. And you're *so* good at what you do, Maggie. And I'm so in love with you that I'm sure I'd follow you blindly off any bridge. And that frightens me.'

A tear slipped down my cheek.

He took a shuddering breath. 'It frightens me that I had to lock myself in a bathroom and beat up a mirror to stop myself from going after Gus and beating up him instead. When I saw his arms around you, his lips on yours right where mine had been less than an hour earlier … I've never wanted to hurt a person before, not like that.' He was drifting away from me, his eyes growing distant with his words. Quentin was putting walls up I had never seen before.

Another tear escaped as I watched the soul I had tortured so unforgivably finally fall apart and call foul.

We were one another's true match, and the science behind the tech proved that true matches were fiercely possessive and protective of one another. My actions proved this as much as his. But even so, I knew Quentin wouldn't feel this conflicted – even as my true match – if he had faith in me. And with that thought, I knew what I had to do. It was going to break me, but I had no choice.

'You should be frightened,' I said, straightening to face my fate. 'I *am* capable of horrible things, Quin. And I know that in the coming days the chance of me hurting you …' My words caught in my throat. 'You're right not to trust me.'

Quentin looked up, caught off guard by my admission.

'I haven't earned it. I've done the opposite,' I continued.

'What are you saying?' he asked, his tone low, his eyes narrowed suspiciously.

'I'm saying that I'm stepping away. I'm giving you the control when it comes to us.'

'And what am I supposed to do with that?'

I half smiled. 'That's up to you, Quin. But I'll be here, waiting for you. Forever, if that's what it takes. So you take your time. I can tell you until I'm blue in the face that I love you with every fibre of my being and that you can trust me to never betray you again. But we both know words only go so far.'

I gently touched his bandaged hands. 'We're all done here.'

He looked at me, his eyes sad as I wondered if my words were about more than just his hands. Was Quentin finally done with me?

He pulled himself together and stood. 'I'll go get cleaned up and sleep on the couch,' he said.

I nodded, taking that as my cue. I put away the medical supplies and headed for the bedroom I'd claimed as mine while he stood in the middle of the living room, half watching me, half staring aimlessly.

I paused before closing the bedroom door and caught his eye. 'When you saw Gus and me kiss, you said you could tell what he felt for me?'

He clenched his jaw. 'I could. Clear as day.'

I nodded. 'I noticed you never mentioned if you could tell what *I* felt for him.'

Something in his eyes softened. Something that made me hold out hope that there was still a chance. That maybe I hadn't ruined him completely.

And I realised in that moment that even if I couldn't get him back to *me*, I would do whatever it took to give Quentin back to himself.

Seventeen

Gus and Travis stumbled in loudly at around 3 a.m.

I lay in bed, still wide awake, as I listened to them knock over furniture and start clanking about in the kitchen.

When I heard voices, I moved to the door.

'Let's get this over with. Just do it. Take your best shot,' Gus slurred loudly. I could almost see the sway of his body through his voice.

Christ.

I threw my sweater on over my singlet and grabbed the door handle, figuring things were about to get messy.

'Go to bed, Gus.' It was Quentin's voice. Strong. Commanding. Leaving absolutely no room for argument.

'What happened to you?' This came from Travis, who was also clearly intoxicated. Good to know they'd been having a merry time. 'Where's Maggie?' he snapped. I could hear him moving across the living room. Deciding I'd simply had enough for one night, I quickly leaped under the covers and closed my eyes just as the door banged open.

Footsteps neared and a hand clumsily pushed the hair back from my face as I worked hard to keep my breathing shallow and slow.

'Is she okay?' Gus asked from somewhere further away.

'Of course she's okay! I would *never* hurt her!' Quentin. Vehement.

'She looks fine,' Travis said from beside me.

'Then leave her be,' Gus slurred. 'If she wakes up, she'll be pissed. She barely sleeps these days as it is.'

'And how the hell do you know that?' Quentin snapped just before I heard my door close softly.

I opened my eyes slowly, making sure I was alone again before I catapulted out of bed and shuffled back to the door to listen.

'I know because I've slept in the same place as her since we got her out, Quentin. I've heard her pacing the hall every night to avoid closing her eyes and then, when she's too exhausted to fight it, I've sat up and listened to her scream her way through nightmare after nightmare. That's how I know.'

I heard a large thump and grabbed for the doorknob again.

'Jesus Christ!' Travis huffed, as if caught between shock and laughter. 'Did you see that? He just fell right over. Passed out on his feet!'

'Just get him away from me,' Quentin warned.

I heard some mumbling that I couldn't make out and then the sound of scuffling noises, which I figured was Travis dragging Gus into one of the bedrooms. At least, I hoped that was what I was hearing. Either way, I wasn't going out there, so I got back into bed and settled in for the nightmares everyone seemed to know about.

At some point during the night, when the montage of faces – the negs I'd turned my back on in order to save my father – was almost overwhelming, I felt something like a force field go up around me, shielding me from the worst of it until gradually the images faded and I emerged from the dream to feel something warm wrapped around me, holding me tight.

In the morning, I was alone.

But I woke with a sense of resolve.

I couldn't be the person everyone wanted. I could only be me. And right now, the only version of me I could cope with was the one who got things done. It was game day. Tonight I'd be going back into the tunnels. From here on out, I needed to stay in control, otherwise people I cared about were going to die.

With that thought, I got up, dressed in leggings and a long T-shirt and headed out to the kitchen. Quentin was passed out on the sofa. Travis was stirring a cup of coffee at the table.

'Got one of those for me?' I asked.

He passed me his and got up to make another.

'I expected you to be dead to the world for a few more hours at least,' I said.

Travis shrugged. 'I never sleep in.'

I nodded, sipping my coffee. 'What time are your men going to be here?'

'Not until around 2 p.m. I didn't want to give them too much time to think about what was going down.'

I nodded again. Travis was a pro.

'You going to take me down, Travis?'

He paused from dropping a spoonful of sugar into his cup and put down the spoon. 'You've got some of the most backwards relationships going on around here and you're worried about me flipping on you?' He shook his head. 'I've given you my word.'

I stared at him. 'Have you given anyone else your word?'

He pressed his lips together, irritated by the accusation. 'I haven't spoken to your father since I gave him my final piece of intel after that night on Roosevelt.'

I scoffed. 'Except for when you went to get your money zips, right?'

'Wrong, Maggie.' His eyes darted to the side. 'I never collected on the job. If I could go back, I never would've done it. Believe what you want, but I'm sorry for what happened to you and for the part I played in it.'

Lost for words, I nodded and stood. 'I'm … I'm going for a run,' I said, backing away towards the elevator.

Once outside, I felt better. Being outdoors was officially my favourite place now. If I'd had it my way, I would've had a home without a roof, or better yet, had my home on a roof somewhere. The less walls and ceilings in my life, the better.

I broke into a jog and headed towards the Muay Thai centre. Master Rua took me through a light work-out in one of the back rooms while I filled him in on the basics of the plan.

'When?' he asked.

I opened my mouth to tell him it was tonight, but held back at the last second. 'It's better if you don't know specifics.'

He wasn't happy. First I'd refused to tell him where our new place was for fear that he was being monitored – despite his assurances he'd checked the centre for bugs – and now this.

'You need more help than black-market thieves,' he said.

I shrugged, moving through my exercises. 'It's the best I have, and now that Quentin has left his family I can't wait around. They'll come for him soon. I need to get him out of Arlington sooner rather than later.'

'You're thinking too much about this boy and not enough about staying alive.'

I jabbed, he blocked. 'Not true. I'm thinking about making things right.' Jab, jab. 'And this is going to work.'

Master Rua took it easy on me, insisting I keep up my strength. Before I left the centre I gave him the two money zips that had been bugged with action alerts. I hated parting with so much money, but the other zips had enough on them to keep us going for a while if we were careful, and I couldn't take the risk. I warned Master Rua that trackers would be activated as soon as he tried to use the zips, but if he could find a way to de-bug them, he was welcome to the money. He didn't seem interested in the idea and assured me he could dispose of them safely. I wasn't surprised the money didn't tempt him.

He pulled me into a quick hug before handing me a bag of my favourite breakfast pastries. 'Fight hard, Maggie. If you insist on taking the fight down to their level, there will be no negotiations, no second chances, you fight only to win.'

I nodded, swallowing hard at his words. I knew he was telling me that tonight I'd have to be willing to cross that final line, to kill someone. But still, I wasn't sure if I could accept that killing was the answer.

Before I pulled away, Master Rua pressed something else into my hand.

I looked down to see an envelope and glanced at him questioningly.

'A courier brought it to me today. Made me sign for it.'

I nodded, looking at my name written on the front. It was Sam's writing.

As soon as I got back to the loft, I went straight to my room, closed the door and ripped open the envelope.

Hey little sis,

I know you said no contact, but I needed you to know we are safe. We've got the hazers and are staying well hidden. We'd been moving about every few days just in case, but we've decided to settle in the latest place for a couple of weeks. So far there has been no trouble.

Mom's finding things hard, knowing you're out there and all alone. Every time we move she begs for us to go back and get you, but I always say no. I think she's starting to hate me and, well, I'm starting to hate me too. I know I promised you I'd be back, but something tells me you're better off without us there for now.

Just come find us soon.

I've got one of those old-fashioned phones you told me to get. Had to pay an arm and a leg for it. Anyway, I've written the number below. I know you won't call until it's safe. Just … call soon, okay?

We miss you, Mags.

Sam.

There was a knock on my door.

'What?'

'Maggie, you might want to come out here.' It was Travis, clearly speaking at a level that was only intended for me to hear.

Rolling my eyes, I tucked the letter into my pocket – along with my concerns that Sam and Mom were taking a risk staying in the one place – and went out to the living room. Gus looked like he'd just woken up and was helping himself to a glass of water in the kitchen.

He saw me just as the bathroom door at my end of the long room opened and Quentin walked out dressed for the day, a towel in his hand.

Quentin's eyes went straight to me then, after a beat, moved on to Gus.

Gus cautiously walked out from behind the kitchen bench.

Quentin hung the towel over one of the chairs and met him in the middle of the open space while Travis and I watched on, not sure if we should be worried or not.

'Quin,' Gus said.

'Gus,' Quentin said. 'Feeling better?'

'Feeling crap, actually.'

Quin nodded. 'But okay?'

Gus ran a hand through his bed-head hair. 'Yeah. About last night, I don't remember most of it, but Travis told me that you wouldn't get into it with me. Thanks for not –'

I gasped.

Travis made a low whistling sound.

And Gus never got a chance to finish his sentence because Quentin's fist connected with his face and sent him down in one punch.

I took a step forwards, but Quentin quickly put his hand up, halting me. 'It's okay. I'm done.' He leaned over Gus. 'I didn't get into it with you last night because you were drunk and I knew you wouldn't remember it.' He smiled widely. 'But I'm fairly certain you now have enough of your faculties back to ensure you won't forget that if you *ever* touch Maggie again like you did yesterday, I won't be stopping at one punch. Gus, this isn't a warning, it's a promise. I simply don't have it in me to stand back and let that happen again. Do you understand what I'm saying?'

Gus nodded, dabbing at his bleeding lip.

Quentin dropped down onto the sofa and, seemingly satisfied, used his black-market M-Band to plug in some earphones and activate his music.

'Man packs a punch,' Travis said under his breath while I just watched on, open-mouthed.

I nodded, holding back the urge to scream at the world. I grabbed a tub of ice-cream from the kitchen for breakfast before returning silently to my room. I needed to stay focused.

With barely a knock, Gus let himself in a few minutes later, holding a tissue to his lip.

I put down the blueprints I'd been studying and gave him my attention.

'I'm sorry, Maggie,' he said, leaning against the wall.

There was a part of me that wanted to order him out of my room, to order everyone to concentrate on what we were about to do, but I found myself saying something else entirely.

'Is it true?'

'What?'

'Don't, Gus. You know what I mean. Is it true you have feelings for me?'

He winced as he dabbed at his lip again. 'They kind of snuck up on me. You're not the only one who hasn't had a lot of people in their life before. Not close, at least. You and I had been loving-to-hate each other for so long that when the hate finally went away ...' Something in my throat tightened at his confession. 'And when I found out that Kelsey never really cared, I guess I turned my attention to thoughts of ...' He looked at me. 'I thought it would go away with time. But then you up and kissed me.'

'So it's my fault?' I snapped, riding a roller coaster of emotions. I wasn't equipped to deal with this shit.

'No. It's mine. I just got lost in the moment. Funny thing is ...' He looked suddenly shy.

'What?' I asked cautiously.

'Well, even though I couldn't seem to stop myself from going there in the kiss, it was more because it took me by surprise and I needed to know, you know? But when we were actually ... Well, it wasn't exactly like I imagined it would be.' I'm pretty sure he was blushing.

I smiled. 'I didn't light your world on fire?'

He shifted about, but finally looked up with a quirky smile. 'Not really, Mags.'

I snorted. 'I'm not surprised. I don't love you!' I threw a pillow at him. 'And you don't love me either. At least not like that. I think we're best friends and, considering we are such dysfunctional people, that makes it confusing. I mean, when you love someone enough to put everything on the line for them, risk your freedom and even your life, that's bound to happen, right?'

Gus looked up, nodding slightly.

'I know you've been hurting about Kelsey. I know you care about her and, frankly, I'm pissed that you've been using me as a distraction from that, but here's the thing: I'd move heaven and earth for you, Gus, but I love Quin. Even if he can never love me again. The small amount of time I had that was filled with his love has made me an addict for life. I'll never settle for anything else.'

'I get it, Mags. I promise I won't get between you two again. I'll get my head sorted out.'

I stood up and pulled him into a rare hug. 'I know you will. But just in case you're ever confused again, if you try anything with me, I'm going to hit you *much* harder that Quentin did. We clear?'

He half laughed. 'I have to find out what happened to Kelsey. I know what Alex told you, but … something doesn't feel right. I know we hadn't been together for long, and that I was supposed to be taking off, but … you're right, I did, *do*, care about her. I just can't believe she would cut me off like that.'

Gus and I sat down on the edge of the bed and, for what felt like the first time, we talked. No threats. No blackmail. Just friends. And the more he talked about his relationship with Kelsey, the more I became just as confused as him.

Why *had* Kelsey just tossed him aside?

Eighteen

As planned, Travis's men showed up at 2 p.m.

I recognised one of the guys, Ned, from the night Travis had led us to Roosevelt Island – and then blown up most of it.

Ned was a stocky guy with a goofy smile. But there was something about him that held my interest. And soon enough I saw him pull Travis aside when he thought everyone else was otherwise occupied. I watched out of the corner of my eye as he asked Travis about his well-being and whether he was okay. It left no doubt in my mind that if Travis had given Ned the nod, all hell would've broken loose. Ned was smart, observant and loyal. All skills we would need that night.

The next guy was all brawn and greed. The perfect combination. Hex was a martial-arts expert who walked around with a massive chip on his shoulder. He was angsty and too quick to want a piece of the action, which wasn't ideal, but he was also driven by his desire for money and that kept him in line and stopped him from asking the wrong questions.

The last guy, Liam, was more of a mystery. He watched on silently. He was obviously intelligent and he was blanketed in muscle. The rest of the crew seemed to respect him and often asked his opinion on things, even though he rarely voiced one.

I caught him looking me over a few times and the hairs on the back of my neck stood up, which only served to annoy me. On top of that, Quentin was watching from the other side of the room, looking restless.

'I'm clear on the extraction points, but are you sure this is one of the smaller hubs?' Travis asked, looking over the maps that would guide us to the hidden cell Gus had located.

'More importantly, it's one of the newest,' Gus explained. 'There are no guarantees, but it seems likely that it'll contains a fresh intake of negs from the processing camps. Judging by the size on the maps, we think it'll contain between one and two hundred, which is manageable.' This was important given that we wouldn't be equipped to deal with any of the larger hubs, which could hold up to a thousand prisoners.

'And by fresh intake, you mean …' Travis began.

'More likely to be helpful,' I explained.

'And less likely to kill you with their bare hands,' Gus added. Unnecessarily. Even if it was true.

It wasn't that all negs were difficult. It was becoming more and more apparent that many of them weren't even negs at all. But there was a percentage who were highly unpredictable. And for those who weren't, being locked up underground for such a long time ... well, I knew more than anyone how it could change a person.

'Where do you stand on all of this, Liam?' I asked, keen to move on.

'I stand with my bank account. Pay me enough and I'll do whatever you want,' he threw back. No hesitation. No added info. His voice steady. His body language relaxed. He was perfect.

Too perfect.

I nodded, holding his eyes. 'That works for me,' I lied.

'Right, well, let's break this down into segments,' Travis began, taking control of the meeting. 'Gus will be in the garage of the Archstone apartment building, controlling the elevators and security cameras from his laptop.'

Gus snorted. 'I still don't understand why I have to actually be there. I can control everything from here just fine.'

Both Travis and Ned smiled broadly while Liam and Hex stared him down.

'If things go belly up, you're going to want to be as close to us as possible,' Travis said. 'Trust me, we will be your only hope of getting out of there, and if we get caught they'll be here before you can get away.'

I rolled my eyes. 'And they want you nearby in case we're leading them into a trap.'

'That too,' Ned said, still with the toothy grin.

'Memory alert!' Gus snapped. 'It wasn't us who did the double-crossing last time, if I recall.'

'True. More reason for us to be careful,' Travis threw back.

'Have you forgotten –'

Travis snarled, cutting him off. 'I haven't forgotten anything, but I have to be alive to give a damn, now don't I?'

Gus backed down. Travis was right. Blackmail only worked when there was still a spark of hope that you would get through to the other side.

I pointed to the map of the apartment building's underground parking garage. 'We go in here. We break into teams of two. One team will enter through the metro tunnels and the other two teams will be at this door, waiting for us to open it from the other side.'

'Why don't we all just go through the metro?' Ned asked.

I shook my head. 'Too many cameras to dodge. Gus won't be able to keep them all down – plus with ground security personnel along with all the commuters coming home during rush hour, there'll be too many witnesses for six of us to slip through unnoticed.'

Travis and Ned nodded.

'So who's in my team?' Hex asked.

'Hex, you're with Ned. Travis, you team up with Quentin.' I glanced up to check Quentin was okay with this. His eyes were darting back and forth between Liam and me. He knew me.

'Works for me,' he said.

I bit back the smile. 'That leaves us,' I said, turning to Liam. 'And we're on the metro run.'

Liam held my eyes for a moment, before nodding.

By 6 p.m. I'd locked myself in the bedroom to change and collect the last of my weapons.

I dressed in my usual black uniform and army boots then hitched my hair into a tight ponytail.

Earlier in the day Quentin had snuck out to get me some more clothes. I'd roused on him for leaving the loft and taking unnecessary risks, but he'd just smiled and said, 'I noticed you weren't around when everyone was having lunch.'

I glared at him. Damn it, I should've known he wouldn't have missed anything. Not when it had to do with me. 'I was getting supplies.'

'Uh-huh,' he said, shoving the bag in my chest and walking away, ending any further discussion on the subject.

Now I was wearing the skinny jeans, long-sleeved top and new hoodie – all black – that he'd bought for me. And none of them had come from Target. Who knew black jeans could look so different from black jeans?

I stared at myself in the small mirror. There was no denying I looked badass. The hoodie was more of a panelled vest that zipped tight, hugging what curves I had. And when I pulled the hood up, it sat in place, perfectly hiding me but not hindering my view. I moved closer to the mirror. I'd filled out in the last couple of weeks, regaining much of the weight I'd lost in my prison cell.

I took a deep breath, staring straight into my own eyes.

'You gotta do this, Maggie,' I told myself. 'This is your chance to change your path. To do something right for once.' I pulled away and watched my features morph into something a little grittier, a little more familiar. 'So don't mess it up.'

With that, I spun around, grabbed my backpack that was filled to the brim with weapons and blueprints, stuffed my taser in my hoodie pocket, my tranq gun down the back of my jeans, and joined the rest of my waiting soldiers.

'Liam, you ready?'

Liam nodded, and came to stand beside me.

'Gus, you set?'

'You mean to die?' Gus closed his laptop and threw it in his carry bag. He gave me a pointed look before adding, 'Or worse?'

I raised my eyebrows.

Gus snorted. 'I apologise. I forgot I'm supposed to be clambering to get behind you in your all-new superhero-vixen wear, as though just because we're on the right dirty-rotten team for once, that means we're somehow going to prevail.' He paused and took a breath before carrying on. 'I mean, for chrissake, look around.' Gus waved a finger around the room. 'We're a combination of lowlifes and criminals, led by a she-bitch and ...' he paused at Quentin, 'a guy who basically equates to the devil's spawn.'

I crossed my arms and tapped my index finger.

Gus sighed.

I grinned.

It was like old times.

'Anything else?' I asked.

'No point delaying, I suppose,' he said, hoisting his bag on his shoulder. My grin widened. For Gus, it was a quick turnaround.

'Here,' I said, holding out a small bag to Gus.

He tilted his head and took the bag, glancing inside. 'Seriously? You risked going back to your place to get these? For me?'

I shrugged. 'Yep.'

Gus stuffed them in his bag and flashed me a grin laced with mischief to hide his gratitude. 'Cool.'

'Travis?' I asked, noting that Travis and his crew had gone all out with camouflage paint on their faces. Apparently it made them more difficult to ID on surveillance footage. 'Travis, are you good to go?' I asked.

'All good,' he said as he grabbed his gear. Ned and Hex followed suit.

I steeled my heart and turned back to Quentin, who was leaning up against the wall by the elevator doors. We hadn't spoken much since I'd told him I would leave our relationship in his court. He'd gone out to buy me clothes and had been part of planning the break-in, but that was it. Which meant he still didn't trust me. Or worse, didn't want me.

'You sure you want to go down there again?' I asked, hoping he'd changed his mind.

He smiled sadly, adjusting one of the bandages on his hand – he'd stripped most of them away so he had movement. 'And miss seeing my father finally exposed for what he really is?'

As much as I wished I could keep him somewhere safe until this was done, I also understood that, just like me, he needed to do this.

'I'll see you down there,' I said, turning to follow Liam who was already waiting in the elevator. We were taking the metro, leaving the others with the vehicles.

Just as I started through the doors, Quentin grabbed me by the arm, pulling me back to him. He wrapped his hand behind my neck and dropped his forehead against mine, causing every nerve in my body to ignite.

He breathed in and out deeply, and it stirred the emotions that I would never again be able to deny. Staring into his steel-blue eyes, my breath caught. I got the distinct impression that he was locking this moment of closeness away in his mind. As if he didn't believe there would be another. Suddenly I was frightened in a way I had never been before.

I gripped his arms fiercely. 'Promise me you'll stay with Travis,' I said. 'Don't leave his side.'

He nodded, his thumbs trembling as they grazed my cheeks. I could feel that he wanted to kiss me. But he couldn't. Something was still holding him back. I made the decision easier for him and stepped away.

I glanced at Travis, who had watched the exchange and no doubt heard my words. 'Don't stuff this up, Travis,' I warned.

He locked eyes with me. 'I'm clear on my role, and I don't make mistakes.' It was the best damn thing he could've said. Because as far as I was concerned, Travis's only function was making sure Quentin stayed alive.

Nineteen

Being in the metro reminded me of the time I'd seen a neg jump in front of a train to avoid being taken in by M-Corp security. It also happened to be one of the times I'd been trailing Quentin, preparing to tear his world apart. It was strange how the neg had seemed to instinctively know that the promises of rehabilitation and reintegration were all lies. The instant he'd seen the security team, he'd known he couldn't put his life in their hands.

I was hoping that, like him, there were other people out there in the general population who questioned the legitimacy of the M-Corp brand. The company's public image was a hard one to tear down – people had become accustomed to accepting their technologies and their word. But I had to pray that when we showed people the truth, they would be willing to listen.

They *had* to listen. We were going to give them so much evidence that they wouldn't be able to turn a blind eye anymore. By tomorrow, every free person in the world would be asking the same question: could they take me next? And I was going to make sure they understood the answer was: hell yes.

My father may not have been the victim I'd believed him to be. He'd turned out to be the very opposite. But on my path to finding him, I'd discovered beyond any doubt that there were thousands of people locked beneath the city who *were* innocent. They deserved to have their lives back and be with their families.

As we took the long escalator down to the underground platform in the Court House Metro, my thoughts wandered to the population-control documents we'd uncovered. Gus had kept copies and tomorrow, once we were somewhere safe, they would be leaked to the world. Within minutes, every man, woman and child would know why the Poverty Tax really existed; that M-Corp were using the tax to fund production of a drug designed to prevent third-world countries from breeding; that they were stealing their rights to fall in love and to have children. Destroying their lives, futures, legacies.

Liam followed close behind me. He seemed relaxed, but I knew he was watching everything. If I was sure of anything, it was that this guy was more than a black-market thug. He was too good. I pulled a small bag from my backpack and threw it in a large trashcan before making my way to the other end of the platform.

'There's a good few people around. You sure this is going to work?' Liam asked, looking dubious.

I ignored him, pulled out my handheld cell and called Gus.

'Ready for the fireworks?' he answered.

'As soon as the cameras are taken care of, we're good to go,' I responded.

'Okey-dokey. Cameras ... are ... down. You have sixty seconds to move out of range. Twenty seconds until boom time.'

I hung up, keeping count.

Liam huffed. 'Well?'

I turned my attention to him and forced a smile. 'I have a question I'd like to ask you, Liam.'

'What?'

I pointed down the tunnel. 'Run first. Questions second.'

As soon as I finished speaking, a series of small explosions sounded from the other end of the station. A number of sparks flew high as Gus detonated the package of fireworks I'd just dumped in the trashcan.

Some commuters exchanged panicked looks while others laughed as the colourful and harmless explosions continued. In the meantime, Liam and I had jumped down onto the tracks and run at full speed until we were within the darkness of the metro tunnel.

I concentrated on sprinting until I spotted the concealed doorway that blended almost seamlessly into the tunnel wall.

'Christ. I can't believe that actually worked,' Liam said, barely panting from the hard run.

I shrugged, trying to hide my deep breaths, and focused on the narrow key-slot in the door. I slipped in an electronic card connected to a decoder that had cost more than three months of my old salary. And Gus's.

As we waited, Liam started to get jittery.

'Not to sound clichéd or anything, but I'm pretty sure I hear a train coming our way.'

I ignored him.

'Seriously. Did you guys check the schedule?'

The door finally clicked with the right code and slid open. I followed Liam inside and then the door closed behind us, leaving us in complete darkness.

Before Liam had time to do anything, I pushed him hard into the wall and slammed my elbow against his neck, my other hand pressing my tranq gun into his stomach.

My throat was closing in on me and my heart was racing, but I ignored it and pushed on. 'What you're feeling down there is my tranq gun,' I said, my voice laced with deadly threat. 'You say the wrong thing, you try to fight me, I'm going to tranq you and leave you here for M-Corp to find. And considering what we're about to do, finding you will be a very, *very* bad thing.'

'You wouldn't leave me down here,' Liam hissed through gritted teeth.

'Oh, Liam. You have no idea what I'm capable of doing. Of just how many people I *have* left down here. Now tell me what you are hiding.'

'I'm not hiding anything,' he bit back.

'Yes, Liam. You are.' I'd been around enough liars to know with absolute certainty when I saw one. 'And you're going to tell me, or I'm going to shoot you. This is the last time I'm going to ask. What are you hiding?'

It was so dark that if I hadn't been pressed up against Liam's form I wouldn't have felt the defeat that washed through him, causing his body to slump slightly.

'Take the flashlight from my belt. It's just there near your right hand.'

'Why?' I asked, leaving my right hand – and the tranq gun – exactly where it was.

'Because you want the answer and I'm going to show you.'

'Fine,' I said, reaching down with my left hand until I felt the flashlight. I clicked it on and a small ray of light highlighted our silhouettes and the space between us. Instantly a wave of relief ran through me. I pointed the flashlight at Liam's face. Yep, he was pissed. The veins on his forehead and neck looked like they were about to pop.

'Unbutton the top of my shirt,' he instructed.

I rolled my eyes. 'You've gotten the wrong idea, you idiot –' I started, but was cut off by him shoving me so hard I was flung back onto the opposite wall, my hand going wide.

Liam was on me in a second. Our roles quickly reversed as his pinned my gun hand to the wall and used his brute strength to crush my body.

'All I wanted was some goddamn money and to get it by busting up something M-Corp,' he murmured, more to himself than me.

Suddenly he was off me, stepping back.

Slowly I raised the flashlight to see his face. He was shaking his head, his hands behind his neck. When he brought them down and opened the top two buttons of his shirt, I followed his movements with the flashlight, pausing at the expanse of skin exposed at his collarbone.

The scar ran at least ten centimetres wide. Not a scar. A branding.

'You're a neg!'

He looked down, studying the marking. He dropped his arms. 'When they didn't have tattoo equipment, they improvised.' He buttoned his shirt back up. 'I was military. I had a wife. A son.' He swallowed. 'When Phera-tech started, we rated real strong.' He half laughed. 'As if I needed a damn computer to tell me we had it going on.'

I found myself relaxing my stance.

'I was off on assignment and just before I was due to go home, I was offered a job in the private sector. The details were sketchy – apart from a crazy amount of money, I didn't know much else. Anyway, couldn't figure out how my skills could come to anything good in the private sector, so I turned it down flat. Went home to my wife.' He sniffed and coughed, masking his emotion. 'Made it as far as the airport before I was picked up by M-Corp guards, who switched on my Phera-tech. And wouldn't you know …'

'You rated neg,' I finished for him.

He nodded.

'I escaped from the processing camp. Never made it down to this shithole. I've been lying low in the black market ever since. Travis helps me go unnoticed and stay funded, and in return I do the jobs he asks. No questions.'

'Why didn't you go and find your wife? Take her and your son away?'

His shoulders dropped and I instantly regretted the question.

'You think that wasn't the first thing I did? But they'd gotten to her. Fed her all the lies. Made her believe I was evil or something.' He looked up at the ceiling and I lowered the flashlight from his face. 'She'd killed herself.'

'Oh my God. I'm sorry, Liam,' I said.

'Yeah,' he said, his voice thick but strong. 'Well, now I only have my son and I'm not about to let him down. He's in a good home. Better than what I can give him right now. But with this job and a few others, I'll have enough money to get us both off the grid, so that's why I'm here. For him. And if I get my chance to give M-Corp the middle finger on the way – then that's just fine with me.'

'I don't know what to say.'

'How about you're sorry for shoving a tranq gun in my gut and you're ready to get on with business?' he said. I didn't need to have the flashlight on his face to know he had mustered a smile.

I nodded. 'Sorry for shoving a tranq gun in your gut. Let's go.' I held out my hand with the flashlight, ignoring the slight tremor that came with finally having to accept I was back in the tunnels. Back in the dark.

He gently pushed my hand away. 'Keep it. I'll follow.'

I nodded and started to walk. 'Liam?'

'Yeah?'

'What did you used to do for the military?'

He was silent for a time. I waited.

'Chemical weapon delivery.'

'Oh.'

'Yeah.'

'I'm glad you got away,' I said.

'Maggie?'

'Yep?'

'Can we stop talking and get on with the job now?'

I smiled. 'Yes,' I said with relief.

We walked silently, taking corners carefully as we moved deeper into the rabbit warren of tunnels.

'Jesus Christ,' Liam murmured at one point as the tunnel we were in gradually got tighter and tighter. I didn't respond, just clenched the flashlight in my hand like a lifeline.

'Here,' I said when we finally came across a small alcove. 'This must be the doorway to the parking garage.'

'This is one messed-up place.'

'Yeah,' I said distractedly as I started to check the door for any traps. It was one of the usual tunnel doors, which meant it was unlocked from our side, but needed a code to open from the other side.

I took a deep breath. 'Only one way to find out,' I whispered to myself, grasping the handle and pulling down.

The slide mechanism activated and the door slid open, revealing a smug-looking Travis on the other side. 'What'd you two do, stop for tea on the way?'

I rolled my eyes and stepped aside. 'Hurry up and get in here.'

They filed through, Quentin coming in last, brushing up against my body as he did. He leaned towards my ear. 'Everything okay?'

I knew he was referring to Liam. He'd seen my intentions from the beginning.

I nodded. 'All good.'

He kept moving into the narrow corridor, his hand lingering on my hip.

Luckily the narrow section of the tunnel didn't last too long. As soon as we reached a wider walkway, Ned quickly shook out his arms, causing Travis to laugh quietly. But apart from that, we said little as we all followed the direction we'd learned by heart until we reached a much larger transit tunnel.

'Hell,' Ned murmured. 'I'd heard the stories, but this ... this place is overflowing with bad vibes.'

I nodded. 'Just count yourself lucky we're nowhere near the core,' I said.

'You been that far?' Ned asked incredulously, not knowing that in fact I'd been imprisoned in the core for over a month.

'Yeah. And I'm never going back.'

I felt Quentin's hand grasp mine. No one else could see and I squeezed his hand back. Whatever was wrong with us, we would always be in tune with one another and that drew us together.

I made everyone wait in the side tunnel until I was sure I couldn't hear any transit pods coming in our direction. When I was satisfied, I motioned them forwards.

'We run from here.' With that, I took off, the rest following behind as we ran hard, passing Junction 78, then 79, and finally to Junction 80. It wasn't a huge distance, which was why we'd chosen this route specifically. We'd need to run the entire hub of negs back along this route soon enough.

We found a narrow tunnel to the side, helping us avoid the main junction entrance and the men followed me into it. When we reached a small opening – a ventilation hole – I dropped to a crouch with Quentin beside me. We gave the rest of them a moment to absorb what they were seeing.

You can tell people that there are prisons underground where negs are locked up. You can describe the way they've been dug out of the black rock and resemble giant salad bowls containing a number of buildings. That each hub represents only a small fraction of the many hundreds of hubs that exit beneath the streets where we walk free. You can tell people all you want. Explain the plain grey uniforms. How the negs are forced to remain in bare feet to make them easier to control. How they are made to exist in a world with nothing more than dim light and stale air that's delivered with the following promise: It. Is. Limited.

You can tell people.

Then they see it.

And their world changes.

And grown men suddenly want to cry.

Then, of course, they do what grown men also do. They swear.

'I knew there was a reason I never wanted to come down here,' Travis whispered, crouching beside me.

I nodded as we all continued to stare.

'Definitely one of those things you can't damn well un-see,' Hex said, glaring at me as if it was all my fault.

'You got my respect if you've been coming and going from this place, like the rumours say,' Ned said. 'That's some nasty shit going on down there.'

I didn't respond. I didn't deserve anyone's respect. Sure, I'd been coming and going. But in the worst possible way: every time, I'd simply turned my back and left them all behind.

'Four guards on the entrance,' Quentin said, pointing down to the main entryway we'd sidestepped on the way in.

'Three on the far entrance over there,' Liam added, gesturing to an aqueduct where trucks entered and exited. 'And I'd say we're looking at somewhere between four and six guards inside each of the buildings.' He glanced at me, unhappy with the ratios.

I studied the layout. It was similar to many of the hubs I'd broken into before. And Gus had been right; it only looked big enough to contain a maximum of a hundred or so prisoners. But something about this hub was different. To start with, the walls of the main building were white, but not made out of cement. They looked like they were glass or something. I shuddered. I'd seen similar buildings before. In the core.

'How are we doing this?' Travis asked.

I snapped out of my thoughts. 'It's past curfew, so there will only be two guards inside each building. They run a skeleton shift overnight because the negs are locked in their rooms. The four at the main entrance will be easy enough. We can drop down from above and surprise them from behind. It's the guards on the far side who are going to be the problem,' I explained.

'Hex and Ned, you drop down first and take the guards at the front. Fast and quiet. Tranqs only,' I said. When I saw their lukewarm reactions, I pushed. 'I mean it, guys. You kill them, this is all over. They all have mortality zips, and alarms will start going off everywhere.' Waiting for them to all give me a nod, I went on. 'Travis and Quin, at the same time you drop down onto the rooftop of that building.' I pointed to the main building, which I knew housed the negs. 'You'll get access through the vents, which will take you into the corridors. The main guard will be in the security room down the end of the corridor. You need to be fast in case he's watching the monitors and sees us taking down the other guards.'

They nodded.

I swallowed, fighting my nerves and adrenalin. I handed Quentin the zip program that Gus had written. 'Plug this into the central computer in the security room,'

I told him. 'It has a five-minute activation delay on it. That will give you enough time to find the second guard, take him down and then get into a safe position.'

I stressed the last words because as soon as those five minutes were up, all of the doors to the negs' rooms would slide open and there'd be a level of chaos we could only hope to try to control.

Quentin pulled a rope from his bag. 'We'll get it done.' He locked eyes with me and I felt the urge to grab his hand and run. Suddenly I wasn't sure of anything and just wanted to get him to safety. But I also knew we had to do this. *I* had to do this.

'Guess that leaves you and me with the far entrance?' Liam said, jolting me from my fears.

I nodded quickly. 'We'll use this ledge,' I instructed, pointing towards the walkway carved into the granite walls, which ran the entire length of the salad-bowl-shaped hub. 'If we move fast and go unnoticed, we should get pretty close to the far entrance.'

'Looks like fun,' Liam said, somehow managing to drag a smile from me. The ledge was unforgivingly narrow, and there was no doubt that if one of us fell it would be the end. Not to mention we'd be sitting ducks if someone spotted us and decided on some target practice.

'Okay,' I said. 'When Liam and I reach the halfway mark, everyone else is a go. All clear?'

Everyone nodded, prepping their weapons and anchoring their abseil ropes. Everyone except me had a fully loaded gun – bullets and all – even Quentin. It was their right to be armed, and Quentin had been upset when I'd insisted I only wanted to carry my taser and tranq gun. I'd argued that my current weapons, backpack and equipment were already weighing me down. But I knew he saw right through me to the truth. I just didn't know if I could live with myself if I crossed that final line. Killing a person was the one thing I'd managed to avoid in all this. I wanted it to stay that way.

Twenty

The world around me narrowed in. I felt my muscles contract each time I swallowed; I heard each breath in and out. My sight constricted to tunnel vision and I looked at the guys, knowing I was somehow becoming separate. How I needed to be.

I sent Gus a message, letting him know we were moving in. He replied that he was readying the transport. It was a huge task, detouring an empty train and stopping it in the middle of nowhere. Not to mention preventing any other trains coming that way until we were ready. But no matter how we had looked at it, this was the only way we could think of to get the negs to safety without causing absolute mayhem. And I knew Gus would make it happen.

Nods were exchanged as we took up our positions. Me in front, Liam behind. With one last fleeting glance over my shoulder – not to Quentin because I couldn't, but to Travis, my message clear – I crouched low and ran.

My heart rate increased and I faintly acknowledged there was a time when I would have worked hard on controlling it, just to prove I could. Now, knowing my black-market M-Band would not alert any authorities that I was in a state of panic, I let it slide and focused on moving ahead.

The ledge we were navigating was barely wide enough for one foot at a time and eventually forced us to slow down and stand tall, our backs flat to the rock as we neared our goal – a small boulder jutting out from the cliff. Just big enough to tie a rope to.

As soon as we reached it, we got to work tying the rope and linking up our D-Rings to our waist harnesses.

'They're down,' Liam said behind me.

I nodded, not looking back.

'Let's go,' I said, leaping without another word, knowing that every second counted.

I dropped down the rope fast, barely using the hand behind me to slow the descent. Liam moved just as fast above me.

I hit the ground and leaped aside just in time for his arrival. We had landed behind the building closest to the far entrance. It was a good place for us to hide – in front of the building was an open space about twenty square metres and beyond that stood the three M-Corp security guards who were guarding the aqueduct.

We unclipped from the rope, grabbed our weapons and moved silently, using the cover of the building until the very last moment.

I glanced at Liam, my heart pounding. He moved like the pro he was, and I could see why M-Corp had first tried to recruit him and then not taken no for an answer.

He pulled a chain from around his neck and kissed the gold ring that hung from it. 'I'll go right,' he whispered, and with a mere nod from me we were running, staying in the shadows for as long as we could.

Luck wasn't on our side. The guards spotted us within moments.

They were fast.

We were faster.

Liam threw a smoke bomb just as one raised his gun.

I took down the first guard with two tranqs in the shoulder before he'd managed to take aim. But as he fell, he got off two shots and I grimaced as the noise reverberated around the underground hub. If the others hadn't taken down the rest of the guards, they would now know something was going down.

Liam moved behind the cloud of smoke and quickly out of sight. After a pause, I heard the unmistakeable sounds of flesh hitting flesh and knew he'd found at least one of the other guards.

I looked around for the third guard, but the smoke was thicker than we'd anticipated and I couldn't see a damn thing. I definitely didn't see the fist flying my way until it hit me square across the jaw. I dropped my weapon as I stumbled back a few steps. I righted myself just in time to receive another round of blows, a particularly hard jab going into my side.

I felt something warm slide down my cheek and neck and knew it was blood. But only one thought ran through my mind: *he still hasn't called it in.*

I would've heard if the guard had radioed in the attack. And I wasn't going to let the team down. I staggered forwards and waited, focusing all of my attention on the fight.

Sure enough, his attack came from the right. But this time I was ready. I ducked his fist and spun around, coming up behind him, where I swiftly delivered a hard blow to his lower back. It shocked him long enough for me to lever my body back and jam my foot into his calf, stomping down as hard as I could manage. I was fairly certain I heard a crack. He was down on his knees in seconds. I didn't hesitate, spinning and delivering a fast round-kick that collided with the side of his head, knocking him out instantly. Just to be sure, I found my tranq gun on the ground where I'd dropped it and shot him twice in the chest.

My handheld cell buzzed and I checked the screen.

Zip's active. 5 minute countdown started.

I stared at Gus's message then set the timer on my M-Band. Quentin and Travis had done it. In less than five minutes, the doors to all of the cells would open and the negs would be released.

'The other two are both out,' Liam said, coming up behind me. 'I'm sorry. I lost you in the smoke.'

'It's fine,' I said. It had all happened in seconds, not minutes. 'Let's go help the others.'

We wound our way towards the main building.

'What the hell?' Liam said, stepping away from me to inspect what looked like two water tanks sitting on the bed of a truck.

'What's wrong?' I asked.

'You see those tubes? They're running from those tanks into the main building.'

'And?' I asked, getting impatient.

'Nothing good is in those tanks, Maggie. I ... I told you what I used to do for the military.'

I nodded, watching his eyes dart about and his face turn pale. 'I got a real bad feeling we need to get the hell outta here.' He continued checking out the tanks, looking for God knows what.

But I was already moving. Sprinting towards the main building entrance.

'Quin!' I screamed at the top of my lungs. 'Quin!'

I was moving faster than my legs could manage, falling over myself as I reached the main doors and started thumping on the glass. I didn't have an access key so I just pounded on the door hysterically.

'Quin! Damn it! Please! Travis!' I yelled.

Suddenly they were there, running down the hall. I checked the time. I didn't know what the hell was going on, but I kept banging on the door, screaming at them to move faster. They heard my panic, or saw it. They picked up the pace and reached the doors. My heart stopped.

Liam was now beside me. 'They gotta get out of there, Maggie. Now!' he yelled.

My eyes went wide. Time slowed down. I stared into Quentin's eyes. No. My stomach turned. They needed door-activation keys. They wouldn't have had time to get them.

God. No. They couldn't take him from me.

'No!' I screamed, my voice carrying all my fears.

But just then the door slid open. I blinked as they raced out, Travis stopping only to flash me a grin and the set of swipe keys he'd obviously picked up in the security room.

The doors closed instantly behind them.

'What the hell's going on? The negs will be coming out in a few minutes,' Travis said just as a number of shots rang out from the front of the hub, where we'd left Ned and Hex to take care of the guards.

'They're coming,' I said. 'They're here.'

We started moving back into the depths of the hub, running between the buildings as the sound of gunfire neared and then, even worse, footsteps. Dozens of jogging feet thundering towards us.

'Run!' I screamed. We were heading towards the aqueduct. It was our only hope, even if it was incredibly slim.

Liam led and we ran in single file. I made it with him to one building while Travis and Quentin were caught behind another when a volley of gunfire exploded around us. I jolted at the noise, the sounds amplified in the stone structure, as I desperately assessed the divide that now separated us.

'Quin!' I screamed. 'Run! Now! You have to! Travis!' I implored. 'Travis, please!'

Travis looked right at me. His eyes knowing. Defiant. He pushed Quentin ahead of him and suddenly they were running towards us. Liam had pulled out his gun and was firing bullets randomly to offer what cover he could. But there were so damn many of them shooting back.

They were so close.

Shots fired.

They dodged.

Ran.

Quentin's eyes locked on mine. He was only ten metres away.

Then Hex was there, standing behind Travis with a smile on his face. Gun raised. And pointed right at Travis's head.

'Runnnn!' I screamed.

Travis looked over his shoulder and saw Hex leading the charge, an army behind him.

Liam threw another smoke bomb.

But it was too late.

Gunfire erupted.

Travis launched forwards and to the side.

Quentin went down.

Smoke clouded everything.

I ran into the haze, skidding to my knees beside Quentin.

The shooting suddenly ceased.

He was bleeding. I kicked into gear, ignoring the fact that my insides were breaking apart, and looked him over quickly.

He was shot in the arm.

'Quin!' I snapped, shaking his other arm.

His eyes opened.

'Can you run? You have to run!'

He blinked. Nodded at me. 'Travis?' he asked, getting to his knees.

I scrambled over to Travis, who had landed behind Quin. I tilted his head towards mine only to see his lifeless eyes staring back at me. They'd hit him in the neck and chest. He was riddled with bullets. Bullets that had been aimed at Quentin.

I pried the security passes from his clenched fist and grabbed Quentin's hand. 'He's dead. We need to move.'

We ran through the smoke, heading back to Liam, who'd waited by the building.

'The smoke won't stop them for long,' he said. 'I'm surprised they aren't already through it.' He led the way between two of the smaller buildings, staying close to the walls to keep us hidden.

But he was right.

They should've been on us by now.

They *should've* been shooting us dead.

I looked at the timer on my M-Band.

All of this had happened in just over three minutes.

I pulled up, frozen, as I stared back at the main building.

A red beacon had started to flash on the roof of the building. And then, something that caused us all to gasp: the white opaque walls of the building faded to clear until we had full view of everyone inside. But as if that weren't enough, on the rooftop a magnified hologram flickered to life, showing roaming close-ups of each and every prisoner below.

'There! Look!' Quentin said, pointing to the centre of the building. It was filling up with white smoke.

'It's only in the corridors,' Liam said, sounding defeated. 'Oh, shit.'

I watched the images on the rooftop, scanning through the faces until the hologram paused on one image and I slapped a hand over my mouth.

'Oh my God!' I cried, grabbing hold of Quentin's arm to keep me up.

'What?' he asked. 'Maggie, Jesus, what?'

She was looking around nervously. Her clothes were torn and I dreaded to think what had happened to make them that way. She looked much younger than any other time I'd seen her, but it was definitely her.

'Oh my God, oh my God.'

'What? Maggie, answer me!' Quentin yelled. But I couldn't. I just stared.

My band beeped. The five minutes were up.

Before I knew it I was running, but I barely made it two steps before Quentin and Liam were there, dragging me back into the shadows where they held me down as I watched the doors we had programmed to release the negs to their freedom slide open and let the smoke into their rooms.

One by one, we watched the bodies drop to the ground. And the hologram above zoomed in, showing her face as the vapour hit her lungs and she screamed out before falling. She'd made it no more than two steps from her room.

I watched on, restrained by the arms holding me back as my mind spiralled into a terrifying hell. This couldn't be happening.

Gunfire started up again in the distance. I knew I should be moving, but I couldn't muster the ability to care.

We'd killed them all.

I'd killed them all.

'Margaret,' a voice calmly boomed from the sky. A whimper escaped my lips at the sound of my father's voice. 'Margaret, will you never learn that your actions have consequences?' Even far away, talking to me through a speaker system, I could hear the taunt in his voice. A cruel tone I would never have believed the man who raised me was capable of. 'Once again, you appear to be carrying precious cargo that certain people would like returned. Guards are coming in to apprehend you. Stay on your knees. Do not struggle. I have given permission to use full force. On *all* of you if needed.'

I pulled myself away from Quentin's arms while staying on my knees.

'What are you doing?' Quentin asked, frantically looking around. 'Maggie, what the hell are you doing?' he repeated as I shuffled on my knees away from him.

I glanced at Liam. 'I'm sorry,' I said.

He shrugged, as if a person could actually do something so everyday in a moment like that. 'I knew the risks. It's not on you.'

He was lying, but I nodded and looked at Quentin. 'I love you, Quin. I'm sorry I made you a part of this. I was crazy to think we could ever win against them.'

Quentin shook his head, looking around. The gunfire was getting closer, voices calling out, nearer by the second. 'We need to run!' he yelled at me.

I held his gaze, my eyes saying all the things I couldn't say aloud. There was nowhere to run. No way out. The most I could hope for was that by not fighting them, Quentin would have a chance. I had to believe his family would spare him, that *his* father was capable of mercy.

Quentin was shaking his head and then he launched himself at me, pulling me into his arms as if he could shield me from the world.

Smoke bombs detonated to our left and right while something inside me died. There was yelling in the distance. More gunfire. The arms around me suddenly went slack, Quentin murmuring my name in my ear one last time.

I looked over my shoulder. Liam was lying motionless behind us. I patted Quentin down and found the dart in his side. I looked up in time to see the shooter aim his weapon at me.

Right then, it felt as if God was revelling in his vengeance. And he would get no argument from me.

I looked into the shooter's fierce eyes, knowing he would see nothing reflected in mine. For all my plans, all my hopes, I was no better than those I had vainly tried to fight against.

'You stupid bitch,' he said, right before he cracked the butt of his gun hard against my head.

Alex was right, I thought, as the darkness came to collect me.

I was a stupid, *stupid* bitch.

Twenty-one

A sharp pain shot up my spine and lodged behind my eyes.

I grabbed at my head, flinching when I felt the clump of sticky, matted hair over a huge bump.

It was surreal to wake up. In those final seconds before I'd closed my eyes, I'd somehow come to terms with never opening them again. Now, it felt somehow wrong. And entirely undeserved. And hard. Because as I forced my eyes to open and take in my surroundings, I instantly knew that I was going to have to survive when so many had died because of me.

Tears silently streamed from my eyes as my insides tore apart, slashing me with the certain knowledge that I had failed those negs, those *human beings*, in the worst possible way. I wrapped my arms around my waist and drowned in silent screams.

I was in a truck. It was big, probably a semi-trailer. I could see feet all around me. All in military-issue boots. Flashes of the faces of those who'd just been killed in the neg hub kept bouncing through my mind. I squeezed my eyes tight, trying to stop them, knowing they never would.

'That was some kind of shit-fight in there,' someone said. I thought he was talking to me and was about to look up when I heard someone else reply.

'Never seen anything like it.'

'Can you believe it was her own father ordering that takedown? That's some cold-ass piece of work.'

'We completely underestimated how far he would go. With a Mercer there and all. That guy was crazy enough to take them both down.'

'Shut up, both of you!' came a familiar voice.

'Sorry, man. I know this has gotta be tough on you. We all loved her, but you gotta admit, it isn't all their fault. None of us knew she'd be in that hub and we all agreed on running this thing out to see where their loyalties lay. We knew they'd be walking into a trap. None of us could've known how crazy things would get.'

I heard a scuffle and then pushed myself up onto my knees in time to see Alex head-butt the guys who'd just been talking.

'What did you mean?' I asked croakily, causing them all to freeze and look at me. 'When you said you *knew* we were walking into a trap?'

At least a dozen sets of eyes homed in on me.

Alex dropped his hold on the guy's shirt and turned to face me. 'Did you know she was in there?' he spat.

'No. Did you?' I bit back, not needing to clarify who he was talking about. I could still see Kelsey's face as she took her last fatal breath. It was so clear I could almost reach out and touch her.

He sniffed, defensively. 'We ... We had a good idea she'd been taken, but we were still looking for her in the processing camps. We didn't think she'd be taken underground so fast.'

I staggered to my feet, ignoring the movement of the trailer that was clearly travelling at high speed and stared at the men and women around me until they moved back and gave me some room.

'You knew we were going down there.' Statement. He didn't argue it. 'How?'

'We have people everywhere. We knew everything. At least, we did until you moved locations.'

As the trailer took a corner, I swayed awkwardly and stumbled to the side, putting a hand against the wall of the truck to steady myself. My entire body was screaming out in pain, and yet ... it was nothing. 'You knew we were at Burn.'

He nodded. 'We expected something to go down at the school. We had a tracker planted in your bag that morning and bugged the apartment above Burn the first chance we got once we found out you were there. We thought we had you and your plan covered, but then you went AWOL after you met me.'

'After you *left* me to run for my life with M-Corp on my tail, you mean,' I sneered.

Alex shrugged. 'As far as we knew, you were bringing them to us. I was simply following protocol.'

'Then what?' I asked, wary of where all this was leading.

'It wasn't until this afternoon we got the rest of the intel, and by then we were just scampering to keep up,' he explained, shaking his head.

'Who?' I asked, already knowing there had to have been someone on the inside.

'Me,' said a voice from the back. Men moved aside until Liam came into view. 'It was me.'

I bit the inside of my cheek to stop the tears. I wouldn't cry anymore.

'I knew,' I mumbled. 'I knew there was something.'

He nodded. 'And I'm more sorry than you could know. But you have to believe we didn't know ... We thought this was a standard loyalty check.'

I blinked. 'A standard *loyalty check*? What the ... What is that?!'

Liam flinched. 'You came to us. You wanted in. But it was impossible for us to believe that you hadn't been turned while you were their prisoner. M-Corp never let people go unless they're working for them. And you were holding hands with a Mercer for chrissake. What did you expect us to believe?'

'We ran through all the scenarios,' Alex explained, his voice dead, the pain of losing his sister overlapping with both guilt and blame. 'Even if you were clean, Quentin had to be playing you. There was no way you were both legit. So we decided to monitor you. When we caught wind of your plan, we figured it was the fastest way to flush out any moles. We expected to see one of you show your hand. We expected to catch you out before it ever happened, but then you all disappeared.'

'Until Travis called in his team,' I finished. I wanted to scream. To be sick. All those people … they had just dropped dead in front of us. Because of me. And here they were, laying out how and why they hadn't helped stop it.

Alex nodded. 'Liam was bugged, but we'd adapted his M-Band so he had no link to us in case your tech guy scanned him, which he did. His directive was simple: stay with the group. By the time we figured out exactly *who* Hex was and that he'd be leading a tornado-style shit-storm your way, there was nothing we could do to warn Liam, so we stuck to the plan and mobilised our teams.'

'So you had ways in and out of the tunnels?'

Alex pulled the black beanie off his head and threw it at the wall. 'We always have, but tonight we blew up part of the aqueduct and all of the side tunnel we'd built to connect to it.'

I brushed the hair off my face, trying to put it all together. 'So you knew we were going in?'

'Yes.'

'You knew Hex was a mole?' More sickening evidence of how wrong I'd been to think I was ever in control.

'Yes.'

I even felt distant from myself as I heard my hardened tone. 'You knew M-Corp would be waiting for us and there was a chance they would try to kill us all?'

'Yes,' Alex said.

I was moving before I had a chance to think it through. I launched myself at him and actually made it, throwing punches left, right and centre. When I failed to make enough impact, I resorted to straight-out scratching with my nails.

'They died!' I screamed, ignoring the hands pulling me off him. 'They all … Your sister!'

'You think I don't know that?' Alex boomed. 'You think I don't know what happened down there?'

'You could've stopped it. You could've helped us when we asked!' I yelled, my legs kicking uselessly at him as I struggled against the guards holding me back.

Alex glared at me, wiping the blood dripping from the scratch marks I'd left on his face. 'It wasn't my call,' he growled.

I stopped struggling; I needed to concentrate on breathing to stop myself gagging on the facts. 'You're the head of Preference Evolution. If it isn't your call, then whose damn call was it?'

'I was never the head of Preference Evolution.' He spat a mouthful of blood on the floor. 'I'm just the front.'

I blinked, intuitively dreading where this was going. 'Who?' It came out as more of a whisper than a demand.

Alex shook his head. 'Right now, that's none of your business,' he said, looking over my shoulder. 'Take her down the back.'

Before I could speak again, the two guards restraining me dragged me to the back of the truck and dropped me in the corner.

'If you know what's good for you, you'll stay put and give him some time,' said one of the guards. And for the first time I noticed it was a girl.

She was dressed head-to-toe in combat gear and she would've been in her mid-twenties. She crouched by my side.

'I'm Grace,' she said, her voice softening. 'Try to understand that this is a really hard time for Alex. Right before he went into that hub to pull you guys out, he saw what happened to Kelsey. He's looking for someone to blame and you're the closest. Soon enough he'll turn his attention back in the right direction.' I listened to her talk, watching as she glanced thoughtfully between Alex and me. She cared for him.

'Am I a prisoner?' I asked, prodding at my throbbing head.

'Yes,' said the other guard just as Grace said, 'Of course not.'

Grace shot the guy a stern look before turning back to me. 'We're heading to the Pre-Evo base of operations.'

'I thought you guys were some kind of *peaceful* group,' I said.

At my obvious sarcasm, she sighed. 'We're a little more established than people realise.'

'Where have you taken the others?' I asked, no longer able to avoid the question.

'Quentin is getting treatment for his gunshot wound. He'll be fine. We picked up Gus as well. They're coming in on separate transport.'

At the mention of Gus's name I flinched. 'Does he …?'

'I imagine someone has told him about Kelsey,' Grace answered.

I stared at the floor.

'I'm afraid Travis and Ned are gone,' Grace continued. 'We were unable to retrieve the bodies.'

I swallowed bile. Travis had died following my orders and I was certain he had thrown himself in the line of bullets in order to protect Quin. Now his body was just abandoned down there.

'And Hex, well, he was never on your team to start with,' Grace said softly.

'M-Corp,' I said.

She nodded. 'He's been in your father's pocket for a while. He first came onto our radar when he sold out your location at Roosevelt Island.'

And the hits just kept on coming. 'That was my father?' I'd always thought that attack was against Travis, not me.

She shrugged. 'In a way. He started a series of events that sent the feds to Travis. But, yeah, it was him.'

'And who are you?' I asked.

'I'm just one of many who want to see the world stop going in this direction. And by being here, I have the chance to maybe one day change that direction for the better.'

I nodded, swallowing painfully. She was a do-gooder and unfortunately that didn't inspire any hope.

'So I can just get up and leave?' I asked.

'No,' the guy said.

I looked at Grace, who nodded. 'I'm afraid he's right.'

'Then I am your prisoner.'

Grace shook her head. 'We're under orders not to release you. But that doesn't make you a prisoner. That makes you lucky. If we put you back out there now, after what you did down there … They're coming for you, Maggie. And this time they won't be playing games.'

I looked away. Her words were no surprise. After what we'd attempted to do … I'd always known they'd be coming for us. I'd just expected to have a lot more arsenal to be fighting back with.

And a lot less blood on my hands.

Twenty-two

Arriving at a run-down theatre site was not something I'd predicted. The truck pulled into an underground garage and the troops – because make no mistake, these people were part of a highly trained army – started jumping out and moving through an internal door.

With Grace beside me, we followed the troops until I had to stop and stare. It was like a scene from a spy movie. Apart from the stage, the theatre had been cleared completely. What was once tiered audience seating was now an area full of workstations, weaponry and labs divided by glass partition walls. A false ceiling covered the original ornate ceiling, except in the centre, where they'd cut a hole to accommodate a massive chandelier.

'Pretty impressive, right?' Grace said with a small smile.

I stared at her, trying to let the awful numbness prevail over my need to lash out. I had just watched my father commit mass execution and she wanted me to be impressed with their building? Sure, I had walked past this place on my way to school every day and had no idea that behind the old theatre façade was the most battle-ready, high-tech and intimidating place I'd ever seen, with the exception of M-Corp's core. But right then, I couldn't care less.

'There are living quarters upstairs. I'll show you to where you will be staying for now,' Grace explained, but I'd already turned from her and was walking towards the table in the centre of the room.

Gus sat at what looked like a massive boardroom table, elbows on the polished cherry-wood surface, head in his hands. Two men stood nearby, pretending they weren't watching over him.

I didn't know what to do, what to say, yet I found myself walking all the way to his side and dropping to my knees.

He looked over to me, met my eyes. I didn't turn away. I didn't blink. We just looked at each other. And I waited.

Finally a tear slipped down his cheek and he heaved in a shuddering breath. 'I pressed the button. I opened the doors.'

I shook my head, grabbing his shoulders and turning him square to me so he couldn't look away. 'On my order,' I said unwaveringly. 'It was on my order, Gus. This isn't on you.'

He stared at me for another minute, and though I wanted to curl into a ball and scream and cry, I didn't. I stayed there on my knees, doing all I could to give him whatever strength I had left, even if that strength would go into hating me.

Finally he blinked and looked around. 'You get a load of this?' he murmured.

I followed his gaze. 'Pretty out there. Did you … Did she ever tell you about it?'

He shook his head. 'We never talked about this stuff. Never wanted to cross into the wrong territory with one another.' His voice broke on every second word, and then his shoulders slumped towards me so fast, I barely caught him as he gripped me tight. 'What have we done, Mags?'

I held him, biting down on the inside of my cheek to try to control myself. 'We stuffed up,' I said into his ear.

He trembled even as he gripped me harder.

'But we're not the only ones,' I added softly so only he could hear. 'All I know for sure is we're not free to leave and, until we know more, we stick together. Have you still got those gifts I gave you earlier?'

When he nodded, I let out a little breath. 'I don't know what to do, or where to go, but we'll figure it out. I promise you. In the meantime, if you get worried, don't hesitate to use them.'

Gus glanced around the room filled with every high-tech gizmo you could imagine. He nodded again, sniffing as he sat up, as if he'd suddenly grasped onto a new purpose. 'I've got your back, you know that.'

'I wouldn't blame you if you hated me right now.'

Gus smiled sadly. 'You, me and hate feels a lot like home, Mags.'

I pressed my lips together, barely fighting back the emotion.

Gus glanced towards the ceiling. 'They've taken him upstairs to the infirmary. They wouldn't let me stay with him.'

I stood, squeezing his hand one last time, and turned to see Grace silently waiting to the side. 'Take me to Quentin,' I said to her.

'I don't think that's –'

I stepped right up into her space, my hand around her neck before she'd even flinched. I pressed my thumb into her oesophagus. 'Take me to Quentin now or you are about to have a new way to eat.'

She held up her hands in defeat. 'I'll take you,' she wheezed.

I nodded, letting go of her instantly. That was easy enough.

She half smiled as she twisted her head from side to side. 'You do realise there are over a hundred armed troops on site right now? If I screamed, there would be more weapons than you could imagine pointed in your direction in a heartbeat.'

I shrugged. 'Which way?'

She sighed, then made her decision. 'Over here.'

I followed Grace up the spiral staircase to the next floor. 'This place is huge,' I remarked.

She led us down a series of corridors. 'We've been here about two years now,' she explained. 'But most of it was built about a decade ago.'

'When microchipping first started.'

She looked at me quickly then away, and I could tell she hadn't meant to reveal so much.

She came to a door and used her M-Band to activate the lock. She held the door open. 'You can wait in here. They've taken him somewhere else to clean him up, but he should be back anytime now.'

I walked into the room that contained nothing but a table and two chairs and turned back to Grace. 'I said take me to him, not take me to a waiting room.'

Grace smiled. 'You had your thumb jammed in my throat, Maggie. Did you expect me to argue specifics? And besides, there is someone who wants to speak with you first.' With that, her smile widened and she stepped back out into the corridor, pulling the door closed and locking me in.

I furrowed my brow. I had totally underestimated her.

I moved over to the small steel table and sat in the chair facing the door. I was trapped and frankly it was taking all of my energy not to fly into some kind of hysterical fit. Instead, I stared at the light, grateful for that at least, and I waited.

Five minutes.

Ten minutes.

Half an hour.

Eventually weariness won out and I rested my head on my arms on the table. I didn't even hear the door open. In fact, it wasn't until the chair across from me screeched along the floor that I looked up.

It was a definite time-stood-still moment.

'Hello, Maggie.'

I stared, wide-eyed and open-mouthed. It probably would have been a comical look. That is, if the situation wasn't so mindboggling and not at all funny.

'Holy shit,' I whispered.

Eliza Mercer nodded as she took a seat. 'I'd say that's a fair response.'

'Holy shit,' I repeated.

'Yes. I heard you the first time.' She raised her eyebrows, looking at me patiently. Maternally.

This was it. It was over. M-Corp had won.

'M-Corp are Preference Evolution,' I said, suddenly wondering why it had never occurred to me.

Eliza sat there in her black cargo pants and fitted long-sleeved top. Her hair was pulled off her face in a ponytail and she wore almost no makeup. She looked younger. She looked strong.

I blew out a breath. 'I should've known. M-Corp love playing both sides. Controlling the lust-enhancer market … Hell, the way M-Corp has controlled me should've been enough to clue me in.'

'I'm afraid, in this circumstance, it is not M-Corp that has been playing both sides. Just me.' She watched me carefully.

I half laughed, noting that the sound came across as slightly hysterical. 'Jesus, I know I've made a lot of mistakes, and right now you must all be laughing at me. But if you think I'm going to fall for that …' I shook my head.

Eliza leaned forwards. 'I was once CIA. I was recruited out of school and trained from the age of eighteen. I was like you. Fast. Strong. Quick-witted. And determined to come out on top.'

I swallowed, listening to her words.

'I travelled the world, working undercover. I was a valuable asset. But when I came back to America in between jobs I met a man. He was gorgeous,' she explained, smiling at the memory. 'And charismatic. He didn't know what I did for a living; he thought I was merely a personal assistant to a government department head. I fell in love. *We* fell in love. After a year, he asked me to marry him. I said yes and quit my job. We married and had a family, and I never told him the truth.'

'Why?' I asked, still refusing to believe a word she said.

She shrugged. 'I told myself it was to protect them. Perhaps it was to protect me. Or maybe it was intuition. Whatever it was, I later watched his empire grow and grow, and I wasn't the only one. The year M-Chips were released into the general population, the government could sense its hold on the nation becoming increasingly tenuous. The Mercer Corporation had become so powerful, other countries were turning to it for funding support instead of the government, and M-Corp were only increasing in size. It became apparent that to stand against the corporation would be detrimental, so they did what they could. They set up a sleeper group, one that would appear to have no associations with any government body. This group was given the power and authority to make the ultimate call.'

'What call?'

'That, if and when the Mercer Corporation succeeded in taking human life into their own hands, they would be stopped, using any means necessary. It was a covert department. One that needed to be headed by someone capable of large-scale, clandestine operations and who had no recent history with the government. Someone who had displayed only patriotic behaviour in the past. And, most importantly, someone who was –'

'On the inside,' I finished for her.

She nodded, pleased with my deduction. 'Preference Evolution is not part of M-Corp, Maggie. Preference Evolution *is* the United States of America.'

I tried to ignore what felt like a tonne of bricks landing on my chest. But all of a sudden I was back at the masquerade ball, watching Eliza standing on the balcony talking to the mystery man. The man who later revealed himself to the room. 'You were talking to the President,' I whispered.

She sighed. 'A rare opportunity to deliver some hard news, I'm afraid. I had hoped to speak with you and Quentin that night, but you were being watched too closely and we weren't expecting you to lose our tail so efficiently once outside.'

'You're in charge.' It wasn't a question, but she answered.

'I'm in charge.'

'What about the rest of the family?' I asked cautiously.

Something in Eliza's eyes changed. 'While our love for one another endures against hope, I lost Garrett to greed a long time ago. As a result, he lost my loyalty in favour of my first love, my country. I thought that by staying in the marriage I would be able to influence the boys. I couldn't tell them the truth without endangering them too much, but I'd hoped they would instinctively show opposition when they discovered the truth about M-Corp's activities.' She looked away, her jaw setting. 'Zachery was the first to embrace the company. When he found out about the underground hubs, he simply turned a blind eye and even … began to relish the darker side of the business. He has chosen a path I could not save him from, and the things that he's done …'

Were illegal and most likely brutal. And we both knew it. If her story was true, Eliza was not just spying on her husband anymore, but also her own children.

'Sebastian?'

She shook her head. 'Like Quentin, he had always been so moral. I thought at first he might reject the lures, but … he has only become more immersed in the company over the past year. I feared Quentin would go the same way, that there was little chance he'd find the strength to turn away from the temptations. But then you set him up.' She blew out a breath and leaned back. 'I couldn't believe it. I'd never thought of doing such a thing and, even if I had, I couldn't have brought the extra dynamic you delivered. I worried it had gone too far, but then I saw you at the Mercer Ball,' she rolled her eyes, 'bleeding through your dress for all to see. Yet it was then that I realised; just as I was watching him fall apart, I was also seeing him fall in love.'

My breath caught. 'So you always knew who I was?' It was only half a question. It was pretty obvious what the answer was.

'When Quentin first came home and said he rated well with you, Garrett was immediately suspicious you were a gold-digger.'

I rolled my eyes. Typical.

'But, yes, I've known who you were for at least six months. I even knew who you were looking for, though it took me a while to figure it out. Your mother had done a surprisingly good job of distancing you all from your father. And for his part, your father never mentioned anything about the family he'd left behind, so we'd never thought to worry. Originally I assumed you were searching for a regular neg.'

As I let the pieces fall into place, Eliza went on. 'Part of what I do for M-Corp, and in particular for Garrett, is use our external resources to run background checks on people, so when you first caught his attention it didn't seem unusual that I be the one to look into your history. I delayed telling Garrett who you were for as long as I could, but eventually ...' She held her hands out as if to say, *Sorry I hung you out to dry, but that's life.*

And I suppose she was right. I'd done the same thing myself more times than I cared to admit.

'Why bother delaying?' I asked.

Her lips twitched. 'I wanted to see how things panned out. We've known about you for a while, but not the details, and no one had been able to get close enough to get all of the information – something you proved by setting up Quentin with a disruption drug none of us knew was in your possession. We were also aware you had intel. I guess I figured the time would come when we would talk, possibly join forces, and then … I saw how Quentin looked at you and I began to hope I wasn't entirely alone in my family.'

I narrowed my eyes. 'But eventually you told Garrett the truth about me?'

She nodded. 'The time came when it was impossible to conceal it without threatening my cover.'

I digested this for a moment before looking back at Eliza. 'And then you let us go back down there. You let me be captured and tortured so you could … oh yeah, *see how things panned out.*'

Eliza leaned back in response to the venom in my voice. 'Actually we were blindsided. We didn't even know you and Quin had gone into the tunnels that day. All of our manpower had been caught up dealing with a large group of black-market thieves led by your friend, Travis. On that same day they attacked over a dozen of the lust-enhancer labs, and we were scrambling to work out what was happening and how the hell they'd managed to pull it off. For me, it was even harder, as my responsibilities to Garrett and the company kept me equally busy.'

Oh. 'I sold Travis the lab locations and delivery documents in return for the entry codes and map to the core.'

'We know that now, but at the time we only found out because of an anonymous tip, which we think came from M-Corp themselves. The tip was a ploy to distract us while they were taking care of you and Quentin.'

I rapped my fingernails on the table. 'If they felt the need to offer a distraction, does that mean they're onto you?'

She shook her head. 'Not me. But they're possibly suspicious of Preference Evolution and who we really are. It may have been a test to see if we mobilised.' She shrugged. 'It's one of the reasons we don't have much more time before we make our move.' She softened her features and relaxed her shoulders. 'Maggie, where I have failed with my other sons, you succeeded with Quentin, and for that I will always be in your debt. The love he feels for you has given him the strength to fight for what is right. But now I must ask, Maggie, what of your love for my son? Do *you* love him enough to do what is right as well?'

Call me gullible, but I couldn't help believing her story. Eliza Mercer was the perfect mole. And how she'd done what she'd done for the past however many years, I'll never know. She clearly still loved Garrett – her consistent and public ratings with him proved it. And yet, here she was, preparing to take him down. She'd had no choice but to stand back and watch her sons be consumed by the very thing she was fighting against. And she hadn't been able to say a thing to them.

'What do you want?'

'A few things. Your intel to start. Your word you will stay here until further notice and not attempt to leave the building. Your maps of the tunnels, and most importantly ...' She straightened. 'Most importantly, I need to know you won't tell my son that I'm here or what role I play.'

'Why?' I asked suspiciously.

'I know what you're thinking and you're wrong. It's not because I don't trust him. It's that if he's caught, he'll try to protect me. Or if I'm caught, he'll try to save me. Both ways will end with him dead. He can't know. Not until this is over. And I need your word before I let you go to him that you will keep this from him.'

'Why reveal yourself to me, then?'

She smiled. 'Would you have let it drop? Not knowing who was in charge? Would you have done what people here asked of you without knowing for sure what side you were playing on?'

I put my chin up. 'And you think you've convinced me you aren't just part of some elaborate M-Corp scheme?'

'Need more convincing?' she challenged, standing up and going to the door. She pulled it open before I could respond.

'Holy shit,' I said, standing too.

'She says that quite often,' Eliza said.

Master Rua walked into the room, keeping a cautious eye on me. I suspected he was waiting for an attack of some sort. Instead I shocked him by slumping back into my chair, a tear rolling down my cheek.

'I trusted you.' And now I knew exactly how the Pre-Evo's had managed to keep such good tabs on me.

He nodded. 'And my lies were not as terrible as you are thinking. I am not one of them, merely an ally. I trained you to be a fighter so you would survive. I trained you, Maggie, just like I trained Eliza many years ago. Never have I seen two more alike.'

'Why didn't you tell me?'

He pressed his hands together. 'You were not ready to hear. Now you are.'

I looked between Master Rua and Eliza, and I knew, somewhere deep in my gut, they were telling me the truth.

'I want to let you go to Quentin, Maggie,' Eliza said. 'He's worried and asking after you. But I need your word.'

'You're asking me to lie to him. After everything we've been through and all I've done to him, you're asking me to betray him again?'

She nodded. 'I wish there was another way to keep him safe. But this is it, and it's in your hands.'

I swallowed over the lump in my throat. Looking at Eliza, I could see that she would do whatever it took. She believed there was no other way. I had personal experience delivering a very similar look to people so I knew we had hit her no-negotiation point.

Slowly I nodded. 'Okay.'

'Thank you,' she said on an exhale, and I couldn't help but wonder if I'd just signed my death warrant.

Twenty-three

Quentin was in what looked like a small clinic. He was lying shirtless on a single bed, his upper arm wrapped in bandages. His eyes were closed when I walked in, but as I approached, they flickered open.

I dredged up a smile. 'Thought you were sleeping.'

He shook his head. 'Just waiting for you. Are you okay?' he asked, looking me over.

'You're the one who was shot.'

His eyes bore into me in the way only his could and my body reacted – even now, even with everything that had gone so terribly wrong, I still responded with relief and joy at being close to him.

'You know what I mean,' he said.

'Better now,' I answered, quickly clenching my jaw to stop it quivering. The truth was, I was not okay. All I could hear was my father's voice telling me about consequences as I watched all those people die.

Suddenly his hand was pushing the loose hair back from my face. 'Hey,' he croaked. 'I thought we agreed no lies?'

My heart ached. 'I killed all those people,' I whispered, my body shaking with the confession.

Quentin looked down. 'Fighting back doesn't make us the villains, Mags. We tried. And yeah, we failed. But that can't be an excuse to give up. We just have to find another way.'

I met his eyes and saw that just as much pain and memory was haunting him. 'How can you think that?'

He shrugged and forced a smile. 'You taught me.'

I squeezed my eyes shut for a moment and took a deep breath. How could he still believe in me after all I had done?

'What time is it?' he asked, taking in his surroundings. The walls of the room were white and he was lying in a steel cot with plain white sheets. I perched on the edge of his bed because there was nothing else in the room except a trolley with some medical supplies and a glass of water.

'Nearly 1 a.m.,' I said, offering him the glass.

He pushed himself up and took a grateful sip.

'How is it?' I gestured to his shoulder.

He shrugged, then winced a little. 'It's just a flesh wound. Unimpressive, I'm afraid.'

I reached forwards, letting my finger slide down the scar on his forehead that had always fascinated me. 'Another scar for the collection,' I said.

He smiled. 'I was fourteen when I got that one. Sebastian took me rock climbing. He was messing around and his foot slipped. I caught him before he fell.

My head hit the rocks and he was so heavy I was sure my shoulder was going to pop out of its socket, but I held on. I honestly thought we were done for, but somehow we grappled our way to safety. I remember my father yelling at Sebastian at the hospital for putting me in danger like that.' He smiled at the memory. 'But my mother pulled me aside that night. She told me that wounds could be worn like a badge if received during acts of honour.' His smile faded. 'I should probably find a new hobby. We both should.'

I nodded.

'Gus?' he asked.

'He's here.'

'Liam?'

I swallowed. 'Here too. He was their insider.'

Quentin nodded. 'I guess I shouldn't be surprised. So, did they save us or capture us?'

I looked around. We were seemingly alone, and yet, I knew they would be monitoring us somehow. 'Saved us, I think,' I said.

'What about Alex? I heard the soldiers talking when they brought me in. It was his sister in there. He must want us dead.' He grimaced, shifting again.

'He definitely hates me. But he's not in charge.'

This got Quentin's attention. 'Who is?'

I swallowed, focusing on his eyes for strength. And love. Then I took a deep breath, let it out and said, 'Your mother.'

'My ... my *mother*?' he checked.

I nodded and spoke quickly. 'I wasn't supposed to tell you. I promised I wouldn't. But I promised you first.'

The doors crashed open.

Quentin and I looked from the doors to one another.

Time slowed down as Quentin's hands interlocked with mine. Men were rushing into the room, weapons drawn. All the while Quentin stared at me and simply said, 'No more lies.'

I half smiled. 'No more lies.'

And then they were on me, pulling me away from him and dragging me out of the room. I let them. There was no point fighting them, but I kept my eyes on Quentin and my heart bloomed, knowing I'd made the right decision.

He deserved the truth.

'Mother!' I heard him yell as they dragged me down the hall.

'You're some piece of work, you know that?' a voice snapped at me, waking me up.

I'd been locked in a room and left for what I'd known would be a while. It hadn't taken me long to give in to my weariness and lay down to rest. I'd been relieved to discover the room had a small en suite, considering I'd woken up more than once needing to be sick. I hadn't been able to fight the tiredness, but my nightmares had certainly been able to fight me.

I sat up, still fully dressed in bloodstained clothes, blinking awake my sluggish eyes – one of which was basically swollen shut from last night's fight – and checked my M-Band. It was mid-morning. I'd slept on and off for almost eight hours.

'I'm sorry, Alex,' I said, my voice hoarse as I took in his rigid form just inside the door. He had a few bruises and scratch marks on his face from when I'd attacked him and his eyes were red-rimmed as if he'd been crying, but right now they were filled only with fire. Good for him.

'If you've snuck in to kill me, now is probably a good time. I really don't have the energy to kick your ass.'

He threw a bottle of water at me, not blinking when it hit me in the stomach. 'That's all you have to say! You don't even care, do you? You killed my sister!' His voice ran at me like daggers.

I got to work on opening the bottle, concentrating on that instead of my guilt. Alex didn't need to see me wallowing in self-pity, even if he thought he did. Finally I looked up. 'Yes. I did. But so did you. We are all responsible and if there was a way to go back, I would. But I can't.'

'Are you trying to tell me that if you knew she was there, it would've stopped you going in?'

I shook my head, sitting up. We both knew it would've only encouraged us to go after Kelsey. Gus would never have left her in there. 'But maybe we would've tried something different,' I argued. 'Especially if we'd known we weren't alone out there. Maybe if we'd known the truth about the Pre-Evo's, we would've come to you – oh, but wait,' I deadpanned. 'We did.'

Alex pinched the bridge of his nose. 'I wish I'd handled that meeting so differently,' he said, the fight draining from him. He probably wished he'd just put a bullet in my head that night. He sighed. 'Maybe if I had, things would be different.'

I stood up, noting how everything ached. 'You'll always look at me and see the person who took your sister away and that's okay. I deserve that. But Grace was right when she said you need to shift the main blame where it belongs. M-Corp has to be stopped. Clearly I suck at any and all attempts I've made, but look at this place,' I said, flapping my hands around. 'You actually have the firepower and manpower to take them on. If anyone can stop them, it's you guys. What I don't get is why the hell you are all sitting around here.'

'It's not that simple,' he gritted out.

I shook my head, leaning over to jam my feet into my boots. 'It is. And every day you delay, someone else's sister or brother pays the price!'

Alex ran a hand through his hair, looking between me and the door as if he was considering something. Then he took a few steps closer and locked eyes with me. 'There's an antidote,' he said softly.

And that's when all hell broke loose.

The lights shut off.

Shouts sounded from out in the hall, people were being ordered to cover the entry points.

One voice, however, boomed above all others. 'You will bring her out here to us, or we'll set these off all day long. You can't begin to imagine how many of these things we have, or how many places we've hidden them!'

With that, another wave of sounds followed: feet scampering, guns being cocked, whispers and straight-out orders being shouted. It was mayhem.

'I may not be able to see you, but I can feel you smiling,' Alex said, close by.

I broke into a short laugh. I couldn't believe they'd gone so far. It was strangely … uplifting. 'I think you should do what Quentin says,' I suggested.

'Jesus, you two have some kind of twisted puppy love going on,' Alex mumbled, taking hold of my upper arm.

'Something like that,' I said, now completely failing to withhold my smile.

'Tech bombs?' he queried.

'Yep.'

'He's going to keep setting them off, isn't he?'

'Yep,' I said.

'How many do they have?'

None. I knew that in order to create the current level of pandemonium, Gus would have set off the only two he had.

'Enough,' I replied honestly, because Alex was already leading me into the hall.

Seemingly unfazed by the lack of light, Alex navigated us through the maze of corridors. 'Watch your step,' he warned as we began descending the spiral staircase.

As we neared the bottom, the generator must've kicked in and emergency lights powered up, casting the main room in a dim red glow, reminding me of those final moments in the underground prison. I ignored the chill running down my spine.

In the centre of the room, Quentin and Gus sat at the head of a large table with about forty armed personnel, all looking incredibly pissed, surrounding them. Gus and Quentin looked surprisingly relaxed.

Quentin saw me first, and suddenly he was moving, pushing through the troops as if they were holding nothing but toy guns as he kept his eyes fixed on mine.

'Hey,' I barely managed before he had me in his arms, my feet off the floor and his lips on mine.

His hand slid to the side of my face, cupping my cheek, and he kissed me like he never had before. Like he'd let go completely. And as his lips pressed deliciously against mine and mine softened against his in return, I felt it. The walls that had come up between us, the layers of mistrust that I had created, the ones I thought we could never break through, all came tumbling down.

Before I realised it, my legs were around his waist and the kiss deepened to something that was so much more than physical. It was our connection, a true love that would never be broken no matter how much it was tested. He was my everything. And, in that moment, I knew I was his.

Finally I dredged up the willpower to break the kiss and drop my forehead to his. 'We have an audience,' I said, lightening my hold on his bandaged arm.

'I don't care,' he said. 'I don't care.'

'Did you see her?' I whispered.

He nodded. 'I can't believe it and yet, I can, you know?'

I returned his nod. 'Do you trust them?'

He took a deep breath and kissed me lightly on the mouth, then cheek, then ear, where he whispered, 'I trust they fight for a cause. That they are who they say they are. But for the rest, I trust us.'

Gently he put me on my feet and we turned to see the entire room watching us. No one looked impressed. And a lot of weapons were pointed in our direction.

'Probably a good call,' I murmured back, making Quentin grin.

He took my hand and squeezed. 'We'll pick this up again later,' he promised, then looked over at Gus and said, 'Thanks, man.'

Gus shrugged. 'They shouldn't have taken her away like that,' he said matter-of-factly. 'Especially when they obviously need us,' he added, eyebrows raised. There were a lot of angry faces surrounding us, but no one took him up on the challenge.

'I assume you're all done with the theatrics?' came Eliza Mercer's voice. I looked over, noticing her for the first time, standing to the side with her arms crossed. She was dressed in a pencil skirt and silk blouse with pearls draped around her neck. She was Mrs Mercer.

Quentin put his shoulders back. 'You're one to talk when it turns out your entire life has been about jumping from one stage to the next,' he scoffed, pointing at the theatre.

Eliza flinched.

Quentin didn't give her a chance to respond. 'You've made your decisions and if you expect me to ever try to understand them, then you had better start by respecting the hell out of mine. And that all starts with one simple rule: you, and anyone here, doesn't dare separate me from my family.'

'And by family?' she asked, her face giving nothing away, reminding me of the Eliza Mercer I had first met.

Quentin squeezed my hand. 'I mean, Maggie.' He glanced at me briefly. 'And Gus.'

'Really?' I whispered.

He considered for a moment then gave a resolute nod. 'Every family needs a Gus.'

'Even though he likes to blow things up?'

Quentin shrugged. 'It has its uses.'

Gus snorted, but didn't argue.

'I guess I deserve that,' Eliza said.

'No, Mom. *I* deserve it.'

After a beat, she nodded and looked at the troops. 'Lower your weapons. You have my word, Quentin, you and your … family will not be separated again.' It was as though each word tasted like acid in her mouth. 'Gus, could you please deactivate the rest of the tech bombs so my team can get back to work?'

Gus smiled. 'Power will come back on in about two minutes.'

'And the others?' she snapped.

'What others?'

I gotta give it to Gus, he delivered the line with a perfect poker face.

Eliza turned back to Quentin and me. 'There are no others.' It wasn't a question. When we said nothing, she surprised me by smiling. 'All right,' she addressed the room. 'Can we all get on with business now?'

I took that as my cue and stepped forwards. 'Absolutely,' I said. 'Why don't we start with you explaining to us what the hell the antidote is?'

I heard Alex groan behind me and took a second to glance over my shoulder and see him shaking his head. I gave him a tight-lipped smile. 'Sorry.'

I'd figured, what the hell. He couldn't hate me any more than he already did.

It took over an hour to get everything back online, even with Gus helping them out. At first, they'd told him not to touch anything, but after listening to him rant on about how he could have their systems up and running a lot faster if they just gave him a computer – well, eventually Eliza held a gun to his head and gave him one. Gus was right.

I'd used the time to shower and change, grateful to finally be rid of the underground blood and dirt. And now we sat at the central table. Gus, Quentin and me on one side; Eliza, Alex, Grace, a guy called Michael and another guy with a thick Australian accent – whose name I'd already forgotten – on the other. Despite the long-winded introductions, all I caught was that Michael was some kind of big-deal scientist, and the Australian did something involving weather or aviation, or both.

My eyes kept drifting back to the scientist. I recognised him from somewhere.

'Maggie, did your father ever discuss his experiments with you?' Eliza asked.

I bristled at the question, fighting my instinct to always defend my father. I sat back in my chair and took a breath. 'He started by discovering ways to temporarily increase pheromone ratings. He picked people who rated consistently below average and used them as his test subjects. I only saw one experiment where things went … the other way.'

Quentin took my hand and I let him.

'In the experiments where the test subjects showed improved ratings, did you ever stay around to gauge how long this change lasted for?' Michael asked.

I studied the man, with his overgrown white hair and few days' growth. He was in his late sixties at least, maybe older.

'Maggie,' Alex said, bringing me back to the conversation.

'A couple of times,' I answered, still looking at Michael. It was right on the verge of coming to me. 'The change only lasted about an hour. Once a little longer, but not much.'

They all nodded as if they'd expected this answer.

'I know you,' I said to Michael. And when he smiled, that was the last piece I needed. He was older and covered in more hair, but there was no mistaking it. 'Dr Peterson, right?'

Michael nodded. 'I didn't think you would remember me. You were quite young when your father and I worked together.'

Looking at him, I couldn't deny the ache in my heart. It was almost as if I were looking at the man that my father could have been. If it had been my father who got that big promotion instead of Michael, maybe our lives would've been very different.

I mustered a small smile. 'I remember you. You used to bring cookies.'

He laughed lightly. 'I did. My wife fancies herself quite the baker.' He quickly sobered. 'I ... Your father was my colleague, but also my friend. I never believed he could be capable of so much ... I'm very sorry for the position you now find yourself in.'

I swallowed the lump in my throat and nodded. 'Thank you.'

He gave a short nod and cleared his throat, looking back down at his papers. 'What we're telling you is highly sensitive and classified. We have a plan in motion, but until that plan has played out, we can't risk having people on the outside with any knowledge of it.

So if you don't want to hear it, now is the time to say. And if you do, prepare to settle in, because no one leaves these walls until we're done and, apart from what goes through Eliza, there's no communication coming in or going out.'

Quentin and Gus looked at me. Great. My call.

I was through with doing things my father's way – based on statistics, on science and verified facts. 'Chance favours the bold,' I mumbled. 'Give it to us.'

Eliza nodded, taking the lead. 'The drug your father first started to develop was in fact the antidote to the drug he later discovered. Originally he toyed with changing ratings, both in positive and negative directions, but the effect only lasted for a limited time, like the negative disruption you used on Quentin.'

'Did you know all along about that?' Quentin interrupted.

Eliza looked down. 'Yes. And I can't even apologise for it, because what Maggie did ultimately brought you to us. But I am sincerely sorry for the pain you've felt along the way.'

Quentin stared at her in disbelief, but said nothing more.

'The original drugs were only effective for a short time, but he continued to develop them,' Eliza went on. 'Now he can take an individual who's rating perfectly normally and turn them neg permanently.'

I nodded. 'We saw the population-control documents. Is that what this is all about?'

Eliza looked surprised, but took it in her stride. 'We underestimated you and the people who were helping you, Maggie. Master Rua warned me not to, but I admit I undervalued your intelligence.'

I stared at her, waiting for her to get on with it. Compliments really weren't going to fly at the moment. Sensing this, she moved on.

'What this permanent disruption does is change our genetic makeup. It makes a person someone they are not. All the qualities, for better or worse, that are dominant in those who naturally rate as negs eventually develop in individuals treated with his disruptions.'

I nodded. 'I'm following. We figured it worked something like that.'

Alex leaned forwards. 'You have to think it all the way through. Consider what it would be like to live in a country of negs. To be surrounded by an army of negs. To have a government strong-armed by negs. And then there are the things to consider right here. You think we don't want to just start breaking negs out of their underground cells? You think we haven't been over and over thousands of scenarios that involve us going in, guns blazing?' He pushed his chair back and stood, planting his hands on the table. 'But we can't!' he hissed. 'We can't release that many negs into the public with no plan to help them or their families who'll suddenly be dealing with someone they barely recognise, let alone all of the trauma the negs will carry with them from their time underground. We can't send them back out into the world, knowing they have been changed forever and won't be able to make the same choices they once would have.'

'It would be anarchy,' Gus said.

Alex clenched his jaw and nodded.

'And before long, a military solution would be unavoidable,' Eliza threw in.

'What about in the countries where they've been treating people out in the open? How can they even do that?' Quentin asked.

'They've been releasing the disruption from the air,' Michael answered. 'The vapours filter down and infect people randomly.'

'Crop dusting,' I said, knowing that would've been another of my father's ideas. He had once been a pesticide developer. Who would've thought that his job could lead to this?

'In a way, yes,' Eliza said. 'And the minority who seem to be controlling the world now are also controlling who will breed. But they are being reckless with more than just the lives of those they turn neg. They expect the negs to simply grow old and die and the world to be none the wiser about why breeding habits changed so drastically, but there are a significant percentage of people turned neg who'll become volatile and violent in the near future. We've already had riots breaking out in Bangladesh, Nigeria and Zimbabwe. They've been covered up so far, but there will be more, and we fear it could lead to a modern world war – waged with technology, driven by the wealthy, and fought by the innocent victims of M-Corp.'

'Survival of the fittest,' I mumbled, remembering my father once using that phrase. At the time I thought he'd meant he was against it. What I now realised was that he was trying to figure out how to enforce it.

'In its crudest sense,' Eliza agreed.

'So this is where your plan comes in, right?' Gus said. 'I mean your antidote or whatever the hell it is. You clearly have a solution, so out with it – give us the showstopper.'

Alex glared at Gus. 'I never knew what my sister saw in you – other than a potential source.'

Gus snorted. 'A potential source?' Gus tilted his head in a way that had all of my internal alarm bells ringing. 'Well, now that you mention it, she did spend quite a bit of time pumping m–'

Alex started moving and I slapped my hand over Gus's mouth and delivered a death stare to both of them. 'Not now!' I pointed at Alex with my free hand, stopping him from taking another step. 'You have no idea about their relationship and you should have more respect for your sister than to be cruel to someone she cared about.' I jabbed a finger at Gus. 'And you! You … You should just have more respect in general!'

When he nodded, I lowered my hand and looked back at Eliza. 'Well? Is Gus right? Do you have a solution?'

'Of course,' she said. 'We have the solution and a way to make it all happen, and we're happy to take you through the ins and outs. We're just missing one thing.'

'What?' I asked plainly, hoping that if I gave them a simple question I might get a simple answer.

'The antidote.'

Twenty-four

I tossed and turned that night, getting up to loosen the tightly tucked sheets first, then throwing my pillows on the ground, only to pick them up a few minutes later. I don't know why I bothered. Being uncomfortable wasn't the reason I couldn't sleep. It had more to do with knowing what lay ahead – which was nothing good – and the fact that I would never be able to close my eyes again without seeing that building with the glass walls, and the people as their doors slid open and smoke filtered in.

I blew out a breath and sat up.

After another round of unsuccessful sheep-counting, followed by a stint of huffing while pacing the room, I threw on my hoodie and snuck out the door.

It was close to 2 a.m. and out in the hallway all was silent. I poked my head around the corner and saw the guard posted at the end of the hall. I'd been warned he would be there – not to 'confine' us, but to protect the sensitive material within the building. I guess it was fair enough we weren't allowed to roam unsupervised.

I moved back and headed towards the door beside my room. While I was pondering whether or not I should knock, or turn tail and bee-line back to my room, his door swung open and Quentin stepped into the hall.

He was in the midst of pulling a T-shirt over his head and I got a full view of his chest and side muscles. Suddenly all I could think about was that kiss from earlier. Being wrapped in his arms. I flushed red.

As soon as the T-shirt cleared his face, his eyes locked with mine and our connection sucked all the air from around us. My mind took a backseat to the intense desire that I had fought and tried to quash for way too long.

'I was coming to see you,' I breathed.

Quentin tilted his head and gave me a roguish smile. 'Well, you damn well better not have been headed to Gus's room,' he said with just enough lightness so the growl didn't carry too much bite.

I opened my mouth to respond. But Quentin was already in motion, his long legs closing the gap in three strides and suddenly my back was up against the wall. His hands tangled tightly in my hair, and his mouth seized mine in a way that brooked no argument. There'd be no more fighting this thing between us and my insides cheered as I pulled him closer, my hands matching the roughness of his as they explored every inch of his body.

Apparently my roaming hands did something right because Quentin made a throaty sound and abruptly lifted me. As I wrapped my legs around his waist, he half turned, half stumbled towards the opposite wall, my back hitting hard, but by this stage neither of us cared. We were entirely lost to the passion that had built and built, determined to have this time together before it was possibly all too late.

My hoodie was ripped off first, leaving me in a white tank top and boy shorts. Quentin groaned when he looked me over and I couldn't help the blush. I possibly should have considered putting a bra on.

Determined to even the stakes, I grabbed at his shirt and yanked it over his head. Of course, Quentin didn't blush at all, and why the hell would he? He looked exactly like a guy who'd spent years earning his black belt in karate should. Perfect.

When he caught me staring, he threw me a smile and I rolled my eyes. He touched my black-market M-Band, which was currently vibrating with pulse-rate alerts. 'I love that I can do this to you.'

'You need to shave,' I said for some reason. Jesus, what was wrong with me?

He smiled, seeing through my lame defence instantly. 'I do,' he agreed, placing me on my feet and taking my hand. Gently he led me back to his room and closed the door behind us. I barely had the chance to register that his room was the mirror image of mine – bed, timber wardrobe, slim desk and one steel chair – before I was back in his arms, his face brushing mine so that his stubble grazed my cheek and neck, sending tingles down my arms. 'Does it bother you?'

'Hmm?'

I felt his smile on the curve of my neck. 'That I need to shave?'

Was he *kidding* me? 'I'll survive,' I whispered, my quivering voice giving me away.

'Couldn't sleep?' he murmured, continuing his explorations, which had me basically melting into his arms.

I swallowed, lost in this closeness, in his scent, his touch. 'Couldn't sleep,' I confirmed.

Quentin chuckled, causing more damn goosebumps. 'I'm glad you came looking for me,' he said, his voice deliciously low. He continued the slow torture as he whispered in my ear, 'I owe you an apology.'

'Apology?' I managed to squeeze out. Frankly I would've been good with holding off the chitchat.

'For shutting you out and not trusting my gut when it screamed at me that, even after everything that happened, you were the *best* thing in my world. For fighting the truth.' He moved around, his lips brushing mine as he spoke. 'That I love everything about you – your strength, your heart, your stubbornness, the way you hit first and ask questions later, the way you would do anything for the people you love.'

I wanted to argue and explain I wasn't a good person, but then his lips were on mine and my body took control, moulding to his. No more words. No more questions. Just the truth of our love. It might have been dredged through the mud, lit on fire and buried beneath a world of secrets and betrayal, yet somehow it was as strong as ever, *stronger* for us having felt its loss.

I gripped Quentin tightly, giving everything of myself to this moment, to him. Suddenly my feet were in the air and my back was being eased onto his bed. Quentin hovered above me, his hands pushing my hair off my face, his nose nudging mine.

I fought for breath, lost entirely in his eyes. 'I love you, Quin. I don't know …' My voice caught. 'I couldn't have survived this whole thing without you. You made me keep fighting when all I wanted to do was give up. *I'm* the one who's sorry.'

My eyes were welling up and Quentin swiped away the tear that ran free as he murmured, 'Shh. We are *so* done with apologies.' He kissed me lightly, his hand trailing down to the base of my tank top. 'No more talking.' His eyes locked with mine, patient for my response. I knew what he was asking. No pressure, it was entirely my call.

A few thoughts flashed through my mind – mostly to do with vanity and guaranteed awkwardness – but they quickly vanished as I stared into his eyes, eyes that were still more steel than blue, and that was exactly what I needed. Quentin didn't need me to save him; he was strong in mind and body all on his own. I was not his crutch. I was his choice.

Suddenly impatient, I quickly tapped my M-Band screen, opening the medical zip that came standard with all M-Bands, and activated the contraceptive zip. As

Quentin watched, I grinned and reached down to help speed up the process, pulling off my tank top. When I glanced back up, he was biting down on a smile. 'We don't have to do anything you're not comfortable with,' he said softly.

'Quin?' I said, drawing his lips back to mine. 'No more talking.'

He kissed me as he chuckled and then we got on with … no more talking.

'Are you scared?' Quentin asked me in the early hours of the morning.

We were still in his bed, exhausted but determined to continue talking and touching one another, the same way we had been for several hours now. We'd covered many of the conversations we'd been avoiding. He told me about what had happened in the core after we'd been separated and I'd been imprisoned. How my father had him drugged and locked up at first. He told me how he'd felt really unwell when he'd come around, and that even after his father came to get him he didn't feel right for a few days. I explained that I'd had similar experiences after being sedated underground. I thought it was odd we'd both felt so unwell and worried that my father might have done something to us.

'Right now, I'm not scared at all,' I said, curling into him. At that moment I was in a state of contented bliss – which, in the circumstances, spoke volumes.

He pulled me closer, as if that was actually possible. 'You know what I mean,' he said, kissing the top of my head.

Seriously? I had died and gone to heaven and he wanted to talk about being scared? I sighed. I'd known the conversation would get there eventually, but I'd been enjoying pretending we were just a normal couple who'd just done this amazing thing together – because, call me a sap or whatever, but for a very long time nothing about my life had been normal, and what had just happened between us was so much more than just sex. And it had definitely changed things. I was now aware of a new level of closeness between us and I would never settle for anything less.

But ignoring the plan that Eliza, Alex and Michael had described to us in detail last night, including exactly what role they wanted me to play, was something I couldn't ignore forever. Just thinking about it made me hear their voices again.

'We've looked at it from every angle,' Eliza explained. 'But in the end, the only way we see a possible victory is to launch a fast and multi-pronged attack. We need to get a number of sites within our control, secure the antidote and then ...' Eliza paused, glancing at Alex.

'We have to have faith that they want this too, Liz,' Alex said in a way that made it clear they held one another's trust. Alex looked at me before adding, 'And I believe they do.'

His declaration threw me off kilter. Probably on purpose since I definitely didn't expect the next words out of Eliza's mouth.

'Once we secure the antidote, the only way we can protect the flow of information and have any hope of disabling M-Corp's armed forces is to cut off the head of the snake,' she said.

The words were followed by a pin-drop silence.

It was Quentin who spoke first. 'You want to kill Dad?'

Eliza took a deep breath and let it out at a measured pace. 'Yes, Quentin. I believe it's the only way. I believe that nothing short of ending his life will stop the terror he's inflicting on others. I have stood by for too many years to take any chances.'

'What about Zach and Sebastian?'

She shook her head. 'We're hoping to subdue them and then work out some kind of deal.' She heaved a heartfelt sigh. 'I wish it wasn't this way, Quin. I wish ... a lot of things, but if we get the antidote and we have the opportunity, my orders will be to take Garrett down.' She turned to me. And I knew before she said it. 'And he isn't the only one.'

Shaking off the memory of last night's meeting, I refocused on the warm arms encircling me. 'Yes,' I confessed. 'Mostly I'm scared I'll fail and cost more lives. Every time I go down there, something bad happens.'

Quentin kissed the side of my neck. 'And?' he whispered.

I closed my eyes. '*And* I spent years doing nothing but trying to save my father and now I'm part of a team who plan to destroy him. I'm not scared of what has to happen, I'm just scared that if it comes down to him and me, I won't be able to …'

Quentin stroked my back and kissed the top of my head. 'Hey, they said they wanted you to draw him out, that you had the best chance of finding the antidote. No one said anything about you pulling the trigger. That's not going to happen, Maggie. No way. And besides, I'll be there with you. I'm not letting you out of my sight.'

I nodded into his chest. He was right, and yet … I couldn't help thinking that somehow things would go exactly as I feared.

'We should probably get dressed,' I said, not moving an inch.

'We probably should,' Quentin said, not making any move to get up either.

'You *definitely* should,' said a new voice that shocked the life out of us both.

I made a grab for the sheet, covering myself as Quentin shielded me with his body. 'Mom! Seriously! You could learn to knock!'

Eliza shrugged, glaring at both of us. 'For all you two know, I could've been out there knocking for the past four hours.'

I gulped as a terrible thought occurred to me. 'Please tell me these rooms don't have surveillance cameras,' I squeaked.

'If they do, I'm about to go and beat the shit out of whoever has been monitoring them,' Quentin growled.

Eliza rolled her eyes. 'The rooms have no cameras.'

I let go of the breath I'd been holding.

'But the hallways do,' she added.

I blushed bright red, remembering where all of this began last night. Quentin, apparently unbothered, simply chuckled.

'Get dressed and meet us downstairs. We have strategies to work out and I only have an hour before I need to head out to attend a charity event with Garrett. Clothes have been left in your cupboards.' With a final glare she closed the door.

'Oh my God,' I groaned, sinking under the sheets.

'Don't worry about it,' Quentin said, getting up. 'The last person I'm concerned about right now is my mother. Her days of controlling my life are well and truly over.'

I groaned again, refusing to resurface. 'She's a highly trained undercover spy who has carte blanche from the United States Government. Right now she's more powerful than the President and she just caught me naked in bed with her son.'

Quentin started laughing. 'Actually,' he said, 'I've been thinking about that. We've never told anyone about our rating and I was wondering if we should maybe ...'

I threw the sheet back. 'No!'

Quentin took a step back from the bed, his hands raised. 'Okay. Just a suggestion,' he said, still smiling. But I could see the hurt.

I crawled on my knees to the edge of the bed. 'It's not that I don't want to tell people we're together, or that I love you, or any of that … I just …' My father's words replayed in my head. He'd warned me that society would never accept that Quentin and I were a true match. We'd only just worked everything out and the idea of creating a new problem … I couldn't. 'I just want to keep the true-match part to ourselves for now – well, us and Gus.'

'And your father,' Quentin added. 'Do you expect him to keep it a secret?'

'I don't know what my father will or won't do. I have no idea why he's bothered to keep it a secret at all. But for now, can we not say anything? Once this is all over, if I'm still here –'

'Maggie!' Quentin snapped, cutting me off.

'Okay.' I nodded. 'That was stupid. What I meant to say was that once this is all over and we are getting on with our happily ever after, then you can tell anyone you want. Please?'

Quentin studied me for a moment, tracing his finger down the side of my face. 'Happily ever after, huh?' he said, his voice suddenly rough.

I leaned into his touch. 'I'm thinking we both go back and sit our final exams, then move out to the country where my mom and Sam will have a small farm. We can help them run the property. We'll have to rent at first, but with all of us working, we should be able to get something nice. Maybe we'll build a little cabin on their land to stay in when we visit, or we could go to university, or both. There are some great universities close to good farming land.'

'You've got it all worked out.'

I wrapped my arms around his waist. 'All open for discussion, of course, but … yeah. I gave it some thought when I was underground.' I frowned. 'I probably gave it too much thought, to be honest.'

Quentin stared at me and I wondered what he was thinking. But then his face broke into a gorgeous smile and he pulled me closer, peppering me with kisses. 'As long as you're there, it sounds like the kind of place a person could spend forever.'

I smiled.

Yes. It sounded like paradise.

Twenty-five

Everyone was already well into discussion by the time we made it to the table. By the looks we received, and the wink Grace gave me as we walked by, it was clear they knew why we were late. I felt my cheeks burn.

When I saw Gus, I sobered quickly. Damn, could I be any more insensitive? Flaunting my relationship with Quentin straight after what had happened to Kelsey?

As if he could see right through to my guilt, Gus rolled his eyes at me and turned to Quentin. 'You're a brave man, my friend.'

'I hope that isn't jealousy disguised as sarcasm,' Quentin returned, his tone even and yet the threat unmistakeable. I tensed. Things between Gus and Quentin had settled down as if the events of the other night were forgiven, but now I wondered if I'd been wrong.

Gus's eyes flicked between Quentin and me and I could tell he wondered the same thing. For about a second. Then he simply smiled and shook his head. 'Comforting and oddly enough … not at all.' His smile transformed to something more familiar, something that already had me narrowing my eyes. 'But I just have to know ...' he said, raising an eyebrow. 'Did she leave bite marks?'

I glared at Gus as he laughed, and then at Quentin who was barely containing himself.

Ha, ha, very funny.

'As much as I would love to continue this particular line of conversation, could we please, for the love of God, get back to the small matter of bringing down the most powerful entity in the world?' Eliza barked.

Gus snorted. 'I suggested she just divorce the guy, take half of everything and bring the company down that way.'

I blinked. 'Is that a terrible idea?'

Quentin and I sat near Gus as Alex groaned. 'Okay, here's a little survival 101 for you people,' he said, using a condescending tone that made my hackles rise. 'Divorcing a man like Garrett Mercer and ultimately making yourself his public enemy really only ends with one outcome.'

'Tragedy strikes,' Grace threw in dramatically. 'Out on highway five tonight, slippery roads and hazardous conditions proved too much for motorists, causing a multi-car pile-up. Five lives lost, one of whom was the well-known Eliza Mercer, wife of devastated M-Corp chief executive Garrett Mercer ... Blah, blah, blah, you get the picture.'

I nodded. 'Got it.'

'So you're willing to risk Maggie's life, sending her up against her father, but not your own, is that about right?'

Quentin said quietly, looking at his hand resting on the table as if it was taking all his energy to keep it still.

All eyes bounced between him and Eliza.

Eliza's expression was neutral, giving nothing away. 'I risk my life every time I sleep beside him. Every time I make up an excuse about where I've been so that I can be here, like now. Every time I've diverted his attention from you or your brothers to protect you from the truth.'

'And you want me to thank you now? For all the lies?'

'You can hate me all you want, Quentin, but don't be so narrow-minded to think yours was the only life sacrificed in all this. Don't forget that for as many years as I can remember, I have lived a lie and have had very few people that I could turn to and trust. If you think it's easy to watch your children gradually move away from what's right and drown in a world of wrong, you are very mistaken.' The conviction in her voice, even as it shook, was enough to have everyone sitting back.

Finally Quentin nodded. 'I can't imagine how it's been for you,' he conceded. 'But I also can't ignore the fact that you made informed decisions, one of which was to give your children no choice at all.'

Eliza straightened the papers in front of her, avoiding any eye contact. 'Shall we move forwards?'

Everyone nodded, including Quentin.

'How am I going to get to my father?' I asked, hoping to redirect the focus and give Quentin a moment to get himself together. Processing disillusionment was something I was well and truly familiar with. 'Is he even here? Doesn't he spend most of his time in New York? And if he is, won't he be secured in the core?' I asked, ignoring the shudder that ran through my body at the thought of that place.

'He is definitely here. Since you were first identified as a problem, he has been under orders from Garrett to remain until you are taken care of,' Alex said. 'But, yes, he will be in the core. Which is another reason why it has to be you.'

I scrunched up my nose. 'Why?'

Alex shifted in his chair uncomfortably. 'You're the only one who's been in there.'

I didn't bother hiding my disbelief. 'Except for Eliza, of course.'

Eliza shook her head. 'I've never been to the core, Maggie. Garrett never wanted me there for reasons I'm sure you can imagine. He knows I know what goes on and that outwardly I don't oppose it, but that doesn't mean he lets me see it all in motion. I don't even have access.'

'Yes, you do,' Gus offered.

'No, I'm afraid I don't.'

'But you do,' Gus insisted. 'We got in using Mercer DNA – Quentin's to be precise. There is no way his DNA would've worked just by matching with Garrett's; it had to have been compatible with yours too, which means ...'
He held out his hand, not needing to finish.

Eliza's mouth fell open. 'I didn't know.' I watched her carefully for any sign of deceit, but all I saw was genuine shock.

'Well, it's probably so that you can access the panic chambers,' Gus explained.

Eliza stared at Gus. Alex and Grace were doing the same thing. 'Panic chambers?' she queried.

Gus rolled his eyes and fixed an incredulous look on the Preference Evolution team. I couldn't help but smile. 'You people really should've started talking with us when we offered. Someone bring me a computer and I'll show it to you on the blueprints. And ...' he glanced around, 'any chance we can get some coffee?'

'And doughnuts?' I added quickly. 'Or anything greasy.'

'Cheeseburgers would work,' Quentin threw in.

Somewhat stunned at Quentin's unhealthy food choice and most definitely more in love with him because of it, I nodded enthusiastically. 'Cheeseburgers would be perfect.'

I watched as Eliza's jaw clenched. She really didn't appreciate that we were there and that we had skills and intel to offer. She might endure it to get the job done, but it was also becoming more and more apparent that the two roles she played – wife of Garrett Mercer, and head honcho spy – were actually not entirely dissimilar. Before she could hide it, I saw her glance in my direction. The intensity in that one look told me everything. She hated that Quentin was with me.

Grace placed a laptop in front of Gus and he got to work.

'Can I ask you a personal question, Eliza?' I asked, crossing my arms.

'Go ahead,' she said with a sigh.

'What happens if this entire plan plays out and we take them down? What's your intention once all the steps are taken to implement the changes you've outlined? If Garrett is gone, that would put you in a very high position of power, so I want to know, what are you planning to do?'

Eliza stood and started to pace behind the chairs. 'It's a fair question, but the answer, I'm afraid, might not be as radical as you would like.'

I shrugged. 'Try me.'

She watched me carefully. 'Okay. If you want me to say that the world of M-Bands, that the technology that created this way of life will be extinguished, I can't.'

I wasn't expecting that at all, but I nodded. 'Go on.'

'The technology will continue. Microchipping now plays its part in the world and, for the most, that's a good thing. M-Bands, likewise, offer many conveniences and health advantages that people won't want to part with.'

'And Phera-tech?'

'You tell me, Maggie. What do you think the world will be willing to settle for? Have you seen the way society has changed since Phera-tech has been available? How many relationships have been broken and formed? Will people simply go back to a world without it?'

I wished I could answer her with a direct *yes*, but I couldn't and she knew it. I wasn't a fool. Life had changed so much over the past eight years. It seemed like such a short time for our way of life to shift so drastically, but I suppose that's how it has often been in history. I also knew it would be impossible to turn back the clock. We couldn't ask people to pull out their M-Chips and pretend their lives had not already become dependent on this technology; it had become the modern way of life.

'So what *are* you proposing?'

'I'm proposing that we fix the problem first. We need to help the people who've been taken and locked away, and we need to help the third-world countries that are being overrun by negs before war breaks out. We play out the plan and then, when we're ready, we tell the world the truth: that they were lied to about what was happening to the negs and how many of them there were. We admit that the people governing the technology were corrupt and that lives were lost. And then we ask them to stand with us. To give up a convenience in order to save lives. If we can get the majority on board, we have a program we can use to adapt Phera-tech.'

'What does it do?' Gus asked, looking up, intrigued.

'It doesn't reveal any ratings lower than fifteen per cent.'

'No one will know who the negs are,' Quentin said.

Eliza nodded. 'And we will go back to accepting that in society we are not perfect, but nor should we be.'

'And M-Corp saves the day?' I said, my bitterness shining through.

'You have no reason to trust me, Maggie, but I'm going to ask that you try your hardest to have faith in the fact that I have thought this through and have a plan.'

'And you will be the new head of M-Corp?'

'I will,' she said, and I had to give her points for not backing down.

Gus chose that moment to spin the laptop around. 'There you are. Panic chambers. They're not far from the core lab and have similar entry and exit points. I assume they're there in the event of some kind of attack.'

Alex nodded. 'Garrett must have had them added on in the last two years. They were never on the original plans.'

Gus shrugged. 'Well, they're there now and I'd be willing to make a hefty wager that when this all goes down, that's exactly where Garrett and your lovely sons will go.'

Eliza passed the laptop to Alex. 'Let's plan a way in based on the assumption I'll be able to access the outer door of the panic chambers with my DNA. Have we got codes that will get us in that far?'

Alex nodded, getting up from his chair. 'Should do. Let me get the guys on it and we'll work something out. But we can't assume we'll get in everywhere without triggering some kind of alarm. Maggie and Quentin got in last time because no one was expecting a breach, but now they'll be more prepared, and there are a number of nearby hubs, not to mention core security, that we'll have to deal with.'

Gus tapped his fingers on the table and I watched him knowingly as Eliza and Alex continued to theorise.

'Gus?' I said quietly.

'There is a way ...' he said to me.

'What?' I asked him quickly, glancing at the rest of the table who were still oblivious to our conversation.

Gus locked eyes with me and something in my gut twisted in an all-bad way. Gus gave me a wry grin before addressing the table. 'If you can give me the right access codes, I can write a program to shut off the hubs.'

Everyone stopped what they were doing and stared at Gus.

He shrugged. 'I've been studying the design for a long time. The hubs were originally created by the government, correct?'

Alex nodded. 'Yes, they were designed as a system of bunkers in the event that something terrible happened and they needed to move people below ground.'

'And, of course, being American, it was designed with defence in mind,' Gus continued.

Grace leaned forwards. 'Yes. They call them hubs, but really the system is more like the hull of a ship. If one hub is attacked or infiltrated, it can be shut off from the core.'

Gus smiled. 'The main doors to the core section – where you'll find Maggie's father and the panic chambers – are impenetrable. Once you are on the inside and those doors close, no one else will be able to get through. If I can hack the security programs and take over the system, I can make sure all the security personnel are shut down in their hubs or, at the very least, outside the main doors.'

'Are you sure?' Eliza asked.

Gus nodded. 'If you have the right codes and access intel, sure.'

'That would make things a lot simpler for processing afterwards as well,' Eliza murmured to Alex.

'How long will it take?' Alex asked Gus.

'Two days, give or take. I'd already been working on the bones of the program, I just never had all the pieces of the puzzle.'

'Get him everything he needs,' Eliza ordered Alex.

Alex was already up and walking. Grace went to follow him, but then paused and looked at Gus. 'There's already a betting pool going for where we'll find Garrett. I'll throw in your call and take your bet later on.'

'Be ready to lose big,' he said, sitting back with a grin.

Grace returned the smile before she took off to catch up with Alex.

'Quentin,' Eliza said, drawing our attention back in her direction. 'I know you'll want to be with Maggie, but I was hoping you might reconsider. Liam will be down there to keep her safe and they'll be able to move faster through the tunnels if it's just them. Not to mention that she has more chance of pulling this off if it looks as though she's come alone.'

Slowly Quentin stood from his seat. I could feel the tension rippling off him and wanted nothing more than to wrap my arms around him. Instead I inched back in my seat and watched him take the time to stretch before settling his attention on his mother.

'I want you to know that I forgive you,' he said so quietly she had to lean towards him a little. 'You had to make impossible choices and I accept that you did the best you could. And I can't tell you how relieved I am to know that not all of my family are the monsters I'd come to believe they were. In time, you and I might even be able to forge some kind of relationship based on truth and trust. But let me give you the first hint on what is never going to happen,' he said, his voice becoming increasingly dark and threatening. 'You, along with any other person in this place, are not going to send the one person I love and trust completely into the pits of hell and tell me to sit up here, twiddle my thumbs ...' he hit his fist down hard on the table, 'and wait for someone to come and tell me she is never coming back! Are we clear, Mother?'

Eliza tried to hide her surprise. She didn't know what we were to one another. But I did. And I knew that every word Quentin had just spoken was the truth. It was why I hadn't bothered trying to tell him to stay behind myself. We'd gone too far for that. We were in this thing together now and *no one* was going to tear us apart.

Twenty-six

I sat on the work-out mats, massaging my calves. I'd made serious inroads since I'd been released from my underground prison, but my muscles still often cramped in response to the workload. From the corner of my eye, I watched Quentin kicking at the commando dummy. We'd been working out for a while and had reached my favourite stage – the one where I pretended not to care that he'd lost his shirt.

Eliza had been mostly absent over the last two days due to keeping up appearances with Garrett, Sebastian and Zachery. When she did manage to send word through to Alex, it was to inform him that Garrett's behaviour was increasingly volatile and that he was frustrated by the lack of progress they were making on locating both Quentin and myself. The descriptions of Garrett's mood swings would've had me more concerned if Alex hadn't reassured us so completely that no one would be able to track our location – not even through direct satellite. The computer systems in the theatre had been designed to act as a kind of magnetic field. First, they pulled in signals and then proceeded to bounce them all over the world. By now, it would be sending their GPS department up the wall.

That Quentin and I were the focus of Garrett's attention wasn't a surprise to anyone. Part of Eliza's cover was to show panic for her missing son's well-being. So while she didn't want to feed Garrett's paranoia or encourage him to take steps to find Quentin or me, she had to act like she was expecting results. I didn't envy her position.

Eliza knew Garrett's priority was to find us so that he could silence us. More than anything, he was worried we would go public, and he knew I had a certain amount of supporting evidence. Not to mention his son by my side.

There was a warrant out for my arrest – they had pinned the explosions at Roosevelt Island on me, describing me as a 'violent criminal'. Anyone with information that could lead to my whereabouts had been encouraged to call the authorities. And, of course, the authorities had all been notified to pass any information directly to M-Corp.

Everyone, apart from Eliza, remained on a communications lockdown to avoid any intel leaks, and Quentin and I had been doing our best to get on with preparations. On the third day, there was a funeral service for Kelsey and we had a small gathering to remember Travis as well. It was pretty lame given that none of us knew him all that well, but I couldn't let his death go by unrecognised. The more I'd gone back over the events of that terrible night underground, the more I was sure that Travis had stepped into the line of fire to protect Quentin. I'd never know why. But he had.

Quentin and I trained a number of times during the day, preferring to spar with one another rather than the other commandos. It wasn't that we didn't believe they were after the same goal, or that they weren't nice, once we managed to break the ice; it was more that ... any excuse to partner up or be close was all we needed.

From behind me, a pair or arms snaked around my waist and pulled me to my feet. My body, which already knew those arms so well, willingly folded back into him with complete trust. Once I was on my feet, he started to shuffle backwards, planting a small kiss laced with intention just below my ear.

In between the training sessions, visits to the labs to talk with Michael, and running through the blueprints and attack plan with Gus and Alex, Quentin had taken to wrapping his arms around me and sneaking me back to his room, or mine, or behind a corner or even a quiet hallway – despite my arguments that there were cameras – just to press his lips against mine for whatever small amount of time we managed to steal. I could feel how his entire being relaxed the moment we were in contact and had come to understand that he needed me in his arms just as much as I needed to be there.

He backed up in small steps, making me smile as he made quick work of getting us away from any prying eyes, and scooting me around the corner and into the equipment room.

'Hey,' he breathed, still holding me in place, my back to his chest. Slowly he ran a hand down my side and then across my belly, finding the base of my T-shirt and lifting it just enough to let his fingers graze my skin, causing instant heat to wash through my body.

'You're all sweaty,' I said, in a fake attempt to sound grossed out. Out of the corner of my eye I could see a group of troops testing one of the plastic containment shells. They'd been having problems with getting some of them to fully inflate.

'So are you,' Quentin replied, bringing me back to him. I could feel his smile as he ran his lips down my neck.

Suddenly I spun around in his arms, tired of leaving him with all of the control. And, of course, that was exactly what he'd been waiting for – the moment I turned he pounced, his lips crashing against mine, his arms wrapping around my lower back so tightly that it was blissfully painful. In the back of my mind I knew we were too caught up in one another. That this fire between us was dangerous and possibly the very thing we should fear the most – and yet, I didn't care. I needed this. Us. Someone to fight for. And yes, I'd be lying if I didn't admit that there was a part of me, buried deep, that relished what we had, because loving him so completely gave me the strength I needed to go back down there. To face this final act with the kind of conviction that could only come from knowing there was someone I was willing to die for.

Quentin pushed me away slightly, breaking the kiss, his breathing heavy and his eyes locked on mine as if he knew my thoughts, knew what his love was giving me the strength to do.

'Where are you?' he whispered.

I ran my hand through his hair, my thumb down the scar on his forehead. 'I'm right here. With you,' I responded.

He searched my eyes, looking for my deepest, darkest thoughts. I let him have my eyes, but showed him instead my deepest desires and my truest love. And with that, I saw him come undone – his control slipped away and his lips crashed back to mine.

Quentin had become my world quite some time ago, but now he knew it and that frightened me. We were aware of one another's every move and somehow we seemed to move in sync, a crackling energy always pulsing between us, so intense I'd swear at times I could literally see it encircling us.

My betrayals had been forgiven. I knew that. But they had not been forgotten. How could they be when there was still so much to process? I knew that time would be the only thing that would fully cure us. That and normality, and that meant getting through this fight against M-Corp. It meant making it to the other side.

I would do whatever it took to get him there. Even if it meant he went there without me.

The door flew open and Quentin reluctantly let me go as Alex, Liam and three other commandos walked into the room, unfazed by how they'd found us. They were used to it by now.

'Weapons training in five minutes down in the firing range,' Alex stated, grabbing his gun from the armoury cages – the other three men doing the same. The lower levels of the theatre consisted of three floors, the bottom one taken up entirely by a large shooting range.

Quentin pulled his bag out from under the bench and threw on a shirt while I started massaging my calves again.

Alex handed us both a gun and was halfway out the door when he looked back at us. 'You two are incredibly annoying. You realise that?'

I nodded guiltily. Quentin not so much.

'You also realise that in less than twenty-four hours we are moving out?' he snapped.

We both nodded again.

Alex gave a grunt. 'Be downstairs in two minutes.'

We had been locked in the theatre with over a hundred commandos for almost three weeks by the time I found myself pulling on my army-issue boots and tying my hair back in a tight ponytail before readying my weapons.

This was it.

Game day. No. It was Super Bowl night.

I hadn't seen much of Gus in the first week or so, but five days ago, the entire theatre – every room – had been blasted with the song Gus had decided should be our anthem back in the apartment above Burn. It had taken him longer than he'd predicted to finish the program, but the moment I'd heard the opening lines to 'Uprising', I knew he'd cracked it.

Since then, the entire place had been a flurry of activity. Eliza coming in and out when she could, and Alex and Grace preparing all the troops into various teams.

The first team had left in choppers three hours ago to get into position for the initial strike.

Unfortunately it had become increasingly clear that the Pre-Evo numbers just didn't stack up. Even once we'd pulled in all of the other operatives they had positioned around the country, we still only had a full team of about two hundred. Yes, they were all highly trained, but without Gus's program there was little hope for success. And they knew it. Which was why Gus had been appointed twenty-four-hour bodyguards, just in case there was a traitor amongst them. Or amongst us.

Consequently I had only seen Gus during evening meals. But he seemed to be happy playing his part and would quickly disappear, back to work.

Quentin and I had settled into a quiet acceptance. We were doing this and there was no point thinking of all the things that could go wrong. For me, this was my last chance to make things right and I knew I had to give it everything I had.

'Ready?' Quentin asked softly from where he'd been loading his bag on the bed.

I nodded, looking at him in the mirror. 'Ready.'

And yet, neither one of us moved.

'Mags, I … I've been thinking that if I get the chance down there, if we come across my brothers …'

I bit down on the inside of my cheek. I'd been waiting for this.

I turned to face him and closed the distance. 'You'll do what you think is right. Things are going to get crazy down there, Quin. In the end, you're going to have to trust yourself. Trust your instincts. Whatever you decide, you have my support.'

He swallowed, taking my hand in his. 'I've been over it in my head so many times and I can accept all of it, except for Sebastian. Zachery was always a power-hungry bastard. And my father … well, I get it. But Seb … we were always together. I can't believe he would choose this life if he had a choice.'

I squeezed his hands. 'Do you trust your mother?'

He shifted uncomfortably. 'She came to see me yesterday. We talked.'

'About?'

'About why she made the choices she made. About the future she believes we can help give the world. It all made sense.' He shrugged, but I could tell whatever she'd said had helped bridge the divide between them.

'I'm glad you gave her a chance,' I said, meaning it.

He stepped back and let out a breath as he rubbed the back of his neck. 'As for the trust part? I honestly can't be sure.'

'Then trust yourself. You'll know. If you see him, you'll know.'

Quentin nodded. 'It's crazy how much I love you. Just promise me you'll look after yourself down there. It's already taking every ounce of strength I have to let you do this in the first place.'

'Let me?' I questioned, raising my eyebrows.

His brow furrowed. 'You know what I mean. Last time we went to the core I lost you. I never knew if I'd get you back and every day you were gone I couldn't get the images out of my mind of what you were going through. I didn't know if you were alive, dead, in a neg hub. I conjured every terrible and unforgivable thing and imagined it was happening to you.' His body was shaking. 'So, yes, it's goddamn almost impossible to force myself not to lock you up somewhere safe where only I can ever find you.'

I had to bite my teeth together to stop my quivering jaw, seeing him come apart like that and seeing the ghosts of all he'd been through during that time …

I placed my hands on either side of his face, sharing my strength with him. 'I'm sorry. I … I'm so used to doing everything alone that I forget sometimes that my choices should be ours.' I ran my thumbs over his cheeks and mustered the strength to bare just a little more of my soul to this man. 'It's going to be okay, Quin. We are going to do this together,' I explained, trying to keep my voice steady. 'It isn't possible we could be separated from one another. And I know this because I've got so much love to give you it will take more than any ordinary lifetime. But there are people down there, locked away, and our fathers are responsible for that. It falls to us more than anyone to stop the suffering and the lies. So let's get this done and then we can get on with living, okay?'

Quentin's eyes cleared more and more as I spoke and when I finished he was watching me with awe. 'You amaze me,' he whispered. 'I don't know what I did, in this lifetime or any other, to have earned this chance with you, to be your true match. But I promise you I'll never take it, or you, for granted.' He pulled me in for a kiss. 'When this is done, I'm going to give you everything.'

'Paradise will do,' I said with a smile.

He rested his head on mine. 'With you, paradise is easy,' he whispered.

Sirens started in the hallway outside our room. The signal that it was time to move out.

Quentin stepped back, passing me my bag, then grabbing his own. He smiled sadly as I opened the door. 'I suppose this is the part where one of us says it's time to save the world, right?'

I shook my head. 'Let's settle for just trying to restore a little of what's been taken.'

Twenty-seven

When we entered the main room, it was overflowing with troops dressed head to toe in black. Fully loaded weapons attached to their backs and waists. Much like us.

The plan was intricate and we were only a small element. Observing the way Eliza and Alex had orchestrated the multi-pronged attack highlighted how inept my little missions over the past two years had really been.

But despite our team – just Liam, Quentin and myself – being the smallest and least qualified, we were all acutely aware that if we failed, the entire plan fell apart. Nothing like a little pressure.

While Quentin checked in with Liam, I headed off in search of Gus but soon spotted someone and made a bee-line in his direction.

'You're not a part of this, are you?' I asked.

Master Rua turned to face me, his eyebrows raised. He appreciated manners and I had none. It had been a constant problem for us.

I crossed my arms, refusing to backtrack.

Master Rua sighed. 'Nice to see you too, Maggie. You think I'm too old?'

Yes!

'Yes,' I answered, aloud this time.

Master Rua gave me a rare smile. 'With all hands on deck and both the tech and science teams being moved to the secure mobile site, I'm here as a point of contact if anyone gets separated from their teams and is forced to return,' he said, pointing to the tech geniuses and scientists standing around with their equipment waiting to be moved out to the bus that had been set up as travelling headquarters.

I read between the lines. He was here in case we were ambushed and there were any survivors who made it back. I nodded, lost for the right words.

Michael, who had just sent off another pallet of supplies, noticed us watching and came over.

'Maggie, Alak,' he said with a nod, using Master Rua's first name.

Master Rua nodded in greeting.

'Everything set?' I asked.

Michael held his hands out. 'As much as possible until we have the actual antidote in our possession. Our two main labs in Canada have been prepped and we have the mobile units equipped with as much of the chemicals we think we're going to need as possible. If your teams are successful, we believe we can have the antidote produced within eighteen hours – possibly sooner.'

I knew this part. This was one of the elements of the plan that fell to me. 'If I can help you find out what the active ingredient is,' I said.

Michael sighed. 'I know we're asking a lot of you, Maggie. But it really would make a difference if we had that information as well as a sample of the antidote. It would save us a lot of time if we didn't have to break it down to identify what's in it.'

'And once you have the capability to produce it?' Master Rua interjected, saving me from having to make any more promises than I already had.

'We believe we can have enough of the antidote replicated for America within thirty-six hours and for the rest of the world within seventy-two to ninety-six hours. Then we hand over to aviation and weather control.'

Within the underground networks around the world, it would be simple enough to administer the antidote. But in the third-world countries already affected on mass the hope was that, just as M-Corp had released the negative disruption from the air, they would also be able to deliver it from the sky. But this time by seeding the clouds, with the antidote embedded in the mix.

Someone in a lab coat called Michael's name.

He sighed. 'Well, we're all loaded and set to push off.' He took my hand in both of his. 'Good luck, Maggie.' And then he was gone in a sea of white coats.

'The punters keep complaining you haven't been showing up for the fights,' Master Rua said. 'You were always a sure bet.'

'So the centre isn't just a front?' I asked, voicing the question I had been wondering since first seeing him with Eliza.

'I'm a Muay Thai instructor. That is all I have ever been. I just happen to have played a role training some influential and powerful people. At times I have been brought in to consult or be part of tactical training. If I believe in the cause, I offer my services.'

'And that's good enough for them?'

He shrugged. 'Eliza trusts me, and trust is a rare thing in this world. It cuts through a lot of red tape.'

I glanced at Quentin who was talking with Liam. 'Yes,' I said, swallowing the lump in my throat, remembering all the lies I'd told to gain Quentin's trust in the beginning. 'It does.'

'Now is not the time to dwell, Maggie,' Master Rua chastised, reading my thoughts.

I half smiled. 'Sorry if I'm costing you money by no longer fighting for you.'

'You should be. You should also be apologising that my days are now considerably less entertaining.' His smile dropped. 'And I imagine they never will be again. Am I correct?'

I swallowed, thrown by the display of emotion from my combat mentor who had also become one of the few people *I'd* learned to trust.

I looked into his probing eyes and nodded. 'Once this is done, I'm done. I can't live this life forever. It will eat me up and spew me out.'

He clenched his jaw and looked away. 'At least you are strong enough to know it.' I followed his line of sight to Eliza. 'You're a good girl, Maggie. Remember that when you are down there tonight. But also remember that even the best of us must fight to win.'

'Nicely put!' Gus said, surprising me from behind. 'We should have that put on T-shirts.'

I turned around, looking him up and down. Then burst out laughing. 'What the hell are you wearing?'

Gus's smile morphed into a scowl. 'You don't like it?' he asked, adjusting his black fedora before patting down the bulletproof vest that sat snugly over his trooper uniform.

'Gus, you're in combat gear. What the hell?' My laughter was quickly subsiding.

Gus did *not* do combat gear. He never needed or wanted or was willing to wear it because, quite simply, Gus did *not* do combat.

He rolled his eyes at me. 'What? I totally make this work. It's suave but tough – it says a lot about me.' When he saw that my features had set into hard lines, he sighed. 'Looks like you've got one more in your merry little suicide group.'

'What?' I barely got the word out.

'Calm down. I don't plan on actually involving myself in any real physical work. Think of me as more of a sightseeing passenger. One who will watch on with mild interest and not participate in any of the moral-boosting, life-risking activities.'

'Gus,' I snapped. 'What the hell is going on?'

332

Gus licked his lips and took a deep breath. 'They need a genius on the inside and, well, you didn't cut it.'

I crossed my arms, on the verge of dragging him out of the room and beating some sense into him. Gus must've sensed he'd pushed my final button because he shrugged. 'Once you've found the antidote, who did you think was going to hack the files?'

'You. But I figured you'd do it by remote computer, like always.'

He shook his head and sat on the edge of a table. 'Not this time, Mags. That M-Corp central computer is a monster. It would take weeks to attempt anything by external hacking. Think about all the times you've had to go down there for us to find information and how rarely we found anything of use.'

This was true.

'I have to access the real thing, and if the plan plays out as it should, it won't be a problem. Liam will have your father in hand, I'll get down and dirty with the mainframe, and you and Quin can sit back and put your feet up.'

My face went slack.

He smiled. 'What? Afraid I'll steal your limelight?' He gestured to himself. 'I can totally see how you would be worried. Just seeing how badass I make this outfit look is enough to worry anyone. I can already see the superhero movie adaptation.'

I rolled my eyes and whacked him on the shoulder. Gus grabbed a black marker off the table and before I knew it, he reached forwards and drew a line down my face.

I leaped back in shock.

Suddenly he was laughing hard.

Master Rua grunted and walked away.

Then I was laughing too.

Nothing was particularly funny. The last thing I wanted was Gus – who couldn't save himself from a stray cat – going down into those tunnels of death. But there we were, goofing around.

Armed with a pen in each hand, we'd tagged each other several times and Gus had me pinned to a chair, basically straddling me as he continued his attack, when Quentin suddenly appeared by my side.

We both froze. I knew Gus, like me, was wondering how uncomfortable things were about to get. But the instant my eyes met Quentin's, my concerns evaporated and I knew all of that stuff was behind us. Of course, that didn't stop him from grabbing a fluorescent orange highlighter and streaking a thick line down Gus's cheek in my defence.

A few minutes later we all stood, pens drawn, as we stared one another down waiting to see who would make the next move. By then all three of us were covered in a marker–biro–highlighter combination.

Alex stormed straight through the centre of our circle with a dozen special ops guys on his tail. When he saw my face, he didn't try to hide his frustration. 'Hadn't realised we were taking a break for playtime, kids.'

Gus and Quentin burst out laughing and instantly retaliated, throwing several uncapped pens towards Alex. Most missed – a number of special ops scary dudes copping their misfires. When we saw that the biggest, scariest-looking soldier of them all had a smear of pink across his nose, none of us could hold it in. Even Alex couldn't suppress a smile as they walked away.

Like I said, nothing was particularly funny at that moment, but we all knew this might be the last time we'd all laugh together. Hell, it might be the last laugh, full stop.

Twenty-eight

'Bring back memories?' Quentin murmured in my ear, causing goosebumps to run down my arms.

'Hmm,' I said, staring straight ahead at the field we'd been dropped off in, and then turning to look at the two silver Ducati motorcycles beside us.

'Are they the Diamond off-roaders?'

'Yep.'

My mouth was dry with anticipation. These bikes were the hottest thing on two wheels I'd ever seen. They weren't supposed to be available to the public for another six months and to someone like me, never. But that hadn't stopped me salivating over them since I'd read the first road-testing article a year ago.

While I stared at the gorgeous bikes, already envisaging the ride I was about to go on, Quentin passed me a helmet and then jumped on the first one. Before I knew it, Liam positioned himself on the other one and told Gus to jump on behind him.

My brow furrowed and I looked around. 'Where's mine?' I asked.

Quentin pursed his lips. I could see he was working hard to hold himself together as he patted the back of his bike. 'I knew I'd get you on the back of a bike sooner or later,' he said with a smirk.

My excitement fled fast. I appealed to Liam. 'Come on, surely we could have gotten enough bikes. We'd be faster that way.'

Liam just turned on his engine. 'Only thing slowing us down right now is your ego!' he called out.

Gus gave an exaggerated nod as he got into position behind Liam.

Sulking, I threw on my helmet and got on Quentin's bike. 'Just so you know, I'm a terrible passenger,' I said.

Quentin chuckled. 'Never would've guessed.' He grabbed my arms and wrapped them around his waist. And, hello there … Whatcha know? Riding on the back of his bike suddenly had my interest as I snuggled in close.

As it turned out, Quentin was an excellent motorbike rider and he took the lead, driving along the same off-road path we'd taken a couple of months ago without nearly as many close shaves as I'd caused us.

When the airport came into view in the distance, I signalled for us to stop. I took off my helmet as I waited for Liam's bike to pull up alongside us.

'Remember to avoid being seen by any cameras or security personnel,' I instructed. I was stating the obvious, but I felt responsible for making sure this entryway into the tunnels worked. After all, I'd been the one who'd insisted on using the same route as I had before. Eliza and her team had taken a different route to keep us separated. Eliza had worked out their entry point: through a vaulted underground bank that was majority-owned by M-Corp. After some investigations and Gus hitting up a few of his black-market contacts, they were able to confirm there was a hidden door to the tunnels in the vault at their Market Street branch in Leesburg, only twenty miles northwest of the core. Eliza's team had left an hour before us to allow for the distance and should have already been well within the tunnels.

Liam, Gus and Quentin all nodded. We put our hoods up for extra cover beneath our helmets, and then set off again. Everyone knew their part and how to play it, so there was no need to linger.

Arriving at Dulles International Airport felt like opening the floodgates to all the memories I worked so hard to ignore. Images flashed through my mind: the airport guard, the transit pods, seeing my father, losing him *and* Quentin in the space of minutes and then ... the darkness.

I swallowed the lump forming in my throat and tried to pull myself together. I couldn't afford to go there.

When I finally focused on my surroundings, I noticed that the airport scene was quite different to the last time I'd been there.

I glanced around the baggage area, which was considerably quieter than I'd ever seen it before. As we walked further in, I saw that someone had cordoned off the last conveyor belt with white plywood, creating a false wall around it. Nailed to the boards were signs apologising for the inconvenience caused by the airport's recent renovations and redirecting travellers towards temporary baggage conveyor belts on the floor above.

'Wow,' I murmured, glancing at Liam as he navigated his way past passengers.

'Yep. We're good for some things,' he said, looking around to ensure no one was following us. He continued forwards, walking us straight past a number of security guards who all just happened to turn in the opposite direction when we walked by, not one of them looking at us for even the briefest moment. Whoever Pre-Evo had connection with at the airport was major.

'All clear,' he said, holding open the makeshift door in the white plywood wall. We moved quickly through the door and Liam kept a lookout before shutting it behind him and securing a padlock on our side. The instant we heard the click our shoulders collectively dropped a couple of inches, some of the tension relieved for now. Getting caught at this stage of the game really wasn't an option.

'I can't believe this hasn't drawn the attention of M-Corp security,' I said, gesturing to the fake renovation area.

'You're assuming they have someone constantly monitoring the airport,' Liam said.

'You don't think they do?' I asked.

His response was a shrug.

'They aren't all-seeing, Mags,' Gus threw in. 'They'd have access to the airport security cameras, but I doubt they have anyone whose sole job it is to sit and monitor this particular feed.'

I suppose they couldn't monitor *all* the sites they kept under surveillance twenty-four seven, but still ...

Sensing my need to move, Liam held out his hand towards the carousel and I took that as my cue.

'This way,' I instructed.

Crouched low, we made our way along the black conveyor belt into the back area and found the hidden doorway. Liam used a more advanced decoder than the one I owned and within twelve seconds the door slid open and we jumped into the concrete room beyond.

'This is different to last time,' Quentin remarked, looking around at the large room that had been empty on our last visit, but was now overflowing with boxes.

'A delivery must've just come in,' I said, looking at the faux-pharmaceutical boxes.

'You mean ...' Gus gulped. 'All of these boxes are filled with lust-enhancers?'

'That'd be my guess,' I said.

Gus's mouth dropped open. 'Okay. Am I the only one considering our options here? I mean, think about it. Load up a few boxes, take what money we have and ... you know, we're at the airport anyway. Just a few box-loads would get us millions on the black market.'

'You really want to do that?' Quentin asked knowingly.

Gus looked away, and I knew he didn't want to be caught showing emotion. He had his own reasons for making this trip and it wasn't all about the greater good. Despite his own ignorance of the fact, Gus had loved Kelsey. 'Not exactly, but if everyone else was keen …' He shrugged. 'I'd completely understand the temptation.'

'Are we ready to move on?' I asked with raised eyebrows.

Gus nodded and Quentin moved to my side.

'The first tunnel is narrow so we stay in single file – at times you'll have to walk side-on. There are a few tight corners, but if I slow down just be patient, it's because I'm checking ahead. No talking unless absolutely necessary.'

'I should take the lead, Maggie,' Liam said, stepping forwards.

I blocked him with a hand on his chest. 'Not gonna happen. I know the way, you only know the map and, trust me when I say, the real thing is different. Plus, I want you coming up the rear to cover Gus.'

'I'll ignore the crudeness of that statement because I'm fully in favour of what you really mean,' Gus said quickly. 'In fact, when in doubt, Liam, think of me as your protectee – the one you throw your body in front of the moment any bullets start flying.'

Liam grunted but moved to the back. And that left me with the lead, and Quentin close on my tail.

Stepping into the tunnel, I ignored the pressure in my chest and forced myself to breathe the familiar stale air and continue forwards. But when Liam stepped in and closed the door behind him … everything was suddenly pitch black and my body simply stopped functioning.

We'd decided in the planning process that flashlights might expose us and therefore had agreed to go in dark. Clearly not one of my better ideas.

Struggling to find air, I leaned against the wall and blinked rapidly, desperate for my eyes to fix on something, anything. But … I couldn't … Who was I kidding? I couldn't do this! I couldn't face these people! I couldn't even walk!

My heart was pounding; I could hear it like huge drumbeats echoing in my ears. I was suddenly there, starving again as all around me people died while I could do nothing but stumble through darkness. My breaths became short and ragged. I couldn't do this.

I had just turned around and decided go back when a pair of hands slid around my waist, startling me at first, but then confidently pulling me in. Quentin.

His warmth surrounded me. His smell. He turned me in his arms so I was facing back down the dark tunnel and pulled me to his chest, whispering in my ear, 'Breathe.'

But I didn't want to. Couldn't. I wanted to launch into full-on panic mode.

'We need you, Mags. Breathe,' he said again, whispering so only I could hear.

Oh God, he was right. Gus and Quin needed me to be strong. They needed me to do this and help right all the wrongs. And I needed to be able to do that.

Slowly I forced out a breath, then took one in, ignoring my shuddering chest and trying again. In, out, in … until

I started to feel my arms and legs again. Until I was able to kept my focus on Quentin's warmth surrounding me and on the job at hand. Until I was able to push aside my fear of the dark and what lurked within.

'I'm okay,' I whispered, as much to myself as to Quentin.

'I know,' he said. 'You've got this.' And it was the conviction in his voice, his touch and faith that broke through the dread that had seized me. With each new breath I felt his strength become mine and I straightened, taking that first step forwards – the step towards my fate.

This is what it was all about – a battle that had somehow become my destiny since that very first experiment my father had included me in at Mitchell's Diner. He had secured my future that night. He had started all of this. And tonight, I was going to end it. Or die trying.

'This way,' I said, a little louder so everyone could hear.

We remained silent from that point until we reached the larger tunnel. We were all hot and bothered from the tiny passageway. Gus basically catapulted himself into the wider area, dramatically gasping for air.

'Jesus, Gus. Lucky there's no one waiting for us with loaded weapons since you didn't even bother to look before stumbling out,' I chastised.

'I hate you too,' he said, glaring at me. 'Let's try not to forget this hellhole is full of fun family moments for … not me, but the two of you,' he said, jabbing a finger at

Quentin and me. 'Honestly, you two take dysfunctional to an entirely apocalyptic level. If I wasn't so damn sure it was going to end badly for me, I'd be impressed.'

Everyone stared at Gus.

'Should I gag him?' Liam asked.

I looked at him and saw that his expression was deadly serious.

I rolled my eyes. 'We go west,' I said. 'Liam, you take point and I'll keep Gus quiet.'

Liam looked more than relieved to be off babysitting duty and flew into full-on soldier mode. I walked with Gus to make sure he didn't get himself into trouble, but even so, I could feel Quentin's eyes on me, watching over me protectively.

When we hit a junction, I led them to the nearby call station. 'Cameras there and there,' I pointed. 'Once we put a call in for the transit pods, the cameras will automatically activate.'

Gus scoffed. 'Not with me down here, they won't.'

He pulled out his small laptop and started typing away – frankly I had no idea what he was doing, but he seemed busy so I turned my attention back to the tunnels and kept watch.

'How is this going to work?' Quentin asked.

'I'm hacking into the system – but before I trigger it, I'm kind of tiptoeing first to a different section – or in this case a different junction,' Gus explained absently, pulling out a notebook where he'd written the access codes Pre-Evo had given him. 'Once we activate the system, we'll be able to bring a pod here, but the pod's zip drive will show that it's gone to a different junction and the cameras will activate in that junction too.'

Yes. Gus had mad skills.

He finished up, seemingly happy, and then we waited as Liam plugged in his earpiece and radioed in for a report. When he finished getting the details, he filled us in.

'The first strike is underway. They've taken the Barclay Street building. No sighting of any Mercer family members or your father, Maggie.'

I took this in, bouncing up and down on the balls of my feet.

The first strike had been in New York City. As we waited for the pod, the M-Corp offices in New York were currently being raided and secured by what would look like – to anyone on the outside – a privately organised crime group who were shutting down the tech and taking personnel hostage for some kind of financial gain. The idea had actually being inspired by our little tech bomb display in the theatre.

It was a risk, hitting that site first, and many of the most accomplished soldiers had gone to be part of the strike force. The plan was to take the site hard and fast to stop word getting out that M-Corp was under attack. Eliza had made the ultimate choice to take out their New York office and I couldn't argue with her decision. It would go a long way towards making the underground vulnerable.

'They've taken the entryways and shut down all comms,' Liam passed on as he paced. 'It looks good.'

I nodded, half listening as Quentin asked Liam a few questions. Right then I was starting to slip away. I was becoming disconnected from my surroundings in that way that I had mastered. In those moments when lives were on the line and objectives meant everything, it was what I had to do. It was what made me perform at my best.

My breathing steadied. In contrast to my meltdown in the dark, I now felt centred and encouraged my mind to slide into battle-mode.

'Gus, they want to know about the other group. Did they manage to call a pod? Are they in?' Liam suddenly asked, simultaneously talking with us and into his radio.

Gus started tapping his laptop, his face illuminated by the screen, his eyes scanning whatever information it was feeding him. After a few moments, he nodded. 'They're en route. I'm just shutting down all the other pods now so we don't have any surprises. They'll have to notify us if they want to activate another one after this.'

Liam nodded, relaying this over the radio while I stared at Gus, wide-eyed. 'You can shut down all the pods?'

He nodded, barely looking up.

My hands fisted and I spoke through gritted teeth as I took a menacing step towards him. 'Then why the hell was I always running for my damn life down here every time one of those things came along? Not to mention the broken bones from all the falls I had when trying to hitch a fricking ride!'

Quentin blinked. 'You broke bones hitching them?'

I rolled my eyes. I may have let Quentin believe that I'd never had a problem jumping on and off the high-speed pods when I first taught him how to hitch a ride. 'Get over it. You worked out how to do it just so you could prove a point. If you'd known I'd face-planted in the ground for the first half-dozen attempts, it would've just given you an excuse to fail.'

Gus smiled. 'Ah, Maggie. I've missed you.'

I glared. 'Explain. Now.'

Gus simply shrugged. 'It was more fun that way.'

Quentin barely got his arms around me before I launched myself at Gus. I swear to God, in that moment, I was well and truly prepared to strangle him.

Gus sucked in a breath and leaned back into the wall behind him, even as he laughed. 'There might've also been the little matter of having to hack into the system personally to make it work – which means by tomorrow M-Corp will be able to find the footprints I'm currently leaving behind,' he explained, hands raised in surrender.

I eased back, but not all the way.

Gus sighed. 'You would've blown your cover after one visit if I'd done it that way.'

I let Quentin pull me back a few steps. 'Oh,' I said. 'Sorry about … that.' I motioned to the space between us that I had just been filling.

Gus shook his shoulders out. 'No problem. I'd be lying if I didn't admit that every broken bone brought a special kind of delight into my life.'

'Gus,' Quentin warned.

'*At* the time,' Gus clarified. 'When you were blackmailing my ass from here to kingdom come.'

'Things were simpler then,' I grumbled.

'Yes. I'll always look back on that time fondly,' he replied sarcastically.

A few minutes later an empty pod pulled up and the doors slid open.

'Taxi, anyone?' Gus asked, looking way too smug.

I leaped aboard, grateful that I wasn't going to have to attempt to teach anyone else how to hitch a ride on a pod. To start, there were too many of us. And, frankly, I wasn't even sure Gus knew *how* to run.

'It will only take about fifteen minutes,' I explained once we were all inside the sleek white pod and the doors had closed.

Liam raised his eyebrows questioningly, but once we got going his look of doubt quickly faded. The pods were wicked fast.

While we moved, Liam pulled his earpiece out, saying something about the radios not working in the pods.

'Jesus Christ.' Gus whistled, looking around the pod and taking in the junctions we were zooming past. 'It's like a video game down here.'

'Yeah, except the bullets are real,' Quentin offered.

'And you only get one life,' Liam threw in.

Twenty-nine

Whthe pod pulled to a sudden stop and the doors opened, we were ready.

Liam leaped from the pod, gun raised, and didn't hesitate to fire directly at the four M-Corp guards that we'd spotted on approach. Quentin and I followed him out of the pod to the muted sounds of his weapon firing with a silencer. By the time my feet hit the ground it was already over. The four guards were down and motionless. And a second later the mortality zips on their M-Bands triggered high-pitched alarms.

Liam was ready and pulled another small weapon from his vest, aiming and then shooting fast at the four M-Bands.

'Electro-shots?' I asked.

He nodded. 'Kills an M-Band's external activity immediately. Won't stop the alert getting to its destination, but it will stop the GPS from sending them straight to us.'

'Damn,' Quentin murmured. 'Was that absolutely necessary?'

Liam had done the right thing. Exactly what our orders were. If they were M-Corp, don't question, just shoot. Letting a guard get to a gun would be bad enough – we all knew first-hand they didn't hesitate to take lives – but risking one calling for aid on their radio would spell disaster. And yet, I understood Quentin's reaction.

Liam kept his big-ass gun pointed ahead as he cleared the way forwards. I covered the space to our right, Quentin moved instinctively to the left and Gus – helpfully – remained in the pod until he was given the go-ahead.

My heart thumped so hard I was sure the others would be able to hear it as I scanned for M-Corp soldiers. I had a weapon in each hand. Gun in my left. Tranq gun in my right. I knew it was wishful thinking, but part of me still hoped I'd be able to avoid killing anyone directly.

Straight ahead were the doors to the core lab. To our left were four tunnels, with another four to our right, all of them curving off like the legs of a giant spider, and here we were in the belly of the beast.

'Clear!' Liam whispered to the rest of us, and Gus immediately got to work on his computer again. After a few moments, two massive doors descended, one each to block off the four tunnels on either side, leaving just the tunnel we'd travelled in on as our access in or out.

This had always been part of the plan. I knew that as these two doors descended, similar steel doors were lowering between all of the hubs, closing off each community of negs and their captors, thereby controlling the number of forces our troops would have to face and effectively redistributing the numbers in our favour.

'Just like the hull of a ship,' Gus murmured, looking anywhere but towards the four bodies that lay heaped on the ground.

Liam wasted no time, hooking his earpiece in and requesting a status update. But as he started to listen in, the expression on his face had us all moving closer.

'Repeat!' he ordered.

Something had gone wrong.

I held my breath, looking beyond Liam to the doors that led to the core lab. We were almost there. I couldn't turn back now.

'New York was secured and they took down the corporate offices in Washington, but someone must've gotten word out. Eliza's pod was ambushed as soon as they arrived.'

Instantly Liam, Quentin and I had our guns raised and our backs to one another.

Gus, meanwhile, turned sheet-white. 'They know we're coming.'

'Not necessarily!' I snapped, wanting to curb his panic before he went into free-fall. 'If they knew about us, there would've been more than just four guards waiting for us when we arrived. And the guards weren't ready for us at all. Liam, what's happening out there?'

Liam was listening to his earpiece frantically. 'They're under attack. They've linked me to the feed. I can hear them!'

And then we heard it too. In the distance the unmistakeable sound of gunfire echoed through the tunnels. Quentin flinched. I turned to face him. His eyes were wide and he looked ill.

'Oh, shit!' Liam kept repeating as he listened in. 'They have them,' he said, his face crumpling. And after another tense minute: 'Eliza kept her radio on as long as possible. The last thing I heard ...' He swallowed.

'What?' Quentin demanded.

'I'm fairly certain it was your father's voice.'

'What did he say?'

'He said that all this time he'd thought it was Sebastian who was the weak link, and then I heard her cry out.'

'Then what?' Quentin snapped.

'The line went dead.'

We all stood. Frozen for a moment. What the hell did this mean? Where did we go from here? The team leader and primary group were down, possibly dead.

But then I looked at Quentin again and I saw everything I needed to see right there in his eyes. The fear, yes, but also the love for his mother that he might try to deny but would never be able to completely hide. And suddenly, I knew.

'Are we the closest to them?' I asked, embracing the familiar calm settling over me.

Liam nodded. 'Teams are trying to get to them, but they were positioned in other areas for the next strike. And with the doors down ...'

'Tell all but one team to hold their original positions.'

I dug into my backpack and pulled out one of the empty vials I'd brought along. 'Quin, I need you to fill this with your blood. I'm sorry, I don't have a syringe, so you're just going to have to make a cut.' I held out my pocket knife.

'Why?' Quentin asked, staring at the vial, still lost in his thoughts.

'Because I'm going to need it to get into the core lab while you and Liam go get your mom and help her finish what she started.'

Quentin stiffened, his eyes darting about as he ran through all the possibilities. After a moment, he shook his head. 'I'm not leaving you.'

I ignored him and turned to Liam. 'If you run, how fast can you get there?'

'Five minutes,' he replied, confirming that we were much closer than the other teams.

'Do you have enough firepower?'

'I've got enough ammo to take out a village.'

I nodded. 'Then shoot first, Liam.'

He raised his eyebrows. 'You really think I need to be told that?'

'No, but I'm saying it anyway. Get Eliza out of there and secure Garrett Mercer if you can.'

Liam looked uncomfortable. I could see he wanted to do exactly what I was suggesting, but it went against orders. 'What about you?'

'We'll wait here for fifteen minutes. Hopefully you can get back to us by then, but either way, I'm going in and we tell all the other teams to proceed on schedule as well.'

Finally Liam nodded. He had no choice – we needed Eliza if the plan was going to work. I turned back to Quentin, who was still shaking his head. I placed a hand on his cheek, stilling him.

'It's okay, Quin. You're allowed to want to go to her. She's your mom and you'll never forgive yourself if you don't try. Liam needs you. I'd bet my life if Garrett is there, he's taken them into the panic chambers. Liam needs backup and he needs your DNA.'

'What about your backup?'

The sound of a gun being cocked behind me made me turn to see Gus, holding his weapon like a pro.

'She has backup,' Gus said.

We all stared at him, but he didn't bat an eye.

'What?' he said. 'Just because my weapon of choice is a computer, doesn't mean I won't do my part. I've been down to the firing range just as much as the two of you and I'm willing to bet my average is higher. Just go, Quin. Maggie's covered.'

I was still staring at Gus when Quentin heaved a sigh. He grabbed my hands in his and squeezed. 'I'll be back. I'll get her out of there and I'm coming back for you.'

I nodded, forcing a smile. 'You know where I'll be. Now open a vein for me, baby,' I said, holding out the vial.

Quentin grabbed the pocket knife and sliced across the back of his forearm, letting the blood drip into the vial until it was full.

As soon as it was, Liam was moving out at a run. Quentin grabbed me and kissed me quickly, whispering a promise of paradise before taking off after him.

Once they were out of sight, I turned back to Gus. 'You've never been to the firing range, have you?'

'Nope.'

'And you have no idea how to shoot a gun, do you?'

He smiled. 'None whatsoever. I can't believe that cocking-it thing actually worked,' he marvelled.

'You did good, Gus.'

'Of course I did good. I'm the glue that holds this plan together.'

I rolled my eyes. 'That might be going a little far.'

'I don't think so,' he said, replacing his gun with his computer and getting back to work.

'What are you doing now?' I asked, leaning back against the wall as I counted the seconds go by.

'Trying to hack into the radio frequency. It's not easy, given that Alex wanted to ensure M-Corp wouldn't be able to do it, but without Liam, we're out of the loop here.'

'How long do you think it will take?'

He stared at the screen, glancing up briefly with a look of unhappiness. 'Longer than I'd like.'

I sighed. We were disconnected and that was that.

After another period of time, noises suddenly started to come from Gus's computer. Voices. Orders being shouted.

We can't locate units 7, 12 or 15, sir.

Unit 7 is our priority. Send any available forces to the main lab.

Copy that.

'Gus?'

He shook his head, still tapping away. 'I … I couldn't find our frequency. This must be M-Corp's.' He glanced between the dead guards and me.

'What do you think the chances are *they're* Unit 7?' I asked, already knowing the answer.

'Pretty darn good.'

I nodded, pulling out the vial of Quentin's blood.

'Do you think he'll be in there, Mags?'

'Yes,' I said, trying to ignore the shiver that shook my body. 'Especially if he knows something is going down. He'll want to get his files and protect what's his. Plus,' I added, pausing in front of the massive doors, 'he'll think he's safe in there.'

'Except if he knows *you* are coming for him.'

'My father's not afraid of me, Gus.' I wished I had better news for him. I stared back down the dark tunnel, knowing that troops would get here soon. 'How long since they left?' I asked.

'Ten minutes,' Gus replied.

I sighed and set about opening the doors to the core lab using Quentin's blood and the codes we'd been given from Pre-Evo. 'Let's go.'

Gus looked ill. 'But it hasn't been fifteen minutes yet!'

'They're with Eliza. They're fighting. What happens from this point won't affect what I'm here to do, Gus.'

The outer doors slid open soundlessly and I entered the decontamination chamber, Gus following hesitantly.

Once the doors closed behind us, I set about using the same codes and blood sample to activate the timed inner door before turning to Gus.

I placed the leftover blood in Gus's hand and used the three-minute delay on the door to give him instructions.

'Can you wire this so no one can get in – not even with the right codes and DNA?'

Gus nodded quickly.

'Do it. Stay in the chamber for as long as you can. Troops are most likely coming from the tunnels, but you'll be safe in here.'

I pulled his gun from its holster, checked it was loaded properly and cocked it again before holding it out in front of him. 'Point at the baddies. Shoot. If they move again, shoot again. Got it?'

He stared at me. 'I … I can't shoot someone, Maggie. You're … you're all strong like that and I get it – bad people and all. I do. I don't even care that much being around it and somehow part of it. But I couldn't live with myself if I was the one who …'

I swallowed the lump in my throat, understanding all too well what he was saying. I wanted to tell him it was okay, but that wasn't what he needed to hear. So instead I gritted my teeth and shoved him in the chest. 'You shoot them, Gus. Or they will shoot you dead without another thought. Regret it all you want later – at least you'll be alive to hate yourself. You get me?'

He blinked quickly as if he was trying to hold himself together. I took that for understanding. 'If the inner door opens and it isn't me, you shoot. In the meantime, keep working to get onto the Pre-Evo frequency and send out a message to let them know we're going to need backup in the tunnels.'

He looked as if he was about to faint, so I slapped him. Hard. He reared back, grabbing his cheek. 'Jesus Christ, Maggie. You are such a bitch sometimes!'

I half smiled. 'You'll never have to see me again after tonight if you don't want to, but for one last time, Gus, *please* just do as I tell you.'

He raised his eyebrows. 'Or what? You're going to hurt me?'

I shook my head. 'No. But *they* are going to kill you.'

He nodded sharply. 'You make valid points.'

The decontamination chamber beeped.

I pushed Gus back against the wall, out of sight. 'Stay!' I whispered.

His brow furrowed and I knew all of a sudden he'd stopped worrying for himself and it was now solely for me. I rolled my eyes at him and turned back to the inner door, which slid opened silently. I waited a beat. This was it. I pulled out my gun and my tranq gun and stepped into the lab.

The doors closed silently behind me.

Thirty

The gun was jammed against the back of my head the instant I took my second step into the room.

Holding my hands out to the side, I felt strangely calm as I was relieved of my weapons and roughly patted down by the guard behind me. Unsurprised by the turn of events, I stared ahead, directly into the same brown eyes my brother and I shared. The eyes I had grown up looking into with naive wonder and trust. The eyes of the man I had gone to the ends and depths of the earth to rescue, only to discover I had never known this man at all.

'Hello, Dad,' I said evenly.

Seeing my father before me with his raised gun and arrogant expression made me want to be sick. All I saw now when I looked at him was death. I couldn't begin to imagine how many lives he had ruined, taken, prevented.

The guard continued to prod at me, checking my pockets and finding my smoke bombs and my standard tools. When he moved around to my side, gun still pressed firmly to my head, I glanced at him and was startled to note it was one of the guards who had released me from my cell. I remembered the creases around his eyes. Like the last time I'd seen him, it was clear to me he did not want to be there. Yet he was. He had learned that no matter what his feelings, they did not count. And the look of resignation reminded me that so many negs had given in to this life. Had been so entirely broken that no task would be too awful or gruesome. He would do whatever he had to.

Then again, so would I.

Another guard appeared at my other side. This time I wasn't surprised to discover it was the other guard who'd moved me out of my cell.

'Glad to see you don't stink as much this time,' he sneered at me.

My eyes narrowed.

Seeing him was a reminder of the complexity of the situation. For, fight as we might for those who'd been wrongly turned neg and even for those who genuinely rated as negs but didn't deserve to be judged and convicted for it, there were others who were undoubtedly sinister. Who embodied every unhinged quality of a neg, in the worst possible ways.

Looking into his eyes, it was clear. This man was not resigned to what he must do. He welcomed it. Hungered for it.

I relaxed into my captor's tight hold. 'You should've kept more guards with you, Dad,' I suggested conversationally.

My father chuckled. 'Oh, I think I'm doing just fine, Margaret.'

Feeling the gun at my temple, resting easier than before, I took my chance. I slammed my head back into the guard behind. Stepped forwards fast. Leg back. Grabbed the other guard in front of me by one shoulder. Swung forwards, my knee hitting his most sensitive target. My fist was already moving, straight on, for maximum impact. My flat knuckles smashed into his nose.

'You mean him?' I said to my father as we watched the guard, who hadn't even had time to grab for his balls between the two hits, now on the ground. Blood ran wildly from his nose and he gagged on it then passed out cold.

The guard behind me had yanked me back by my ponytail and belted me hard across the face – a price I happily paid – before attempting to restrain me again. But I was already pulling back and spinning out of his hold.

He got in an extra jab to my gut, I'll give him that, but from there, the fight was mine. With two hard hits to his face – one with my fist, the other with my elbow – it gave me the time I needed to both grab the gun from his waist and then lever my body back to deliver a round-kick to his head. With the help of the nearby wall which his head collided with, he went down, just as unconscious as his buddy.

I had the gun aimed at my father even as I took a moment to right myself and assess my handiwork, focusing on the first guard who still had blood gushing from his nose.

I licked my cut lip. 'You might want to roll him onto his side so he doesn't drown,' I suggested, turning back to my slightly horrified father. Violence was clearly nothing new to him. But coming from me … it was enough to make him falter. 'They might've been able to push me around when I was starving to death, but I've been having three square meals a day, Dad. And for someone who has been following my every move, you've severely underestimated me if you think *this* is "doing just fine",' I said, parroting his words back at him.

He quickly recovered his game face as he straightened and focused his attention away from the bloodied guard and back to me. My stomach flipped when I saw the overly confident and cruel smile curl his lips.

'Actually, Margaret, I wasn't referring to the guards,' he said, adjusting his hold on his gun to press a button on his M-Band. It activated the dark tinted glass wall behind him which slowly faded into clear glass, revealing what lay beyond.

'I was referring … to them.' A look of triumph settled over his features. 'Besides, as I hear it, the troops are needed elsewhere right now.'

My shoulders dropped. My throat closed in tight and my eyes stung with unshed tears as I stared at the glass prison behind my father.

'What … what have you done?' I whispered, unable to tear my eyes away from the sight before me. Samuel and Mom were bruised and battered, their clothes dirty and torn. Blood had dried down the side of Sam's neck and they both stood with their hands banging against the glass, yelling to me a jumble of words I had no hope of hearing since the cell was obviously soundproof.

I hadn't heard from them since Sam's letter, but we'd been cut off from communication in the theatre and I'd thought they were safe. Never had I thought ... Not my own father! Even after everything I'd learned, I never believed the threat to my family – *his* family – would come from him.

'Put the gun on the ground and kick it away,' he ordered.

I did as I was told, keeping my eyes on my family the entire time. 'I'll kill you if you hurt them,' I warned, hoping that my voice conveyed the absolute truth in my threat.

My father sighed with little heart. 'I never wanted it to come to this, Margaret. I never drew attention to you or Samuel. If you had just left well enough alone, you'd be on your way to a good university by now, just like everyone else your age.' He paused to adjust his aim and glanced at his M-Band. 'Unfortunately for you, you have become a problem I can no longer afford.' He jolted his arm in warning. What he didn't realise is that I didn't care what he did as long as the gun was pointed at me and away from Mom and Sam.

'How did you get in here again?' he hissed.

I took a slow step towards the nearby desk where a glass of water sat on the edge. 'I've made some new friends,' I explained.

'Preference Evolution,' he scoffed. 'Fairly pathetic friends. I expected more from you.'

I held my hands out. 'You know all about them, then?' I asked, taking another small step.

'Stop moving,' he snapped. When I nodded, he went on. 'I know they think they have a chance against us, but they don't. It doesn't matter what their little raid achieves tonight or who they have helping them. It won't get them anywhere. Garrett can push a button and clean out every hub within minutes. Do you think he would hesitate taking your friends down at the same time?'

I glared at him. I knew all too well what their interpretation of 'cleaning' meant. Just hearing him talk about gassing so many innocent people to death was the final confirmation that my father was a monster. On the upside, his answers also confirmed that, for all he thought he knew, somehow Eliza Mercer had managed to keep the true identity of Preference Evolution a secret all this time.

I shrugged, playing along and trying to keep my eyes from darting to Mom and Sam. 'Possible, but I met their leader the other day and she seems to think they have a real shot at bringing you lot down. I've got to say, hearing it from her ...' I baited. 'Well, it gave me a shiver, you know?'

He glared at me. 'She? Who the hell are you talking about?'

I smiled knowingly. 'She's very convincing.'

My father shook his head. 'You're talking about Alex, aren't you? Well, we know all about him. In fact, you gave us a fabulous opportunity to unhinge him recently.'

I nodded slowly. 'Killing Kelsey like that was a very clear statement. Unfortunately for *you*, it only pissed Alex off. And apart from that,' I flashed a quick smile, 'he's not the one in charge. Gotta admit, that part surprised me too.'

My father's eyes narrowed. For the first time, I had his interest. He cocked his gun. 'Who's their leader? Tell me now and stop wasting my time!'

I took the final step towards the desk, showing my father that I knew he wasn't about to shoot me right this second, not when I had information he wanted, and gestured to the glass of water. 'May I?' I asked.

He huffed in an oddly parental way, which only served to annoy me. 'Help yourself,' he said.

'Not poisoned?'

He smiled. 'The time for anything other than a bullet has passed.'

I grimaced. 'Sadly I feel the same way.' I picked up the glass and took a small sip. Water.

'Who is it?' he pushed.

I leaned towards him, now only a metre or so away. Sensing I was going to give him what he wanted, he mimicked the movement.

'Eliza Mercer,' I whispered.

When his eyes flew wide and he reared back, I threw the water in his face and leaped on top of him, causing him to topple to the ground.

Straddling him, I took my opportunity and struck him with clean strong hits to the face. Right. Left. Right. A cut on his eye started to bleed down his cheek. And when he screamed out, my right hand shot forwards, clasping his cheeks, my fingers digging in deep to keep his mouth open.

Then from a small concealed pocket on the top of my shoulder – in the past two years I'd noticed that pat-downs rarely included the tops of shoulders – I pulled out the flat plastic vial Eliza Mercer had given to me that afternoon.

I popped the lip and shoved the contents down my father's throat, blocking his nose until he was forced to swallow in order to breathe.

When he had consumed the contents, I leaned forwards and whispered into his ear, 'Now you're a neg too, Dad. You just swallowed one of your own disruptions. The permanent kind. I hope you like it down here.'

He flinched.

I stood up, smiled down at him and turned to look at my family. I could hear him shuffling and grunting behind me, but I kept my back to him and ignored Sam's wide eyes as he pointed.

Sure enough, my father didn't disappoint.

'Very clever, Margaret,' he said, causing me to look over my shoulder and find him back on his feet, gun raised. Did he really think I'd expect any less?

'Thank you,' I said. 'I've been looking forward to this moment ever since Eliza told me she could access a supply of your disruption. Kill me, Dad. If that is what you need to do.' I shrugged. 'Nothing I chose to do today was going to stop that. But at least now we know your actions will be solely because you're more evil than any neg out there – because killing me won't help you. You're as dead as anyone else in this room.'

My father clenched his jaw and shook his head. 'Do you honestly think I would surround myself with these disruptions every day, would risk my life without having a protection plan?' He started entering a series of numbers into his M-Band. A click sounded on a nearby wall and a concealed door began to open up, revealing a hidden vault.

He reached in and removed a tray that must have held about a hundred tiny vials and placed it on the desk.

'An antidote?' I whispered. 'There's an antidote?'

He pulled out one of the small vials and shook his head at me, as if disappointed. 'Still a child.' He threw the contents of the vial into his mouth and swallowed.

'It's that simple. Just swallow it?' I asked, feigning just the right amount of confusion.

He shrugged, increasingly confident now he'd taken the antidote. 'It can be swallowed or absorbed through the skin,' he gloated. 'Yet another display of my brilliance.'

I nodded thoughtfully, trying to contain my pleasure at getting the information I had come for. 'How much of it do you have?' I asked carefully, knowing this question might be one too many.

I remembered thinking: *Yep, too many*, as I watched his eyes narrow.

The shot came so fast I'm fairly certain I felt it before I heard it.

Thirty-one

'I should thank you, Maggie. If it hadn't been for you and your friend, I might've had a small supply problem on my hands. Perhaps,' he mocked, 'perhaps your return to my life was a blessing in disguise. For me.'

The force of the bullet had thrown me back a few steps. Hunched over, I slowly straightened, unable to stop the small cry of pain as I peeled back my hand from the wound in my left shoulder.

There was a lot of blood.

Too much.

I pressed my right hand against it as firmly as I could manage and, grimacing, I looked at my father. 'You should have aimed a little lower, Dad. You would've shot me through the heart and I'd be dead by now.'

He shook his head, looking slightly regretful for a brief moment. 'At least this way you can all say goodbye.'

I looked at Mom and Sam who were pounding frantically – futilely – on the glass. Mom had slid down to her knees and was screaming uncontrollably while Sam had tears streaming down his face.

Seeing them made it all so much worse.

I heard the noise of static – my father was talking into his M-Band radio. 'Status report!' he ordered.

'Intruders at the panic chambers apprehended and dealt with,' came the reply. 'We are now en route to your lab and expect to encounter more resistance.' It took me a few beats to place the voice. But when I did there was no doubt it was Sebastian Mercer.

I watched as my father pressed another few buttons. He glanced at me before talking into his band again: 'And Quentin?'

A breath caught in my throat while there was a pause on the other end.

Finally the response came through – the voice was distorted, leaving no doubt that my father had activated his truth zip, which would alter Sebastian's voice to a high-pitched squeal if he was lying, as opposed to the low gravelly response that meant truth.

'My brother is dead,' he said.

The oxygen left my body, I started to lose my vision.

No.

Not Quentin.

I'd … I'd know. I was sure of it.

I looked at the blood seeping through the gaps between my fingers and considered just letting go. It would speed up the process of what I knew was going to happen anyway.

But then my father spoke again.

'Who killed him?'

'I did,' Sebastian answered. 'Shot to the head.'

Truth.

'Keep his body intact,' my father ordered sharply before shutting down the connection.

On hearing those words, something snapped inside of me.

I looked at Mom and Sam, and for the first time fully grasped their fate. Just as Sebastian could kill his own brother, my father would kill not just me, but his entire family.

'Just remember,' my father said, as if reading my thoughts, 'you left me no choice.'

I stumbled on the spot. 'You're my father!' I screamed. 'My choices were made out of love for you!' Tears rolled down my face. 'How could you have been so loving to me when I was a child and so evil now?'

His face gave away nothing. 'I can make another family, but I can't replace what I have here. I've worked too hard and I'm right on the verge of having everything. You think I've been playing second fiddle to Mercer all this time without looking at the bigger picture?'

I blinked. What the hell was he talking about?

'What plan?' I asked dully.

He shook his head. 'Yet again you disappoint me. What was the number one rule, Margaret?'

I didn't need to think for long. 'Information is power.'

He raised his eyebrows and nodded. 'Mercer has been so busy managing his kingdom and selling his tech to anyone and everyone, he forgot to keep his eyes on the future.'

I was starting to lose my ability to focus. But I knew this was important. 'But not you,' I said.

'Not me.'

'You always said that the technology was a disease.'

He smiled. 'And nothing is more valuable than –'

'The cure,' I finished for him.

His smile turned wicked. 'It was so easy. All I had to do was sit back while Mercer convinced countries, governments, the private sector to come on board. Garrett Mercer is one conniving son of a bitch – even I was amazed when he sold the population-control remedies. And none of them stopped to consider the science or its repercussions.'

'The riots?'

He half laughed. 'Only the tip of the iceberg. The world is on a fast track to anarchy and devastation. The term "world war" will be brought to a new level as battles become not about country or honour, but about basic animal instincts to kill or be killed. The negs have grown in number to become a plague upon the earth. And I am their god.'

I sucked in a sharp breath. 'You're insane.'

'No. I'm a genius.' He raised his gun again. 'But I will give you some peace of mind before you leave us.' He took a deep breath and pressed a number of buttons on the mainframe computer, which caused a machine within Mom and Sam's cell to start powering up.

I didn't need to ask what the machine was. I'd seen similar ones rolled into the hubs on cleaning day. He was going to gas them, but I wasn't going to say it aloud. Mom and Sam didn't need to know.

He looked back at me. 'At least you can know that you and your true match – along with other true matches – helped make all of this possible. Take solace in the knowledge that a future exists because of your contribution.'

Sluggishly my mind tried to put together what he was saying, even as I watched him pull out a long syringe.

'I would have preferred to keep you both alive at one point,' he mused. 'But since your match is already dead ...' he shrugged, 'and you're well on the way, I'll make do.'

I scrunched my eyes closed, trying desperately to think through the pain. I was missing something. The value? Quentin and me? The syringe?

'The ... the antidote?' I stammered.

'Took you long enough.'

'The true match.'

He nodded me on. And then I saw it, his *need* to tell me. For me to know how clever he was. 'You mingle the disruption with the combined pheromone secretions of a true match and it causes the outgoing signals to stall and reboot. Like restarting an engine, but on new fuel.'

'What about for the people who are truly negs?'

He shrugged. 'No cure for that.'

'H-how many are not really negs?'

'Enough.'

'How many?' I gritted out again.

He paused. 'In America, maybe seventy per cent. Around the rest of the world?' He pondered. 'Considerably more.'

The blood was dripping from my fingers and pooling on the ground. I stumbled over to the cell holding Mom and Sam. Their hands were up against the glass, both of them crying openly. I wanted to tell them it would be okay. That I would get them out of there. But I couldn't.

'I love you,' I mouthed.

'We love you too,' Samuel mouthed back.

I dropped to my knees and placed a hand up against Mom's. She was screaming and Sam fell to her side, rocking her back and forth.

'It's touching,' my father said from behind me. 'Your love for your family. It truly is. What I don't seem to have, you possess in spades. But you've taught me my lesson well, Maggie. I can already see Samuel's need for vengeance written all over his face. You decided their fate when you took this path. You cannot save them.'

I dropped my hand from the glass and stealthily reached into the top of my boot, pulling free the small knife the guard had not found. Giving it all I had, I spun around and threw it at my father.

But he sidestepped in time and it barely nicked the edge of his thigh.

He looked at his leg, then to the knife on the ground and chuckled. 'Pathetic to the end.'

I got to my feet, refusing to look weak in front of him. 'I might be pathetic, but at least I'm loved. All those who once loved you now despise you. I hope your money and power keep you company because that's all you'll ever have!'

He glared at me and raised his gun. 'Goodbye, Margaret.'

The shot sounded out, harsh and loud.

My vision blurred and I fell to my knees as another shot sounded. I dropped to my side, surrounded by the silent screams of my family.

After a few moments, I heard footsteps approach and opened my eyes a little to see a shadow looming over me.

'Mags!' A booted foot kicked my leg. 'Now really isn't the best time for a nap.'

I opened my eyes all the way. 'Gus?'

He rolled his eyes. 'No. You're in heaven and the first thing you get to see is me. Now get your ass up and help me out here!'

It was then I noticed he had his hand pressed to his stomach. Wincing with the pain, I pushed myself up and staggered to my feet. My father was lying a few metres away. He wasn't moving.

I looked back at Gus. The arm still holding his gun was trembling and he was deathly white. He remained focused on my father's motionless figure rather than what I thought was the more pressing matter of the fatal amount of blood pouring from his gut. But then I remembered what he'd said to me about using the gun.

Watching Gus carefully, I swallowed the scream clawing at my throat and held out my hand for him to give me the gun, which he did willingly.

'Stay here,' I instructed. He didn't argue.

I walked over and bent down by my father to check his pulse. Not that I needed to. I could see his shallow breaths, the colour of the blood, his half-open eyes. He only had moments left. When I stood up again, I aimed the gun at his chest and shot.

Once.

Twice.

'Jesus Christ, Maggie!' Gus murmured. But I could already hear the relief in his voice that he hadn't been the one to take my father's life. And I'd never tell him – or anyone else – otherwise.

And if stealing my father's last breath made Gus's a little less pained, then I could live with that.

I tucked the gun into my back waistband and made it back to Gus just in time to fail at catching him. We both fell to the ground, him in my lap.

There was so much that I had faced. But this was simply too much. Knowing that Quentin was most likely …

I cried openly, sobbing as I tried to see how bad Gus's wound was. He shoved my hand aside.

'No point,' he said, voicing what I already knew.

I bit my lip to try to stop the sounds coming from me as I looked for some way, *any* way to stop this from happening. But it was impossible.

'How'd you get in anyway?' I half asked, half scolded.

'When I heard the shot and you didn't come out afterwards to give me the all clear …' He let out a breath. 'I listened until I heard your voice come from further away … took my chance you weren't near the entrance and hotwired the door to open without activating the entry alerts.' He shrugged. 'I slipped in. Hid behind the entry desk until …'

I nodded, lost for words. He'd risked everything to save me.

'Plug this into the mainframe,' he instructed, holding up the other end of a cable that fed into his laptop.

Knowing I had to do this, I reached up with the cord and plugged it into the driver.

Gus leaned against me and tapped a series of keys on his laptop. 'Let's get your family out of there before that machine starts spitting out gas,' he said. Within ten seconds the machine inside Mom and Samuel's cell shut down completely, and a few seconds later the door opened.

Mom and Samuel rushed out, sliding to the ground beside us.

'Oh my God! Maggie, I thought he'd kill you!' Mom said.

I hiccupped on a sob as I shook my head. 'Gus saved me.'

They both nodded. 'We saw, Mags,' Sam said.

My chest convulsed with sobs as Gus's breathing became even more shallow. He passed me the laptop. 'Whatever you type in here will go to a safe place, Mags. People will find it. Send them the message with everything you know about the antidote. Even if none of us make it out of here, the solution will.' He pointed his shaking finger to another button. 'Press here and enter the code when you want the world to know.'

I blinked. 'You don't trust Pre-Evo.' There was no way he'd have all of our intel set up and ready to go if he did.

He swallowed painfully as my mom checked his wound quickly, then his pulse. 'Much easier for them to lie than tell the truth. This is the system I originally set up.'

'What's the code?' I whispered.

He tried to smile. 'The Maggieverse.'

I nodded, clenching my jaw as I stroked the hair back from his face. 'I'm so sorry, Gus. I failed you too.'

He shook his head slightly. 'Nah. Never think that. Might not be hanging around, but at least we've got what we came for.'

Mom gave me a look that said it all.

'You're my best friend, Gus,' I said, tears falling.

He tried to smile. 'Only friend.'

I nodded, finding it hard to talk. 'Love you always,' I managed.

He closed his eyes. 'Love you back, Mags. Always have.'

I bit down on a moan as Gus let out his last breath. I rocked him back and forth, repeating the cries: 'Please don't go. Please don't leave me too.'

I don't know how much time had passed when Sam gently pulled me back.

'He's gone, Mags. He's gone and you're bleeding real bad.' He started tying what looked like a ripped-up lab coat around my shoulder. I was numb to the pain now, even when he pulled the knot tight.

'Sam?' I said quietly, watching as Mom covered Gus with another lab coat. 'Sam?' I repeated, when he didn't answer.

'Yeah?' he said, finishing the makeshift bandage on my shoulder.

'You need to keep Mom safe.' I took a step back to assess my weapons. I was vaguely aware that my body hurt, but I had no energy to care about it. 'The two guards are unconscious but alive by the door.' I gestured to the one I'd hit in the nose. 'He won't be getting up anytime soon, but keep an eye on the other one.' I handed him Gus's gun and then patted down the unconscious guard, grabbing my taser first. But then I paused, put it back and found my gun instead. After another brief moment, I took the guard's gun too.

'Mags,' Sam snapped, now following me around as I got organised. 'You were on the ground taking your last breaths a few seconds ago, in case you've forgotten. What the hell do you think you're doing?'

'I'm going to find Quin,' I said matter-of-factly.

Sam gulped. 'Quin? As in Quentin Mercer? What the hell does he have to do with all this?'

'She loves him,' my mother threw in, now joining us. When I raised my eyebrows, she smiled sadly. 'I was listening.'

I sighed, picking up Gus's laptop. 'Did you hear everything?'

They nodded. 'We just couldn't *be* heard,' Sam said.

'So you know about the antidote?'

'Kinda. I wasn't really focusing on that part,' Sam said.

'I caught most of it,' Mom offered, and I knew her medical background would help.

I pointed to the still-open vault and the tray of vials on the desk. 'I need you to type everything you know into this message box, including everything about the antidote.'

'Is that it there?' Mom asked, stepping up to the task.

I nodded. 'It can be swallowed or absorbed through the skin. If they can't make enough with what's there, tell them ...' I grabbed at my shoulder, noticing the blood had already soaked through the lab coat. 'Tell them the formula is Dad's disruption recipe mixed with an equal dose of pheromone secretions from a true match.'

Mom and Sam froze, putting the pieces together. 'But your father said you ...' She blinked and looked back at the antidote. 'That's you?'

I looked down.

'That's why you're going after him,' Sam said. 'He's your true match.'

I felt the tears brimming in my eyes. 'They said he's …
but I have to see for myself. Can you get the message out
and then stay here until help arrives?'

Mom nodded even as she grabbed me, pulling me to
her with a mother's strength. 'You don't know he's out
there. How can you ask me to let you go? You're my
baby!'

I eased myself out of her arms and stepped back,
meeting her eyes. I hoped she would see my love for her
along with the determination. 'I'm not asking, Mom.'

She gasped and I knew she saw the side of me that I'd
always kept hidden from her. The part that could be cold
and calculating. The part I got from my father.

'Don't open the door for anyone unless you're sure
you can trust them,' I said.

'And if no one comes?' Sam asked.

I swallowed, wishing there was a better answer.
Wishing I could tell them I would be back. 'If no one
comes in the next half-hour, open the doors, stay armed
and take the tunnels east. You heard Gus give me the
password?'

Sam nodded.

'Good. Make sure you keep Gus's laptop with you, and
hidden from *everyone* else. If I can't … Make sure that the
file gets activated as soon as you're away from here.' They
had heard enough and understood what I was saying. I
pulled a hard-copy map out of my vest. 'Use this.'

Sam took the map, resting his hand on top of mine
briefly before I hit the button to open the door to the

decontamination chamber. When I met his eyes, I saw that he knew this was it.

I half smiled at them. 'At least I'll know that, after all my failures, I helped in the end.' I looked away as I added, 'Don't come after me.'

They watched, conflicted but knowing they had to do as I asked. The antidote had to get out there and the world deserved the truth, otherwise it was all for nothing.

'I love you guys. I'm so sorry I dragged you into this.'

I hit the button for the door to shut. As it slid closed, I heard Sam call back, 'We love you too, Mags.'

It was a bittersweet goodbye.

Thirty-two

In the chamber I kept my back to the wall to remain hidden for as long as possible, holding the two fully loaded automatic guns ready as I waited for the doors to open.

I knew there would be troops out there; already I could hear the muted sounds of rapid gunfire. The question was, how many? And would any of the good guys be there by now? And then it struck me: I was on the good side. A team.

How the hell did I become a team player?

Breathing deep, I ignored the pain in my shoulder and tried to refocus, reminding myself that in some small way, we had won. I might not get out of these tunnels alive and it might not be the victory we'd hoped for, but if I knew anything about Gus's skills, it meant that right now Sam was sending a backup of the antidote information to a place where the right people would find it. We had the answers; they would not die down here with us.

I closed my eyes and kept my concentration, opening them just as the doors began to part. Waiting until the last moment, I exited the chamber, guns at the ready.

The side tunnels were still blocked off and the main tunnel was immersed in smoke. All that I could see in front of me were two M-Corp guards on their knees by the doors, obviously trying to rewire them and override Gus's handiwork.

Judging by the smiles on their faces, they thought the fact that the doors had just opened signalled their success. They clearly weren't expecting me to come storming out and deliver two fast shots, hitting both of them in their thighs. They both collapsed to the ground, screaming out. But I was already moving into the thicket of smoke and their screams were quickly absorbed by the deafening sounds of gunfire.

'Shit!' I said as I ducked and ran, getting my hand on a wall and using that to guide me and keep me upright. I didn't know how long I had left in me and I could barely see ten metres in front of me. A damn big problem, considering I had just stepped into a war zone.

Bullets hit the wall nearby and I looked around to see where they had come from. The tunnel lights were all but out, and flashlights created random beams of white light against the smoke. I was able to make out the most of what was happening in the central zone. Which was basically a shit-fight.

Shots were being fired and one set of troops was moving in on another. But for the life of me – with almost all dressed in black and faces covered by oxygen masks – I had no idea who was who.

A lone figure far down the tunnel passed through a beam of light, and intrigue had me moving towards it.

A shot rang out and I pushed ahead, still using the wall for support as I stumbled towards what I could now see was more than one person. They were further away than I'd first thought. On my way I passed an unusually short side tunnel and could see it opened to a nearby hub. As I neared the entrance, what I saw caused me to stop and stare. Below me the hub, which had the usual salad-bowl design, looked standard enough. What *was* different was that in the centre of the hub was a massive plastic structure, like a blown-up sphere, and within it stood hundreds of negs. I looked a little closer and noticed there was also a small group of guards sitting with their hands tied behind their backs.

The containment shells had always been part of the plan, but seeing them in action, feeding clean oxygen into the bubble to ensure that no matter what gasses were activated the negs would not be 'cleaned' like my father had threatened – well, it made me want to fist-pump the air. It fleetingly occurred to me that I'd left behind my backpack – and the mask I'd packed – but obviously the air I was breathing at that moment was okay. And later ... I was fairly certain there would be no 'later' for me.

As I rounded the corner back into the main tunnel, I froze and almost lost my footing.

There was more light down this end of the tunnel and I could see better, enough at least to recognise Eliza Mercer standing with a gun raised, facing her husband, who was also armed.

'I thought it would be easy,' she said. 'I thought that after all the terrible things you've done, pulling the trigger would be a relief.' Her hand was shaking.

'You can't kill me, Eliza. After everything we've been through.' He shook his head. 'No. You won't kill me.'

'Are you sure you even know me, Garrett?' she taunted, standing taller for the threat. And when she did, her eyes moved to the side and she saw me. Like the pro she was, she barely paused before looking back at him. But I saw her fingers spread and sensed her plea. I stayed where I was.

'Our high ratings would suggest I've always been aware of your strength, if not always your activities.'

She adjusted her stance. 'I've never known how you managed not to go down in your ratings with me. After all this time and all you have done,' she said.

I could hear the satisfaction in his voice as he answered. 'Because you and I are two of a kind, Eliza. I realise that now more than ever. We are willing to do whatever it takes to make the future right.' He lowered his gun slightly. 'I started rating negative with many people a long time ago, but there were always more that I rated well with because they want what I'm prepared to give them. A stronger world, with better people. I'm not the bad man you think I am, and you know that in your heart. We're the same. *That's* why our ratings have held.'

She shook her head even as her arm wavered. I could feel her conviction slipping away.

'You're right,' she said softly. 'Maybe you aren't the bad person I think you are. But I have to know for sure.' She dropped her gun. I had to cover my mouth to stop from shouting out.

Garrett's arm was in the air before I'd taken a step. The shots came in rapid succession. Sharp. Loud. Then, in the echo, I heard Garrett Mercer sigh. 'I'll always love you, Eliza. But I will not die for you.'

Eliza's eyes flashed with surprise as she clutched her stomach and I realised she honestly believed he wouldn't kill her, that somehow their love would be enough. She staggered and looked up, her eyes fixed on mine and I knew. She had the answer she needed. The answer she was willing to give her life for. And I knew what she was telling me.

Pounding footsteps sounded a little further down the tunnel and I knew my advantage would soon be lost.

I raised both my guns and somehow pushed off the wall.

Everything hurt. But most of all my heart. It was tearing apart and dying fast in these tunnels of doom. All I wanted to do was squeeze my eyes shut and wish the world away. But I didn't. I held my hands as steady as I could and watched Garrett – who had just murdered his wife – and Sebastian Mercer, who had just skidded to his father's side. Neither had noticed me. And for once I was grateful for their arrogance.

Sebastian was out of breath. 'Dad!' he screamed. 'Dad, no!' He grabbed his hair with one hand, his gun resting comfortably in the other.

I didn't hesitate. From somewhere I found the strength and will to finish this. To cut off – like Eliza had wanted – the head of the snake.

'Hey!' I yelled, causing them both to spin in my direction.

My first bullet hit Garrett Mercer in the chest.

The gun's kickback felt like a ball of fire slamming into my arm and caused me to stagger. But I straightened and ignored the pain. The second and third bullet came fast, hitting just below the first. Garrett barely had time to look up in shock and register who the shooter was before he went down.

My teeth chattered and my body trembled, fighting me as I forced it not to give up. Not yet.

I adjusted my aim towards Sebastian, opening and closing my eyes a few times to steady my focus.

He dropped the gun he held by his side and raised his hands. 'It's not what you think,' he said quickly.

'Did you or did you not shoot your own brother?' I hissed through ragged breaths before I let out a cry of agony that had nothing to do with my physical pain.

He looked around nervously, keeping his hands up. 'Yes, but –'

I shook the gun, cutting him off.

More shots sounded around us. Troops were shouting out commands about closing in the perimeters. The coded commands told me that it was Pre-Evo soldiers.

We were winning.

Just one last thing to do.

I straightened my arm and shook my head at Quentin's murderer. 'He was your brother and he loved you!' I said, my finger putting pressure on the trigger just as I heard the voice of a ghost.

'Maggie. Don't shoot him,' he said. Calm. Soft.

My finger hesitated and I squeezed my eyes tight again, thinking I was imagining his voice.

But then, I heard it again. Closer. 'Mags. Please.'

I flinched and looked over my shoulder to see a form approaching through the smoke.

He was limping, a gun hanging loose in his hand by his side. He was dirty with tunnel soot and had a deep cut close to his left eye, but he was alive.

When his face cleared through the fog, I felt the tears pour down my face. 'You're here,' I whispered.

Quentin nodded and furrowed his brow in that perfect way of his as he looked me over, his eyes lingering on my shoulder where Sam had tied up the lab coat.

I shook my head, increasingly confused, and kept the guns trained on Sebastian. 'No. Sebastian told my father that you were dead, that he killed you … He was talking through a truth zip …'

'I told your father I killed my brother. And I *did* kill my brother, Maggie,' Sebastian said, causing me to jolt. 'Just not this one,' he said, his genuine sorrow bleeding into every word.

It still took me a beat to get it. 'Zachery?'

He nodded.

'Sebastian was playing both sides like Mom,' Quentin explained, coming a little closer but still moving cautiously. 'They just never realised it. He's been working with a group of the United Nations. Maggie, he's not with them.'

'I never was,' Sebastian threw in with a hesitant smile. 'I've being implanting my own team down here for the past six months – all of them working from within M-Corp's ranks. I'm aligned with the British arm of the UN and used my work trips to hide what I've really been doing.'

'But your father?' I said, shaking my head, worried Sebastian was tricking us. 'You ran to him. You stood by his side, *armed*, and he wasn't afraid of you.'

Sebastian nodded in a placating gesture. 'He never knew. He never realised I'd given my team the green light. He never knew, Maggie. I swear to you, I would have shot him in the head if you hadn't done it first.'

I glanced nervously at Quentin, who now knew I had killed his father. I was on the verge of being sick, but somehow the adrenalin kept me going.

'Please, Maggie. I need to help my mom,' Sebastian pleaded.

I glanced at Eliza, who wasn't moving. I couldn't tell if she was breathing or not.

I dropped my guns. Sebastian leaped over his father's body and rushed to his mother's side. Quentin instantly had me in his arms. I had no strength left. Everything was numb.

'Where the hell is Gus?' he growled, looking around in frustration. 'He should be with you!'

My voice shook as I replied. 'He saved me, Quin. He saved my family.'

The air left his lungs even as he continued to hold me. He knew what I was saying.

'How badly are you hurt?' he asked.

I took in as much air as I could and forced a half-smile. 'I'm okay. We got the antidote. Go check on your mom,' I said. Then, using what felt like the last of my strength, I nudged him towards her. 'Then find my mom and brother. They're in the core lab and they have everything Michael will need to make the antidote.'

Quentin's brow furrowed as he looked between his mom and me. Finally he took a step towards Sebastian, who was crouched over Eliza and calling for medical support teams on his radio.

I swayed back and forth a few times, the darkness beckoning. The last thing I saw was Sebastian stand with Eliza cradled in his arms and then the world around me faded away to background noise. I heard snippets of commands and even a distant cheer. I vaguely registered the pain when my knees hit the gravel.

The world went dark and I heard the only voice I wanted to hear call my name over and over. It was urgent and yet I was suddenly calm. I let it lull me to sleep.

Finally to rest.

Thirty-three

I drowned in the dreams. The nightmares. Always the same.

My eyes are open wide.
But I can't see.
I'm shaking and starving.
I hear my breathing.
My heartbeat.
I hear the ventilation fan.
I am alone, and yet …
A hand suddenly grasps my arm, fingers digging to the bone.
Then he is there, close to my ear, his whisper echoing off the walls until it becomes a chant that swirls around me like a tornado.
'You chose this path, Margaret. You forced it when you should've left well enough alone.'
My father's voice mocks me. Then suddenly he is injecting something into my arm.
But this time the dream changes. I see now, he is not injecting me but withdrawing. Taking part of me. Using me.

I look to my right and suddenly Quin is there. There are trays of needles around him too. He looks sick. Tired.

'Quin,' I whisper.

'For the greater good, sacrifices are often made,' my father says.

The faces come. Images of all the negs I have failed. I see them all clearly – so many. And finally, I see Kelsey. I see Travis.

I see Gus.

My father pulls me up so I can see the chaos that is my own doing. He laughs and points at Quentin who crumples to the ground. 'You have ruined him too. Left him with nothing.'

I shake my head hard. 'No. He has me! He has me!'

My father laughs. It is evil.

'But you have given up. You are dying.'

Suddenly they are gone and I am back in the cell. Alone. In the dark. Starving. Quivering.

This dream is different to the others. This dream comes with a choice. I can feel in my bones, in my veins, the life pumping through me and slowly fading away.

I am tired. Have been tired for so long. Rest beckons and, though I know I do not deserve it, it lures me. Pulling like a magnet when every other direction feels thick, like pushing through wet cement.

I inch towards the darkest of the dark.

But my hand will not go with me. It stays behind me, as if something is holding it, pulling me through the cement.

I look back.

The faces are all there. The memories. The past. The heartache. The truth of all of my mistakes. It hurts to look. But then I feel his hand in mine.

It squeezes. It begs.

I cry out to the darkness. But there is no answer. Only choice. Mine.

I am dying. I know.

But I'm not dead.

Death no longer lurks like in the other dreams, it dances all around me, so confident in its victory.

And then I am pushing towards the faces, through the pain I know I will carry with me for all of eternity. I push through it all. Because he is my choice.

He will always be my choice.

He is not just my match. He is my heart, my love, my redemption.

He is paradise.

I start to convulse. Fighting the dream and searching for reality. I know when I am getting near because it is agony. Inside and out.

Suddenly I feel the strain of my struggles and my body breaks out in a sweat. It is cold and only spurs on my battle against the demons that have me trapped.

Then I hear him. 'Breathe. You have to breathe. You have to breathe so you can come back to me.'

His voice is getting closer.

I fight for him. I will fight forever.

'Maggie! Feel my hands, Maggie. Feel my hands in yours.'

He has said these words before. And like before, I clench my hands. They are empty, and yet …

I feel something. Distant.

Then he speaks again and his voice is close, whispering to my heart and to my will. 'I love you, Maggie. With everything I am, that's the one thing I have always been sure of.'

The one thing.

I push. It hurts. I scream. The pain is so intolerable I know I am close.

And then finally, after what feels like lifetimes of struggle, I feel it, clasping my hand, urging me on. Home.

I open my eyes.

He is with me.

Quentin pressed his forehead against mine, his chest convulsing a few times.

I swallowed. My throat was raw, but I tried to speak. 'Hey,' I managed.

He took a deep breath and looked up. I could see the tears in his eyes that he was trying to hold back. 'I thought I'd lost you. You … you …' He looked around, lost for words.

It was then that I noticed we were not alone. There were a number of people around me. I thought they were doctors, but I wasn't sure. Most were in combat gear. A few in white coats. From the hard metal table I was lying on, my eyes darted left then right. We were in another lab. There was equipment all around me, but this was not a hospital.

I flinched.

'Still … underground?' I asked, even though I knew.

Quentin seemed to sense this and instead answered my unspoken question. 'We have control. We couldn't move you, Mags. You'd lost too much blood. They needed to do a transfusion.'

I nodded, trying to clear my foggy mind. 'Who?' was all I could manage. 'How?'

He knew why I was asking. 'Me. Turns out most true matches have the same blood type, which comes in handy when you're AB negative,' he said with a small smile.

'Oh.' Then another thought occurred to me. 'Mom? Sam?'

'We're here, Maggie,' Mom said, appearing behind Quin. She was wearing gloves and one of the white coats.

'Your mom has been taking care of you. She was amazing,' Quentin explained.

I closed my eyes and wasn't sure how much time passed before I opened them again, but they were both still there. 'I thought … you and Sam were supposed to get out.'

Mom nodded. 'Your friend Grace came to get us once all the shooting had finished. She brought us to you. You didn't think we would really just leave you behind, did you?'

'But … What about …?'

'The information about the antidote has been passed on to the right people. As for the other thing, Gus's equipment is safe whenever you are ready. But right now you need to rest.'

How could I possibly rest now?

I looked at Quentin and he raised an eyebrow.

'Your … mom?'

Quentin dropped his head and shook it.

'I'm so sorry. I should have …'

He ran his hand down my cheek. 'She knew what was at stake. I'm pretty sure she walked into these tunnels knowing she wouldn't be walking out.'

But would he still feel that way when he knew I'd just stood there and let it happen? I looked around at all of the other people buzzing around the lab. Then I saw Michael talking with another white-coated woman.

'How long?'

'Just over twelve hours,' Quentin answered.

My eyes widened. 'The antidote?'

Michael looked over then, his eyes meeting mine, and he smiled. 'We got it. Thanks to you, Maggie. We have the cure. We're just about to run the first batches through the tunnel water pipes. Would you like to watch?'

I licked my lips and nodded. Mom tried to argue, but Quentin helped me sit up and they turned my metal bed towards the huge monitor screens. There were dozens of them, all focused in on the neg hubs. Within each hub, the containment shells had been deflated and the negs had been returned to their prison cells.

I'd always known they wouldn't be released straight away, but still, it was hard to see that, after everything, they were still locked up like animals.

'Ready?' Michael called to the room.

After a series of replies, he hit a button and across all the screens we could see fire sprinklers raining down in the negs' prison cells.

'We needed to keep everyone locked up to ensure they would be in the right place to receive the antidote,' Michael explained.

'How much do they need?'

'Barely anything. Once it hits their skin, it will start to work.'

'Do we have enough?'

Michael paused and looked at me then Quentin. 'We were lucky with the supply we found. It will be enough to create the initial doses, and we have teams tracking down true matches around the country so we can gather more of their combined pheromones.'

I glanced at Quentin, who quickly put a finger to his lips, and then back to Michael, who gave me a wink before looking back at the monitors.

Somehow they'd kept our match a secret.

I let out a breath and watched in amazement as negs stood beneath the sprinkler systems as the antidote rained down on them.

'By tomorrow we will know who really is and isn't a neg,' Michael commented.

'But I thought we were going to stop the tech from telling us that. Aren't *we*?' I questioned, feeling groggy again. That was the promise Eliza had made.

'She needs to rest,' my mother said from behind me.

'Wait. I want an answer,' I said stubbornly.

'Maggie, that is the plan, yes. But it's complicated. Some of these prisoners were actually moved here from state and federal prisons for crimes they'd been convicted of. We need to be sure what and who we are dealing with.'

It seemed simple enough to me. If they were in prison before, then they should either be given pardon because of what they'd been through, or be sent back to a normal prison where they could have visitors and not be locked underground like sub-humans. But I didn't have the energy to argue.

'Why don't you rest, Maggie? We promise it is all in good hands,' Michael said, seeing my unease.

I watched him for a beat. He was a good guy. But bureaucracy complicated even the most basic solutions. Slowly I nodded, casting one more look at the monitors, and let Quentin wheel my bed to the side of the room.

I grabbed Mom's hand.

When she saw the look in my eyes, she sighed and nodded, looking over her shoulder to someone else. A few seconds later Sam was by my side.

'Hey, sis.'

'Hey, Sam.'

'Thought you weren't going to make it there for a bit. Should've known you'd be strong enough to put death in its place.'

I smiled. 'Thanks. Do you still have what I left with you?'

He nodded and discreetly pulled Gus's small laptop out from beneath his shirt. But when he tried to pass it to me, I was suddenly woozy and my hands slipped away.

'She needs to rest!' Mom snapped. 'This can wait.' She started to push Sam and Quentin away. But Quentin didn't budge. And Sam pushed back.

'Give it to Quin,' I said to Sam.

Sam looked dubious and I knew he wasn't sure if Quentin could be trusted.

'Please, Sam,' I whispered. 'Please.'

Thankfully it was enough and he handed it over. Quentin took the laptop and gave me a quizzical look.

'It's the program Gus developed for the first time we went in. It has everything. The proof. The pictures. The truth.' My vision was blacking out. 'Enter the password and the world will know.'

'Maggie, Jesus, I don't know. Maybe we should wait until you're better. Until we're out of here at least,' he said, looking around. 'I need to be sure you're safe.'

I shook my head softly, knowing I would lose consciousness soon. I pulled his hand towards me and he got the idea, leaning close. 'Then get me out of here. Your parents are gone, Quin. You and Sebastian are the heirs. You have all the power. Everyone who's a part of M-Corp answers to you now.'

The last thing I saw was Quentin's eyes flash with understanding. And fear.

Thirty-four

That was the last time I saw Quentin Mercer.

When I woke up, I realised he'd done exactly as I asked and moved me out of the underground. I was in an ambulance, Mom and Sam beside me. I didn't stay awake for long – just enough to say his name and see their eyes drop. I knew it then. So I closed my eyes and went back to sleep.

The next time I woke, I was in a hospital-style bed, but I was on a small plane. No. A helicopter. Mom and Sam sat nearby. I looked around, but we were alone. I closed my eyes.

Finally I opened my eyes and found myself in a real bed, large with a thick wooden frame. I could hear birds and possibly a rooster crowing in the distance. But what had me sitting up was the smell.

Definitely bacon.

I moved fast. Then very, *very* slowly. I was dizzy and weak. Once I'd adjusted to sitting up, I took in my surroundings. I was in a bedroom. It was a beautiful combination of modern and country style: lots of cherry wood, a beautiful cream rug and an open fire with crackling embers. It felt like being in someone's home, not just some random house.

And bacon smells were wafting into the room.

I was wearing blue pyjamas. Not mine, yet they were silk and fit me perfectly.

I still had a drip connected to my hand and carefully pulled it out and then studied my M-Band. My blood pressure was high, but otherwise my vitals looked steady. Next I inspected my shoulder. The wound was covered in a white bandage and the skin across my upper arm and chest was all badly bruised. When I experimented with movement, I quickly decided I wouldn't try again.

Despite the aches, my body seemed in working order and after a few minutes I made it to my feet, using the bed for balance. My eyes filled with tears and my breathing faltered with the sudden realisation that I was alone. Sure, there was someone cooking bacon somewhere, but I knew. Just knew it wasn't him.

I forced the tears back and took a step, then another and kept going through the first door, which I gratefully discovered was a bathroom. I ran a hot shower and made a point not to look at myself in the mirror. I knew I looked terrible; there was no need to catalogue any more bruises.

I don't know how long I was in the shower. Long enough to end up sitting. Long enough to let the tears fall. Long enough to relive pulling the trigger. First my father. Followed by Garrett Mercer. Long enough to remember I'd been too slow to save Eliza, and that I would never see Gus again. But not long enough for any of it to be okay.

Back in the bedroom I found a wardrobe full of clothes and managed to pull on a pair of sweat pants and a long-sleeved tee. The clothes still had the tags on them, and once again everything fit me perfectly

In the hallway, the first thing I noticed was that the house was seriously big. There was a set of stairs in front of me, and when I looked to my left I could see a long hall with four doors on either side of the hall and the same in the other direction.

I followed the bacon smell downstairs and entered an open living area, which took my breath away. It was dominated by massive caramel-coloured sofas that looked as though they would be heaven to sink into, with a stone fireplace and a luxurious cream rug in the centre of the room. Running down the side of the room was a twelve-seater dining table in the same cherry wood that was used in the bedroom. The backdrop was a long wall of floor-to-ceiling glass doors, which opened up to a massive wrap-around veranda – and why wouldn't it, when beyond the house was nothing but stunning rolling hills that appeared to be bathing in the setting sun?

It was surreal to be in such a beautiful place when I felt submerged in such ugliness. I kept going into the kitchen, which was an equally spectacular combination of country meets modern. I found my mother at the stove with two pans in front of her, and the breakfast bar set out with three plates.

I cleared my throat.

She spun around, surprised, but when she saw me she just smiled. 'I figured if anything would get you up, it was bacon. Even if it is dinner time.'

I sat gingerly at the enormous breakfast bar. 'Where's Sam?' I asked, my voice croaky from disuse.

Mom started to dish up food. 'He's out on a ride. He'll be back any minute.'

'Ride?'

'He says it's because he's enjoying being around horses again. But just between us, I'm pretty sure he's enjoying being around the very pretty stable hand a lot more.'

'How long have we been here?' I asked, then quickly added, 'Where are we?'

'Charlottesville,' Mom said with a warm smile.

Where we used to live.

'Quin did this,' I said, feeling my throat tighten.

Mom nodded, her smile turning a little sad. We were home. Quentin had sent us home. Albeit to a much bigger house.

'We got here on Sunday. It's Wednesday night.'

I almost fell off the chair. 'I've been out for three days?'

Mom shrugged, pushing a plate towards me. 'Give or take.'

'What does that mean?'

Mom looked everywhere but at me.

'Mom,' I pushed.

Eventually she leaned her forearms on the bench and looked at me. 'We had to sedate you for part of it.'

I swallowed. 'Why?'

'The nightmares, Maggie. When we sedated you, they didn't seem to be as ... violent for you.'

'Oh,' I murmured, suddenly feeling way too exposed.

Mom eased back. 'Eat. You need your strength.'

The door flew open and Sam walked in with a girl – who I assumed was the stable hand – behind him.

'She's awake!' he said merrily, throwing his cowboy hat and coat on the hooks.

The girl came in and confidently extended her hand to me. 'Good evening, Ms Stevens, my name is Sky. Mr Mercer hired me when he took over the property. I run the team here. There are ten of us, but Mr Mercer mentioned you would either decrease or increase the numbers when you were ready. In the meantime, I want you to rest assured that I will keep the stables running and the stock moving.'

Holy shit. 'Stock?'

'Yes, Ms Stevens, we have twenty thousand head of cattle. Well, thirty if you count the next-door property.'

'Next door?' I said, trying to make sense of it all.

'Yes, Ms Stevens.'

I looked at Mom, entirely confused.

'Where Sam and I are staying,' she clarified softly.

'You mean ...' I looked from Mom to Sam, who nodded at me.

'Yep,' Sam said.

'So this house …?'

'The paperwork is still being finalised apparently, but yeah …' He shrugged with a goofy smile. 'Once the sale is finalised, this place is all yours, Mags. Though, until you're back on your feet, we're all staying in this house.'

'Where is he?' I asked.

Sam looked at Mom. She cleared her throat and started handing food to Sky and Sam. 'Sit, eat,' she instructed and then looked back at me.

'He sent us to the hospital first and as soon as you were stable they flew us up here. He organised everything and had people and transport waiting,' Mom explained.

'Yep,' Sam said. 'Kept us all under armed guard the entire time. Within a day he had the properties ready, furniture and clothes delivered, staff on hand. It's been crazy.'

'Where is he?'

Mom sighed. 'He's in DC, darling. With everything that happened and then the massive aftermath, there was no way for him to be anywhere else. The world is demanding answers. He said to tell you he'd be here as soon as he could.'

'Has anyone heard from him since we left the underground?' I asked, including Sky in my questioning. They all shook their heads.

'The last we saw, he was being taken into custody,' Mom explained. 'But the news reported that he and his brother were cooperating with the government and UN in closed-door discussions. They have no idea when that will end.'

'Is he in trouble?'

No one was able to answer. I had to fight my gut reaction to leap out of my chair and charge back to DC to help him. But Quentin didn't need me to rescue him. He was so much stronger than I'd ever given him credit for.

Another thought occurred to me. 'Am I? I mean … after what I did. Do they know about Garrett? That I … That I was the one who shot him?' Not to mention my own father.

'They know, Maggie. We've been half expecting the police to show up here, but no one has. Not for that reason anyway,' Mom said.

I turned to Sky. 'Did he give you any indication when he'd be coming here?'

Sky looked uneasy. 'Not exactly. I only spoke to him when he first acquired the ranches. But on Tuesday morning an additional twelve security personnel arrived, so he's obviously keeping tabs on things. I'm sure he'll be here soon.'

I shook my head, struggling to keep up and already feeling like I needed to go back to bed. '*Additional* security? Why do we need security?'

Sky dropped her fork. 'She doesn't know?'

Mom shook her head. 'She'd only just woken up when you two came in. I haven't had a chance.'

'Tell me,' I demanded.

*

'*My name is Gus Reynolds. I'm twenty-three years old and I'm an M-Corp programmer – or at least, I was.*' He smiled knowingly. '*I'm pretty sure I was fired. And if not, consider this my resignation.*' His smile faded and he was suddenly serious. '*I have dabbled in some black-market trading, I won't deny it. I have listed and documented all of my crimes for the world to see so that when others attempt to discredit me, you'll already have all of the facts. Simpler that way.*'

I hiccupped through a tight breath, watching Gus on the video that Mom and Sam told me had been running continuously on the internet and television since 6 a.m. on Sunday morning.

I noticed that he was sitting in his room at the theatre. He had filmed this in the days before we'd gone back into the tunnels.

'*I'm not a perfect person. But I don't regard myself as a bad person either. I know the difference between right and wrong, and I know that there are many types of wrong – the worst of which is the wrongdoing that hurts innocent people. So if you will indulge me, a slightly crooked, extremely brilliant hacker, for a few minutes, I'm going to tell you a story about a girl who lost her dad and had her world fall apart. And then I am going to tell you the story about the woman she became. And if you are watching this, there's a very good chance that either she or I or both of us are dead. If it's me, Maggie, and you are watching this – it's not your fault.*' He flashed a sorry smile. '*We both know I'm not like you. I'm no hero, so if I went down, it was probably for the only reason I'd be willing to, and that's okay with me. And if you went down, then at least the world will get to hear the truth because I'm fairly certain that by the time they see this, you will have done exactly what I always knew you were going to. Because this is the story of a girl who saves the world.'*

Tears streamed down my face as Gus told my tale. He'd detailed and kept everything since we'd first met; he showed clips and evidence and entwined everything into the tale – all of the facts, all of the truth. He exposed the hubs, the clean-ups, the lies. He exposed all of the murdering, the labs, the hidden doors, the parking garage system. He showed maps and blueprints and footage from my M-Band of me in the tunnels, footage I'd forgotten I'd taken or not realised he'd swiped from my M-Band.

He showed it all.

The truth of the neg camps the world believed were rehabilitation farms, the images of negs screaming as they were branded. He explained what my father had done and who he was, holding nothing back. He confessed my sins against Quentin and explained the disruption process; how I had fooled the heir to the most powerful family in the world and how Quentin had been the biggest surprise of all. That finding him in the thick of all the corruption had given me the strength to become what Gus always believed I could be. He spoke of my heartache at finding out my father was the villain and not the victim. He showed footage of me turning up to his apartment with a bullet wound in my stomach. Him, gluing and stapling me back together.

He told the world about the population-control documents we'd found, about what M-Corp had planned to do. *Was* doing.

He showed me, frail and almost starved to death, staring at the dust mites dancing in the sunlight that first day I was out of my cell and in the apartment above Burn. He showed me lying in Quentin Mercer's arms, holding onto him for dear life. The only thing he didn't reveal was that Quentin was my true match.

He talked briefly of Preference Evolution, but avoided going into any detail, explaining that they were on the good side, but that it was their right to tell their story in their words.

'It hasn't all been pretty. But when you are just one girl fighting against something that's so mighty the rest of the world has chosen to turn a blind eye – well, it can't be pretty, can it? But now that you know the ugly truth, ask yourself this: what would you have done? I know I could never have shown her strength. Even at her worst, she found a reason to keep fighting. And that reason is us and our right to exist. I hope that we're worth it.'

The image of Gus's face faded away and a scrolling message came up on the screen.

Following the shock revelations that have come out in the past week, the military has seized control of M-Corp. Negs in the US and many countries around the world have already been treated with the antidote, and those who do not have previous prison sentences to serve out have been released back to their homes and families. Those countries that have not yet been treated will receive the antidote within the coming days.

All military personnel are currently being treated with the antidote and are being vetted before being released back into active duty. Counselling and therapy have been made available to all affected.

To the families who have lost loved ones due to the heinous crimes committed against humanity, there are no excuses for those who have caused your suffering. You have our deepest sympathies and this government's promise that every and all steps are being taken to bring those responsible to justice and to ensure such a travesty is never repeated or forgotten.

A new law has been passed, reinstating all funds and employment to any negs who were taken away from their homes and families. Compensation will be provided under the new International Reynolds Freedom Law.

We thank you for your patience in this time of change and ask you to bear with us until we can bring more information your way.

The Presidential message ended and then images flashed on the screen showing countries that were clearly third world; people living in small clay homes, hills in the distance and what looked like smouldering fires. The pictures showed a military presence; soldiers dressed in British army uniforms.

As I watched, people kneeled on the hard ground, their heads raised to the sky as they faced a shower of rain. They welcomed it like a cleansing.

I glanced at Mom. She nodded, sensing my question. 'They've been seeding the clouds. Raining down the antidote.'

The plan had worked.

My heart gave a squeeze as more tears fell. I nodded, biting down on my fist, watching as these people were given back their chance at life, the chance my father stole.

I wanted to be happy for them, and I was relieved, but, selfishly, my heart hurt. Quentin was gone and I feared how long the government would keep him. M-Corp was now his and Sebastian's responsibility and I had no idea what that meant for the future. Even if the government had seized control of the company, there was still so much he would be needed for, so much that would keep him away.

'What about Gus?'

Mom clasped my hands in hers. 'Oh, darling, you've been through so much. I'm so sorry about Gus. He obviously cared for you deeply, the whole world can see that.'

'Did they ... Where is he?'

'The government took custody of his body. We appealed to have him released to us, but they waited to see if any other family members claimed him. When no one did, they signed him over to our care yesterday. He's at a morgue in Arlington and we were waiting for you until we finalised the funeral arrangements.'

I nodded tightly. 'Tomorrow? Can we talk about it tomorrow?'

'Yes, of course.'

Then I remembered. 'I still don't get why the security?'

Sam stood up and held out his hand. 'I'll show you.'

Thirty-five

My forehead creased, but I took Sam's hand, letting him gently pull me to my feet and lead me outside. 'We're just going to the top of that small crest,' he said, motioning to a hill about twenty metres away. It was dark now, but the lighting from the house was enough for me to see where he wanted to go.

'Okay,' I said, letting him help me.

As we walked, I noticed my brother still had bruises on his face and arms, but most notably, he was different. Not just his clothes, though seeing him back in jeans and a flannel shirt was nice, it was everything; the way he walked, the way he spoke, every vibe coming off him.

'You're happy,' I said.

'Very,' he agreed. 'I missed this place. I feel like I can finally breathe again, you know?'

I cast my eyes down quickly and nodded. But I wasn't sure I did. I wasn't sure breathing would ever come naturally to me again.

Quentin wasn't there. And Gus was gone when it should have been me.

When I reached the top of the crest, I gasped. The fence line of the property was still a fair way away, but I now had full view of it. And, more importantly, of the thousands of people crowding behind the fence on the roadside, while on the other side a large number of security were keeping guard. Beyond the fence, a number of portable lights had been set up and I could see piles of blankets and food supplies.

'Oh my God,' I said, starting to panic. I would have dropped to my knees if Sam hadn't had his arm around me. 'What do they want?' But already I knew. They were coming for me. They wanted me to pay for my sins, answer to my crimes. 'And why the hell are we feeding them?'

Sam gave me a squeeze as Mom and Sky joined us on the crest.

I started to back away. 'They'll storm the place. We should get away from here. It's not safe. Mom, you shouldn't be here.'

Mom smiled softly. 'Can you take a little more walking, Maggie?'

I nodded. 'Of course. We need to get moving!'

Mom took my other arm and together she and Sam started walking – but in the wrong damn direction!

'Not this way!' I said. 'We need to get out of here.'

But Sky was on her radio, obviously talking to the security guards, who started to turn around and noticed us coming their way.

'Just trust us, Maggie,' Sam said with a small laugh.

As we got closer, my heart sped up. I couldn't breathe as I waited for the people to push down the fence and charge us. But they didn't.

In fact, they were all calm. All silent. Watching as we moved closer and closer. One of the security guards jogged towards us and suddenly I felt a wave of relief.

'Liam?' I asked, not sure if I was seeing things.

He made it the last few steps and gave me a toothy grin before pulling me in for a hug. 'Wasn't about to let anyone else watch out for you until you were ready to get back to the job yourself.'

'Who are all these people, Liam?'

He glanced at Sam. 'She doesn't know?'

Sam shrugged, looking as though he was enjoying himself. 'No idea.'

Liam laughed and pulled out his radio. 'Tell them it's her,' he ordered.

'Liam!' I yelled, but it was too late. Why the hell was no one running?

But then I saw the guards talking to the crowds. I heard the murmurs and saw the movements until they travelled beyond where my eyes could see.

A flickering light.

A candle.

Another. And another.

And then hundreds.

Until there were thousands.

As far as I could see, spreading out like a wave of earthly stars.

The breath whooshed from my lungs.

'They've been keeping vigil, Maggie,' Mom said, tears in her eyes. 'They're here to thank you.'

I was speechless, and even if I wasn't, there was no way I could speak over the lump in my throat.

'A lot of them are wrongly accused negs,' Sam said. 'Liam thinks some are true negs who have never committed any crime. Many of them are the families of negs who've come to thank you for saving their loved ones when they couldn't. They started arriving by car after Gus's message went live. Then on foot. Then, they just stayed. Quentin sent security, but no one has caused a problem. Liam organised to keep everyone warm and fed while they waited for you.' He pointed to a group of a few hundred near the top fence. 'That's the line of volunteers, Mags.'

I shook my head and squeezed out the words. 'For what?'

'To work for you. Anything. Everything. You gave them back their lives and they want to know if there's anything they can do for you. They refuse to leave.'

And then the voices started, soft at first but quickly building into a thunderstorm of sound. It only took a few of the words for me to recognise what they were singing.

I grabbed Liam's hand and listened as thousands of voices sang 'Amazing Grace'.

Tears poured down my face.

Tears of guilt, mostly.

'Take me down there, Liam,' I said, my voice trembling.

'She's too exhausted,' Mom argued, but Liam just gave her a big smile then lifted me in his arms, cradling me easily as he walked me towards the singing crowds. Once there, he gently put me down and kept his arm around me while I walked along the fence line as far as I could manage, thanking people for being there and telling them I was sorry for everything they had been through.

The shame was devastating. I didn't deserve their praise and wanted to hide away, but *they* deserved for me to face them.

If only they knew everything, they wouldn't be singing songs. If they knew how many I had walked away from. About Sarah – how she'd been shot dead in front of me because I'd failed to get her out. I shook my head. Gus might have told my tale, but still … They didn't know all the people I'd left to their terrible fate.

I didn't last long, and as I started to fade Mom was there, gently telling Liam I'd had enough for one day.

Liam watched me for a beat, but then nodded and instructed the security guards to inform the rest of the crowds that I was going to have a rest and that I would visit again tomorrow. This seemed to satisfy them, and then he picked me up and carried me in his arms all the way back to my room in that ginormous ranch.

'Your son?' I asked as Liam pulled up the covers for me.

He smiled proudly. 'He's here. Staying in one of the guesthouses with me. He wants to meet you.'

'I want to meet him too,' I said groggily, my eyes closing, only to flash open again. 'I have guesthouses?'

'Four permanent ones,' he said. 'And we have set up some temporary caravans on the property for the extra security.'

'How big is the property?' I asked.

'Roughly? About thirty thousand acres, I believe.'

'Oh. Right,' I said, my eyes closing before I could even begin to process the fact that this place was about twice the size of Manhattan. Because if I had to process that, I might also have to acknowledge the fact that despite all the crowds … I felt entirely bereft.

Over the next two days, I caught up on all that had happened. The world had woken up on Monday morning to Gus's face streaming on every single media platform known to man, in every corner of the world.

Gus had been right when he described himself as a brilliant hacker – no one had quite worked out exactly how he'd done it. The initial feed only aired for about forty minutes before they managed to bring it down, but it was enough. The world knew and then the feed started to come back online. Two hours after that, CNN started the continual loop that I had seen. Their ratings had never been higher.

The world now knew that Phera-tech was a corrupted technology; that the simplistic system of rating one another had turned into a control mechanism that was taking lives and stealing rights.

Negs had been released immediately because of the immense public pressure following Gus's message. It appeared that the world was no longer willing to go quietly into the night.

Talk shows were now dominated by negs telling their gruesome tales. One even came on talking about me, that he had met me and begged me to take him out of there. I watched, remembering the night I had gone in and found him. It turns out he was a real neg and was happy to admit it to the world along with the fact that he had never done anything criminal or violent – except for when he had been underground. I sympathised with him when he confessed he would carry that guilt with him for the rest of his life. Most of all I was surprised when he told the host that he understood why I'd done what I'd done and that he believed I'd made the right choice. I shook my head, watching.

Following leads from all the seized M-Corp files, police had uncovered sweatshops around the world where those in charge had used the disruption to turn workers into negs – leaving them as little more than slaves.

The news reports indicated that there had been a number or arrests made from within the Mercer Corporation and that the company was now working in full cooperation with the US government and the UN.

But, of course, there was still so much more to do. That's where the reports always ended. *So much more to do.*

I had been slowly getting my strength back and starting to move around a little more. I spent as much time as I could visiting with the people on the fence line and helping the security guards bring supplies.

On Saturday morning, I sat on the sofa with Mom and Sam, all of us nibbling on the omelette Mom had made. She still couldn't cook and the thing was more charred than should be possible, but Sam and I scooped a handful of cheese on top and told her it was superb. Soon enough Liam and his five-year-old son, Jacob, joined us and we turned up the volume just as Jacob spat out his first bite of crispy omelette.

CNN had now returned to their normal broadcasting. They were filming a press conference at the White House; a common occurrence at the moment.

I half watched as the President began to speak, knowing that there would be a lot of talk we'd already heard. But eventually he started talking about Phera-tech and that was when I tuned in.

'… We have reached a point where we need to make some decisions. As a country, but also as a world and as a species. We should have done this before it all began. We should have listened to the warnings. We were wrong. But now we have a chance to make things right. There is a technology that we can offer the world, but it's now your choice – *your* vote – that will make the difference. So I'm going to hand over the microphone to someone you already know quite a lot about. His part in the exposure of what has really been happening with this technology was instrumental. Ladies and gentlemen, Quentin Mercer.'

Cameras started flashing everywhere. It was the first time anyone in the general public – including me – would see him since the news broke. They'd had him in lockdown, and rumours had started running rife as to what he and his brother were up to.

The camera zoomed in as a door to the press conference room opened. My heart pumped double time as I sat rooted in place. And then, there he was.

He was safe and perfect and I had to bite my lip to stop the cry that came from my soul. His black suit and crisp white shirt made him look strong and much older than his eighteen years. But his face was gentle and beneath the powerful exterior I could see the tiredness his eyes betrayed.

He came to the stage and shook hands with the President. They exchanged a few quiet words and then Quentin stepped up to the microphone. He paused, looked out to the press and then turned to the camera.

'My father was a criminal. He took the wrong road and many people paid the price for his wrongdoing. As his son, I offer you my deepest apology, but I know that means very little right now. There is no excuse for what he did. No punishment great enough. But I believe there is a way to move forwards. A way for us to show the people of this world who would take our freedom from us that we are not going to stand by and let that happen.'

At first I struggled to listen to what he was saying, too busy taking in the sight of him – every single inch. He was beautiful – even the wound near his eye that was neatly stitched. When I did start paying attention to his message, I was struck by how much strength flowed from each word. He was most definitely in control and I knew I was watching the beginning of greatness.

'It is hard to stand before the world and admit that my father was the worst kind of person.' He dropped his eyes. When he lifted them, he gave just a glimpse of his sorrow and I felt it in every part of my body. 'To admit that he killed my mother. And to admit that I'm glad he's gone.'

Oh, Quentin.

'If the system worked, my father should have rated as a neg, but he never did. Perhaps he rigged the system, or perhaps the system is flawed. Perhaps it was something else.'

I was struck by his words and the fact that, like his mother, he had come full circle, back to the technology and how it had let them down in so many ways.

He took a deep breath and stared into the camera. 'It is hard to admit these things. But it is made easier by being able to tell you that my mother was the *best* kind of person.' A small smile broke through his serious expression. 'She worked as an undercover agent for the government, working from the inside to find a way to stop the great injustices that were happening. She risked her life every day and, in the end, gave her life for this very purpose. It is my mother's example that both my brother, Sebastian, and I look to for guidance as we pave the road ahead.'

He relaxed into his stance a little, the small movement making his speech more personal.

'Yes, we found a cure for the immediate problem. And that's great. But that doesn't stop the bigger problem we've created. My mother had a vision that we could live in a world that had both technology *and* empathy. In the days before her death, she told me how she believed we were capable of both, as long as we put our humanity and compassion before advancement. She believed if we could do that we would be able to tap into a greater evolution of mankind than any of us could comprehend. And I agree. Over the past week, we have been testing a technology that Eliza Mercer developed, and thanks to the input of Gus Reynolds in the final weeks of his life we believe this technology is now ready to be introduced to the world. So what does it do?'

Quentin smiled and I knew he had the world in the palm of his hand.

'Well,' he went on, 'in a nutshell, it will limit Phera-tech so that ratings under fifteen per cent are no longer displayed, thereby preventing negative ratings completely. But it will also limit the higher ratings, maxing out at ninety per cent. We believe nothing in life should be so definite that a person could be willing to kill for it – both the *good* and the *bad*. In addition to this alteration to your M-Bands and to Phera-tech, the laws requiring a minimum monthly register of ratings along with the Negative Removal Act will be scrapped. The research shows that negs are volatile and often violent, but ask yourself this – do we not *all* deserve the chance to change and to evolve? I hope you'll agree with me that we do.

'I'm here today not on behalf of the Mercer Corporation, but on behalf of my brother, Sebastian, who is away giving a similar talk in other countries, and on behalf of my mother who is no longer with us. And in order to show you just how true that statement is …' he paused and you could feel the attention of the world waiting for his next words, 'Sebastian and I, as the sole heirs of the Mercer Corporation, have hereby relinquished control and ownership, donating the firm, its wealth and all of its patents and intellectual property to the United Nations. No single entity will be able to make these types of decisions again. A board of trusted international representatives in the fields of science, business, politics and human rights will be entrusted with future decisions. The technology will endure. It must because we, the public, demand it must. But hopefully, if you choose to pass this vote with us, we will find a way to make the technology kinder.'

Quentin stood back and the President took over, explaining that given the urgent nature of the matter, a vote would proceed immediately with all US residents required to register their votes online within the next twenty-four hours.

'Over the next hour, all M-Bands will automatically update with a "vote" zip complete with instructions. We've kept it as straight forward as possible and the results will be announced this time tomorrow.'

The President then opened the floor to questions, of which there were many. But I had stopped listening. All I could do was watch Quentin as he was ushered from the room by security guards. It was clear the government were still keeping a tight hold on him, ensuring he spoke to none of the press or answered any questions. How long would they keep him hidden away?

Thirty-six

It was Sunday – a week since we'd raided the tunnels – and it was funeral day. I didn't know how I was going to get through it. I didn't even know if anyone would come. Gus and I didn't exactly have a lot of friends, so when the funeral company had asked me for the guest list I'd baulked. He didn't even have any family that he cared for, and knowing how he'd felt, I hadn't put them on the list.

I stood in front of the distressed mirror in my bedroom, feeling just as worn. I was wearing a long navy-blue dress and had my arm in a black sling. I barely recognised myself anymore and was frustrated that I looked so lost. I needed to be strong today. I needed to be strong for Gus.

I grabbed Gus's black fedora and put it on just as I heard the front door open and Liam call my name. I walked downstairs slowly, knowing each step brought me closer to the final goodbyes.

'Is it on?' I asked, when I found Liam and my family all standing nervously around the television screen.

Liam nodded, turning up the volume.

The President was speaking, talking about the unprecedented amount of votes that had been received. And about the extraordinary landslide. Sebastian Mercer stood in the background, but I couldn't see Quentin anywhere and that worried me.

'It is with great pride that I announce the implementation of the new restrictions on Phera-tech. As decided by the people of the United States of America, we will no longer single out those who rate as negatives. Ratings below fifteen per cent and above ninety per cent will no longer appear. The Negative Removal Act has been rescinded, as have the laws requiring minimum monthly ratings. As your President, I thank you for taking this brave step towards a better future.'

'Wow,' Mom said. 'I honestly wasn't sure if the public would get behind it. Everything is going to change now.'

Liam nodded, tapping on his M-Band. 'And the UK, Russia, China, Japan, Australia and other countries are delivering equally strong results.'

'This is incredible, right, Mags?' Sam said, shaking his head in amazement.

'Yeah. It's a new world,' I said with a genuine smile, even as I backed up a few steps and pointed towards the door. 'I'm just going to … go for a walk before we have to get going.'

Everyone seemed to understand, and I was grateful they let me go.

I went outside, relishing the feel of the fresh morning air. I wandered towards the crest, noticing that a helicopter had just landed in the field ahead. I figured it was our ride to the funeral.

I stopped just before I reached the top of the hill, not wanting to face the thousands of people I knew were still there. It was such an odd sensation. I'd been alone for so long, running my own game, manipulating others, caring only about my own goals. But now here I was, surrounded by people, about to bury my only friend – and there was only one person I wanted to see.

It was over.

I crossed my arms and closed my eyes, letting the cold seep into me. And yes, more tears fell. I felt like I'd turned into a damn water feature.

I don't know how long I'd been standing there when I started to register the sounds of excited chatter coming from the people at the fence line. They weren't normally this noisy, and when the cheers started to increase, I took a few tentative steps towards the top of the crest.

When I cleared the small hill and saw the other side, my trembling hand flew to my mouth.

The helicopter wasn't there to pick us up. It had been dropping him off.

He was in jeans and a shirt and he was walking towards me, a quirky expression on his face as he squinted into the sun.

I don't know what came over me, but I ran. I ran straight for him, my legs not moving fast enough. Until finally. Finally I threw myself into his waiting arms.

I hit him so hard he stumbled back a few steps, but somehow managed to keep us both upright.

'Hey,' he said, exhaling.

Then, unable to control the overwhelming influx of emotions, I suddenly pulled back and pounded him on the chest. 'I missed you! I don't work right without you anymore!'

'Shh,' he soothed, holding me tightly even as I heard him chuckle. 'I got here as soon as I could. I would never have missed the funeral.'

'Why didn't you call?'

He clasped my face in his hands and forced my eyes to his. 'They had Sebastian and me under lock and key. First for questioning to clear our names, and then to work out all the responsible parties. After that, we stayed to discuss the future of the company and the tech. We could have fought it, but we needed them to trust that we were on their side and … I agreed to all of their conditions as long as they agreed to stay away from you.'

I sucked in a breath. That answered my question about why no one had come for me.

Quentin shrugged, seeing my confusion. 'Gus's statement and the files pretty much explained your role in full. You broke the law a lot, but given the outcome, the President has issued you with a full pardon.'

'So I'm not in trouble?'

He shook his head.

'And what about you?' I hedged. 'Are you just visiting

or …?' I wanted to believe it was finished, that we could be together, but I was too scared to hope.

He bit back a grin. 'Actually, I've come to oversee my investment.'

'The ranch? So you really bought it?'

He nodded.

'With what money? Didn't you and Sebastian give up the company?'

'We did. But that doesn't mean the family didn't own a number of other lucrative and fully legal businesses that we continue to have interests in. We've donated the majority of the family wealth to help with the clean-up, but some companies we'll maintain to generate additional funds, which will go towards helping the families affected. The ranch … Well, it's a working ranch and its profits will go towards good causes too and …' His smile widened as he looked around. 'I'm fairly certain I promised you paradise.'

I swallowed thickly and looked down.

'Maggie?'

'I killed them, Quin. Your dad. Mine. I shot them and … I'll never be able to undo it.' I needed him to know this. To realise that every time he looked at me, he'd know that I was the one who killed his father.

'Would you undo it if you could?' he asked softly, his hand going to a stray lock of hair and tucking it behind my ear.

I shook my head. Because no matter what I had to live with, watching all those people being released from their prisons and seeing the cure rain down on so many innocent victims, I couldn't deny that I stood by my choices.

'Neither would I. I wouldn't undo any of it, not from the minute I met you.'

I nodded quickly, trying to hold back the tears. 'Please tell me you're back. Please tell me you're staying.'

His finger lightly lifted my chin. 'I'm back. I'm staying.'

And then I was in his arms again, his lips on mine and thousands of people who appeared to genuinely care were whistling and cheering.

Despite my attempts to keep him kissing me forever, he finally managed to pull back with another chuckle. 'I'm still going to have to travel back and forth to check on the businesses, but Sebastian is going to take the lion's share. And I figured Charlottesville worked as well as anywhere else, with Georgetown, Washington and Lee, and the University of Virginia all a short chopper ride away.'

I looked at him as though he was crazy. 'I'm not getting a helicopter to university.'

He shrugged and smiled. 'We'll see.'

The funeral broke my heart all over again. But with Quentin at my side, it was bearable. He held my hand as I sat stoically with my family, listening to the service. He knew I couldn't manage much more and he didn't push.

More than a few surprises waited for me at the funeral. To start with, even though it was a private service, they had set up masses of security to keep the general public out. It turned out Gus had become a modern martyr, something that would have highly amused him.

The turnout to the service was pretty much a who's who of not only American politics, but leaders from around the world.

More importantly, when I looked around at my family and beyond them to Liam and Jacob, Master Rua, Ivy, Morris, many of the kids from school, and then spotted Grace and Alex standing at the back, I realised that perhaps Gus, Quentin and I hadn't been as alone as I'd thought. I squeezed Quentin's hand and he smiled warmly.

The service was tastefully tasteless in many ways, exactly how Gus would have liked it. At the end, Quentin and I stood at the exit doors and shook everyone's hand and thanked them for coming.

Ivy and Morris hugged us both and promised to visit the ranch in the coming weeks.

When Alex approached, he surprised me by drawing me into his arms. 'I'm sorry about Gus.'

I nodded.

'For what it's worth, I think my sister loved him.'

'I think he loved her too.'

He let out a breath, as if trying to release some of the pain we all carried with us. But it was impossible. 'We'll be at Eliza's service on Tuesday, but you probably won't see us,' he said, turning to Quentin.

Quentin nodded with understanding.

'Well,' Alex said, stepping back and taking Grace's

hand in his. 'We're here if you ever need us. All you have to do is call.' With his other hand he held out a card.

Preference Evolution
Head of Operations

I looked at him with a raised brow.

He shrugged. 'You never know when we might come in handy.'

And with that and a brief hug from Grace, they were gone. Something told me I would never see them again. And that was okay.

Finally I picked up my hat and took Quentin's hand, readying myself to face the world.

'He would have liked that you wore that,' Quentin said, tucking a strand of hair behind my ear.

I imitated a Gus-like snort. 'He would've hated it and told me I was trying to steal his look.'

Quentin laughed. 'Probably.' He gestured to the door then held out his hand. 'Are you ready for this?'

I took a deep breath and let it out before taking his hand in response.

Together we stepped outside, instantly assaulted by camera flashes and reporters calling out their questions.

We kept our heads down and headed towards the field where the helicopter and my family were already waiting. Liam joined us on my other side and together we walked through the crowds as the press threw their questions out randomly.

'What happens now, Mr Mercer?'

'Ms Stevens, did you always know what your father had planned?'

'Ms Stevens, is it true you were the one to take your father's life and then later also shoot Garrett Mercer?' I flinched at that one, but Quentin held my hand tight and pulled me close.

Then came the next question from a woman right in front of us. 'Mr Mercer, we've now heard much of your turbulent relationship with Ms Stevens. We understand she was the one who informed you about the true goings-on of your family business?'

For some reason Quentin decided to answer. 'That's correct,' Quentin said, slowing briefly.

'And yet she also led you to believe you yourself were a neg?' the woman continued, looking as though she couldn't believe her luck.

His lips pressed together. 'She had her reasons, as the world is well aware.'

'Of course,' she said quickly. 'But what now for the two of you? Are you still in love with her? Even after what she did?'

Quentin stopped completely, causing a hush amongst the reporters. He turned to me and smiled briefly before turning his blue eyes – more steel than ocean – out to the field of hungry press as though he was about to reveal the best-kept secret of them all.

'One hundred per cent.'

Acknowledgements

Many thanks to:

Selwa Anthony – Agent and Trusted Advisor

HarperCollins Australia – Publishing House
Chren Byng – Associate Publisher
James Kellow – CEO HarperCollins Australia
Cristina Cappelluto – Children's Publishing Director
Tegan Morrison – Editor
Kate Burnitt – Project Manager
Beth Hall – Proofreader
Amanda Diaz – Publicist
Tim Miller – Marketing and Book Trailer Wizard
Stephanie Spartels – Cover Designer
Elizabeth O'Donnell – International Rights
Amy Fox – Sales
Jacqui Barton – Education Manager
Janelle Garside – Production
Bianca Fazzalaro – Children's Publishing Assistant

The Horseshoe Curve – Jim Fink

Matt – Husband (thirteen years: each one better than the one before)
Sienna and Winter – Kids (who are growing up way too fast)
Harriet – Always First Reader (and Friend!)
Family – Mum, Dad, Jenny, Phil and all of my siblings and siblings-in-law

As you can see, it takes many people to produce the final product we find on the shelves (or on our e-readers). I am extremely lucky to have such an incredible team to work with and if I have missed anyone's name, please forgive me.

My final thanks is reserved for the readers and bloggers who make this awesome job of writing stories a possibility for me. Thank you for your time, and for your trust. I have loved delving into Maggie's world and I hope you enjoy this conclusion to her story.

An internationally bestselling author, entrepreneur and mother living in Sydney, Australia, Jessica Shirvington is also a 2011 and 2012 finalist for *Cosmopolitan*'s annual Fun, Fearless Female Award. Married with two beautiful daughters, she met her husband, former Olympian Matt Shirvington, at age seventeen. Jessica knows her early-age romance and its longevity has definitely contributed to how she tackles relationships in her YA novels, which include the series The Violet Eden Chapters (also known as The Embrace Series) and the stand-alone novel *Between the Lives* (also known as *One Past Midnight*).

Visit her online at
www.jessicashirvington.com
www.facebook.com/Shirvington
Twitter: @JessShirvington

Also available ...

THE PERFECT LIFE OR THE PERFECT LOVE?   YOU CHOOSE.

Between the Lives

JESSICA **SHIRVINGTON**

THE BESTSELLING AUTHOR OF *EMBRACE*

Sabine isn't like anyone else. For as long as she can remember, she's had two lives.

Every twenty-four hours she 'Shifts', living each day twice. She has one life in Wellesley, Massachusetts, and another, completely different life in Roxbury, Boston.

All Sabine has ever wanted is the chance to live one life. When it seems like this might finally be possible, Sabine begins a series of dangerous experiments to achieve her goal. But is she willing to risk everything – including the one man who might actually believe her?